Cyrus Thomas

The Frontier Schoolmaster

The autobiography of a teacher

Cyrus Thomas

The Frontier Schoolmaster
The autobiography of a teacher

ISBN/EAN: 9783337029265

Printed in Europe, USA, Canada, Australia, Japan

Cover: Foto ©Raphael Reischuk / pixelio.de

More available books at **www.hansebooks.com**

FRONTIER SCHOOLMASTER;

THE

AUTOBIOGRAPHY OF A TEACHER,

AN ACCOUNT NOT ONLY OF EXPERIENCES IN THE SCHOOL-
ROOM BUT IN AGRICULTURAL, POLITICAL,
AND MILITARY LIFE,

TOGETHER WITH

AN ESSAY

ON THE

MANAGEMENT OF OUR PUBLIC SCHOOLS.

BY C. THOMAS.

MONTREAL:
PRINTED BY JOHN LOVELL & SON.
1880.

INTRODUCTION.

THE fact that I had published two local histories which had received the compliment *useful*, more freely with each succeeding year, inspired me with the hope that I might meet the same success in a different field of literature—hence, the publication of THE FRONTIER SCHOOLMASTER.

An experience of twelve years in the school-room having shown me a deplorable lack of interest in schools on the part of the public—a great want of moral support to teachers,—I could think of no better subjects than these, about which to employ my humble pen. But, in order to lead the reader to the common-place and uninteresting subject of school teaching, it was necessary to enliven the journey by the narration of incidents unconnected with the school-room. It was with a hope, too, that some of these incidents might not be without their useful lesson that they were introduced.

The experienced voter will doubtless recognize familiar scenes in the picture of the political campaign, and the young man who is a "hanger-on" at the door of some Government official, waiting **for an** "appointment," instead **of** seizing manfully **on** present opportunities to earn a livelihood, may, possibly, **read in the** experience of the **hero of** this tale, **his** own disappointment and humiliation.

Many **of** the incidents herein described **are facts related** with little embellishment, and if the descriptions sometimes border **on** caricature, **it is for** the sake of pointing a **moral** the **more** forcibly.

Should it be thought **that I** have dwelt at too much **length** on **the** details of teaching, related unimportant **incidents, let me** say in reply that I believe incidents which **affect the** happiness **of our teachers, and** consequently the **great** interests **of education, can scarcely** with justice be pronounced too trivial **for narration.**

The village school described midway of the work may **be** regarded **a** representative one; its character and management **showing** much **too** perfectly **the** condition of a great many **schools in our** own Province **at** the present time. The **fault is not in** our School Inspectors, as some have insinuated; **it lies** wholly in the people; **in** their deplorable **apathy towards** *all* schools; **in** their ambition to accumulate **wealth; in short,** to bequeath to their children **an** inheritance **of broad acres** and fine herds rather than one **of** cultured minds. Could **the** District **of each** School Inspector be **so** limited **that his** visits to schools could be made **much** longer **and** far **more** frequent, I doubt not that his **ability** to **do good would** be greatly enhanced.

The custom of boarding around which is slowly going out of existence is still tenaciously adhered **to in** very many localities.

For the amusement of those who have never had any experience in this novel way of boarding, **I have shown** without exaggeration the discomforts **that** teachers not **un-**frequently experience **where** this custom still exists.

In conclusion, I would **say that if** this story of characters and events in the humble walks of life contributes in a slight degree towards awakening deeper interest in our schools, and thus conduces to their improvement—if it secures for the industrious, care-worn teacher, deserving sympathy from his patrons, or affords to himself any information or encouragement in the discharge of his duties, it will faithfully execute **its** mission — THE FRONTIER SCHOOLMASTER will answer the highest hope of

                              THE AUTHOR.

CONTENTS.

PAGE

CHAPTER VII.

CHAPTER VIII.

CHAPTER IX.

CHAPTER X.

CHAPTER XI.

CHAPTER XII.

CHAPTER XIII.

CHAPTER XIV.

CHAPTER XV.

CHAPTER XVI.

CHAPTER XVII.

CHAPTER XVIII.

CHAPTER XIX.

FRONTIER SCHOOLMASTER.

CHAPTER I.

My aversion to teaching—I am exhorted to teach, but refuse—I
repent, and engage to teach during the winter—My schoolhouse
—Boarding around.

I WAS seventeen. Two of my friends, young men not
older than myself, had recently engaged to teach school,
and had advised me to take up the same business awhile,
in order to obtain means towards defraying my expenses
in climbing the Hill of Learning, but such was my dislike
for the work that I had resolved never to attempt it.

Two things had given rise to this aversion : first, I
remembered distinctly the annoyances to which I had seen
teachers exposed from the thoughtlessness or mischievous
proclivities of their pupils.

Second, I had decided to study law, and, with a boy's
want of reflection and judgment, I looked upon teaching
as a vocation so inferior to that of a lawyer's that I was
unwilling to use it even as a stepping-stone to something
higher.

B

thing to help yourself you can't expect me to do much more for you. I've kept you dressed up and at school, now, for two years, summer and winter, and, if you are not of a mind to teach a few months, you must pay your expenses at Mayfair if you go to school this winter."

"I don't think Frank is strong enough to teach," anxiously interposed my mother.

It was to her that I was chiefly indebted for the comparative ease I had always enjoyed. I was a youth of rather delicate constitution, and she had always manifested considerable anxiety lest I should over-exert myself in attending to such farm labors as devolved upon me to perform; consequently, I had endured but little of the hardships which the neighboring farmers' boys had to undergo.

She had always insisted, too, that my wishes with regard to dress should be fully gratified, so that my expenses while at school really amounted to a considerable sum for a man of small means to meet.

My father was equally pleased to indulge me, whenever he thought it wise to do so, but he was of a more practical turn, and wished to teach me self-reliance, industry, and all the other virtues which equip a young man properly for the battle of life. The little property that he possessed he had acquired by the strictest industry and economy, hence, he had no sympathy for the young man who shrank from hardships, or the one who, with everything in his favor, had made shipwreck of his possessions.

My mother was a widow residing in New York at the time he married her, and, after the marriage, he remained in that city until I was seven years of age, when he was induced, by the cheapness of land in Canada, to remove hither. To the remark of my mother, as narrated above, he simply ejaculated :

" I'll risk him."

This closed the discussion, and soon after this I retired to my chamber to meditate, but not to sleep till after the clock had struck one.

I pondered the situation, realized the impossibility of carrying out my schemes without money, and so surrendered myself to circumstances, and decided to try my success at school teaching.

I did not so much fear my ability to impart instruction to pupils as I distrusted my temper under trying circumstances. I was impetuous, very sensitive, and I hardly felt equal to the task of preserving my equanimity and exuberant spirits in the **face** of the fault-findings of patrons, and insolence of disorderly pupils, to which I **knew** teachers were almost invariably subjected. But there **was** no alternative, so I felt constrained to submit.

The following Monday I was again at school in Mayfair. In the evening I chanced to meet a man named Barnum in the post-office, who was pointed out to me as the chairman of a school committee in a district in Meadville, ten miles from Mayfair. I timidly, and with many misgivings, addressed him. He had seen me, he said, in the village at our Lyceums, school examinations, etc., and believed from what he had seen and heard of me that I was a " chap" that could teach a good school, if I was a " mind tew." I was somewhat encouraged, still I feared that he expected too much of me. He was a wealthy but illiterate farmer, and penurious withal, so that the main object with him seemed to be to secure my services at the lowest possible price. After a long parley the bargain was closed, and I had engaged to teach for three months, build my own fires and " board around " for the sum of $11 per month. I knew the customs of teachers well, so the information that I was to " board around " among my pupils did not surprise me, yet it seemed the most trying part of the labors I had agreed to undertake.

It was a bitter cold Monday morning following that time-honored New England festival, Thanksgiving, that I left the village of Meadville and trudged on foot almost disheartened over the frosty snow to the scene of my future labors. I shall never forget the appearance of the school-house as it first struck me on that memorable morning. It was not unique, for the schoolhouses of northern New England and a greater part of Canada in those days wore the same forbidding aspect ; and it is to be regretted that a quarter of a century has not made the change in these educational institutions which the progress of wealth and intelligence demands. It was an old wooden building without paint or cornice. Many of the clapboards had started from their places, and frequent loud cracks occasioned by the assaults of Jack Frost upon this cheerless structure made me shiver for the urchins who should seek instruction within its walls.

The interior was still less inviting. Three rows of desks on either side of the room, elevated one above the other, offered accommodations to the pupils ; while my own, raised nearly half way to the ceiling, occupied the farther end of the room facing the door. The house was

extremely musty and dirty, and the desks were disfigured
with ink and with all the unsightly notches and carvings
which a boy with a jack-knife is capable of executing.
The only thing that cheered me was the sight of a huge
stove located nearly in the centre of the room. Though
cracked and exceedingly rusty, it suggested the idea of
warmth. With this stove, I thought, and plenty of good
wood, I can bid defiance to **old Boreas** even in this crannied
schoolhouse. I had forgotten that schoolhouses in this
section were always supplied with green wood fresh from
the forest, and that during the first hour or two of school in
the morning the pupils were always supposed to stand five
deep around the stove, while the teacher, from courtesy and
kindness to them, must shiver in the background.

After taking a solemn survey of the building, and
deciphering the **names** of " **John** and Betsey," and " Bill
and Melinda," coupled together on the walls in the rudest
chirography, **I** bethought me of the article in my agreement with the committee which required **me to** build **the**
fires. There was no woodshed, **and the** only thing that
held out to me the hope **of fuel** were several small hum-
mocks of snow near the door, which looked **as if** they might
be sticks of wood left **there** at the close of the last summer's
school.

Inspection showed that my conjecture was right, and
after assaulting these with a long wooden poker which I
had found by the **stove,** and with sundry kicks which
threatened the destruction of my nicely fitting boots, I
succeeded in bringing several of them to a resurrection.

My next difficulty **was** the want of an axe and suitable
kindling. There was **a** house about a quarter of a mile

distant, and to this in no very pleasant humor I repaired. A heavily whiskered man in his shirt sleeves appeared at the door and listened to my solicitations.

" O, you're the new schoolmaster," he said, eyeing me in a most inquisitive manner. " Wall, come in, set down and I'll see if I can find something to start yer fire with· I told Barnum that I'd draw some wood to the schoolhouse last Saturday, but I swan one of my oxen was took lame, and I didn't have time to look up another team ; but I'm gwine into the woods to cut and draw some right off. I'll have enough thar for yer afore night."

I stepped into the house and took a seat before the fireplace. Three or four ragged urchins retreated to a remote corner of the apartment as I entered, where they watched me with impertinent curiosity, and indulged in occasional whisperings and gigglings.

The man, whose name was Johnson, introduced me to his wife as the new schoolmaster, and then retiring in pursuit of kindling left me to listen to her account of the " shiftlessness " of the " folks " in " providin " wood for *that* schoolhouse.

" True as you're settin thar," she exclaimed, waxing eloquent on the subject, " my man had to furnish half the wood for that schoolhouse last winter, and we haint only four young ones to send, when thar's Tom Simpson that sends seven, and he never drawed a stick of wood all winter."

I sympathized with her in her indignation, and described the state of things as I had found it at the schoolhouse that morning.

" Yer orter tore a clapboard off from the backside of the

schoolhouse for kindlin'," exclaimed a precocious boy in the corner, addressing himself to me. "That's the way **the** boys do when we find the fire's gittin' low."

Subsequently, I discovered that that part of the school-room where my desk was located seemed much colder than the other parts, and on seeking the cause, found that the rear of the building was almost entirely denuded of clap-boards—a verification **of** the **boy's** statement that they had been used to resuscitate the expiring embers.

"That's **smart**, Bill," instantly reiterated the mother. "Tear the schoolhouse to pieces to kindle the fire! At that rate we'll have to build another house 'fore long, and then we'll have more taxes to pay. Taxes is eatin' us up now. School teacher's wages is so high that it takes all we can rake and scrape to pay 'em. I hope that old schoolhouse will last **anyway** till my young ones are eddicated."

Bill saved me the trouble of replying by the following rejoinder:

"I don't care, it's a tarnal cold house, and I wish 'twas tore down now. Why, schoolmaster, one day last winter the water pail froze up tighter'n a drum, and Jerusha Cross froze both her ears, right thar in the schoolhouse, when the stove was red hot."

I shuddered, and was indulging in sundry forebodings of the future when Johnson entered with an armful of kind-lings which he transferred to my own arms, and then pre-sented me an axe, which he said he would lend me till school closed to split my kindlings with, and "to chop with a little when necessary." Although the utensil bore the appearance of having been used to chop bones ever since the landing of the Pilgrims, I thanked him cordially for the generous loan, and at once took leave. He accompanied me to the door to close it, and did not allow me to depart without volunteering this consolatory remark :

" You're a light chap to manage our big boys here. I shall expect to hear afore Saturday night that they've pitched yer out of the winder or shoved yer up the chimney."

I was not a little vain of my prowess and agility, but at that moment I was so vexed with the prospect before me that I most cordially hoped his expectations would be realized. Any humiliation I thought would be preferable to that of teaching three months in that place. I think the man must have understood something of my state of feeling when I replied in a most emphatic manner,

" I hope you will ! "

It was nine o'clock ere I had succeeded in kindling a fire, and then the wet, frost-covered wood burned with a slowness which promised but little comfort to the inmates of the schoolroom that day ; but in a short time Johnson arrived with a small load of wood, which he said he had taken from his woodshed, and with the aid of this, the house, before noon, had become endurable.

By ten, about forty pupils had assembled, and I found that this was my average number during my stay here. They were of all ages from six to twenty, presenting various degrees of intelligence and styles of dress. A few were just beginning to read, while many had made some advancement in arithmetic, geography and grammar, and two even studied algebra. Most of them looked neat, though with a few exceptions they were clad in homespun garments ; the girls in dresses of wine-colored, striped or drab woollens, and the boys in gray or striped woollen frocks and trousers. The younger boys with military precision all thrust their mittens for safe keeping beneath the broad belts which secured their frocks at the waist.

My first work after the pupils had collected and I had taken their names was to win their esteem by what I considered an appropriate speech of twenty minutes length. They listened with good attention, and I believed I had made a happy impression. I might still enjoy this consoling thought, had I not overheard Jerusha Cross that evening describing my oratorical effort as a "lot of high flowin' stuff" none of the scholars could understand.

I forgot my woes in a measure in organizing the classes and in striving to get the school into working order, so that noon arrived before I was aware of it. I had not thought of dinner till school was excused and the pupils appeared before me, eagerly devouring the contents of their dinner baskets. I then began to realize that I was in the enjoyment of a good appetite, and remembered that I had taken a scanty and very early breakfast. I sat in my **desk** regarding the situation when a very stout girl, with red face, approached me, carrying in one hand a **basket**, into which the other was thrust, evidently **in quest** of provisions.

"I s'pose you'd like some dinner, wouldn't yer, Schoolmaster?" she asked with a bewitching smile, at the same time bringing forth three large doughnuts from the basket and placing them on the desk before me.

I had hardly time to smile and thank her, when she reinforced this supply with two slices of brown bread and butter.

I had already learned that the girl's name was Jerusha

Cross, and as she walked away from the desk I remembered her as the one whose ears had been frozen in the school house during the preceding winter. A glance at these auricular organs sufficed to show that there was much probability in the boy's story, for they were of enormous size and stood out from her head like wings from a building.

I had always had an antipathy to doughnuts, but I knew when I decided to teach that I must overcome my natural dislike to them, as they had always been regarded in New England as a kind of food specially adapted to the stomachs of school teachers ; whether because they were not expensive, or because they were believed to be conducive to intellectual vigor, I have never been able to learn. I was not long, however, in dispatching those placed before me, neither the bread and butter, and I then sat waiting for the next ten minutes to expire when another girl with a fair, modest face approached the desk and deposited a good-sized apple before me. Without giving me time to thank her she rushed away, blushing, to the group of boys and girls standing near the stove.

Her action had been observed by some of them, and at once a vociferous shout was raised.

" O Nancy's sparkin' the Schoolmaster ! Nancy's sparkin' the Schoolmaster ! "

The expression was instantly caught up and repeated by at least a score of voices, and it was not until I had fiercely pounded the desk with a ruler and commanded silence that the din subsided. The poor girl at the first commencement of the jeering stole away to a back seat in the farther corner, rested her head on a desk and commenced crying. I was indignant at this first exhibition of my pupils' rudeness, and to assure them that I appreciated the present, I at once ate it.

Several days elapsed before the pupils ceased to tease Nancy, slyly, about the schoolmaster, and she seemed to think she had committed such a bold and unfeminine act, that for more than a week she never gave me a chance to speak to her outside of school hours. I lost no opportunity, however, of addressing her kindly, and of encouraging her in her studies, **and I** believe that she **was one of** the several pupils **who when** I left the school regarded me with grateful feelings.

The afternoon wore away quickly and quite pleasantly, so that I began to hope I might go through the school with much less discomfort than I had anticipated. At four o'clock, I excused my pupils, put on my overcoat, and was beginning to wonder where I was first to find "board and lodging," when Jerusha Cross again **came** up to me with the following **question:**

"You'll go home **with me I guess** to-night, **won't yer,** Schoolmaster?"

"To board?" I asked, undecided as to what **reply I** should make.

"Yes," she replied. "**Ma** said she'd like to have yer board **at our** house **this** week, 'cause we're rather short out for **beds,** and Uncle John's folks are comin' from Massachusetts to see **us** next week. **We killed** hogs yesterday **to** be ready for yer."

"How many did you kill?" I asked with all the gravity I could assume.

"Three," she replied, and her eyes glistened with pride at the opportunity given her to proclaim the abundance **in her mother's** larder.

" No, Jerush," exclaimed her brother Sam, a boy of thirteen, standing near, who was evidently an admirer of precision in narration, there warn't three *hogs*. We only killed the old sow and two pigs."

" Well, what's the difference, I'd like to know ? " indignantly retorted the sister. " The pigs was most full grown."

"A pig ain't a hog, anyway," obstinately persisted Sam.

I interrupted the controversy by assuring them that, in either case, I thought the supply would be sufficient for the time I remained with them.

" Yer don't expect to eat a hog and two pigs in six days, do yer ? " asked the boy in amazement. " Yer know yer can't board but two days for a scholar in this deestrict, and there's only three on us."

" In that case, I said, I think a pig will be sufficient."

The boy appearing satisfied with this moderate demand on their winter's store we left the schoolroom, and slowly wended our way to their house. Jerusha walked beside me, and her two brothers followed close behind. The girl was very loquacious, and as we reached the road at once opened conversation as follows :

" Haven't yer never kept school before ? "

" No," I said.

" Well, I should think it would seem kinder queer to yer."

I admitted that it did.

" I don't think I should like to keep school. Ma has always been telling she's going to send me ter the village tew school a couple of terms, and then try and git the school for me up in the Sanborn neighborhood."

"I think that is a good idea," I replied.

"You'd make a great school teacher, Jerush," exclaimed Sam. "Ma tried last fall ter have yer tell how much two bushels and a-half of beans would come tew at ninety cents a bushel and yer couldn't dew it. I'd like ter see yer keep school up in the Sanborn neighborhood; the scholars would ride yer on a rail 'fore you'd ben there a week."

"Shet yer head!" indignantly ejaculated Jerusha, interrupting him.

But the boy didn't "shut his head," and continued:

"'Twas only summer 'fore last the scholars up in that deestrict emptied the water pail down the schoolmarm's back, and last winter they took the schoolmaster out and stood him on his head in a snow drift."

Jerusha made no reply to this revelation of her brother, but after a few minutes said:

"You'll have more scholars next week, schoolmaster; there's a French family that lives up by our house and they've got lots of young ones they're going to send if they can git any thing for em to wear on their feet; they're all barefoot now."

"The young ones can all talk English but six," chimed in Thomas, the younger brother ten years of age.

"How many are there?" I asked.

"Seven," he replied with the greatest seriousness.

Another short period of silence ensued which was also broken by Jerusha.

"Don't yer think," said she, "some folks are awful nasty?"

After some effort to suppress my risibility I replied, " I have no doubt that there are such folks, but I am not acquainted with many."

" Well, I ain't either, but I know Dumas' folks is nasty enough; they eat dogs and cats and skunks and wood-chucks and every thing else they can git."

" They're cussed thiefs too; " said Sam.

" Yes," resumed Jerusha, " last summer, ma missed a whole bag full of dried apples and we knew they took 'em."

" We wouldn't though," said Sam, " if they had'nt like ter hev busted all the young ones from eatin 'em ; but I didn't care so much about that as I did their killin and eatin our old cat. We knew they did that, 'cause thar was a peddler stopped at our house with a lot of skins, and he showed us a catskin he'd just bot of Dumas for six cents. Ma said she thought that was rather cheap, for pa never sold one when he was alive for less'n twelve, and so I made up my mind I'd jest take a squint at it, and I knew right off 'twas our old cat's hide, for he had a black spot on each side and rings round his tail."

" Ma," pursued Jerusha, " would hev had 'em took up last summer, but she thought if she did, jest as like as not they'd pizen one of the cows or burn up the barn."

The conversation concerning this unfortunate French family continued without interruption till we arrived at the domicile of the Widow Cross, which was a mile distant from the schoolhouse. It was a commodious log dwelling with a large frame barn in the rear which bespoke pros-perity. A little farther on was another log house which Sam pointed out as the abode of the incorrigible Dumas family.

A small black dog greeted us as we turned into the door-yard, with numberless sharp yelps and growls, and, as a supplement to this performance, he fastened his teeth to one leg of my pants. The boys came to the rescue in time to save me from being devoured, and as Sam bore him off in his arms he informed me that Trip was a good dog, but that he was "allers cross to beggars when they come round the house."

The widow, who was a tall, masculine-looking woman, not above forty-five, gave me a hearty welcome, and at once invited me to take a seat at the table on which the supper was already placed. There was a bountiful supply of food in the shape of potatoes, pork sirloin, fried, corn and wheaten bread, a small mountain of doughnuts and a heavily laden plate of buckwheat pancakes, well buttered and supplied with maple sugar. Before such a repast my unpleasant reflections once more forsook me, and I listened with interest to the amusing remarks both of the widow and her children.

"I spose," said she, after we were fairly seated, "you never kept school afore."

"No," I said, "this is my first experience in the business."

"Well its payin business," she said; "I wish my boys was big enough and had eddication to teach. How much dew you git a month?"

"Eleven dollars," I replied.

"Leven dollars! well that's good wages. Times aint much now as they used ter be when I went ter school."

"Was it in this place," I inquired, "where you went to school?"

" Yes," she said ; " the old log school-house stood right where ourn does now.   Teachers thought they was gittin good pay in them days if they got eight dollars a month and chopped their own wood.   They took their pay too in sich stuff as they could git.   They ginerally paid em in corn and buckwheat ; sometimes, like enuff, they'd git a little wheat, but thar wa'nt much of that raised in them times."

With accounts like this of olden times—the hardships which the early settlers endured in clearing their lands of the primeval forest, the attacks of wild beasts upon their cattle and sheep, did the widow entertain me during the time we were at supper and while she and her daughter cleared the table and washed the dishes.   Later in the evening, as we sat around the comfortable fire blazing in the fire-place, Sam, after having examined my watch and chain carefully, and inquired their price, remarked :

" Them's a nice pair of boots you've got on, schoolmaster.   What can you git sich a pair for ? "

I gave him the exact price.

" Yer pa," said Mrs. Cross to Sam, " had a pair of thin boots a good deal like them when he was married, and they lasted him 'leven years."

" Do you spose you can make them last you as long as that ? " inquired Sam.

I thought it very doubtful.

After a few more observations respecting the inferior quality of boots and shoes manufactured " now-a-days," the widow said :

" I spose you are used ter sleepin alone."

With some anxiety, not knowing what was to be the next thing, I replied in the affirmative.

"I shall be obleeged to have you sleep with my two boys," she said, "as I'm short out for beds."

I began to wonder where "Uncle John's folks" were to sleep when they came.

"I guess you'll git along well enough," said Sam, "if Tom don't git ter snorin. If he does you'll think the Ole Harry's got yer. I **have** ter git up every night or tew and choke him, **ter make** him stop it."

I concealed my vexation, and replied that I thought we would have no trouble about the matter. **To** study or read much while "boarding around" was an impossibility, but it seemed more than I had bargained for to have the company of any one thrust upon me in my sleeping apartment. But again I resolved to surrender myself to circumstances with becoming grace, if possible, and so I followed the boys to an adjoining apartment which **was** designated as the "square room." There were **a few** chairs in it and a small stand by the bedside, on which Sam deposited the iron candlestick **with** its tallow candle. The boys immediately undressed and generously squeezed themselves together at one side of the bed, that I might have ample room on the other. I did not feel inclined to sleep, and pulling a newspaper from **my** pocket sat down and began to read.

The temperature of **the** room, **however,** did not suffer me to continue this long, and I extinguished the light and joined my bedfellows, now locked in the embrace of sleep.

The widow kindly opened the door a little distance after I had retired, to admit warmth from the kitchen. I could not sleep but turned from side to side and harassed myself with unpleasant thoughts of my position and dark pictures of the future, until I had worked myself into a fever of excitement ; in short, I was in a rage. Tom began to snore ; this annoyed me, and, in a fit of desperation, I jumped from my couch, lit the candle, and sat down without dressing me, on the edge of the bed. I had no motive in doing this, but was prompted, doubtless, like all excited persons, by a desire to do something, without knowing exactly what. But the current of my thoughts was soon changed. No sooner had I placed myself in this position than the detestable cur which had before attacked me, hearing a noise, came through the door and seeing me sitting on the bed in my night-shirt with disheveled hair, approached me, slowly, with surly growls. I remembered what had been said of his aversion to beggars, and the conviction that I was one made his indignities all the more insulting. An angry man sometimes finds relief by venting his spite even upon an inanimate object, and I found consolation in turning the tide of my wrathful feelings against the dog before me. He was in close proximity to me, and evidently intended to commence his work of destruction by burying his teeth in my bare feet. I seized one of my boots by the top and swinging it furiously, brought the heel down with full force on his head. The work was done. He dropped immediately, turned on his side, quivered a moment and then was still. The widow's favorite Trip, the pet of the household, was dead. My wrath had fled. I was alarmed, nay terribly frightened ; I felt that, henceforth, I would be associated in the estimation of the family and all their friends with the Frenchman, the thief, who had killed their cat and stolen their dried apples. What was I to do ? Perhaps I could persuade them that the dog had died a natural death.

But of what disease did he die ? They might have a post-mortem examination, and I thought I must certainly ascribe his death to some disease of which they knew but little. I had noticed a last year's medical almanac hanging up in the room, when I entered, and in my alarm I quickly sought this, in the vain hope of finding in the category of diseases something to which I could reasonably ascribe the death of poor Trip. I ran nervously over the pages and found liver complaint, consumption, bronchitis, dyspepsia, diphtheria, diarrhœa, cholera infantum and swelled neck. If I could now only find *swelled head*, I thought, I would have no difficulty in persuading the widow that that was the disease which brought the dear pet to his untimely end. But I looked in vain; and finally threw down the almanac in despair, deciding to attribute his demise to hydrophobia. His symptoms had not been very marked, but I could with truthfulness assert that when I first came to the house that evening I thought the dog was *mad*, and it would be an easy matter, no doubt, to convince the family that this was a peculiar form of the disease, but rarely known. Hydrophobia, then, was to be the cause of Trip's death, and this decision being made, shivering more with fear than cold, I crept into bed. I was not satisfied, however, with my fabrication; it did not seem quite reasonable; the dog's head might awaken suspicion of "foul play," and then my connection with the affair would be discovered. I projected other plans, and finally hit on the following : I would get up very early in the morning before the family was awake, take the dog to a neighboring wood and bury him in the snow. The boys were sleeping soundly, the widow and her daughter were asleep in the attic, and knew nothing of what had occurred, and my plan seemed quite feasible. They would miss the dog, but would probably attribute his disappearance either to the enmity or hunger of the Dumas family. Consoled by this reflection, Tom having ceased snoring, I dropped asleep.

A rap at the door and the announcement that breakfast was ready was the first thing that roused me to consciousness. I turned over and found that the boys were gone. They had got up so quietly that they had not awakened me. The thought of the last occurrence of the previous evening then came over me and nearly stopped the pulsations of my heart. I raised my head, looked for the dog and he too was gone. They know it all, I thought, and I felt that my only way was to claim that I killed him in self defence. I arose, dressed, and went nervously and with flushed face to the kitchen. As I opened the door, the first object that met my astonished sight was the identical dog that I had killed—Trip. He saw me at the same moment and instantly his caudal appendage dropped, a cowardly expression came over his ugly visage, and he quickly sought refuge beneath a chair in a corner of the room, from which place he peered out at me with a look of mingled detestation and terror. I had scarcely time to say "good morning" to the family when Sam exclaimed,

"What the Ole Harry's the matter with Trip? He acts as if he thought you was a catamount, Schoolmaster."

I only colored more deeply at this remark without making any reply; but I was soon satisfied that none of the family knew of my rencounter with the dog in which he had only been stunned. During the rest of the time that

I boarded with the widow, Trip treated me with profound respect. I seldom caught sight of him except as he viewed me from behind some object, and then there was always an expression of curiosity in his look, as if wondering how long I would permit him to remain on "the shores of time."

CHAPTER II.

THE second day of my stay in the district passed without the occurrence of any interesting or amusing incident. There were two or three loads of green wood at the door of the school house, a portion of which was chopped into stove wood, but the greater part consisted of large logs. I concluded to save what remained of the dry wood, which had been drawn the previous day, for kindling; and in this way I succeeded in getting the house tolerably comfortable every morning before the time school was to commence.

Although fatigued with my day's labor at night, I decided to visit an uncle who resided at the village. I was thoroughly homesick, and it seemed as if I had been absent from home a month. I spent the evening with the Principal of the Academy, a gentleman belonging to the senior class of Dartmouth.

He had taught at Mayfair six months of the previous year, and was now at Meadville for the purpose of earning means to enable him to complete his college course. He laughed heartily at my experience as pedagogue, and gave me an interesting account of his own early experience at teaching. He thought me fortunate in having two boys for bedfellows, affirming that while teaching once in Northern New Hampshire, when about my own age, he boarded at a place where he was obliged to sleep in an old-fashioned bunk, and on waking **in the night** invariably found that his couch was shared by three hounds.

His advice did me good. He persuaded me that by remaining in the school **I** would strengthen my stability of purpose and win a reputation for accomplishing whatever I had undertaken. By "roughing it" for a few months, and coming in contact with different people, I would treasure up many incidents and gain knowledge of human nature which would afford me amusement and profit the rest of **my** life. His logic was not to be disputed, and I went to my school the **next** morning with a lighter **heart** and a more determined spirit.

A week passed, and though I spent three nights of **that** time in the village at my uncle's, I was **always** at my schoolhouse in the morning in time to **attend** to my duties. My dinner was brought regularly by the Cross children, and after the first day it always consisted wholly of doughnuts. Thus far, **I had had** but **little trouble** from disobedience. On two or three occasions, I had felt obliged to shake a couple of mischievously-inclined urchins, but I had in no instance discovered anything that could be regarded as a wilful determination to disobey me. While I sought earnestly to have the pupils advance in their studies, I also spared no pains to gain their good-will, and I felt that I was successful. **The** larger boys at noon were often inclined to address me with a familiarity that was somewhat distasteful, and indulge in jokes at my expense that were hardly respectful, considering my position ; but I had made up my mind to humor their rustic tastes, and thus avoided a collision and won their esteem.

Jerusha Cross was the only one of the girls who gave me much annoyance. She was habitually idle, seldom answered a question correctly, and my reproofs caused her to dislike me.

The first Sabbath after I began to teach I spent at home in Foreston. I was carried back to my school the next morning, but, owing to the distance and the bad roads, as there had been a heavy snow storm, it was some minutes past nine when I reached the schoolhouse. The last of the dry wood had been burned the Saturday previous, and there were but a few sticks of green wood remaining. The boys, according to their custom in such cases, had torn three clapboards from the building, and with this kindled a fire. I scolded them for the act, saying it was the duty of the committee to see that we were supplied with good wood, and in case we were not, instead of demolishing the schoolhouse for fuel, we should go home and wait till wood was furnished.

The wood was soon consumed, and before noon we were suffering from cold.

None of the larger boys seemed inclined to chop, and though I had sent a boy early to inform one of the committee of our necessity, no relief came.

At noon, I dismissed my pupils and went myself to the village. I had had no dinner sent to me that day, from which circumstance I concluded that my term of boarding with the widow had expired.

That evening I chanced to meet that member of the

committee to whom I had in the morning sent the message. I spoke with him, but he was decidedly crusty. Before we separated he said :

" We never had a schoolmaster afore but what could chop a little wood if necessary."

" I am not very good at chopping," I replied.

" Well," he said, "'twouldn't have took yer long ; yer could have chopped enough at noon ter last half a day, and had time ter eat **yer** dinner tew if yer aint no great chopper."

" I had no ax fit to chop with," I replied.

" Why didn't yer send to one of the neighbors and borry one ? A man aint fit tew keep school that can't chop wood enough ter last half a day."

I left him after receiving this information, resolved that I would not chop wood, **and** thinking that such **a** school manager had as much to learn concerning his duties as I had respecting mine.

From that time forward we never had any dry wood, but, by covering the embers well with ashes every night, I had sufficient fire in the morning to enable me to get along with such wood as we had.

I next went to **board with a sociable**, good-hearted old farmer, who **sent** three boys **to school, two** of them older than myself. I had good fare ; **plenty** of nice apples and new cider, and was permitted to enjoy the luxury of sleeping alone. The only thing in which I desired a change was in the quality of my dinner—doughnuts still being regarded by my boarding mistress as indispensable for this midday meal.

I began to get interested in my school. I had inspired the majority of my scholars with an ambition to have good lessons, and, on the whole, they seemed to be doing well.

There were many possessed of bright intellects, and they required no great amount of encouragement and training to bring them up to the standard of cultured men and women. The thing in which they seemed the most deficient was in a knowledge of the art of spelling, nearly all being most lamentably ignorant of this important branch. My second spelling-class consisted of about a dozen members, mostly boys, and the difficulty I experienced in teaching them orthography had caused me to regard this as the most stupid class I had in school.

One day during my second week, there, this class stood before me, and I pronounced from *Town's Speller and Definer* the word *sauce.* The boy whose turn it was spelled,

"S-c-o-c."

"Next," I said, looking at him reproachfully.

After a little deliberation his neighbor spelled,

"S-c-o-c-e."

I looked at him more sternly than at the first, and again said, "Next."

The third commenced,

"S-c-o-s."

"What ridiculous spelling!" I exclaimed. "The next try it."

The fourth boy with considerable show of trepidation slowly spelled thus :

"S-o-c-e."

I was becoming greatly amused, but suppressing my inclination to laugh, I said with an air of impatience,

"If there is any one in this class that knows how to spell this word correctly, let him raise his hand."

Instantly the hand of Josiah Snodgrass went up. He

was a tall boy of sixteen whose unkempt locks of yellow hair rested on his coat collar.

"Now, Josiah," I said, "are you sure that you can spell this word?"

"Yes, sir," he promptly answered.

"Well, proceed then;" and he proceeded in this manner:

"S-o-s."

For a moment I was silent, in which time Josiah cast a triumphant look at the boys in class above him, as if to see whether they were conscious of his superior scholarship, and then I burst into a fit of laughter in which all, except Josiah, joined me. He turned red and white by turns, and, as soon as the tumult had subsided, exclaimed:

"I never went to a teacher afore what made fun of his scholars."

This provoked a more hearty laugh from the whole school, but I soon restored order, and then tried to appease the wrath of Josiah by assuring him that I was not making fun of him, but laughing at the absurd way in which they had all spelled such a common word. I then gave the class a sharp lecture for neglecting to learn the lesson, and dismissed them with the injunction that the same lesson must be committed for the afternoon. The affair soon seemed to be forgotten by all except Josiah, who went to his seat to sulk, but not to study. Observing his manner, I remembered that his father—a man with a face about as intelligent as that of a Polynesian idol—had called some days previous, to speak with me about his son. He complained that former teachers had indulged in altogether too much partiality, consequently, Josiah had been abused, many of the scholars having been allowed to "poke fun" at him.

Two days after the incident in class, related above, had occurred, a boy came in and announced that Barnum was at the door and wished to see me. I went out and found him sitting in his sleigh. He at once made known the object of his visit as follows :

" I've come ter see yer 'bout some complaints that have been made ag'inst the school."

" What are they ? " I asked, considerably excited.

" Wall," he said, " Snodgrass was up last night, and he complained that yer make fun of yer scholars, so they don't like ter go to school t'yer."

I indignantly denied this accusation, then, remembering the incident in the spelling class when Josiah Snodgrass accused me of making fun of him I narrated it in detail, not doubting that Barnum, too, would be amused at the way in which they had spelled the word *sauce*. He only disgorged a quantity of tobacco juice from his mouth, and without even smiling, said :

" Wall I never should hev thought of lafin at that. I spose the boys war kinder fraid on yer the reason they didn't spell the word. Yer spell it s-a-u-s, don't yer ? "

I found it very difficult to suppress a laugh, but succeeded, and soberly said :

" No, it is spelled, s-a-u-c-e."

He looked at me, as if reflecting, and then asked :

" Be yer sure its spelled so in the book ? "

I replied in the affirmative.

" Let's see yer book," he said, still doubtful of my knowledge of orthography.

I went in, procured a spelling book, and then returned and pointed the word out to him.

" Wall," he said, after resting his eyes on it at least three minutes, " 'tis spelt so thar, but books change so we shan't any on us know how ter spell in a few years. In the book I studied when I went ter school the word was spelt s-a-u-s. But that **aint of** no consequence anyway, only you should'nt laf **at** anything when yer keepin school. You're a young man jest commencin business in **the** world, and I kinder advise **yer** for **yer own** good. **But** thar's **some other** things the deestrict **is** findin fault about. They say you're lettin the scholars tear the clap-boards off from the schoolhouse and cut the desks ter pieces with their knives."

I was highly indignant. I denied, positively, having done anything of the kind, and described the condition of the house as I first saw it. To my knowledge, not a boy had defaced **it with a knife** since I had been teaching; and I assured him **that on only** one occasion had they torn boards from the house for kindling wood; and that I had reproved them sharply for the act.

" Wall," he said, " yer orter jest sent out for two **or three** good blue beeches, as soon as yer found out they took the clapboards and made em took off their coats, and gin em an all-killin whalin."

" In my opinion," Mr. Barnum, I said, " your course is not **the** wisest, **and, had the** committee **of this** district always discharged their duty properly, and provided wood, I doubt whether any clapboards would have been torn from **the** house."

"Thar was wood enough here t'other day," he said, " when they took the clapboards."

" Yes, Mr. Barnum, but it was not fitted for the stove."

" Wall yer orter seen that 'twas chopped," he said. " We

allers expect a teacher to chop a little hisself if thar's
any wood ter chop when he runs short."

I felt that forbearance was fast ceasing to be a virtue, for
he seemed determined to find fault with me.

" My business here, Mr. Barnum," I said, " is not to chop
wood whenever the committee neglect to supply us, nor do
I think that I should incur the blame for what the pupils
have done in former years. It is your duty to know the
condition of the schoolhouse, and to visit the school from
time to time to ascertain whether I am managing it properly or not. It is not just that you should base your opinion
of my fitness for the place on the report of some unreasonable and ignorant boy or girl."

Barnum was evidently displeased, but after a moment's
silence he replied :

" I spose 'twould be well enough for some on us to come
inter the school once in a while, but it's a thing we've never
done afore. Fact is, I'm darned sorry I took the office of
committee, and specially of chairman. I didn't want it,
but they kinder forced it onter me ; and now I'm in, I'm
gwine ter dew the best I can fer the deestrict. I've hired
you and gin yer a good price, and I don't want yer to dew
anything that'll give the deestrict a chance ter find fault
with me."

I assured him that I would make every effort to discharge my duties faithfully and honorably, and expressed
the belief that no reasonable or sensible person would censure him for any action of mine. This closed the conversation, and he departed.

At the commencement of the third week I went to
board at a place which was distant about a mile and a half

from the schoolhouse. Here a young man shared my bed, and we slept in an upper room, remote from fire, where the snow sifted through the crevices in the roof, so that it sometimes covered the bed to the depth of an inch. Unused to such exposure, I caught a severe cold, from which I suffered for several weeks. My fare at this place was good, but doughnuts were still provided for my dinner.

An incident occurred this week which afforded a momentary relief to the monotony of teaching, and added another to the list of complaints which Barnum was treasuring up against me.

There **was a** boy in the school, fifteen years of age, named Thomas O'Callaghan. He had never been used to kind treatment and the comforts of life, consequently, was ill-tempered and rough in his manner.

Finding him engaged in mischief one day, I ordered him to come to my desk. He seemed reluctant to obey, and, rising in his seat, insolently declared that he would not come. I quickly walked up to him, seized him by the collar, **at the** back **of the** neck, with the intention of bringing him out with a sudden jerk. He wore an old blue jacket, which hung loosely about him, and **which** evidently had been made for his father, or for some person much larger than himself. To my astonishment, **Tom** never moved with the jerk I gave, **but his** jacket and **the** upper part of his shirt, if he wore one, instantly came over his head, and he stood before the school, stripped to the waist, as if about to take a dive in the waters of some sylvan stream. A roar of laughter burst at once, from every quarter of the house. Tom's face turned scarlet, so did mine. Once more I repressed **an** inclination to laugh, and quickly seizing the

D

jacket by the lower part, generously jerked it back over his head. Tom was subdued. I even began to pity him. He did not wait for me to command him a second time, but went to my desk, and, after receiving as severe a reprimand as I felt like administering, took his seat and devoted himself to his book.

The next morning, about ten o'clock, there was a loud rap at the door, and before any one could answer the summons, the door burst open, and in stepped a six-foot, broad-shouldered Irishman, gloriously drunk. It was Jerry O'Callaghan, Tom's father. He had in his hand a long birchen ox-whip with which he was driving a yoke of oxen to the village, and on arriving at the school-house had entered for the purpose of expressing his dissatisfaction at the way in which, on the previous day, I had treated his boy, Tom. An audible titter saluted him as he came in; but taking no notice of this he walked straight onward to within a few feet of where I was standing and suddenly stopped. Poising his unsteady head for a moment, as if to get a good look at me, he exclaimed:

"And ye're the schoolmasther?"

I was amused, but his muscular frame inspiring me with a degree of uneasiness as to what the result of his visit might be, I answered most respectfully, and with a faint attempt at a smile,

"Yes, sir."

"Bedad ye're the granest lookin divil that I've seen since I came to this counthry."

I was undecided as to the best course to pursue. To order him to leave the house, feeling as I did my inability to enforce the order without assistance, I believed would be folly.

The large boys, doubtless, would assist me, but then to make the school-room the scene of a disgraceful fight was a thing to be avoided, if possible.

I scanned his face and becoming satisfied that he was not naturally, vicious I determined to keep cool and flatter his vanity, in hopes of winning his friendship. The pupils were enjoying the ludicrous scene immensely, and no doubt secretly desired its prolongation.

As soon as I had sufficiently recovered from **my** astonishment I replied to his remark as follows:

" It is hardly fair for you, Mr. O'Callaghan, to make sport of a man's face because he does not happen to have one that looks as well as your own."

" Faith ye're right thin; ye'll niver see the day that ye'll have the honest and intilligent face of Jerry O'Callaghan· Shure they'd niver be makin **a tachir** of the likes o' ye in ould Ireland."

" I believe," I said, "that they have good teachers **in** Ireland."

" Good taichers, is it? **Bedad sir,** they're jintlemin. **Ye** might travel from Cork to Balleymooney, **and** divil the schoolmasther 'ud ye find that 'ud be guilty of tearin a boy's shirt."

During this short eulogy on Irish school-masters, Jerry's face flushed with anger; he dropped his ox-whip on the floor, clinched his fists, and stood trembling with eagerness for an affray. Before I had thought of a reply he continued, " Was'nt it yersilf jist that tore the shirt yistherday off from me poor boy Tom and lift him for an hour undrissed and naked to be laughed at by the boys and girruls."

" I assure you, Mr. O'Callaghan," I said, "that I had no

intention of tearing your boy's shirt. It was merely an accident, for which I am very sorry."

He paid no attention to my defence, but looking towards his boy, said,

"Tom, ye brute ye, come out here and pull off yer coat to show the masther how yer poor old mither had to sit up last night to mind the shirt he tore off yer back."

Tom did not stir, but with a most sheepish air looked steadfastly on his book. Seeing his reluctance, his father again exclaimed, "Tom would ye be disobeyin yer father now? Be jabers if ye don't come out here and pull off yer coat I'll break the hid of ye."

Tom knew too well the meaning of that threat to hesitate longer, and, with an expression of countenance in which shame and rage commingled, he came out and proceeded to take off his jacket.

Pitying the poor fellow, I said, "Mr O'Callaghan, I hope you will not compel Thomas to take off his coat. I have no doubt that I tore his shirt badly, but I assure you that I shall be most happy to pay you for any damage I may have done his clothes."

" Is it pay ye mane? divil a cint ud I be takin. Its only that he may see how me poor Nance had to sit up last night to put a big patch on the boy's shirt that I'd be makin him pull off his coat. Off wid yer coat, Tom."

Obedient to this mandate Tom divested himself of the jacket, and revealed a tattered nether garment of coarse, faded linen, across the back of which was a broad patch of the same material, new and unbleached.

" Did ye iver see the likes o' that now, man?" said Jerry, addressing himself to me, and pointing to the patch. " There's not a woman in this counthry that can patch like Nance; but was'nt it a shame for ye to be makin the poor woman sit up all night to be mendin a hole like that?"

"I am very sorry that I gave Mrs. O'Callaghan so much trouble," I said, "and hereafter I hope that I may be able to imitate the custom of your teachers in Ireland that we may have a good school."

"D'ye know how schoolmasthers corrict their boys in Ireland?" he asked.

"I believe I have heard," I answered.

A new thought seemed at that moment to have struck him, and glancing at the boys his eye rested on the form of William Sargent. He was the largest and best-dressed boy in school, studied algebra, was proud, and withal quite a gallant amongst the girls of that locality. He sat on a back seat, and had been the most amused spectator of any in the schoolroom.

"Come down here, Bill," said Jerry, "that I may show the schoolmasther how they flog the boys in Ireland."

Bill laughed and said,

"I guess not."

"Won't ye now?" said Jerry. "Come down now or I'll fitch ye."

Bill only laughed; but Jerry making a few long strides across the floor and up the alley, seized the young man by the collar and one arm and landed him, after nearly making him turn a somersault, in the middle of the floor.

Bill's face by this time was livid with fear and rage, but probably thinking that "discretion is the better part of valor" he said nothing. Jerry was soon at his side, and again taking him by the arm turned him around so that his face fronted my desk, and then ordered him to stand still.

"Get on his back now, Tom," he said addressing his own boy.

The order not being instantly obeyed, Jerry seized him by the collar and the broad part of his pants and placed him on Bill's back; he pulled forward his legs, one on each side of Sargent's body, placed Sargent's arms around them, and issued an order to the effect that Tom should be held tight·

Thus far I had not even imagined that he intended to inflict actual punishment on any one to illustrate to me the method of flogging pupils in Ireland, and my surprise was great when, after having placed his boy in the position described above, he picked up his ox-whip and quickly dealt him a heavy blow across the back. Tom was not the only sufferer, for the end of the flexible birch had raised an ugly ridge on the arm of poor Sargent. Tom screeched, Bill uttered an appalling, "oh!" and Jerry grinned. Instantly the boy was dropped, and Bill turning round hurled a most furious storm of vituperation and invectives at Jerry in which "Paddie" and "drunkard," were the mildest expressions. Jerry's attention was first turned to his boy.

"Hist," he said, "dont be blubbering like a babby, Tom; show the schoolmaster that ye're an Irishman and don't mind a little batin;" and then he stepped towards Sargent who beat a precipitate retreat toward the poker. As he seized it, however, Jerry seized him and at once bore him towards the door. His appearance as he took his unwilling departure may be briefly described thus: his face was turned towards Jerry, whose carroty hair he was desperately clutching with both hands. His left leg was fast in the arm of Jerry, while his right made frantic but ineffectual efforts to kick him in the back. Jerry's broad grin made it seem improbable that

he intended doing Sargent any serious harm, and, as it was
a relief to have him leave the house, I thought it best not to
interfere. He opened the door with little difficulty and
marching straight onward to his team, he placed Sargent
astride of one of his oxen where he compelled him to sit by
holding one of his legs. The scholars had made a rush for
the door to see what was to be done finally with Sargent,
and now stood laughing at his ridiculous situation. Jerry
turning **his head and** seeing me **at** the **door** exclaimed:
"Schoolmasther, come and hold this gintleman by the leg till
I place one of the girruls on the other baste, and bedad I'll
give 'em a nice ride to the village."

The girls retreated pell-mell to their seats; Sargent managed to release his leg from Jerry's grasp at the moment the
latter's attention was diverted, and slipping off on the other
side of the ox he made rapid footsteps homeward, stopping,
however, at a short distance to express a wish that all Irish-
men, and O'Callaghan in particular, might be driven from
the country to a place the exact location of which has not
been determined.

It was now my turn **to run the risk of** offending the
inebriate. I felt that I had allowed **him to continue** his
performances **too** long while indulging **the** hope that I
could get rid **of** him without serious **trouble**; but he must
be checked, at once, and my first effort must be to prevent
his entering the school-house. He started towards the door,
immediately after Sargent escaped, no doubt with the intention of giving us further instruction about schools in Ireland,
but I ordered the boys to take their seats, and then closing
the door remained outside, hoping that I might persuade him
to leave.

"Mr. O'Callaghan," I said, "you have shown me how you think boys should be corrected; I suppose you are now going to the village."

"Indade, I am sir, soon," he said, "but haven't ye more boys ye'd like to have corricted?"

"Not today, sir, I am much obliged to you."

"Ye're a jintleman, Mr. Styles, only don't be tearin the boys' shirts, and if any iv thim dont behave, sind for me and bedad, sir, I'll break their backs shure."

"Thank you," I said, "I must go now, as I have lessons to hear. Good bye, Mr. O'Callaghan," and I extended my hand which he grasped warmly.

"Good bye, schoolmasther, and long life to ye, and may God bliss ye."

I then returned to my labors, and he departed. Jerry's lesson in flogging proved a more expensive one than he fancied. He was the next day arrested on the complaint of Wm. Sargent, sen., who expressed a strong objection to his son's being used to illustrate how things are done in Ireland, and fined ten dollars and costs. Not having any such sum at his disposal he was sent to the county jail for thirty days.

The distance that I had to walk to my boarding place, and the uncomfortable room in which I was obliged to sleep while there, caused me to visit the village more frequently than ever. I sometimes met there some of my schoolmates, was often invited to evening parties, and the pleasure that I thus experienced contrasted strongly with the loneliness that I felt in the district where I was teaching. On two or three occasions, having slept late in the morning, I denied myself the comfort of a breakfast, in order that I might reach my schoolhouse in time to make a fire and be ready for the work of the day; but, unfortunately, twice I **was** too late to kindle the fire, and this work was performed by the pupils. The last time that this occurred was on the day which completed the first month of my engagement. It was nine o'clock when I arrived and the pupils had nearly all assembled. I proceeded with my work as usual, ignorant of the fact that there had been any particular fault found on account of my tardiness, until noon, when one **of** the older boys **came** up to my **desk** and confidentially informed me of **what** had transpired there in the morning before my arrival. I learned that Barnum came there quite early with two children, and found that there was no fire. Instead of making one, however, he waited until many of the pupils had come in to harangue them about the laziness and inefficiency of their teacher. Jerusha Cross, who was also there early, was the only one of the pupils who joined him in his tirade against **me.** Among other things that **he** said, and the inquiries **that he made,** he asked the following:

" What does he go down ter the village so much **for?** Why don't he stay here in the deestrict where he belongs ? "

One of the boys jocosely answered:

" He probably goes to see his girl."

"Girl," sneeringly exclaimed Jerusha, **" I** wish he'd spark his **'tarnal** head **off!** This makes twice I've come here when thar want **no fire.** I like ter froze my ears agin this morning afore the fire was built."

Her brother Sam excited **a** laugh which dampened her enthusiasm, by the following ungenerous remark:

" Nobody 'd known it, Jerush, unless yer told 'em, if yer had froze off 'bout four inches on em."

After various **remarks Barnum** declared his intention of

visiting the other two **members** of the committee at once, **to see** what **they** thought about calling a school meeting to investigate my conduct, and **gave** it as his opinion that I should be turned **out.** **He** left **a** few minutes before my arrival, and doubtless spent the morning in visiting different **parties to** awaken prejudices against me.

The information thus given me gave me great discomfort. I was altogether too sensitive to treat these fault-findings with the indifference and contempt they deserved, **conse-** quently, I went mechanically through the labors of **the** afternoon, thinking all **the** while what, under the circum- stances, I should do. **That I had** been guilty of neglect of **duty two or three times in** not building a fire in season, I was willing to admit; but I felt **that this was the** only fault which they could with reason **or justice** find against me. I had labored faithfully in school, the pupils **were** advancing in **their** studies, **the** majority of **them were** attached to me, and **it was obvious to** me that I had been more successful than I had anticipated in the beginning, and more successful than even experienced teachers fre- quently are. To call a school meeting, then, to discuss the **propriety of** dispensing with my services, I regarded as an **insult** which my spirit was ill prepared to brook, and I **resolved to** quit the school without delay.

Late in the afternoon a boy handed **me the** following notice, which he said had **been given him** at the door by Barnum.

" Mr. Stiles, Sir, we air goin' to hav a school meatin' at the schoolhous to morrer nite. The comitey think you orter be turned **out For thes reasons :**

furst, you Refus ter **chop wod. .**

secon', you let the boys tare bords off Fromm the hous and whital the benchas.

thurd, you git mad at the scollars **and** tair their clos.

forth, you doant bild.fires **in** The mornin.'

fif, you doant sta **at yer** bordin plases nites. we air sory mr. Stiles for you air **a** young Man and we wod like ter see you git Along wel in the Wurld, but foaks in the Deastrik think you air **stuk up** and wunt Bord with them.

by Order of the Comitey,

Z. S. BARNUM.

That night **at four** o'clock I went to my boarding place, took my valise, and without saying a word to any person relative to my intentions I turned my footsteps towards the village with happier feelings than I had enjoyed for a month previous. I cast one look back as I left the borders of the district, and mentally bade the schoolhouse, Barnum and his colleagues in office a reverential farewell.

I enjoyed the happy thought that I would never again teach school. The future, however, proved this to be an erroneous conclusion, but it was the last of my experience in "boarding around."

I never learned who kindled the fire at the school-house on the following morning, but I was informed that only two men besides Barnum appeared at the "school meatin." One was Snodgrass and the other was Johnson, the man who loaned me the axe and supplied me with kindling-wood the morning that I commenced teaching. The **latter** came for the purpose of telling Barnum in public what **he** thought of his efficiency as a school committee, and summed it up briefly by declaring him "the biggest fool" they had ever elected.

CHAPTER III.

THE next morning I went by stage to Foreston. I had anticipated paternal displeasure at the course I had taken, but my thin appearance and bad cough were in my favor, so that there was little said when I reached home except by my mother, who declared that she knew perfectly well when I commenced teaching that I would not, on account of my ill-health, be able to complete my term of engagement. My father suggested that I had better remain at home a few days until I had recovered in a measure from my cold, and then, if the majority in the place where I had been teaching were in favor of my returning to teach the remaining two months, I should do so. I met the proposal with indignation, and denounced it in terms that, I fear, were wanting in filial reverence. I said that nothing would induce me to enter any school-house again as a teacher, much less the one where I had received such indignities; and I pulled Barnum's unique notice from my pocket and read it to him a second time.

He certainly was not well pleased, and probably thought

me unreasonable and stubborn, still he said nothing. **The** next day he drove to Meadville to hear, I presume, the opinion which people entertained of my school, and of my course in leaving it so abruptly, but I never asked him.

For some days I did nothing in the way of manual labor except to assist about **the** chores, and I spent the remainder of the time chiefly in reading. **On** the following Saturday my father informed me that **he had** engaged three wood-choppers to work for him during the ensuing week, for the purpose of getting **his** year's stock of wood, and he expressed a wish that I would drive the horses and help load and unload the wood. I was not quite pleased with this arrangement, but believing that he intended by putting me to some labor to make me regret that I was not teaching, and at the same time awaken repentance in me for disregarding his wishes, I determined that he should be **disappointed**. I affected to endorse his plan most heartily. I entered **at** once into a calculation of the number of loads I could draw in a week, which was about ten more than the most able-bodied laborer would have thought of drawing. He smiled incredulously, but said nothing. I have since thought that my enthusiasm must have astonished him, for until that time I had never **displayed** much ambition at that sort of work.

Monday morning came, and **with it** came the wood-choppers. I **was** up before day-break, **fed** the horses, and as soon as the first tree was felled and cut up I was on the spot with the team ready to draw it. During the entire week I displayed the same industry, neither evincing any sign of fatigue nor expressing a wish to change my employment.

My father kept the men for three weeks, and I drew all

the wood they chopped.   The wood pile for height and size
rivalled the pyramid of Cheops.   We must have had a four
years' stock, but, when my father was about paying the men,
I coolly argued that he should keep them for another fortnight, as it was quite probable we might burn what I had
already drawn before the next winter.   He gave me a
searching look, as if to ascertain whether I was really a
lunatic, and then in no pleasant tone said :

"I don't think I shall have the horses killed *this* winter."

I regarded his determination as quite reasonable, for
since I began to draw wood they must have lost at least
two hundred pounds avoirdupois.

I went to bed that Saturday night nearly worn out with
my hard labor, but I enjoyed the consolation that I had not
yet been persuaded into a wish that I might teach school.

The next week I did but little labor.   I needed rest, and
enjoyed it greatly.   I had recovered from my cough, under my mother's careful nursing, and having gained a good
appetite from my active out-door exercise, I relished the
delicacies which she provided for my benefit.   There was
only one article of diet which I objected to having placed
on the table, and that was doughnuts.   I had had them
for dinner every day while I was teaching, and as soon as
I returned home I obtained a promise from her that there
should be none placed on the table for two months, and the
promise was faithfully kept.

Towards the end of the week my father presented me
with a new ax, carefully sharpened, and expressed a hope
that as I had had time to rest I would begin to use it on
the following week with some effect on the wood pile at the
door.   At first I did not manifest a great degree of pleasure at the present, for I presumed that his design was to

fit me thoroughly **for the** business of chopping, in order
that I might give my employers better satisfaction than I
did at Meadville, should he prevail on me to undertake the
management of another district school. But a little reflection made it seem more probable that he intended to create
in me so strong a dislike for such labor that I would
soon regard school-teaching as a pleasure in comparison to
it. If the latter was his object, I determined that he should
again be disappointed, and, accordingly, I began to admire
the implement **of** labor he had given me, and expatiate on
the amount **of** work which, with its aid, I would accomplish. I estimated that in six weeks I could fit that enormous pile of wood for the stove, when, in all probability, it
would have taken an experienced and hardy chopper as
many months to do it. He only smiled, and gave a grunt
expressive of his contempt for my feeble judgment.

Monday morning, in the forcible language of Bunyan, I
addressed myself to that wood pile with unwonted zeal. I
chopped without intermission, except to take my meals, till
dark. The next morning I was tired and sore, and, though
I made no complaint, nor expressed a wish **to** desist from
my labor, I decided to work in future less violently, and to
rest two or three hours **each** day, giving this interval to
reading. **By** judiciously pursuing this course, in a fortnight's time I had gained strength wonderfully. My hands
first blistered, and then calloused; my muscles became
hard, and the amount of wood that I chopped in a day was
a subject of comment among all the farmers' sons in that
vicinity. But I was not contented with my occupation.
Thoughts of a collegiate education, of a profession, and how
they **were to** be obtained, constantly engaged my mind, and
caused me to feel but little interest in the labor I was per-

forming; still, I said nothing respecting my desires or plans, and no one knew from my expressions or manner that I was discontented with my lot, or that I had any intention of following other business than wood chopping during the rest of my life. I was thus employed for a month, when, on driving to the village of Mayfair, one evening, and meeting one of my old friends and class-mates, he informed me that he was intending to start in a few days for the village of Shirley, about thirty miles distant, on Lake Champlain, for the purpose of attending school, and expressed a hearty wish that I would accompany him.

I was seized with a strong desire to do so, not only from an inclination to get fitted soon for college, but from fear that he would outstrip me in my studies, as we had always been rival candidates for academic honors, and had long allotted on entering college together. He had the advantage of me, however, from the fact that his ambition was not restrained by lack of means, as his father was a wealthy cattle dealer and speculator.

I first broached the subject of attending school again to my mother, as she was always my intercessor for favors from the paternal side of the house. She expressed a willingness to gratify my wishes, but at the same time gave me little hope of success from her intercession. Her first effort in my behalf was met with a rebuff, as we had anticipated, but in a day or two he began to speak more favorably of my design, and by the time another equal period of time had expired he had consented that I should be a student for a term of eleven weeks at Shirley. According to his custom, at such times, his first act, on consenting to grant me this boon, was to give me a lecture, in which he expatiated on the sacrifice that he was making, dwelt on the necessity of my making a proper use of my time, exhorted me to be careful of my expenditures, and, lastly, tried to impress upon me the necessity of doing something to earn money myself before I could expect any further assistance from him. I felt that this last information meant teaching school again, but grateful for his kindness, I listened respectfully to his counsel, and promised that I would observe his wishes.

In assisting to procure my outfit for school I borrowed a few dollars of a **friend** in Mayfair, and gave **him** an order on Barnum **for** whatever sum he was disposed **to** pay me for my month's **services,** knowing that he would be likely to quibble on the ground that I had not fulfilled the terms of my contract. The friend wrote me in a few weeks saying that he had received nine dollars on the order, Barnum refusing to pay the other two dollars, because, as he said, I had left the school without reason. I considered myself fortunate in getting the sum that I did, and regarded Barnum's excuse for keeping the balance, after sending me the notice that he did, quite characteristic of the **man.**

My hard physical labor **at** home had strengthened **me,** so that I was well prepared for mental labor at Shirley. The Principal of the Academy was an able and **energetic** graduate of Dartmouth, who has since risen **to the** position of President of one of the New England Colleges.

He seemed to like his vocation, and under his tutorship I made good progress, both in the classics and in mathematics.

E

CHAPTER IV.

IT was near the last of June that I was again on the farm in Foreston. Nature was clad in her best, and happy from the success that had attended me during my absence, I gave myself up to the full enjoyment of all the pleasure that can be realized at that season by a lover of nature in a rural home.

The farm, with two others of equal size adjoining it, was shut out from the main road, which ran through Foreston, by a belt of woods, and it was encompassed on the other sides by forests, which stretched away in the distance with various degrees of undulation. Close by, to the eastward, lay a beautiful cultivated valley, about two miles in width, running north and south the whole length of the township, and beyond this rose a continuation of the Green Mountain Chain, whose wooded slope had been invaded by the axe of the settler in only a few isolated spots, and whose crest loomed up against the sky in alternate ridges, bluffs, and rounded peaks. It was a high upland farm, and afforded an extensive view, not only of the nearer landscape, but of hill-

side farms and mountain heights far to the southward in
Vermont. It was indeed a secluded and, to me, a beautiful
spot.

This had been my home since early boyhood, and here I
had learned to commune with nature in her varied forms.
I was devotedly fond of hunting, and before attaining my
fifteenth year I had become acquainted, in my sporting rambles, with every brooklet, rock, morass and lonely nook
within a radius of several miles. I also had **my favorite**
woodland bowers, where I read and studied, and the huge
boulder in the recesses of the forest is now in imagination
before me, on whose summit I used to sit and study or
recite the declamation intended for school in the ensuing
week.

I had never been absent from home so long as I was while
at Shirley, and, on returning, I visited all my old familiar
retreats, viewed **the** farm **and** crops, and inventoried the
stock and fowls with great delight. Though disliking some
kinds of farm work, I took much pleasure in others, **espe-**
cially in raising and caring for stock and cultivating crops ;
and on my return, I immediately went to work with an
industry which gave both pleasure and profit to my father.

To my gratification, he had recently purchased a new
buggy and silver mounted harness, and as he had three fine
young horses, I felt that I was well prepared to enjoy myself during my stay at home. After working till fatigued,
I often found rest and recreation by taking a drive, towards
evening, to Mayfair, or to one of the two villages existing
in Foreston.

The farm work which usually precedes haying having been
completed, and nothing appearing to demand my services at
home, I determined one morning to spend the day in visiting

Spruce Knob, the highest elevation in the township, and which formed a part of the mountain chain to which I have above alluded.   The summit was about five miles distant, and though there was no path, and the climbing was in many places difficult, I had reached the highest point by ten o'clock. As it was covered with a stunted growth of spruce, the only way in which I could obtain a good view was by climbing a tree, and then the view became extensive and grand beyond description.

The uncomfortable position, however, that I occupied, soon rendered my descent to the ground necessary, and after eating my lunch I was prepared to return.   I had brought my rifle with me, hoping that a chance to shoot game of some kind might relieve the monotony of my journey, but no animate object, save a few small birds, had thus far attracted my attention, and, as I neared the mountain crest, not even these disturbed the solitude.

I had travelled some distance on my return, when I came to a rocky bluff which gave me a view of a valley below. Strange farms and a stream of much larger size than the one I had crossed in the morning appeared in the distance. Where was I ?   I was bewildered.   I sat down and took a careful survey of the scene before me, and tried to make things assume a natural aspect, but in vain; it was evident that I had lost my course, and had been descending the side of the mountain opposite that from which I had come up The valley was that part of the township known as Glen- field and on reaching it I would be ten miles from home. My best way then, instead of trying to retrace my steps and run the risk of again losing my course, was to travel on. keeping near the mountain crest until I came to the road which led across the mountain to Glenfield.   With this intention I resumed my toilsome journey through tangled brushwood and over fallen trees until near three o'clock, when I reached the highway. I was much encouraged, but, a heavy shower being near at hand, my **first** thoughts were of some place of shelter. A short **walk** brought me to the summit of the mountain where, in an open space on my left, stood a schoolhouse, in which I decided **to** remain until the **shower had** passed. It was evident that a school was in session, and I was pleased with the opportunity thus presented me **of** inspecting **its** character, as I had not been inside **a** district schoolhouse since I left the one in Meadville. Depositing my rifle in the small woodshed at the rear of the building, I came back and rapped **at** the door, which was opened by the teacher, a young lady about eighteen years of age. A look of surprise first greeted me, which soon gave place to a slight blush and **a** smile **of** recognition. She then cordially extended her hand with the salutation:

"How do you do, Mr. Styles?"

I **was** puzzled, surprised, nay astonished. I had not imagined that I would find a teacher here whom I knew, and to be addressed thus familiarly was to me for a moment an unaccountable occurrence. Observing my puzzled look as I gave my hand she said, smiling,

"Don't you know me?"

"Miss Edgarton," I said, beginning to recognize her, yet hardly certain that I was right.

"Yes," she replied. "Will you walk in?"

I accepted the invitation, remarking as I did so—

"It is a long time, Miss Edgarton, since I have seen you."

"Yes," she said, "nearly **six** years."

She offered me a chair, but, as it was the only one the room afforded, I declined it and took a vacant seat behind a desk.

"I am surprised," she said, "to see you in this place. I hope you did not come to inspect my school."

"Not wholly for that purpose," I replied. "I came in to avoid the storm, but I also had some curiosity to see the school."

"You taught yourself last winter, I believe," she said.

"I only tried to teach," I replied.

"You taught for a longer time than I supposed you would," she said laughing. "I knew that unless you had changed greatly since I attended school with you, you would not like the business of teaching."

"I am surprised at your memory, Miss Edgarton," I replied, "and still more that you should have known anything of what I was doing."

"O, I remember very distinctly the events of that winter when we attended the same school," she said, with a peculiar smile, "and I have often heard of you since."

"Indeed," I said, "I have not been fortunate enough to hear of you often. I learned on two occasions, long after we separated, that you were teaching; and two years ago I heard that you were attending school in Massachusetts, but I have heard nothing respecting you since."

"Yes," she replied, "since I saw you I have attended school three winters in Canada, one year in Massachusetts, and have taught school three summers."

"You must like teaching," I said.

"I do not positively dislike it," she replied, "if I have a school of intelligent pupils in a good community."

"Have you ever had any such good luck as that in teaching," I asked.

"O yes," she said, laughing, "I am often quite pleasantly situated while teaching."

"How do you happen to be in this place," I inquired.

"Simply, because I did not decide to teach until after all the other schools were engaged. I find the people here kind, but I am **very** lonesome."

After a few more remarks concerning teaching, **she** handed me **a** book, saying she knew I could employ myself more pleasantly **in** reading than **in** listening to her uninteresting classes; and then she excused herself to resume the duties of her school. I did not read, however, but listened to the simple recitations of the pupils and noted the different degrees of intelligence that they displayed. But I would not leave the reader to infer that the teacher engaged no part of my attention. I was pleased to renew her acquaintance; and as she sat in her **chair** hearing recitations, or moved about the room assisting the pupils in their studies, and kindly but firmly commanded attention to them, her manner, **features** and figure all **came** under my observation.

She **was a** trifle below medium **height, with** form neither slight nor too cumbrous. She had dark **hair,** hazel eyes, and her features, though not chiselled **on** the model of Circassian beauty, evinced much force of character. She was not handsome, yet there was an intelligence and frankness in her expression which, combined with her genial manner, at once commanded confidence and respect.

The circumstances under which I had formed her **ac**quaintance were these :—

One winter, at the time I was twelve years of age, I was

attending district school in the neighborhood where I resided.
The teacher was a lady experienced in her vocation, possessing good acquirements, and one who exacted industry,
respect and good order from her pupils. But she was
unappreciated by them, and, consequently, by their parents.
Through faults, wholly my own, I was never on good terms
with her, and to avoid a well-merited punishment which she
intended to inflict, I absconded from school. Before my
father knew anything of the circumstances, I petitioned him
for the privilege of attending school in an adjacent district,
representing that the teacher, who was a gentleman, was a
thorough scholar and a most efficient instructor; both of
which things were true. The petition was granted, but to
my dismay the rules which had been so obnoxious to me in
the school from which I had run away were in existence in
the other, and were enforced with an inflexible will and
superior strength. Under such circumstances it behoved
me to forego the indulgence of my mischievous habits and
attend to my books. I found here quite a number of boys
and girls well advanced in their studies, and among them
was Ruth Edgarton, who was boarding at one of her relatives
in this district for the purpose of attending the winter school.
I soon formed her acquaintance, and as there was a degree
of congeniality in our tastes, in the course of a few weeks
one of those strong attachments which frequently are formed
at school had sprung up between us. She was my superior
in scholarship, which fact tended to excite my envy, but
which on the whole operated much to my advantage, for,
ashamed of my inferiority in this respect, I devoted myself
to my studies with unwonted energy, determined that I
would not remain long in the background.

In another respect, too, she exercised a salutary influence

over me. Conducting herself at all times with womanly modesty and dignity, she **had** won the approbation of the teacher, and pride soon inspired me with a desire to avoid in her presence his reproofs. More than once, however, my propensity for fun came near securing me a flogging, but either for want of sufficient proof of my rascality, or from partiality towards me, **of** which I sometimes thought him guilty, I was spared this humiliation.

Inquiring **into the** history of Ruth, I learned that she **was** a native of Foreston, but her father and mother having died before she had attained the age of nine, she had gone to reside with an uncle who lived but a few miles distant in an adjoining township. Here she had been more especially under the tutelage of a maiden aunt, a woman of education and refinement, and exceedingly Puritanic in her notions **of** propriety. Ruth was a great reader, and, like myself at that time, had a decided preference for romance. **During** that winter we read several of Captain Maryatt's, **and** Cooper's novels, and the Scottish Chiefs; the latter **pos**sessing for both of us the most absorbing interest.

At the close of school we separated without knowing anything of each other's feelings **save** what we were able to divine; but **I think it may be** correctly inferred that I was enamoured. I earnestly desired to visit her, but diffidence and fear of ridicule restrained me, and so, during the months of the following summer which I spent at home, I projected many plans to be put into execution when I was older; and with these Ruth was always intimately **asso**ciated. I went more regularly to church than ever before, knowing that her uncle, occasionally in former years, had attended divine service in **Foreston; and I** cherished a hope that he might in future do so, and perchance bring his niece with him ; but my hope was vain, and so we did not meet.

As time wore on, my attachment decreased in fervor; other subjects engrossed my thoughts, and before two years had expired, I had lost all interest in this romantic episode in my history.   As stated above, on two or three occasions I had heard of the whereabouts of Miss Edgarton since we attended school together, but until we unexpectedly met at her school, I had not seen her.

As I conversed with her on this occasion, my thoughts continually reverted to the incidents in our former acquaintance, and as I saw her now before me only a trifle taller, and with face more mature, I confess that an interest in her began to awaken within me, and I wondered that I had not more speedily recognized her.

The rain having ceased, she excused her pupils a little before the usual time, as I presumed to resume her chat with me.   She was curious to know what had led me alone and on foot so far from home, and on telling her of my visit to Spruce Knob, and of my mishap in losing my way, she said,

" You are as full of romance, I see, as you were in your boyhood.   There are not many *men* that would enjoy a trip to the mountain alone."

"You forget," I replied, "that I am still in my boyhood."

" Indeed," she responded, taking a survey of my figure, " I think you are a tall young man."

After a few more unimportant remarks, I asked her where she was boarding, and learned that the house was a mile distant, and that I would have to pass it in returning home.

I proposed that we should take the walk together, to

which she gladly assented. I then went for my rifle, seeing which she smiled and said she would accept me as her guard of honor. We walked slowly, and never perhaps was time more fully occupied with conversation than it was on that occasion. At my request she gave me much of her history since we separated, and the remaining time was employed with reminiscences of that memorable winter.

Before **I was** at all aware of it, we had arrived **at** her boarding place. On bidding her adieu she expressed a hope that it would **not be** six years again before we would meet, and I was thus encouraged to suggest a ride on a certain evening of the following week. The suggestion meeting her hearty approval, I departed, unconscious of fatigue, and was soon absorbed in the most pleasant thoughts of that day's adventures. I reached home just at dark, to the relief of my family, who were beginning to feel a degree of uneasiness at my prolonged absence, knowing as they did the liability of my getting lost in that mountain wilderness.

Pursuant to my appointment, I was at the school-house of Miss Edgarton at four o'clock on the evening proposed. She gave me a cordial reception, and I **doubted** not that, owing to her secluded situation, with the want **of** congenial society, she was glad to have me visit her.

We rode down the mountain to Glenfield amid picturesque scenery, thence, along a beautiful river over rich interval farms, talking incessantly all the while; the scenery **and** books affording us sufficient topics. I was surprised at the knowledge with which her mind was stored. She seemed to have devoured all the authors, and spoke of many of whom I knew comparatively nothing. Biography, history, travels, romance and poetry had **all** evidently employed her leisure hours during the six years that had separated us, and though I had regarded myself as quite a reader, her superiority in this respect made me resolve that I would devote myself to reading with much more than my former assiduity.

It was dark when we returned, and she gave me an invitation to remain and take tea with her, but I declined, intimating, however, at the same time my readiness to take her to her home at any time she might wish to visit it. She expressed herself as highly pleased with the offer, saying that her Sabbaths and holidays seemed very long when she spent them in the district, as she usually did, on account of her inability to visit her home as often as she wished. It was then arranged that I should take her home a week from the ensuing Saturday, as on the evening previous to that she was to excuse her school for a vacation of two weeks.

During the remainder of the summer I saw Miss Edgarton, or Ruth as I soon began to call her, quite often. Her uncle resided about five miles westward from my own residence, on a large, well-cultivated farm, which, from its elevated position, had long been known as Maple Highland. It lay at the base of a mountain, of conical shape, which rose up in solitary grandeur like a pyramid, from a comparatively level section of country while on the other sides it was bounded by gentle wooded hills, which, with the valleys between, formed many pretty bowers and cosy dells. These we often visited together, and meeting thus, amid such romantic surroundings, with youth and hope singing their melodies in our hearts, the reader will not wonder that our interest in each other grew strong and deepened as time rolled on.

CHAPTER V.

THE summer wore away, and as **the** autumnal months
advanced thoughts of how I was **to** employ myself during
the winter constantly perplexed me. My brother-in-law
urged me to enter his office, at once, **as** a law student; my
father suggested school-teaching, but, **as** I felt that I was
not ready to do the former, and determined **that if** possible
I would not again **try** the latter business, I was forced to
look about for other employment.

I had relations in Albany, N.Y., and the thought occurring to me that by visiting that city I might possibly obtain
a situation of some sort which would afford me an opportunity to pursue my studies at an evening school, I proposed
the plan to my father, and after much hesitation and many
objections he reluctantly acceded to my proposal.

I was unused to city life, and had but a faint conception
of the numbers of men, young and old, in worse circumstances than myself, who flocked to the **large** towns and
cities, and laid wait with untiring watchfulness for every

place of profit—places, too, which often **were** of a low and unpleasant character, **and** afforded to the occupant but **a** scanty sustenance. **Mine was the** experience of thousands of young men from the rural districts who seek employment in the **city** without the prestige of wealth **or of** influential **friends. For nearly** two months I **tried,** effectually, **to** secure **a** situation. I became familiar with **all** the streets, **and** learned all the places **of** business in that antiquated **Dutch city, in my** efforts to obtain employment, but in **vain.** I watched the advertisements in all the papers, and **no sooner did I find one** that held out, to me a ray of hope **than I was on** the spot and humbly offered my services ; **but,** invariably, the place had either been given to another **before my arrival, or else I was** required to invest money **and** run the risk of its **being a** profitable investment. **I was humbled ; I** felt that I had made a foolish mistake in **not** accepting such **a situation as** I might have obtained at **home,** and so, sadder and wiser, I took the train one morning for the land **of** my adoption.

It was near the middle of December when I returned, **and** the schools were mostly engaged, but fortunately for me **a teacher** was wanted in the district where I resided, and **the** very evening that I reached home one of the school **managers came** in and offered me the situation. I was ready **to accept it on** any terms, but determined to do the best I could **with him, I** expressed no desire to teach, unless I could **enjoy the** privilege of boarding, permanently, at one place.

This was an innovation for which he was unprepared, and he considered himself obliged to confer with others concerning the matter before he could accede to my proposal. Had **it not** been for my desire **to** employ my evenings in study,

I would have had no great objection to "boarding around" in that district, as the inhabitants were all in comfortable circumstances, lived in good houses, and always provided for the comfort of their teachers. I believed, however, that I could carry my point, and so I permitted him to depart with the understanding that he was to let me know his decision at the end of two days. At the expiration of that time he returned with the information that my terms were accepted, and **I** was forthwith engaged for four months at twenty dollars per month. I was to commence my labors on the following Monday, and though the walk to my school was a long one I decided to board at home.

The day following my engagement I drove to Maple Highland, indulging in pleasant anticipations of meeting Ruth and rather pleased withal, that circumstances had combined to place me so near her home during the winter. I had corresponded with her while I was absent, and the last letter I received from her conveyed to me the information that she would not teach that winter, but would remain at home. My disappointment then may be more easily imagined than described, when I learned from her family that she had left a few **days** before for Montreal, where she intended to spend several months or a year perhaps in a convent, for the purpose of perfecting her knowledge of French. I could scarcely conceal my vexation. Why, I thought, did she not let me know of her intention that I might have seen her once, at least, before her departure? For the moment I forgot that she did not know as yet of my return, and that she was not at all certain that I intended to return, for chagrin at my ill-success, while in Albany, had prevented my saying much to her in my last letter respecting my intentions. Further explanations dissipated my unreasonable vexation, but did not in the least diminish my disappointment.

I knew that she had long intended to complete her study of the French language, of which she already possessed some knowledge, and it seemed that an opportunity had recently presented itself which she saw fit to embrace. An uncle of hers from Massachusetts had visited them, bringing with him his daughter, a little younger than Ruth, whom he was intending to leave at a convent in Montreal for the purpose of study. Fearing that she would be lonely there among strangers, he insisted that Ruth should accompany her, and as an inducement offered to defray her expenses,—an offer that she could not wisely refuse.

I returned home in a disconsolate frame of mind. I had anticipated much pleasure from visiting her during the winter, in fact, I felt that this would be about the only relief from the monotony and loneliness of my winter's work, and now that this solace was denied me I contemplated my labors with sad, solitary feelings. But I was beginning to learn that it is wise to submit to disappointments with patience; and summoning to my aid all the resolution that I possessed, I believe that I soon yielded to the circumstances with becoming grace.

I commenced my work the following week under favorable auspices. Having been a pupil at the same school up to a period of four years anterior to the time that I was inaugurated as teacher in it, I knew all my pupils except a few of the younger ones. My popularity with my schoolmates in former times seemed not to have been forgotten, and many of the older boys and girls who left the school about the same time I did to engage more constantly in their labors at home, were induced at the prospect of my

teaching to attend school again that winter. Only one dissenting voice was raised at my engagement.

This was that of a woman who indulged in the prophetic declaration that, owing to my " quick temper," I would
" kill all the scholars before spring." The sequel, however,
did not show the fulfilment of this prophecy. I labored
diligently to instruct my pupils, they became attached to
me, and as I met with no annoyances I soon experienced
a degree of contentment and pleasure in the situation.

I believe that this was the only school I have ever
taught where the satisfaction that I gave could be declared
perfect. I employed my leisure hours in study, and the
four months that I taught proved to me a period of
mental as well as of pecuniary profit. But the business
of teaching seemed to be then, as it has been ever since, ill
fitted to my temperament. Like nearly all similar institutions in this country, the school-house had no proper
means of ventilation ; it alternated between extremes of
temperature, in consequence of which I frequently caught
cold. Before half the term had expired my appetite was
impaired, I grew dyspeptic, nervous and thin, so that I
was cordially glad when my school closed. Previous to
that event, the school manager who hired me endeavored
to obtain a promise that I would teach the school on the
following winter, at a liberal increase of wages, but I gave
the promise that I would do so only in the event of my not
finding more congenial employment.

Not long after I commenced teaching, a letter, post-
marked " Montreal," reached me, which I nervously opened
and read as follows :

F

MONTREAL, 21st Dec., 1854.

DEAR FRANK,

You may be assured that I was not a little surprised, last night, when I learned from a letter which I received from home that you have returned, and are now teaching in your own district in Foreston. I trust it is needless for me to say that my surprise was mingled with vexation that I did not know your intention before banishing myself from home for the winter.

I had no doubt you would secure a good situation in Albany, notwithstanding the discouragements that attended your first efforts, and that a long time must elapse before I would have the pleasure of seeing you again. Indeed, in the fits of despondency which I believe are peculiarly my own, I had often persuaded myself that with your social nature, and fondness for adventure, you would soon become attached to the gaiety and excitement of city life, find more congenial society than in your country home, and thus forget the friends of your boyhood. Thoughts like these, together with the prospect of little to engage either my mind or hands during the long months of a Canadian winter, did much toward leading me to decide on accompanying my cousin to this place.

Do not imagine, however, that I was prompted wholly by despair, or even loneliness, for I knew it to be a most excellent opportunity to continue my French and music. My uncle, too, was so anxious to interpose my staidness and orthodox theology between his only daughter and all Romish proselytizing—of which I think he was needlessly fearful—that I could not well refuse him ; especially, as he offered to pay all the school bills.

I am sure you will like to hear what our life here is

like. First, allow me to assure you that it is very pleasant. When I came I must admit, prejudiced as I had been by reading and hearing of the wickedness of the Romish Church, I felt a sort of dread of—I knew not what. I shall never forget the first night spent here; the wind howled and shrieked around the dormer-windows, which are on both sides of the long dormitory where the girls with their attendant guardian **nuns** sleep. I could easily imagine the shrieks and groans to be those of heretics writhing in the torments calmly ordered and witnessed by the diabolical members of **some** Romish Inquisition holding a session somewhere on the premises. My cousin was nearly frantic with nervous apprehension that night. Added to the shrieking of the wind, there was something so weird in the appearance of the immense dimly lighted room with its rows of ghostly looking little beds. Indeed, I could scarcely persuade her to remain during the first week we **were** here. Accustomed, as she has been, to the almost unrestrained freedom of the American school girl, the **dullness** and monotony of convent life was too great a contrast to be borne with equanimity. **Since** the arrival of several American girls, however, she has become not only reconciled, but apparently quite happy.

We have Professors for music, German and Italian; the other teachers are all professed nuns.

"*Ma tante*" St. Euphrasie, who has our French class, is a bustling little old lady; her spectacles and feeble voice being the only indications of age, and her face is as smooth and fair as an infant's. She often approaches me, **and** laying her shapely white hand on my shoulder, **says**, "Ma chère Demoiselle Ezhairton." I am certainly very grateful for the kindness she shows me.

A description of our work for one day will suffice, for in this respect all the days are alike. We rise at 6 o'clock, and go to the chapel for early mass or prayers, where we remain until the breakfast bell rings. From the refectory we go to the class-rooms, where we remain until dinner, which is served at twelve. In the afternoon we have two hours of study, lunch, another hour of study, tea, recreation until nine o'clock, then prayers. An irreverent American girl blessed with the unappeasable school-girl appetite says, " We ought to be good, we get so much prayer and fasting."

I like these low-voiced, fair-faced nuns ; they seem worthy to wear the mantle of those noble French women who, braving alike the dangers of an ocean voyage, the rigors of an almost Arctic climate, the thousand discomforts of colonial life, come to christianize and civilize their dusky sisters of a savage and often hostile race.

The aim of the Convent School seems, first, to make their pupils Christians—not of our pattern certainly— still Christians—and then ladies in the best sense of that misused word.

The nuns are so graceful, courteous and dignified, it is no small pleasure to come in daily contact with them ; the virtues of the foundress remain with her successors.

But to change the subject, I sincerely hope that you may be successful in your labors, and that you will be sufficiently interested in them to escape the loneliness which you felt last winter.

Were I at home, I should cherish a hope, though fostered by conceit it might be, that an occasional visit to Maple Highland would afford a pleasant relief to the dreariness of your stay at Foreston ; but as it is, I trust that the work of furnishing me with frequent accounts of your doings and with **all the** local news may serve nearly the same purpose.

Your sincere friend, ·

RUTH EDGARTON.

It is needless perhaps **to say** that **I was** not backward in accepting the invitation **to write, so** cordially given. My letters **were both** frequent and long, and the entertaining replies which they elicited certainly afforded a pleasure which nothing save a **personal** visit with their authoress could surpass.

CHAPTER VI.

I HAVE alluded to a small village in the southern part of Foreston. It perhaps scarcely deserved the appellation, for besides a mill, a mechanic's shop, a store and post office, it comprised not more than a half dozen dwellings; but two or three years previous to the opening of my story, when the post office was established, it was dignified with the name Arklow.

At a little distance north of the village, embowered in evergreens and shrubbery, stood the neat residence of Dr. Sutherland, an English gentleman who besides being a physician held the various offices of collector of customs, postmaster and magistrate. He had held the office of collector of customs at this place for several years, during which time he had become popular in the practice of his medical profession.

Early in the spring, soon after my school had closed, I chanced to call at the post office when the Doctor proposed to me that I should enter his office as clerk. He informed me that he had for some time felt the necessity of procuring assistance, and that he knew of no one whose services he would more gladly accept than my own.

I was a little surprised, from the fact that I had never felt particularly well acquainted with him; in truth, as **he** appeared to me somewhat stern in his manner, and was looked upon by the people of that section as quite an aristocrat, I had always regarded him with respectful deference, and had never conversed with him except **on** a few occasions when he opened the conversation himself. It might have been my reserve and the respect I had shown him which won his favor. Be this as it may, however, I **was** flattered with his offer, but, as **the** salary was small, **I** hesitated in accepting it. He urged, assuring me that I would have but little to do, and consequently would find much time to study; offered me free access to his library, the use of a horse and carriage, and lastly assured me that he would immediately apply for a commission for **me** as preventive officer, which when obtained would empower me to seize contraband goods. The particular benefit resulting to me from these seizures would be that a share of the proceeds **arising** from **the sale** of the **goods** would be my own. The offer was one which in my circumstances I could not afford to treat lightly, **and so my** objections were soon laid aside.

Scarcely **a** month had passed after I entered the Doctor's office, before I was duly appointed preventive officer, and was thus in a position to win no little notoriety in my efforts to prevent infractions of the Revenue laws of the country. The office was, and is still, unpopular. Very few who have held it have ever been accorded the respect, much less the friendship, of their neighbors. Yet, it cannot be denied that this unpopularity has always resulted from meddling officiousness and acquisitiveness on the part of the officers themselves. It was not my desire to render myself odious to the farmers and mechanics around me, consequently, in accepting the office, I resolved that I would remain in ignorance, as far as possible, of the small amount of smuggling which these persons did in providing their families with the necessaries of life. It was only to professional smugglers, or those who boldly violated the law for the purpose of great profit, that I decided to give any attention; and, though this course would lessen my chances of making money, it would certainly preserve me from the hatred and contempt of my fellows.

Many weeks passed away, and no opportunity was given me for exercising the prerogative of my office. The duties of my clerkship were few and easy, so that I had ample time for other labors and for frequent social chats with the Doctor, whose affability was always displayed whenever he was permitted to remain at home of an evening.

The first incident affording relief to this monotonous life occurred about two months after I had received my commission.

It was a bright, moonlight night, and the Doctor was absent from home. I had gone to my room, and was preparing to retire to rest, when, chancing to look out to the yard below, in front of the office, I beheld the figure of a man, stealthily approaching and casting frequent glances towards my window. My first thought was of burglars. Immediately extinguishing the light, I drew the curtains near together, leaving, however, space enough to enable me to observe his movements.

After standing a few moments, apparently listening, as if to satisfy himself that all the inmates of the house were at rest, he cautiously retraced his steps and entered the highway, which was a few rods distant. Disarmed by his departure of all fears of attempts at burglary, I went to bed. Scarcely twenty minutes had elapsed ere my attention was attracted by the rumbling of wheels which were slowly passing in the road. The incident itself would have been regarded as unimportant, had I not noticed that, after passing the house some little distance, the speed of the vehicle was considerably increased; indeed, it was soon obvious that it was being driven at a rapid rate. Coupling this circumstance with the fact that a man had, but a few moments previous, secretly reconnoitred the premises of the Custom House, I was certain that some one was smuggling. It was quite probable that he had kept his team in a valley below the house, and, after assuring himself that he could pass the Custom House without danger of discovery, had driven on.

I arose, dressed myself, went to the barn, saddled a horse and started in pursuit. Although he must have had the start of me by two miles, or more, I had no doubt that I would soon overtake him; but to my surprise I galloped on three, four and five miles until I arrived at the village of Foreston, without seeing anything of the team I was pursuing. I stopped at the two hotels of the village, and made enquiries, but no person had arrived, nor had anyone noticed a team passing. Being personally acquainted with the parties of whom I sought information, I had no suspicion of being deceived, hence, I was led to the conclusion that the smuggler must either have taken one of the roads branching off from the main road, or else he had put up at some one of the farm-houses which I had passed. In the former case his chance of eluding me was good, in the latter, if I started out

early in the morning he would very likely be discovered.
Relying on the latter thought, I rode leisurely back to my
quarters, peering carefully into all the sheds that I passed.

In the morning, as soon as I was certain of finding the
farmers up and about their chores, I was again in the saddle,
determined to spare neither time nor labor in bringing this
offender to justice. After riding nearly three miles, I
commenced my enquiries, and learned from two or three
individuals, whom I met, and at two or three different farm-
houses, that a team had passed, rapidly, about the hour that I
designated on the preceding evening. One man averred
that he saw it, but, strange to say, it was near the village,
and the time about two hours later than that mentioned
by the others.

This led me to the belief that the smuggler must have
been concealed somewhere on the road for a while, and had
resumed his journey after my return. This belief was
strengthened at the first hotel, to which I arrived in the
village, as I was there informed that a team, driven rapidly,
had passed about an hour after my departure the night
previous.

Thus encouraged, I spurred on; and thinking that, after
the caution he had displayed, he would not be likely to stop
near Foreston, I rode directly to a thriving village, fifteen
miles north of Arklow. I drew up at an hotel, and in a
few moments afterward, stepping out to the barn to give the
hostler some directions which I had forgotten, I found a man
there, surrounded by several others to whom he was endeavoring to sell a harness. He had six of them, silver
mounted, in an express waggon, beside which he was standing, and I felt sure that he was the man of whom I was
in pursuit. My arrival was scarcely noticed, and I found

little difficulty in interrogating the hostler, unobserved, from whom I learned that the harness peddlar had arrived **at** the hotel that morning, from the south, some time before daylight.

After receiving this information I joined the group of men and listened to the vender **as** he expatiated on the superior quality of his goods, and anxiously urged the man, with whom he was talking, to purchase. **The** seller **was a** tall, spare **New** Englander, with red hair and whiskers, and a most unprepossessing face, and his remarks were frequently interspersed with oaths and coarse jests. Stepping up to his waggon, to examine his harness, I soon engaged him in conversation, in the course of which I carelessly asked him where the articles were manufactured. He seemed prepared for the question, and gave me the name of a remote **town** in Canada.

" Indeed," I said, **" I was not** aware that they make such harnesses as these in that place. By whom were they manufactured ? "

" I made 'em," he replied. " My name is **Towner."**

" Have you been in that place **long** ? " I asked.

" Five or six years," he replied, eyeing me with considerable curiosity.

" You must carry on quite a business there," I said. " Do you employ many **men** ? "

" Three or four," he answered, gruffly.

" Well, since you are **a** manufacturer in that town, and doing so much business, I can find your name in R—s' Gazetteer, which was published last year."

" I spose so," he said, trying to appear indifferent ; " I don't know whether my name is thar or not."

I then **left him, and,** stepping into the hotel, enquired for a copy of the "Gazetteer," to which I had alluded. It was handed me, and I immediately searched the list of names in the town to which Towner said he belonged, without finding his own. Returning to the barn, I said:

"I don't find your name in the 'Gazetteer,' Mr. Towner."

"Wall," he replied, somewhat angrily, "you took a good deal of pains; what did you want to find it for?"

"O," I said, "if I should buy a harness of you, I would like to know all I can about the manufacturer. I might wish to recommend some friend in want of a harness to you."

"Wall," he said, "you can ask anyone that lives in my section about me. But if you want ter buy a harness, young man, I'm jest the chap that ken sell yer one, cheap."

"To tell you the truth, Mr. Towner," I said, "I have some suspicion that your harnesses were manufactured in the States. Now, if I buy one, will you give me a written guarantee that it was made in Canada, so that I shall have no fears of its being seized by the revenue officers?"

"Wall, it seems to me that you air —— pertickler, but, of course, I kin dew it."

"I shall require you to make oath to your statements if I buy one, Mr. Towner, and then I shall take immediate steps to learn all I can about your manufactory."

"Wall, if it's gwine to be so much trouble tew yer, I don't think you'd better buy one."

The man, by this time, began to show considerable uneasiness, and the bystanders, to whom I was an entire stranger, were regarding me with much curiosity.

"Without wasting any more time in parley, Mr. Towner," I said, "I must tell you that I think this is smuggled property."

"You've got a good deal of brass for a young chap," he said. "Who in thunder air you?"

"I am a revenue officer," I replied, "and as such, I shall seize this property at once, unless you show to me that I am wrong in my suspicions."

He turned white, and after looking at me for a moment, in silence, seemed suddenly **to** regain his self-possession, and broke into a hoarse laugh.

"**Wall,** young man, you seem **tew be** pretty sharp," he said; "tew tell the truth, these harnesses was made in the States, but the duty is paid on 'em. You see, I knew you Canada chaps hate **us** Yankees so, that you'd buy a good deal quicker if I could make you believe they was made on this side of the line."

"Indeed, Mr. Towner, you have made a very frank admission; but since you have paid the duty, of course you have a permit with you."

"Yes, I've got one," he said, seeming to have **lost his** inclination to dispose of his goods, as he began to **tie up** the harness which he had been displaying.

"Will you have the kindness to let me see it?" I asked.

"O, yes, of course," he said, **taking out** his pocket-book and beginning to fumble **amongst his papers.**

After spending at **least** ten minutes in this search, he took out his memorandum book, and gave that a careful examination. This being replaced, he thrust his hands nervously, first into his breeches-pocket, then into his vest, and, finally, into the different pockets of his coat, after which he exclaimed, with a bewildered look, "I swear, I guess I've lost it."

"I am sorry," I said, "but of whom did you obtain your permit?"

"Dr. Sutherland," he replied, "at Arklow."

"When did he give it to you?" I asked.

"Last night," he answered, "when I come along."

"I am sorry to tell you, Mr. Towner," I said, "Dr. Sutherland was not in his office yesterday. I was there all day, and you entered no goods there."

"Yes, but I met the Doctor on the road. Hold on! I recollect now. I put the permit in my valise, and I left that about three miles back here, where I stopped this morning. If you'll jest ride back there with me, I'll show yer the permit all right."

"Your story, Mr. Towner," I said, "is simply absurd. Dr. Sutherland could not have given you a permit on the road had you met him. Besides, he was not in the direction in which you came yesterday. But, to show you all fairness, you can leave your waggon and goods here, and I will give you two hours in which to get your valise."

"All right," he said, then turning to the hostler, added: "You'll see to this load," and at once stalked out.

Fully assured that he intended to get away with his goods and return to the States, I saw the necessity of watching him. Securing a small upper room in the hotel, from which I had a fair view of the barn, I sat down by the window and began to read. I noticed, on sitting down, that the barn doors were already closed, and there appeared to be no one around. Half an hour afterwards, the doors suddenly swung open, and a rough looking young fellow appeared in Towner's waggon just in the act of driving out. To rush down was the work of a moment, and I seized the horse by the bits ere he was half way across the yard.

"Where are you going with this team?" I fiercely demanded.

"I'm gwine ter drive it down here a piece, for another man," the fellow answered, confusedly.

"You'll oblige me by getting out of that waggon," I said. "I seize this team for an infraction of the Revenue laws of this country, and unless you wish to get yourself into serious trouble, you'll have nothing to do with it."

The fellow sullenly got out of the waggon, and gave me the reins, upon which I turned the horse about and drove into the barn. Ten minutes afterwards, Towner appeared on the scene. He had lost his self-possession, and was greatly agitated.

As two or three men, besides the hostler, were now present, Towner called me aside, and thus addressed me :

"See here, young man, you've got me. You're sharp, no mistake ; but, now, if you'll let me get out of this country with this team, I'll give yer fifty dollars."

"Not if you were to give me five hundred," I replied.

"Say one hundred," he urged.

"I shall do nothing of the kind," I replied.

He then assumed a threatening tone.

"Perhaps," he said, "you don't know who you've got tew deal with."

"I think," I replied, "that I've had a good opportunity to know something of you."

"Not so much as you will know," he said, with an oath, as he turned and left the barn.

The landlord being present, I asked possession of his barn for an hour, which being granted, I locked it, kept the key, and then waited a short time for dinner. After this, engaging a man to ride my own horse, I seated myself in the smuggler's waggon, and drove back to Arklow.

Pursuant to the requirements of the law, the property seized was sold in a few days at vendue, the proceeds amounting to three hundred and fifty dollars.

Towner was one of the bidders, but it was not struck off to him. I had learned, previous to this, that he had frequently visited other parts of the Province, to dispose of smuggled property, and up to this time had been very successful. The harnesses which he had with him on this occasion he had obtained on credit from a certain firm in Vermont, but whether he ever paid for them is still to me unknown.

It will suffice to say that this seizure, besides resulting in some pecuniary profit to me, gave me a little local fame, and obtained for me the thanks of the head officials of the Customs Department.

About a month after the occurrence of this incident, as I was, one day, sitting alone in the office, a stranger, past middle age, drove up to the door, and, dismounting, entered. After making many inquiries, relative to the duty on different articles, he finally wished to know the duty on boots and shoes. I informed him that there was an *ad valorem* duty of fifteen per cent. on these articles. He expressed some surprise and regrets that it was so high, saying that he had a lot in Mayfair, which he had brought from the South, for the purpose of selling them in Canada. He seemed to be deliberating for some time, and, then, expressed his determination to sell his goods in Vermont rather than import them under so high a tariff. This information given, he drove away.

Towards evening of the next day, he returned, having in his waggon a small box of boots and shoes on which he wished to pay the duty; saying that if he found he could sell these to advantage, he might bring over all that he had. I gave him a permit, but he seemed in no haste to leave, and sat for a long time in the office, engaging me in conversation. As night approached, and he still remained, I began to wonder, **and,** observing **him** more closely, **I** thought he seemed nervous and ill at ease. The suspicion flashed across me that he **was** detaining me for some purpose, and I knew of no object he could have in doing this, unless his stock **of** goods was being smuggled into the country by some other **route.** Three miles west of the road **on** which the Custom House stood ran another nearly parallel to it, and leading through a section but thinly populated, and in many places through strips of woods. Another road starting from Mayfair intersected this **at** nearly right angles, some distance south of Arklow, thus affording smugglers a very convenient **way of** avoiding the Custom House. It had been **my** practice, since I had been in the office, to ride frequently over to this road, especially in **the** evening, to find, **perchance,** some one seeking profit by transgressing the **law;** but up to this time I had been unsuccessful. The singular manner of the person **in the office led** me to the determination to visit this road at once, and stepping **out** of the back door I went to the Doctor's gardener, who **lived** but a few rods distant, and requested him to remain in the office during my absence. He complied, and a few minutes later I was galloping rapidly away. I first went southward until I had come to the road branching off towards Mayfair, but meeting no one, I wheeled and galloped northward. I had ridden perhaps three miles in this direction, when I thought I heard the rumbling of wheels ahead of me.   Halting to listen, although it was now quite dark, I descried some object moving just a little in advance of me.   Starting on again I immediately came up with a two-horse waggon heavily laden with boxes.   Riding alongside, I accosted the driver with a friendly

"Good evening, sir."

"How are yer?" was the reply.

"You seem to have a heavy load," I said.

"Yes, heavy enough," was the gruff answer.

"I suppose you have nothing dutiable in your load."

"No, I guess not," he said, and after a moment's pause asked, "why? what if I have?"

"O nothing, I said, only if you have, since you have passed the Custom House, and are evidently smuggling, I shall seize your team and load."

"Dew yer think so?" he insolently asked.

"I *know* so," I replied.   "Will you have the kindness to stop your horses?"

A sharp crack of the whip, and a loud "Get up, thar," addressed to his horses, was the only notice that was taken of my request.

Obedient to his command, the horses started off on a trot. Knowing from the language and manner of the man that he was a brutal fellow, ignorant of the law and regardless of the consequences of transgressing it, I had little doubt that he intended resistance, and I determined to bring matters to a crisis at once.

Riding up close to the horses, I seized one by the bits, and immediately sliding from my saddle, I reined them to the

side of the road. The driver swore, and ordered me to let go
the reins, but finding that his order was disobeyed he jumped
from the waggon, and, stepping forward, struck at me fiercely
with the butt of his heavy whip. The darkness was not so
intense as to prevent my getting a glimpse of the descending
whalebone, and, dodging it, the blow was received by my
horse across his neck. He immediately sprang, and pulling
away from me, started on **a gallop homeward.** My assailant,
who **had** been nearly knocked over by **the horse** in his
escape, now rushed towards me again **to** renew the assault. I
had drawn my revolver, and before he had time to strike
again I dealt him **a** blow on the temple with the butt **of**
the weapon. He fell insensible to the ground, and instantly
mounting his waggon, I drove on a few paces to a convenient place for turning round, **and then urged** the horses
into a brisk **trot** for the Custom House.

Half a **mile below,** I stopped at the house of a Frenchman, and, giving **him a** dollar, **obtained a promise** that he
would go immediately **and** care for the man whom I had
left by the roadside. On riding back, two **hours** afterward,
to learn the result **of** the Frenchman's **mission, he** informed
me that he met **the** smuggler, before **he reached** the spot I
had designated, **walking** back towards **Mayfair.**

It turned out **as I** had anticipated. **The** team and load,
which consisted of several cases of boots and shoes, belonged
to the man who had visited the Custom House. He had
engaged a low fellow, in Mayfair, for five dollars, to deliver
his goods at a certain house on the Canadian side of the line,
from which he was about three miles distant when I overtook
him. The owner of the goods, himself, had undertaken to so

entertain me at the office, that I would not be likely to leave it till after the man he had hired had fulfilled his contract.

The sequel of this incident was that he obtained his property, on the day of sale, by the payment of six hundred dollars.

CHAPTER VII.

WEEKS rolled by, and the leaves of the forest were assuming their autumnal tint, when I received a letter from Ruth, informing me that she would be at home in the following week. I had not seen her for a year, and it was with no small degree of pleasure that I drove, one afternoon, when I supposed she was at home, to Maple Highland.

A cordial greeting awaited me, though something of that reserve and embarrassment was felt which often characterizes the meeting of young friends after a long separation. The confinement of Convent life, together with close application to her studies, had withdrawn the usual bloom of health from her cheek, which could only be replaced by more active life and country air.

Shortly after my arrival, Mr. Edgarton, Ruth's uncle, accompanied by a well-dressed portly gentleman, entered the parlor. The latter was introduced to me as Mr. Niel. I was somewhat curious to know the character and history of the   er, and what relation he sustained to the family in which he appeared to be visiting, and my curiosity increased gradually, as I chatted with him upon the various topics of the day, on all of which he seemed to be well posted. Although possessing a good degree of general intelligence, he was not scholarly, and a slight degree of rusticity of manner, and his bronzed complexion, led me to the conclusion that he might be a well-to-do farmer. His side whiskers and hair were sufficiently sprinkled with grey to indicate that he was approximating to forty, and I naturally inferred that he might possibly be a *pater familias;* but the interest that he seemed to take in Ruth, and the scrutiny with which he observed her actions, still further increased my curiosity, and I adroitly managed to elicit from him the fact that he was unmarried. The slight feeling of uneasiness, which this information caused me, was in no degree diminished, by the fact that he still remained in the parlor after Mr. Edgarton had retired. The presence of a third party being somewhat embarrassing, to me, at least, I proposed a ride to Ruth. I fancied that I discerned a very little hesitation and confusion, on her part, at my proposal, but be that as it may, if there were any such indications of uneasiness they instantly disappeared; and after asking Mr. Niel, with grace and dignity, to excuse her, she proceeded to her apartment to array herself for the ride.

The effect of my invitation to her displayed itself much more plainly in the visage and manner of my companion. His small grey eyes assumed an unwonted lustre, his florid face took on a redder hue, and the taciturnity into which he seemed suddenly to have fallen, showed that he felt little interest in the matter to which I was calling his attention. Still he was gentlemanly, dignified, and when Ruth again appeared, and we were about setting off, he cheerfully and cordially wished us a pleasant ride.

The eagerness with which I sought to know something respecting this stranger, as soon as we were fairly seated in the waggon, I think must have surprised Ruth, if it did not amuse her; but without the portrayal of any emotion, she gratified my curiosity.

Mr. Niel was a bachelor-farmer of good repute and considerable property, residing in the township of Carrollton about twenty miles distant.　He had long been acquainted with the Edgartons, and in former years, had sometimes visited Maple Highland.

He was a near neighbor of another of Ruth's uncles, who lived in the same township, and she had occasionally met him when she had been there on visits.　In returning from the Convent, she had tarried with her cousins in Carrollton two or three days, and happening, while there, to meet Mr. Niel at an evening party, he expressed a desire to see her family, and offered to take her home on the succeeding day. Regarding him as an old friend of the family, she accepted the offer, and was accordingly driven to Maple Highland in a fine carriage, drawn by a handsome span of bays, the day before I visited her.

"Is he never going to marry?" I asked, with all the nonchalance I could assume.

"O, no, I think not," she said.　"He was once engaged to a girl, when he was quite young, but she died, and he seems never to have shown any inclination to marry since."

I felt slightly relieved, but wishing to know more, I said, after a moment's silence—

"He is rich, I suppose."

"Not rich, in the general acceptation of the term," she said, "but in **very** good circumstances. He lives in a very pretty house, with an Englishman and his wife for servants, and, besides **looking** after his stock, he **spends** much time in experimenting with **crops and in** reading and studying works **on** agriculture."

"**A sort of** *gentleman*-farmer," I suggested.

"**Yes**," she said, "I think **that is a good** description of his occupation."

The subject now changed, though I could not refrain **from** thinking of **my** new acquaintance during the intervals **of** silence, and **wondering** whether he had really given up **all thoughts of** marriage. I **could** readily imagine that, **even with** his advancing **years, he** might prove a dangerous **rival to a** much **younger man** in poorer circumstances; **for a pretty house with servants, a fine** farm, stock, a carriage **and horses, are things not** usually overlooked by a girl in selecting her **future home,** and especially by her parents or guardians.

Tea awaited us on our return, and it seemed to me that Mr. Niel, while **at the** table, put forth a special effort to render himself agreeable. **He talked to** me incessantly; asked a great many questions relative to Custom House business, **said much** respecting the legal profession, towards which, **he said he** had heard I was directing my thoughts, and **wound up with a** very lucid and interesting dissertation on **agriculture. Before I left, he gave me a** pressing invitation **to come** and spend **a week or** two **with** him at his home, **which I promised to do** as soon as time and opportunity **would permit. In truth,** he had so impressed me with an **idea of his ability and** importance **that** I believe I felt a **slight degree of jealousy** on departing, knowing that he was **still** to remain a guest of the Edgartons. I could not forbear wondering, in no very pleasant frame of mind, how long he would prolong his stay, and what degree of friendship existed between him and **Mr.** Edgarton. But, my thoughts reverting **to** Ruth, I felt that I really had no cause **for** distrust. She knew nothing of deceit, and I saw her then, more clearly than I had ever before seen her, a paragon of constancy—the embodiment of all that is noble in woman. I had never, formally, proposed to her the uniting of her fortunes with my own, from the fact that I wished to accomplish much before I could feel that I was in a position to offer her a pleasant home. I felt that such an event could only occur at some distant day; but I believed she fully understood me, knew my intentions, and I scarcely doubted that she would await my pleasure with true womanly devotion.

On reaching home that evening I found the Doctor's family in something of a bustle over the arrival of Mr. Baxter, a lawyer from Montreal, who had recently appeared as a candidate for the office of representative of our county in the Provincial Parliament. It is to be hoped that, at no distant day, the student of history will smile at that feature of Canadian politics which permitted a stranger to represent, in the legislative halls, a section of country of which he knew **but** little, and for the interest of which he, doubtless, cared still less; but the custom at that time had but few opponents and even at the present it is so far **complied** with as to reflect discredit on the intelligence and independence of Canadian voters. "Men, not measures," seemed to be the predominant idea engrafted in the minds of the yeomanry when called upon to exercise the right of suffrage, and frequently, a man, unqualified morally for discharging **the** duties of a high and responsible office, had only to disburse lavishly the sums which his political friends had furnished him, and to promise impossible local improvements and improbable and impossible reforms, to secure his election. Baxter was a man of this stamp. A demagogue, ready on the one hand to kneel with oriental devotion at the shrine of aristocracy, or, for personal gain, to truckle with the **meanness of a** sycophant for the patronage of democracy. McClintock county seemed to offer a fair field for the gratification of his ambition. His friends informed him how easily it had fallen a prey to their wiles in former campaigns, and persuaded him that he had only to visit the county a few times, throw out a few hundred dollars and make generous promises, to obtain a triumphant entrance into the parliamentary chambers. Such was the man, and such the **auspices** under which he appeared, when he came out to ingratiate himself with unsuspecting and unsophisticated **rate-payers.**

The Doctor **gave me an** introduction to him, and, though pleased with the honor, I felt something of the embarrassment peculiar to **young and** inexperienced persons when in the presence of a magnate. He soon put me at my ease, however, and flattered me with his patronizing air, especially when he expressed a wish that he might have **a** confidential talk with me in the course of the evening. I say that I felt flattered, still the fumes of his breath awakened **a** suspicion that he might be in an unusually friendly mood, and that, possibly, in a normal condition, his reserve and **dignity** would inspire me with reverential awe.

Later **in** the evening, while I was reading in the office, a family **servant** entered and announced that Mr. Baxter wished to see **me in** the parlor. I accordingly answered the summons, and found the candidate and the Doctor alone. The latter said as I entered,

" Mr. Baxter wishes to talk with you."

"**Yes,**" said that gentleman, " the Doctor has given me a very favorable impression of your worth, and, although you are quite young, he has recommended you as one that can aid me in the work in which I am at present engaged."

I felt a little bewildered, and blushed at the compliment, but quickly replied,

" I shall be most happy to serve you, Mr. Baxter, in any way I can."

" You speak French, I believe," he said.

" Not very good French," I replied. " I learned something of their *patois* when I was attending district school, and am still able to carry on a conversation in that tongue, though quite imperfectly."

" And you know most of the *habitants* in this township, I suppose," pursued my interlocutor.

" Many of them," **I said.**

" Well," he continued, " my time is so limited that I cannot see many of them at present, and I wish to employ you to see them for me ; and I shall give you **quite a** sum of money to distribute amongst them and the English-speaking farmers of the township ; and I wish it to be deeply impressed upon them that these donations are directly from my own hand, and **are** made from a heartfelt desire that I have to aid them to build up these Townships, and to see the people here thriving and happy. You understand me ? "

" Certainly," I said.

" And, as a proof of my sincerity," he continued, " and of the interest I take in agricultural matters, you can say that I intend to purchase a large farm somewhere in this section, at no distant day, and reside here permanently. The scenery here **is** beautiful, beautiful!" he repeated with emphasis, "and I know of no place in which I would like more to live."

"Wouldn't it be well, Mr. Baxter," here interposed the Doctor, "to caution Mr. Styles a little against using your name too freely in disbursing the money you give to him, and also to exercise much discretion with regard to the character of the individuals to whom he gives it?"

"O, I gave Mr. Styles due credit for discretion in these matters," said Baxter, and then, turning to me, continued:

"Of course you understand that our statutes prohibit anything pertaining to bribery in elections, and I would very carefully avoid any imputation of the kind in my own election. Impress upon the electors the idea that these simple presents are given solely from my appreciation of a noble peasantry, and from my sympathy for them in their struggles to open up a new country. Yes, sir, I admire the honest and sturdy yeomanry of any country," and then, as if inspired with the contemplation of their virtues, he dramatically pronounced the oft-quoted lines of Goldsmith,

> " Princes and lords may flourish or may fade,
> A breath can make them, as a breath has made,
> But a bold peasantry—their country's pride—
> When once destroy'd, can never be supplied."

After waiting a moment, perhaps for applause, he said:

"With regard to the last suggestion of the Doctor, about the persons to whom you give the money, please remember and sound them well before you offer them any pecuniary assistance. Ascertain, first, what their ideas are about the necessary qualifications for a representative, that is, whether they possess intelligence enough to desire that a city gentleman, an experienced lawyer, should represent them in the council chambers, or whether they are so ignorant that they prefer to entrust their interests to some country clod-hopper who has scarcely been beyond the borders of the county. These are the things, Mr. Styles, upon which I wish you to exercise your discretion."

"I certainly hope, Mr. Baxter," I replied, "that I shall act with proper judgment in doing the work which you may assign me."

"I have **no fears** about that, **Mr.** Styles, no fears whatever; but, say, Doctor, havn't you a little more of that wine **?** **It's** very nice."

"Certainly, excuse me," said the Doctor, rising, "I was not aware that we had emptied the bottle."

I then noticed that a bottle and glasses were standing on the table. The Doctor left the apartment for a moment and presently the servant brought in two more bottles of sherry. The Doctor filled two glasses, when Baxter asked, with a little surprise,

"Is not Mr. Styles going to take a glass with us?"

"Mr. Styles is almost a teetotaler," replied the Doctor, "he seldom takes even wine."

"But you surely will take a glass with me," said Baxter, and he extended to **me one well filled.**

I did not care for it, yet, in compliment to him, I quaffed it.

"I am not strictly a teetotaler myself," said Baxter. "At home I *sometimes* indulge in a glass of wine, yet I *believe* in temperance, and am strongly in favor of prohibition. Should I be elected to parliament, one of my first labors will be to introduce a prohibitory liquor bill. A stringent prohibitory law, Mr. Styles, is what this Province needs;" and he tossed off his glass with the air of one who **was** perfectly unconscious of the fact that his practice was greatly **at** variance **with his** teaching.

"Perhaps it would be well," he added, "for you to say to the temperance men of this section, when you meet, that I am heartily in favor of temperance, and shall do all in my power, if elected, to make liquor selling a serious offence—a high crime in the eyes of the laws of this country. A good idea, eh, Mr. Styles?"

"I shall certainly be pleased to tell them what you say," I replied.

"The Doctor tells me that you intend studying law, Mr. Styles."

"I have thought of it," I said.

"Well, sir," he said, with an air of great earnestness, "if you like, I shall be most happy to receive you as a student in my office, but, if you prefer something else, something that will pay sooner, you might obtain a good situation in one of the Government Departments. A clerkship such as I could procure for you would pay twelve or fifteen hundred a year. How would you like that, eh?"

"I think I could appreciate a situation of that kind," I replied with a smile.

"There is no reason, Mr. Styles, why you should not have one, not the slightest reason, and I'll tell you what I'll do. If I am elected as representative of this county I will see that you have such a position within three months."

"You certainly are very kind, Mr. Baxter," I replied, "and I trust that you will find me grateful for any service you may render me."

"Gratitude, Mr. Styles, is not what I am seeking. I am a philanthropist in my way. I always like to do good; and whenever I see that I can aid one of my fellows I am only too happy to do it. But," he continued, "we will speak of this thing hereafter. To-morrow I wish you to go with me to Hilton, to introduce me to parties there, and do whatever you can to further my interests in the approaching election. The Doctor cannot leave his business, and he has very kindly offered me his carriage and horses, and advises that I take you with me."

" I shall be very glad to accompany you," I said.

The remarks of Baxter were now chiefly addressed to the Doctor. He made many inquiries respecting the political aspect of the county, and concerning individuals whom he wished to see; all of which were answered with politeness, yet with some reserve and caution. It was quite apparent to me that the Doctor was not favorably impressed with his guest, and that he placed no great degree of confidence in his extravagant promises, and boasts of patriotism and philanthropy. His office precluded him from taking an active part in politics, but he was a strong partizan, and always aided, as far as consistent, those whose political views accorded with his own; and, however much he might prefer some other candidate to the one now in the field, loyalty to his party prevented him from opposing, in any way, the man of their choice.

Baxter continued to indulge in frequent potations of sherry, **and** as **the** evening advanced he expatiated more freely **on his exploits** in the past, and the grand works to be achieved **in** the future.

The Doctor appreciated his wine for dinner, but he partook sparingly of it **on** this occasion, and, as I declined further invitation **to** imbibe, the two bottles were **almost** wholly appropriated **by** Baxter. His loquacity had in **no** degree abated at twelve o'clock, when I thought proper to retire, and as I bade him good night he paid me another installment of compliments, and expressed much pleasure in view of spending the morrow in my company.

The events of the evening had been to me, boy as I was, far too exciting in their character to suffer me, even when in bed, to fall asleep. I had taken but little interest in Canadian politics, and knew comparatively nothing of the tricks and deceit of unscrupulous politicians. An experienced, conscientious man would doubtless have treated with disdain a proposal to employ him in the work in which Baxter desired me to engage—a work which was virtually the bare-faced corruption of voters; an effort to lead the ignorant to prostitute the right of suffrage to ignoble purposes. But I did not take this view of it. I was too much of a novice to exercise a nice discrimination between right and wrong in these matters, and I saw no particular harm in acting the part which had been assigned me.

Though I was not so dull as to believe that his "trifling donations" were prompted wholly by "patriotism and philanthropy," I thought that if he could thus gain the good will of men and secure their votes, he had a right to do so. I felt grateful to him for his attention, for the confidence he reposed in me, and especially for his unsolicited offer of aid in the future, and had I been possessed of a vote, he would have received it with my whole heart; and I argued that if it was right for me thus to shew my gratitude, it would be equally right for those on whom he had bestowed other or similar favors. I cannot say that I admired the man. There was much in him that awakened suspicion that he was not altogether just what he professed, yet respect for his social position inclined me to the belief that he would spare no effort to fulfil the promises which he made. It did not occur to me that a man of his pretensions, receiving the patronage of prominent government officials, a candidate for a responsible office, could be so regardless of honor as to offer to one of my age and circumstances boons which he had not both the ability and willingness to bestow; and so I flattered myself that a clerkship commanding twelve or fifteen hundred a year required only the contingency of his election to office to be mine. The acceptance of such a position would prevent my studying law, but it would not do to discard a certainty for an uncertainty, and besides being lucrative it would soon enable me to offer Ruth a home with all the comforts she could desire.

CHAPTER VIII.

AT 10 o'clock on the following morning I sat beside Baxter in the Doctor's carriage slowly ascending the mountain. As he was desirous of talking with the farmers along our route, we halted occasionally for this purpose. In these brief interviews, he displayed the same patronizing manner that he did on the preceding evening. He was profuse in promises and wild in his asseverations of friendship for the farmer. The greater number of these men, flattered by his attention, listened credulously to all he said, and without hesitation pledged him their support; but now and then one of more experience and broader intelligence received his proposals cautiously, and offered rational objections to non-resident representation. Too inexperienced in political matters, however, to refute his bold assertions, and too timid in his presence to express their honest convictions, they said but little, though wisely deciding to delay their decision with regard to voting until they had watched the progress of events.

Though conscious now that I possessed all the while a sort of inner conviction that there was a want of sincerity in the man, a hollowness in his pretensions, I tried to stifle it, and in my **boyish** enthusiasm afforded him all the aid I could. I liked the work in which I was engaged. **A** new era seemed suddenly **to** have dawned before me; my ambition was pursuing an entirely different route.

The sight of the schoolhouse where I first met Ruth as a teacher seemed **to** suggest to Baxter the necessity of more educational institutions in **the** county. Though each township already had a High School within **its** borders, which, from scarcity of pupils, **was** but poorly attended, Baxter, in his o'erflowing philanthropy, believed that **these** schools should **be** multiplied. He argued that every section of a township where there were mills and **a** store, **in** short, where there **was** any prospect of a village, should have **a** High School regularly endowed. To establish these schools, and to obtain a liberal government **grant** for their support, was, of course, among the laudable **works which as a** repre-sentative **he was to accomplish. As we descended the** mountain, a **rough road or path leading back into the** forest to the cabins **of two or three settlers suggested** another way of benefitting his constituents. **The immense** quanti-ties of bark **and** lumber in **these** boundless forests needed but **good** roads through which to **be** hauled to market to become a source of wealth to the poor men dwelling in this section. **This** wooded country required to be opened **up;** roads must and should be made.

I had forgotten to **say** that he had not neglected **in** a few instances to forward his interests by presenting small **sums** of **two** or three' dollars **to** individuals with whom he conversed. It was noticeable, however, that these "presents" were made only to those of little intelligence, who at first seemed rather undecided as to the party they should support in the political contest; never to those whose pride or principle might lead them to decline it, or to those who evinced a decided determination to learn the ability of the respective candidates, and consider their claims to the office. He was not a novice in the art of reading men; he seldom made a mistake. Though in disbursing these sums there was no bargain made, no intimation that they were given only as a testimonial of good-will and friendship, the recipients, as a matter of course, felt in duty bound to reciprocate the favor, and in no exceptional instance failed to assure him of their unqualified friendship and support. That they fulfilled these promises is probable; but that they forgot them if offered larger or even equal sums by the opposing party is easy to conjecture. After stopping a short time at the hotel in Glenfield we drove on to Hilton and halted at the door of the inn, a respectable looking building with quite an array of barns and sheds adjoining. The place also sported a bowling alley, and like most country taverns had its complement of rough looking loungers.

The host, whose name was Fogg, a tall, middle-aged Yankee, with shrewdness and a desire for money-catching stamped in every lineament of his visage, and portrayed in every action, received us courteously, and, at once, in the most obsequious manner, avowed his readiness to do all in his power to help Mr. Baxter in securing office. The latter, after ordering dinner, requested the landlord to invite several of the most prominent men, whom he wished to meet, to come in and spend the evening. The request was readily complied with, and as the shades of night drew around us about a dozen rustic looking men assembled. The parlor, a large room containing an oil-cloth instead of a carpet, and furnished with a rustic lounge and several chairs of varied styles and ages, was devoted to the use of the candidate for the evening.

Although I was recognised by the men from the fact, as I afterwards learned, that they had seen me at the Custom House, I knew the names of but two of them, hence the work of giving them an introduction to Baxter fell on Fogg. This ceremony performed, they seated themselves around the room, with hats on, and mutely stared at the candidate, seemingly waiting for the denouement. This silence, however, was of short duration, for the bar-tender soon entered with glasses and a decanter of whiskey, which speedily dispelled all signs of reserve, and made even the most taciturn vie with his neighbor in loquaciousness. After they had all accepted the landlord's invitation to drink, Baxter, seated near the table in the centre of the room, began to explain to them the object of his appearance among them. They listened with breathless attention, for a short time, until he began to expatiate on the beauty and fertility of the country and express his ability and willingness, if elected, to do much towards benefitting its inhabitants, when he was frequently interrupted with cries of "Hear! hear!"

Twenty minutes having been thus consumed, and the decanter having been replenished, a short pause in the speech afforded Fogg an opportunity to suggest another "drink." He evidently felt that he had a moneyed customer, and was determined to make the most of it. No dissenting voice was raised, so Baxter first accepted the invitation, and then the patriotic rate-payers followed.   Black looking, short-stemmed clay pipes were now brought forth from jacket pockets and leisurely filled with tobacco.   The men seemed to have settled down to the determination to have an enjoyable social evening, and they puffed away for the next half hour, never removing their pipes from their mouths save to utter some exclamation of approval.

Baxter, perhaps from the inspiring effects of his potations, delivered the last part of his address to them in a standing posture.   Nearly suffocated by the tobacco smoke and the unwholesome fumes of the apartment, at the close of the address, I slipped out, unobserved, into the sitting room, and placed my chair near the open door, where I could easily see what was done and hear all that was said.   A drink was the first thing in order, and then after they were again seated one of the party said,

" Come, Steeple, let's hear from you ; Mr. Baxter wants to know how we stand, and as you're a magistrate and a man of business, you orter speak fust."

The individual addressed was a spare man of medium height with long black beard and locks which seemed never to have been clipped since his boyhood.   He required no second invitation to speak, and knocking the ashes from his pipe he thrust it into his pocket, rose quickly, and spoke as follows :

" Yes, Jones, your'e right; Mr. Baxter wants to know how we stand, and for one I'm willin' to let him.   I never had much chance for book larnin' and can't talk like a lawyer ; but if I can't I know a thing or tew, and I tell yer what it is, boys, I've made up my mind that Mr. Baxter's jest the chap we want ter represent us next session in parlyment."

"Hear! hear!" "You're right, Steeple!" vociferously shouted several of his audience, and for a moment there was a deafening noise from the stamping of feet and the clapping of hands. Steeple continued :—

"We all know, boys, **what** kind **of a** representative **we** want in parlyment. We want **a man** that kin talk—a man what's **a** gentleman. **You all know, boys,** how't some years ago the folks **of** this county, **cluded** ter send one o' their **own** number **ter** parlyment, and, gentlemen, who did they send ? why they sent old Sam Gibson—a farmer like me and you. He had more money than any on us has got —probly three times more'n all on us together has got. He had lots of mortgages out on twelve **per** cent. intrist, but it took some ont ter git his lection ; but he got it ; and what did he dew **when** he got inter parlyment. Why, he **want no** whar. You **know** its a fact, boys, that he was **so** tarnal stingy that he **use ter take his** provisions from hum and sleep in a barn to save expense. **They say,** tew, that he use ter go right inter the House **durin debates with** his old woolen frock on. **Yes, he was** fur savin' the dollars **to let** out ter poor devils fur twelve per **cent.** intrist. But **them** lawyers and big-bugs in parlyment didn't **take no** more notice on him than they would of **a nigger. They** used ter have their **good** times **and big** dinners ; **but dew** you spose he was **ever** invited ?"

"Not *much*," emphatically replied one of the audience.

"No, not *much*," repeated the speaker. "Now, we don't want ter send no more sich chaps as that ter parlyment. We want a man that wont sleep in a barn—a feller that when they hev any big doins or a champagne dinner, he'll be invited. **Sich a man kin dew** something for his constitooents—and, gentlemen," he continued with great earnestness casting a glance at the same time towards Baxter, " we've got sich a man right here afore us."

" Hear! hear!" again shouted the listeners.

" I aint afeard, boys," resumed the orator, " ter say that I'm fav'rbly impressed with Mr. Baxter, and fur one I shall vote for him, and I b'lieve he'll be 'lected."

Steeple now sat down amidst great applause, which having subsided, one of the party exclaimed,

" Now, Jones, 'tis your turn tew give us a speech." Jones did not hesitate, but springing quickly to his feet said,

" I aint no public speaker, boys, nor a magistrate nuther, but you've never known Jones ter back down in a 'mergency, and he aint gwine ter dew it now. I quite agree with Squire Steeple that Mr. Baxter is the man what we want fur our next member."

" Hear! hear!" once more broke in the audience.

" I quite agree with the Squire tew," he continued, " that Mr. Baxter is a gentleman. He aint afeard of spendin' a dollar or tew, and he aint one of yer stuck up kind nuther. He 'pears ter be like one on us, if he is rich and eddicated, and that's what we want. We want a man that when he's 'lected won't feel tew big ter talk with us if we happen ter go ter Montreal and need a leetle help 'bout bizness. Yer know, boys, that my ole hosses hev been nights and days in 'lection times, and hev carried more'n one load to the polls and ole Bill and Topsy air good for pullin' more loads over this ere mountin yet. You kin be sartin that I shall go fur Mr. Baxter." Jones now resumed his seat, and after the decanter had been once more called into requisition, it being definitely settled that all present pledged themselves to support Baxter, they proceeded to count up the rate-payers, who, in all probability would co-operate with them in sustaining their candidate; and they arrived at the conclusion —which must have been most satisfactory to Baxter—that there were not more than half a dozen out of nearly a hundred in that section upon whom they could not positively rely.

At this juncture I seemed for the first time to have been missed, and I **was** made aware of the fact by the voice of Baxter asking—

" What has become of Styles ? "

I arose, and standing in the door, said,

" I am here, Mr. Baxter."

" O I thought you had deserted us," he replied.

Attention now being directed to myself, Steeple exclaimed,

" Come, Styles, **we** haint had no speech from you yet, and **we** must hev one."

" Yes, yes, that's so," **chimed in** several voices.

" I am not a voter," I replied, " and besides I never made a political speech."

" That makes **no difference, young** man," **said** Jones, " we've hearn of you, and they say your smart **at** trappin' smugglers. Now **a** chap that kin **dew** that kin make a speech."

" No, no," interposed another, " we don't want any custom officer to make speeches ter us. We smuggle for a livin' in this place, we dew."

" Shet up, Busby ! " immediately spoke up his nearest neighbor, " I tell yer the boy's gwine ter speak tew us."

" A speech, Mr. Styles," said Baxter with a smile.

" Pitch in ! " vociferated others.

I felt embarrassed in the presence of Baxter, more especially from the fact that I was taken by surprise and was at
a loss for something to say; but being desirous of displaying my readiness to assist him, I did not like to decline, and
thinking, too, that possibly he was too nearly intoxicated to
observe any fault in my diction or any lack of ideas, I
mustered courage and began.

"I assure you, gentlemen, that I deem it no small compliment to address you on this occasion. It is only recently
that I have formed the acquaintance of Mr. Baxter, and like
the rest of you I am impressed with the opinion that he
intends—I hesitated slightly, for I disliked to speak contrary to my honest convictions—or at least he desires to do
much for this county, and I trust that he may. A lawyer
—a man familiar with the statutes of the country and with
legislation, is certainly to be preferred as our representative
to one who knows nothing about these matters; and as the
one whom rumor leads us to believe will appear in the
field against Mr. Baxter is neither a lawyer nor a practical
legislator, he certainly in this respect has not the same
claim upon your votes. Mr. Baxter has expressed himself
as ready to do whatever it is possible for him to do to promote those things which will contribute to the wealth and
prosperity of the country. He has declared himself the advocate of better roads in this section; the friend of the farmer,
the promoter of schools, churches and temperance reform."

"Git out!" exclaimed a rough voice. "We don't want
any old fogy temperance lecterer for our representative.
Baxter aint no sich chap as that."

I glanced around and discovered a sardonic grin on the
face of the landlord, while Baxter, as if unconscious of what

I had said, was fumbling for papers in his pocket. **I saw** that I had thoughtlessly repeated his remarks, with regard to temperance, to the wrong crowd. Endeavouring to mend the matter, I continued :

"I mean to say that he has declared himself in favor of a prohibitory law, **if the country** needs it, or, —— that is, if his constituents require **it**."

"Well, that's better, young man," spoke out the same gruff voice; "but the country don't need it, and his constitooents don't require it."

"You may be assured, **gentlemen**," I said, "that Mr. Baxter will **not** oppose the **wishes of** his supporters in this, or in any other matter."

"Mr. Styles is right," exclaimed Baxter.

"That's all square 'nuff, young man," exclaimed another of the electors, "but you said suthin' 'bout churches. Now we don't want no more churches nuther. No, sir'ee; I don't go in fur churches. We've got ministers 'nuff to s'port now. P'raps you don't **know,** boys, that my ole woman has been kinder hangin' round these meetins they hev up in the red schoolhouse; but she has, and so ole Tompkins, the preacher, thinks he must **come a visitin'** 'bout **once a** week, and git his dinner, **and** have his hoss fed, **and that** aint 'nuff, but she's got **ter** pack **him off with pertaters,** or meal, or one stuff **or** nuther. I tell yer, boys, I'm down on this thing. No churches fur me."

As soon as he had thus relieved his mind, I said,

"I hope you will not misapprehend me, gentlemen. **My** object in speaking **of these** things was to show you how perfectly willing Mr. Baxter seems to be to do whatever his constituents wish him to do. He certainly has no desire to labor in opposition to your interests, and trusting, as I do, that he may accomplish much for our mutual benefit, I shall labor most heartily with you to secure his election."

I sat down, and instantly Steeple rose to speak.

" I tell yer, boys," he said, " that the young man is right. All he wants is ter have us understand that Mr. Baxter is a gentleman, and that he's willin' ter help us. Now, he aint gwine ter build churches and make us pay fur 'em ; nor he aint gwine ter send ministers out here fur us ter s'port, 'less we want 'em ; nor he aint gwine ter lay out roads where we don't want 'em ; nor dew nothin' else that's gwine ter be agin us."

" Hear! hear!" yelled the company, and Steeple encouraged went on :—

" Now, as fur Tom Snyder's talkin' 'bout feedin' the minister's hoss, and 'grudgin' him suthin ter eat if he needs it, I think that's a leetle tew small pertaters fur this crowd."

" Hear! hear!"

" Now, I may be agin taxin' ter build churches, but if a preacher, or any other decent man comes tew my house and wants suthin ter eat, or if the ole woman wants ter giv him a few pertaters or a little Injun meal, or anything else, he'll hev it, and thar wont be no fuss 'bout it nuther."

" That's you, Steeple, no pigs in this crowd," said Jones. Snyder smoked his pipe, savagely ; the rest cheered.

" Now, boys," resumed the speaker, " its gittin' late, and we orter go home, and let our representative go to bed ; but afore we go I propose that we give three cheers fur him."

For the next three minutes it seemed as if the neighboring mountain must be shaken to its base, with the noise that ensued. As soon as the cheering had subsided Jones rose and said :

" I propose three cheers for the landlord."

Again the deafening cheers went up.

" Now three cheers for the Queen," suggested another.

An earthquake of tumult succeeded.

" Come, boys," said Fogg, " its my treat 'fore you go."

" Hold on," interposed Ruiter, " we must give three cheers for the young custom officer."

" Young man," he said, addressing me, " we shall send you to Parlyment some time," and before giving me time to reply he gave the signal **for** cheering, and **at** once the shouts arose.

The party now dispersed, with the exception of two who had imbibed too freely to be at all inclined to leave, and they patriotically swore they never would go home till Mr. Baxter was " 'lected."

Tired and disgusted with the whole scene, I immediately called for my room, and retired.   It was my first experience at electioneering, and I fervently wished that it might be my last.   I could but feel that there was something terribly debasing in the whole work.   What I had witnessed was only one of the least flagrant cases of man leading his fellow man into temptation—an instance of intelligence, for the emoluments of office, pandering to the prejudices and appetites of ignorance—cool, deliberate encouragement of vice.

I surmised when I heard Baxter request the landlord to invite some of the most prominent men of the locality to his house that evening, that the latter, in observing the request, might possibly consult the interest of his own pocket in the matter, and that, consequently, *pre-eminence*, in his estimation, would consist in ability to drink the most whiskey; and the sequel showed that my estimate of the man was not far from correct. I knew that there was another class of men in that section quite different, morally, from those that we had met that day at the hotel, but as their number was small, I believed that it mattered little, with regard to the success of his election, whether Baxter saw them or not.

In the morning, after breakfast, Baxter called for his bill, which amounted to the modest sum of fifteen dollars, and he then handed Fogg twenty dollars more with the remark—

" I leave that with you, believing that you will see that it is used in my interests."

" You may be sure of that, Mr. Baxter," was the emphatic reply. " You can *count* on me."

Baxter then gave him a few directions, after which we entered the carriage and drove off to a man named Woodbury, quite a respectable farmer and an active temperance man, withal, who lived but a short distance from our direct route to Arklow. I suggested to Baxter the idea of visiting him, and the suggestion meeting his concurrence, we drove to his domicile.

Woodbury was different in many respects from the majority of those men that we had thus far met. He had made the most of his little stock of book learning, and, by observation and a considerable amount of reading, had acquired sufficient knowledge, so that he was looked upon by his neighbors as a man of education ; and by those of higher culture as a man of intelligence.

Spending no money when he thought it unnecessary, always at home except when pressing business called him hence, and outspoken in his opinions, especially with regard to intemperance, he was not at all popular with a certain class in Hilton; his frugality being regarded as *stinginess*, his lectures to the intemperate as meddlesome interference with the rights of others, and his stay-at-home propensity as a want of appreciation of fun and goodfellowship. This outline of his character and reputation I had delineated to Baxter ere we arrived at his house, so that I thought he was sufficiently posted to take the most direct path to Woodbury's good graces.

We found him at work near his house. He received us somewhat coolly, I fancied, but after the salutations had passed he invited us to go in and take a seat. Baxter declined—want of time and press of business being his excuse—and immediately introduced the subject of election. When he paused, Woodbury said:

"You came into the place yesterday, I heard."

"Yes," was the reply, "and I am surprised that I did not see you at the hotel. I met quite a number of the rate-payers there, last evening."

"I knew nothing about the meeting," said Woodbury, "till early this morning. I heard, then, that they had quite a time at Fogg's, last night."

I glanced at Baxter, but he, in no wise disconcerted, quickly replied—

"Yes, a very pleasant meeting. I find, Mr. Woodbury that your people here are wide awake about election. They seem to understand well what the interests of their country demand."

"Well," said Woodbury, "I don't know who was there last night, but my impression is, that if it was the crowd that usually patronizes Fogg, they thought the country needs whiskey more than anything else."

"Indeed," replied Baxter; "why, those whom I met last evening bore the appearance of being honest, industrious farmers. Several of them spoke, and expressed very sensible opinions as to the character of the man whom they would choose to represent them in Parliament. I am very sorry you were not present, Mr. Woodbury."

"I never go into Fogg's house," was the reply; and then, turning to me, he said:

"Now, Styles, why didn't you come and stay with me last night instead of taking Mr. Baxter over to that *Rum Hole?* I could have got quite a number to come in, and a class of men who know quite as well, I dare say, what we need as any who were at Fogg's."

I was taken aback somewhat, but replied—

"Really, Mr. Woodbury, it did not occur to me that you would like to entertain us, and I supposed Mr. Baxter would prefer going to the hotel, it being the most central place. I am sure that I would have enjoyed staying with you, and I have no doubt Mr. Baxter would, had he known that he could have accomplished the object of his visit here as well as he could elsewhere."

"Most certainly, I would," said Baxter, "and I only regret that your generous desires were not known before we had made other arrangements. But I trust that we shall be better acquainted, Mr. Woodbury, for I venture to hope that I shall find you a powerful supporter of my interests in the coming elections."

"Well, I don't know whether you will or not," replied Woodbury in a frank and independent manner. "That depends very much upon circumstances. You are a stranger to me now, and I shall want to know more about you before I can pledge myself to support you."

" I approve of your caution, Mr. Woodbury," said Baxter, "and admire your frankness. I certainly desire that every man in this county shall know for whom he is voting, and I exhort you to make all the inquiries respecting me that you may think proper. Should I be elected, I shall feel myself bound to labor earnestly for the benefit of my constituents, and I believe that I can accomplish much for their good."

" I have no doubt of that," was the reply, "but if you accomplish one-half of what you promise to do for us, you will do more than any other representative I have ever seen."

" Do you insinuate, Mr. Woodbury, that I am trying to deceive you ? "

" Not intentionally, perhaps ; but representatives are but human, and may themselves be deceived. Though your desire to effect great things for your constituents may be strong enough, you are but one amongst a large number. Your power to do good is very limited, and I hope you do not take us all for such fools that we believe you can do any great thing for this county."

Baxter was for a moment staggered by these frank expressions of the honest farmer, but he was not to be easily put down, and summoning all his assurance he returned to the charge.

" Very true, Mr. Woodbury, I am but one, but I have a vote, to say nothing of my influence with others, and by recording that vote on the right side, I shall at least be able to show my good intentions."

" That is all right, Mr. Baxter, you speak now with reason and modesty, and you have only to assure me that your vote always will be cast on the right side, or on the side which your judgment and conscience tell you is right, in order to secure mine."

"I wish that I had some way of assuring you, Mr. Woodbury."

"I wish you had," was the blunt reply, and then looking the candidate squarely in the face he asked,

"What is your opinion of the temperance question, Mr. Baxter?"

The latter with an attempt at a most gracious smile, but with some faint indications of uneasiness, replied,

"I am a very firm believer in temperance, Mr. Woodbury."

"No doubt of it," said Woodbury, with a hearty laugh; I never knew a man who wasn't, but that is not the question. Are you strictly a temperance man, one who not only advocates total abstinence, but practices it?"

"As to being fanatical on the temperance question, I do not think I am," said Baxter, "but believing that the liquor traffic is a great curse to our country, I can heartily give my support to any strict prohibitory law, and shall not fail to do it whenever the opportunity is presented."

"Well, you stand then about as I had surmised. Like thousands of others you dislike to be very active for fear of being considered a fanatic, and too fond of your beverage to deny yourself for the sake of a good example to your fellow men; you go about preaching one thing and practicing another. Do you know, Mr. Baxter, that I regard these moderate drinkers as the greatest curse to the temperance cause that exists?"

"Do you think the temperance question the only one to be considered in selecting your representative?" asked Baxter, with a slightly sarcastic laugh.

"By no means, sir," was the reply, "but I regard it as the most important one; and looking at this matter as I do, I shall vote for no candidate for office who is not a thoroughly honest, temperance man."

"Do I understand you to mean that unless **he is a** teetotaler, he cannot be an honest temperance man?"

"That is precisely what I mean."

"Even if he does everything in his power to obtain the passage **of** prohibitory **laws, and in** other ways promotes temperance?"

"If **he** still neglected to abstain wholly from the use of intoxicating liquors himself, I would not regard him **as an** *honest temperance* man."

"And you would **not** vote for such a man?" still queried Baxter.

"Not if by doing it **I** could be made Governor General to-morrow," was the reply.

"Well, I trust that posterity will appreciate you," said Baxter, beginning to show displeasure, "but I doubt whether many in this age take such **a narrow view** of temperance as you do."

"O," replied Woodbury, with a good-natured laugh, **"I** don't expect **to be** appreciated by **men like you**; but if I do labor under that disadvantage, **I shall at least** have the pleasure **of** knowing that I have **acted** according to the dictates **of** my conscience."

Baxter merely bade him "good morning," and then we returned to the carriage.

For some minutes he maintained a moody silence, **as we** drove homeward, but at length he broke into a **hearty laugh** and asked,

" Have you many such men as Woodbury in this county ? "

" I think not many," I replied.

" It is to be hoped that you hav'n't," he answered.

Had I possessed the fearlessness and candor of Woodbury, I would doubtless have given utterance to my convictions by replying,

" It is to be regretted that we have not," but, like the majority of people similarly situated, I only smiled and said nothing.

We reached Arklow at noon, and though we had been absent but little more than twenty-four hours, it really seemed to me a period of a week.　I certainly was glad to get back to the quiet scenes of my labor, and it would have afforded me great pleasure then to know that my work at electioneering was at an end, but I had the consolation of thinking that whatever remained for me to do in this line during that campaign, I would be permitted to do alone, and consequently in such manner as I preferred.

On the evening of that same day several of the citizens of Arklow met Baxter at the Custom House, but as they were a different class of men from those we met at Fogg's, as might be supposed, the evening was spent in a different manner.

CHAPTER IX.

On the succeeding day, quite early in the morning, Baxter,
in the presence of the Doctor, handed me $200 in bank
notes, and after giving me some brief directions, and expressing many wishes for my success, he jumped into the
carriage waiting for him at the door, and set out to a remote
part of the county.

Left alone with the Doctor once more, I narrated to him
in detail the incidents that had occurred during my visit with
Baxter to Hilton—not forgetting to repeat the patriotic
speeches delivered at Fogg's. He had a keen perception of
the ludicrous, a hearty appreciation of a good joke, and to
him the political meeting, as described, bore so much the
semblance of a well-conceived burlesque, that he never tired
of alluding to it, and years afterward it afforded him the
subject of many a hearty laugh.

"Such ideas of fitness for the office of representative!"
he ejaculated, half an hour or so after I had detailed to him

the story of our adventures, and he was pacing his office
in the enjoyment of his usual morning smoke. " Well," he
continued, "they are as rational perhaps as those of many
others we meet, whom we would naturally suppose were
well informed."

" Possibly," I replied.

" Yes," he said, "and Baxter will find very many such
men in this county who will enthusiastically support him,
and "—here he paused, and looking steadily at me he continued—"he will be elected."

There was a degree of emphasis on the last sentence
which, considered with his manners and previous remarks,
conveyed to me the impression that he regarded such an
event as something to be wondered at and regretted. I had
not before heard him utter a word which gave me an inkling
of the estimate that he had placed upon Baxter. I have
already said that I believed from his manner he did not
admire him, but this was a suspicion which I strove hard
to consider groundless.

I did not like to question him with regard to his opinion
of the man. Pleased with the assurance that he believed
he would be elected, and fearful lest, if I questioned him,
he might say something which would undermine the air
castles that Baxter had inspired me to erect, I chose to
change the subject of conversation at once.

As it was now Saturday, I decided to postpone my electioneering labors till the ensuing week, and spend the
evening of that day in the society of Ruth. I was actuated
not only by anticipation of the pleasure of seeing her, but
I confess to a little curiosity to know how long Mr. Niel
remained, and also to a desire to lay before her the new

projects that had possessed me. Relying much, as I always had, upon her judgment, and regarding her advice as something not to be discarded, I felt that it would afford me much profit and pleasure to talk freely with her concerning my engagement with Baxter, and also of his promised reward.

She seemed unusually glad to see me that evening, from the fact, I presumed, that she was somewhat lonely, her relatives having gone away for a few days on a visit, leaving her—with the exception of a man and maid servant—the only occupant of the house.

After the salutations had passed, and she had given me a humorous account of her housekeeping experiences of the past two days, with as much *sang-froid* as I could display, I asked when Mr. Niel departed. The pleasant smile which had previously lit up her face at once disappeared; her eyes dropped, and I fancied that there was something slightly pettish in her tone when she informed me that he did not leave until the afternoon following the day when I met him. Her manner excited my curiosity, and I longed to have it gratified.

" He seems to be an intimate friend of your uncle," I remarked.

" Yes," she replied, with eyes still downcast, as she employed herself busily with a piece of embroidery, " uncle esteems him highly."

" And like a dutiful niece, I suppose you feel bound to esteem him highly," I ventured still further to remark.

" I esteem him as a friend of the family," she answered, still plying her needle rapidly, and after a moment's pause, glancing inquiringly at me, half laughing, she said, " but why do you ask ? "

" Is it not natural," I replied, conscious that the blood had mounted to my cheek, " that I should feel an interest in your friends ? "

" Perhaps," she said, " but Mr. Niel is not a very *particular* friend of mine."

There was a frankness, an earnestness in this declaration which reassured me. Whatever I had before observed that roused my curiosity, I felt was of little consequence. Her words always carried with them conviction of truthfulness, and as they had done so with more than usual force on the present occasion, I cared not to question her further respecting a subject of which, I fancied, she for some reason did not like to speak.

" Well, Ruth, we will dismiss Mr. Neil," I said, " and as you have volunteered to give me an account of your doings since I saw you, I will tell you of mine, and I might as well inform you that I have a long story to tell."

" Indeed, you excite my curiosity. I hope you hav'n't been chasing smugglers again."

" No, smuggling has been a matter of little interest to me for the last few days."

" Pray, do tell ; you puzzle me."

" I have embarked in politics," I replied laughing.

" Politics ! " she exclaimed, " why I thought you detested politics."

" So I do, and now more than ever, but if you can endure it I will give you a history of my two days experience in political life."

" I will try," she replied.

I then recounted to her my meeting with Baxter, the proposal and the promises he had made me, my visit with him to Hilton, and his subsequent doings up to the time of his departure. I carefully avoided saying anything of my impressions of him, **and in** order to do this I omitted whatever I thought might tend to prejudice her against him. **My** account, too, of the meeting at Fogg's was only a faint picture **of** what actually occurred, but with a pure woman's instinctive horror of vice, she looked reproachfully at me **when I had** reached this point in the narrative, and asked,

"Did not your conscience reprove you for being a witness **of such a** scene?"

The reader already knows what my impressions were on **the** occasion to which she referred, hence will naturally divine that my answer to the question was in the affirmative.

She listened quietly and soberly to the remaining part of my story, evincing no gladness at what she must have felt I regarded as good luck. I was perplexed, not to say chagrined, at her apathy.

"You **do not** congratulate **me**," I said, laughingly, after **a** short silence, "on my success in business."

"Do you really regard it as success in **business?**" she asked in **a tone of** seriousness, **almost sadness.**

"Why **should I** not?" I inquired.

"I hardly know," **she answered,** "but tell me, do you really believe that Mr. Baxter is an honest, good man?"

The question was a hard **one.** **I was** almost annoyed with her for having asked **it.** I could not answer in the affirmative, and disliked to answer negatively, so I equivocated and said:

"I am not sufficiently acquainted with him as yet to know just what I believe of him."

"But do you think **it** is quite right to do what he requires **you to** do?" she still pursued.

"O, you women," I replied, "have too delicate consciences to deal in politics."

"That may be," she answered, "but I have little fear, Frank, that you will do wrong, if you act according to the dictates of your conscience, in engaging in politics."

"I am glad to know that you think so well of me," I answered, wishing heartily just then that Baxter's money was in his own pocket.

"And so you will go to work on Monday," she said, "to induce people to vote for him?"

"That is what I have agreed to do," I replied.

"Well," she continued, "I only hope that you will find him as conscientious in fulfilling his promises to you."

"I cannot now believe that I shall find him otherwise," I answered.

A short silence ensued, which she broke with the following apparently anxious inquiry, at the same time laying her hand on my arm.

"Tell me, will you find it necessary in your labors to have other meetings like that you had at Fogg's?"

"No," I replied, smiling at her fears, "I hope not. I shall be alone, and shall usually meet the rate-payers at their houses."

"Well, it will be pleasant for me to think of that," she answered, with an appearance of relief, "and I am sure it will be more pleasant for you."

"Yes, you may be sure it will," I answered.

The subject of conversation now changed. It was late that evening ere I bid her adieu, and the reader will scarcely wonder that I never fully realized how or when I reached home, when he learns that I performed the journey under the emotions called forth by plighted love.

CHAPTER X.

My first labors in the interests of Baxter, after his departure, took me to two or three French settlements on the mountain slope in Foreston.

The inhabitants were mostly new comers, from the parishes along the Richelieu and St. Lawrence, and were generally ignorant and poor, but hardy and industrious.

Plunging into this mountain wilderness, and settling on rough, stony, yet productive land, they had toiled with hopeful, happy spirits; and with the proceeds of their ashes, shingles, and sometimes sugar, purchased the necessaries of life.

To many of those who had been a few years in the township I was personally known, and from these I learned the circumstances and character of their neighbors, and was thus the better able to decide where my "donations" were the most deserved and were the most likely to relieve the needy. They always received these small sums with every indication of unbounded gratitude, and though I never attempted to extort a promise from any one that he would vote for Baxter, I never bestowed a present on one who was not instantly profuse in his declarations of friendship for him, and loud in his expressions of determination to be early at the poll.

But the habitant was not the only one that I accosted. I often met and talked with the English-speaking citizens, and now and then held a long parley with one better informed than his neighbors, and possessed of an opinion of his own. Thus the entire week was consumed, and at its close I had obtained sufficient information concerning the political status of the township to feel sure that nine-tenths of its rate-payers would vote for Baxter.

It was already understood that a man named Farmer, living in the county, was to be the opposing candidate, but thus far he nor his friends had displayed much interest in his success. He was an able agriculturist, and, with the exception of being better educated, was in every respect a man similar to Woodbury, whom I have already described. The nomination of the candidates was to take place at Mapleton, the *chef-lieu* of the county, on the Wednesday, after I had completed my canvass of Foreston.

On the day previous to the nomination, I was again alone in the Custom Office, engaged in reading, when I was a little surprised by the arrival of Mr. Niel, who drove up with his stylish bays before mentioned. I was the more surprised from the fact that I had never before seen him at Arklow.

He appeared delighted to see me, and, as an excuse for coming there, said that he had called to enter a few simple articles that he had just purchased across the line, in Mayfair. I was not a little puzzled to know why he had taken the trouble to purchase such common articles in Mayfair, and then why he had chosen to enter them at Arklow instead of going to the Custom Office where he usually did his business, and which was located on by far the nearest and most direct route to his residence. I made no effort, however, to gratify my curiosity, and extended to him all the courtesy that I commanded; and as he seemed in no haste to depart, after dispatching his business, I invited him to remain and dine with me; an invitation which he seemed pleased to accept.

During his stay he appeared intent on winning my favor. As on the occasion when I first met him, so now, he asked me many questions relative to myself, talked freely on the subjects in which he thought I felt the most interested, and expressed many warm wishes for the successful issue of the labors in which I was engaged. He said nothing about Ruth, but enquired particularly after Mr. Edgarton's family, and I took no pains to conceal from him the fact that I had visited their residence since I had met him there. Again he urged me to visit him, and, as he left, obtained a promise once more from me that I would spend a few days with him at his house as soon as I could consistently do so.

I certainly was in a quandary. I could assign only one reason for his extraordinary interest in me; but as I had the assurance of Ruth that he was no particular friend of hers I felt secure; and in the other matters that were pressing upon my attention, he and his visit were soon forgotten.

On the morning of the nomination, actuated by a feeling of interest and curiosity, I drove, in company with the Doctor, to Mapleton. Baxter, with two or three politicians, from Montreal, who had come out for the purpose of addressing the electors, had arrived before us. We had besides a posse of roughs who had been conveyed hither for the purpose of cheering and making other demonstrations in his favor, and to do whatever they could to the annoyance and detriment of his opponent. It may not be known to the reader that formerly politicians often employed such characters to do similar work on similar occasions, and as the custom has not yet been fully abandoned, Baxter alone cannot be censured for descending to such a demoralizing and disgraceful act to consummate his schemes.

After dinner, the crowd, upon which whiskey already displayed its effects, repaired to the County House, in front of which the speaker's stand was erected. After that gentleman had been duly nominated, loud cries of " Baxter ! Baxter !" rose from various parts of the throng, and with flushed face and pompous manner he strode to the front of the platform, doffed his hat, brushed back his hair, and in stertorian tones commenced his address.

I shall not attempt to repeat it, believing that it will suffice to say that it was long, rambling and bombastic ; pregnant with protestations of patriotism and pledges of fidelity to his constituents.

Prolonged cheering followed, and then two or three voices called for Farmer. That gentleman, a stout, intelligent looking man, clad in rather coarse but substantial apparel, came forward from the rear of the platform, and would, no doubt, have made a sensible and effective speech had he been permitted; but his appearance was the signal

for the roughs from both the city and country to commence
a series of assaults as disgusting to the respectable, unselfish spectator, as it was discourteous and injurious to the
speaker. **Groans,** yells and insulting epithets, hurled at
the candidate, followed **each** other in such rapid succession
that he never got further than "Gentlemen electors—"
although perfectly **cool and** undismayed, **he** stood long
before them **waiting for the tumult to subside.** He calmly
folded his arms **and surveyed the scene like** one conscious
of rectitude, and possessed more **of** pity **and** shame for
them **than of** indignation **and** rage at their conduct.
Several times, **when there was a** lull in the uproar, did he
attempt to proceed, but just as often did his enemies shame-
fully prevent him. Once, in the course of the proceedings,
Baxter, with a show of candor, stepped forward, and, with
a smile on **his** countenance, which to me seemed one of
satisfaction at the conduct **of his** supporters, asked that
they would kindly refrain from any acts of disturbance,
and permit his good friend, **Mr.** Farmer, to address them.

"Indeed, gentlemen," **he** said, **"conscious, as** I am, that
my friends **here on the** platform, **who are yet to** address
you, will easily **overthrow whatever Mr. Farmer** in his
wisdom and eloquence may say, I **earnestly** entreat that
you will give **him the privilege of speaking.** However
weak his **cause may be, I am** sure **that a** statesman so
distinguished, **a** man of such vast and varied learning,
cannot fail to say much that will edify us, and I assure
you, gentlemen, that **I am** anxious to listen to him."

Baxter resumed **his seat,** and loud cheers followed.
Farmer stood, meanwhile, **his** cheek for the first time
flushed with indignation, **and his** frame quivering with

eagerness to reply to this irony and ungentlemanly satire upon his obscurity, and I secretly hoped that he might be allowed to speak, feeling sure, as I did, that he would convince Mr. Baxter that he had *caught a Tartar.* But it was in vain that he attempted it.

The roughs, as if well assured that Baxter's request was a mere sham—a hypocritical show of fairness—were more demonstrative than ever in their endeavors to prohibit his opponent from speaking. Convinced that it was a pre-concerted plan to give him no hearing, he finally retired from the platform. Some one then ventured to call for Woodbury, his staunch supporter. The cry was caught up and repeated by a few others. That gentleman came forward, but only to be jeered and hooted from the platform. One of Baxter's friends, from Montreal, was then called out, but just as he was about to commence his address there was quite a move in the crowd, and a large number, who proved to be Farmer's friends, walked off. Disgusted with the treatment which that gentleman had received, and too respectable to seek retaliation by the same ignoble means, they chose to retire, leaving the speaker to address those more desirous of listening.

Falling into the ranks of those departing I also moved away and returned to the hotel. I was not surprised to learn from indignant remarks that many who were leaving had come there strongly inclined to support Baxter; but they had become so thoroughly disgusted with the day's proceedings that they were now resolved to support his opponent. One man, in particular, affirmed that on the preceding evening he had expressed the strongest determination to vote for Baxter, but now, if he were offered the best farm in the county, he wouldn't vote for a man who would "uphold such rascality."

I very gladly refrained from participating in politics on this occasion. I met **many** during the day who knew the part I had **taken in** furthering the interests of Baxter, and they congratulated me **warmly on the** present appearances of his success, **but as I inwardly felt** that it was not a subject for **congratulation, I had but little to say** to them in **return.**

An hour after I had returned to the hotel, **Baxter** and **many of his** friends came in. **He seemed in the** most exuberant **spirits, and for the second** time that day shook me **warmly by** the hand, thanked me for the generous way in which I had supported him, and added that he had every evidence that I had used the money he gave me to a "noble purpose." I had **my** doubts about the purpose being a very noble one, but said,

"I **endeavored to use it, Mr. Baxter,** where it would contribute to your **interests.**"

"Well, Styles," he said, "**continue to do your best for me,** and you'll **find it all right after the election.**"

He was now called away by a friend, and the Doctor's carriage being in **readiness for us that** moment, I saw him no more.

Not many days after the nomination, **the** election occurred which occupied two days. Having **no** vote to cast, I remained at home, and from the office window observed the waggon-loads **of** enthusiastic, shouting electors, who during the time **were constantly** going to and from the poll at Foreston.

Notwithstanding **his confident assurance of** success

K

Baxter found that his victory was not so easily won. More than once during the first day of voting did his friends have reason to fear the issue, but stimulated by these fears to greater exertion, and goaded to a reckless and bare-faced use of money even at the polls, they finally succeeded in electing him by a small majority. Foreston, as I had opined, went strongly in his favor, other townships were about equally divided in the number of votes they cast for the respective candidates, while Farmer's native township, in which he still resided, went almost wholly in his favor— a fact which gave evidence of the worth of the man, and the esteem in which he was held by those to whom he was intimately known. It was generally conceded that Baxter's victory would have been far more easy and brilliant had it not been believed that he secretly instigated and encouraged the shameful persecutions inflicted upon Farmer on the day of the nomination.

CHAPTER XI.

MONTHS had passed away since the occurrence of the events recorded in the last chapter, and we were once more on the verge of spring. I had remained in the Custom Office all the while with very little to do, and had whiled away the time chiefly with my books. I had made no money except the little paid me as salary, and having added many—and some of them expensive—volumes to my library, and newly replenished my wardrobe, the not over large amount of money which I had in the fall had dwindled down to a small sum.

I had neither seen Baxter nor heard directly from him since the day that he was nominated, and though in the newspapers I had carefully read the proceedings of Parliament, hoping that his name might frequently appear as a prominent and influential member, thus giving me faith to believe in his ability to fulfil his promises to me, I was in a measure disappointed. All that I ever learned respecting him served to convince me that, while he possessed a little ability, he was by no means a prominent man in his party.

Believing that he knew both my desires and necessities, I felt that inasmuch as he had voluntarily offered to assist me, and I had performed the labor he had assigned me, it belonged to him to fulfil his promises without a reminder of them, hence, I had modestly refrained from visiting him; but as time rolled on, and I began to feel more and more the need of remunerative employment, I decided, at the suggestion of the Doctor, to address him by letter.

I said nothing in this of what had passed between us, but politely solicited his aid in securing a position.

" Did you remind him," asked the Doctor, as I was about posting the letter, " that the three months, in which time he was to place you in a situation, with fifteen hundred a year, expired long ago ? "

" No," I said with a laugh, " I trust that he is not ignorant of the fact."

Three weeks passed, and no answer came. Again I sat down and wrote him, this time making a little stronger appeal to his kindness, and even gently hinting that he had formerly inspired me with a hope that he would give me one of the many situations he had at his command.

I thought that he certainly could not accuse me of sarcasm, if he remembered what he had said while at Arklow, and during our ride to Hilton.

Under the circumstances, I was quite willing he should believe that I regarded him the Autocrat of the Province, having the power to give away every position of emolument in the government.

Ten days more elapsed, and still no word came from him. I would have pursued him no further but for the advice of the Doctor.

"If I were you," said he, "I would visit him. **He,** no doubt, is very busy, and thinks it will do to answer your letters when he has more time. I will write him myself also, reminding him **of** his promise to assist you, and if you see him about the time that he receives the letter, I have no doubt he will **do** his best to aid **you**."

This advice seemed good, **and** having reason to believe that Baxter would **be in** Montreal in the following week, I determined to **see** him. Pursuant to this plan I reached the Canadian Metropolis on Tuesday, and at once repaired to his office.

He received **me** quite coolly, in short, in a manner which afforded a striking contrast to his friendly patronizing air towards me but **a** few months previous, and instantly I felt **a** sort of conviction that all reliance upon him was useless. Imputing these feelings, however, to an over-sensitive nature, I resolved not to relinquish my suit until I had obtained from him some expression, either **fovorable or** unfavorable, to my designs.

He **was writing** when I entered, **and** after turning his attention to me sufficiently long to **say**, gruffly,

"Good morning," and "you **want** to see me, I suppose," he handed me a daily paper, saying as he did so,

"Here, busy yourself with this for awhile, I shall soon be through," and **then resumed** his work.

I *busied* myself with the paper according to his injunction for at least an hour, although long before the expiration of that time I had **ceased** to feel any interest in the matter

of its columns, and was only wondering when he would be
through, and what would be the result of my interview with
him.   Occasionally, in the interim, I cast a side glance at
him to ascertain whether his work was not nearly completed,
and twice I observed him looking askance at me, and I could
not forbear the thought that he was secretly hoping I might
become wearied, and retire from his presence without sub-
mitting him to the annoyance of attending further to my
wants.   Be this as it may, however, I remained, and after
awhile I had the satisfaction of seeing him throw down his
pen.   He sat for a moment seemingly absorbed in thought,
then whirled about his chair facing me, yawned, and said,

"Well, how's the Doctor?"

"Quite well," I replied. "I presume you have recently
received a letter from him."

"Yes," he said, "I received a letter from him a day or
two ago."

He then pulled out his watch, glanced at it, mused a
moment and then asked,

"How long are you going to remain in the city?"

"I wish to return as soon as possible," I answered "to-
morrow, at latest."

"Pshaw! man, what's the use of being in a hurry," he
said. "I have found, young man, that there is never anything made by being in a hurry. I presume it has been
quite awhile since you were in Montreal."

"Yes," I answered, "three years."

"Three years! O, well then, you will want to stay and
look around for a time. I am very much pressed with
business to-day, indeed I am unusually pressed, and as I
would like to have a long talk with you, I wish, if possible

that you would call to-morrow. Where are you staying?"

"At the American House," I answered.

"Well, that is a good hotel," he said. "Now, why not come in to-morrow and see me? I will be at the office early, say at half-past nine, eh?"

"I can do that, if it will be inconvenient for you to talk with me before," I replied.

"Well," he answered, "you see how it is; I have a great amount of work to do just now, and this afternoon I expect two or three different parties in to see me on important business."

"Very well, then," I said, "I will come in the morning if you wish, at half-past nine."

"Yes," he answered, as he turned again to his work, "at half-past nine."

At the appointed hour, on the following day, I was at the office. The office boy had only half completed his work when I arrived, but I sat down and waited for Baxter. At ten o'clock he had not made his appearance, but his partner, who came in shortly afterwards, informed me that he had been unexpectedly called out of the city and would not return until evening. It is needless to say that I was sadly disappointed. I felt the humbleness of my position. Had I been regarded as a person of any importance by Baxter, he certainly would have informed me by note, or otherwise, of his departure, and mentioned some other hour at which he could meet me; but he had done nothing of the kind, and like all other hangers-on at the door of an important personage, I must await his pleasure. I had experienced nothing so humiliating since I was dependent for a livelihood on the whim of a school committee.

That day I spent like the preceding one, in strolling about the city. In the evening, determined not to be thwarted in my design of talking with Baxter, having found out the residence of that dignitary, I repaired thither. I found him at home, but he was in a state of partial intoxication. He seemed much surprised at seeing me, as was evident by the expression with which he greeted me.

" Why," he said, " I thought you had gone home."

" You must have thought," I replied, " that I had but little desire to see you, Mr. Baxter."

" O, I didn't suppose you were very anxious," he said, " but come, now, what can I do for you ? "

I saw that he was in a mood when I could approach him, so I answered good naturedly,

" Well, Mr. Baxter, to tell the truth, I am out of employment, and just in the position where I can appreciate a situation with fifteen hundred a year."

" O, my dear sir," he said with a laugh, " that is a very large salary. There are but few men in Montreal who are getting as much as that."

Being convinced that I had but little to lose from his displeasure, I determined not to be over modest in my appeals to him.

" Indeed," I said, " Mr. Baxter, you led me to infer, last fall, that it would be an easy matter for you to obtain a situation for me which would command that salary."

" Yes, yes," he answered, hurriedly, " no doubt it would at that time, but business is very dull now; and you have no idea how many there are in Montreal with nothing to do who would be very glad to get even seven hundred a year."

"Perhaps," I suggested, "that they have no man of influence, like yourself, to assist them."

"You are mistaken there, young man. I can point you to any number of young men, well educated and most highly connected, who are looking in vain for employment."

I made no reply, and he soon said:

"You were not born in Canada, I believe."

"No, I was born in the States."

"Well, there is another difficulty," he said; "we always feel it our duty to assist those first who were born either in this country or in Great Britain. I was myself born in the old country; and love of my native land always makes me feel under a little more obligation to aid those who are the most nearly allied to the old flag."

I felt insulted, and immediately said:

"Indeed, Mr. Baxter, your loyalty didn't assume this form last fall, when you thrust your friendship on me, and of your own free will pledged yourself to give me a situation, with a good salary, within three months."

"Ah, but you forget," he exclaimed, with some degree of excitement, "that times have changed, wonderfully changed since then. If my election had not cost me so much, possibly I might find it easier to do something for you. Have you any idea what that election cost me?"

"I have no doubt that it cost you or your friends some money," I replied, "but the part that I acted certainly cost you nothing, save the violation of your promises, and it has cost *me* something."

"*You!*" he exclaimed, in a tone of contempt, becoming angry at my plain language to him. "Pray, what has it cost you?"

"Humiliation," I answered.

At this, he burst into a fit of derisive laughter, which having subsided, he exclaimed:

"Well, come now, young man, let us know to what humiliation you have been subjected."

"To the humiliation," I answered, "of having been induced to work for your interests, only to find myself repaid with contumely."

"O, it's pay you seek, eh? Well, make out your bill, and I'll try and settle it."

"Do not add further insult to injury, Mr. Baxter," I said; "if I am to understand that you have neither the ability or inclination to assist me, as you promised, my business with you is finished;" and I rose to depart.

" I am sorry, my dear sir," he said, with an air of affected sympathy and regret, "but I do not see how I can possibly assist you."

"Had you been kind and gentlemanly enough to have said this much to me, by letter, after I had twice written you, it certainly would have saved me the trouble and expense of coming to Montreal on this occasion."

"Yes, yes, I presume it would; but the deuce of it is, you country chaps don't realize how much we business men of the city have to do. You think that, like yourselves, we can sit down at any time and answer letters; but as I don't like to have you offended, I propose to bear a portion of your expenses here myself, and we'll be friends in future, eh? Here are five dollars," and before I fully realized what he was about he had placed the bill in my hand.

Throwing it disdainfully from me, I said:

"I trust, Mr. Baxter, that when you have returned to

your normal condition you will realize that, however great my necessities, I am not to be subjected to insult and then be conciliated by five dollars; and I trust, too, that my experience with you will prove one of the most profitable lessons of my life."

I did not wait for a reply, but as I stepped into the hall, closing the door behind me, he gave vent to another loud guffaw, as if hugely enjoying my display of indignation. It was dark and raining quite hard when I left his house, and the reader may naturally imagine that I performed my walk to the hotel with despondent, unhappy feelings, but, on the contrary, I returned with more buoyant step and lighter spirits. Disappointment of what we are hoping to receive is often far less unpleasant to endure than the tantalizing, feverish expectancy which precedes it.

Such, in a measure, was my experience, but as for a long time I had never really expected much from Baxter, of course my disappointment was nothing compared with what it might have been had not my confidence in him gradually diminished since first we met. As the reader knows, I had applied to him in this instance only at the instigation of my esteemed friend, the Doctor, and now that I had assured myself that I could no longer hope for aid from Baxter, I was relieved, satisfied.

One thing I had accomplished; I had learned the man, thoroughly tested the value of his promises, weighed his moral worth, and this, thought I, is something.

It was indeed to me a good lesson in the art of reading men, which imparted, thus early in life, proved profitable to me in after years. This man, who but a short time before, I, in my inexperience, had regarded with awe and almost veneration, had, from a moral point of view, dwindled into a pigmy that I could but despise. I learned from him that dignity and honor are not always to be found in high social positions.

The feelings of anger which his treatment aroused soon died away, and I almost began to regard the whole thing in the light of á good joke. Though never for a moment excusing his rascality, I felt that I was but little entitled to sympathy. My confidence in him as a man of integrity and honor was shaken in the very commencement of my acquaintance with him, still I gave him my humble support, and engaged in labors at his request which my conscience disapproved, and now that he had shown himself in his true colors, and deliberately snubbed me, I could but honestly feel that my reward was just; indeed, I think that I treated the thing far more philosophically than I have other troubles which have since presented themselves.

My business with Baxter having thus been brought to a termination, I left the city the following day, and went directly to Carrollton, in order to spend a day or two with Mr. Niel, and thus fulfil the promise which I had frequently made to visit him as soon as I found a convenient season. Happily I found that gentleman at home, and delighted to see me. His hospitality exceeded anything that I have ever since witnessed. His house, servants and horses were all at my command, and he seemed displeased if I was not continually making all, not excepting himself, contribute something to my comfort and pleasure. As it was about the commencement of the sugar season—a time when the roads of Canada are usually almost impassable—we could do but little riding; but the disappointment arising from this pri-

vation was more than counterbalanced by the pleasure
derived from the sugar parties that I attended. Three
of these were given by Mr. Niel himself, and as there were
as many more given by **his** neighbors, **we** had almost **a**
daily round **of** fun and enjoyment. Though living in **a**
quiet country place, three miles from **a** village, he had
several intelligent and wealthy farmers for neighbors, **whose**
sons and daughters, refined **and educated beyond** what we
usually expect to find **in the** country, often met **in social**
gatherings, **and thus** made it impossible for **one** sojourning
with them to grow weary **from** loneliness. The house of
Mr. Niel was the most frequent place for these gatherings,
not only because of the hospitality of its owner, but because
it was neatly furnished and commodious, and no doubt he
encouraged them more than he would had he been blessed
with the society of wife and children. I could see nothing,
save the lack of this society, to render my host, temporally,
happy. He was very **far,** however, from being a **light-**
hearted man given to pleasure. **He was** thoughtful, **often**
despondent, and even when he laughed it seemed mechanical
rather than the outburst of a truly happy heart. **He** had
a good library, and I found, as Ruth had already informed
me, that he read much, **especially** of whatever pertained to
agriculture.

My stay with him, which **I had** intended should not be
longer than **two** days, was, **at his earnest** solicitation, first
prolonged to a week, and then I could not release myself
until I had remained another week, and during all this
time he **was** entertaining me like a prince, and securing
more and more of my confidence. I could not say that I
never distrusted him. Believing, as I did, that he **was a**

great admirer, if not an actual lover of Ruth, I could hardly imagine that his friendship for me was so entirely disinterested as he would have me believe. But then, he was so courteous, so kind, so generous in his offers of assistance to me, that whenever a suspicion of his want of sincerity flashed across my mind I was disposed to attribute it to jealousy, and then tried to regard him as a friend. The lesson that I had received from Baxter was fresh in my mind, and I fancied that this, too, was inclined to make me ungenerous, suspicious even of the kindliest feelings and purest motives. He was altogether a different man from Baxter. If he was not just what he seemed, he certainly played his cards with more shrewdness; his acts never being of that transparent nature which would enable you to see that they were prompted by selfishness. Before I had been with him a week, he had learned from me all about my circumstances, what I intended to do, and the fact, which no doubt interested him more than all else, that I was engaged to Ruth, and intended marrying her as soon as other plans which I had laid were consummated. And this confidence he obtained without giving me any thought of ungentlemanly inquisitiveness on his part. He was never obtrusive, never displayed idle curiosity, but first ingratiated himself with me by giving me his confidence, and then won mine, by adroitness which I have scarcely found any other man to possess.

He did not hesitate to talk of Ruth, yet, he never did it to such an extent, or in such a way, as to lead me to infer that he was more interested in her than in other lady friends of whom he sometimes spoke. He related to me the story of his early love, of which the reader knows I had been informed, and, in a manner which conveyed to me conviction of his sincerity, expressed his determination never to wed.

One evening during the second week of my stay with him, as we were seated alone in his library, he addressed me as follows :

" Your desire, now, Mr. Styles, seems to be to go on and complete a college course."

" Perhaps not a college course," I said, "now that I have delayed so long ; I think I would be satisfied to spend a couple of years in some good educational institution before taking a profession."

" And the only obstacle you find in the way is the lack of funds," he said.

" Yes," I replied.

" Well, now," he continued, "you will not take it unkindly if I tell you of a plan of which I have been thinking ?"

" Certainly not," I replied.

"Well, then, it is this. I am not rich in the general acceptation of the term, but I have money at present for which I have no immediate use, and shall loan it for interest, the same as I have other sums for which I hold two or three mortgages as security on estates in this township. Now, if you wish, I would like to loan you whatever you may require to carry out your plans, at six per cent. interest, and give you all the time you need for payment." .

" But you know, Mr. Niel, that I cannot secure you by mortgage."

" I want no security, Mr. Styles, more than your promissory note."

"You certainly surprise me," I said, "and I cannot at all divine how it is that you take interest enough in me to proffer me so great assistance, or that you have so much confidence in me."

"I do not regard it as a very generous act," he replied, "to loan a man who you are convinced is thoroughly honest a few hundred dollars without security; and as for the particular interest which I take in you, I am not aware that it is greater than I would feel in any worthy young man who desires to do something for himself; in short, to be something in the world. I missed a liberal education myself for want of means, and for that reason I can sympathize fully with young men who have the same ambition and are in the same circumstances in which I was then placed. Do you see?"

"I see," I replied, "and your kindness should be appreciated; but besides the question of honesty, there is the risk of misfortune—sickness, death or something else might prevent the payment of such a debt according to the intention of the debtor."

"True," he replied, "we all have risks to run, but in this case, if you live and prosper you will pay the debt. If anything should prevent it, you will have the greater misfortune to bear. The loss of a few hundred dollars in my circumstances will not affect me seriously; but I think it almost useless to speak of such a contingency. You have comparatively good health and constitution, and with your ability, the payment of two, three, four or five hundred dollars will be an easy matter for you when you have completed your studies."

"Well, Mr. Niel," I replied, "I cannot accept your

generous offer before I have taken a little time for deliberation; but whether I accept it or not, I trust you will always
find that I cherish becoming gratitude to you for your
kindness."

"Do not mention it **as an act** of kindness on my part,
Mr. Styles, **it is only an act of** business. I have $200 now
on hand, which I wish **to** place at interest. **If I** loan it to
some man who has real **estate, or** a large amount of personal
property, you certainly would not say **that I** did it from
kindness, **but from** prudence. It would be but a careful
business transaction to make **my** money contribute something to my income, and just for this reason, I propose to
loan it to you, and as **I** regard the security which you can
give me amply sufficient, you should consider that you are
doing me a favor to accept it."

"You certainly argue with the ability of a financier, **Mr.
Niel,**" I replied, laughing; "but **I** doubt whether your
judgment on securities would be deemed good by business
men; but **I** will think of the matter, and let you **know my**
decision to-morrow."

The subject was **then, for the evening, dismissed,** and my
host entertained me **until** a late hour **with** accounts of his
experience **in** business, relating many fortunate strokes by
which he **had** finally placed himself in his present comfortable position.

I did not have to deliberate long to decide to accept what
seemed to me his most generous offer. In reflecting upon
it, I thought his reasoning good, and I saw no cause why I
could not pay the debt, unless I should meet with **some**
dire misfortune. Accordingly the day before **I left his**
house I gave him my note for $200, payable in three years

with interest.   It was stipulated, however, that if I required
a longer time for payment, I should have it, and that I
should also have other sums as I needed them, until I had
received all that I required; the term of payment always
being three years from the time each successive sum was
received.

I believe that my heart never swelled with stronger
feelings of gratitude towards an earthly friend, than it did
toward Mr. Niel, the day that I left his house.   I had
observed him closely, that I might discover, if possible, any
feeling of regret that he had reposed so much confidence in
me. I had even hinted that I was quite willing to release him
from his agreement with me, but so far from displaying any
wish of that kind, he begged me never to mention such a thing
again on pain of incurring his displeasure.   When I bade
him adieu he pressed me to correspond with him, and again
urged me to ask him, without the slightest reluctance, whenever I felt that I required pecuniary assistance.

As I had to pass the residence of Ruth on my return
home, I managed to spend an afternoon with her, and, of
course, gave her a history of my adventures during my
absence, and laid before her the new project of once more
devoting myself to my studies.

She only laughed at the result of my visit to Baxter,
and said:

"I trust that you were not at all disappointed; I
certainly am not; for although I never saw him, the
impression that I had received of him from yourself and
others led me to anticipate precisely such a close of your
intimacy with him, and I am only glad that he has done
you no greater injury."

In speaking of Mr. Niel, I did not tell her how much obligation **I was** under to him for pecuniary aid, but **was** profuse in my encomiums of him, declaring him a generous, intelligent and kind-hearted **man.**

She smiled, mechanically, at my protestations of friendship for him, **and as if** she could not **at** all appreciate my enthusiasm, merely **said :**

"I am glad that you like Mr. **Niel.**"

"But do you not like him ?" I asked in surprise.

"I **have** no particular reason for disliking him," she replied; " he **has** been very kind **to me.**"

"Yes," I answered, almost impatiently, " but you speak with an air which leads me to suspect that you have no very high esteem for him."

"You are, doubtless, too suspicious," she said ; " you know that I can **never display** the **enthusiasm** respecting anything that you **can.**"

I was puzzled. I knew **well that she was** quite as apt as myself **to** express her admiration for one that she really esteemed in glowing **terms;** and **her** apparent caution **on** this occasion led me to believe that, for **some reason,** she did not entertain **a high** opinion **of** Niel. Having, **as the** reader knows, **the** utmost confidence **in her** judgment, he will not wonder that her manner awakened some misgivings within me **as to the real worth of my newly** formed friend, and suggested the thought that, possibly, I might again find myself the victim **of a** selfish **man.** But, then, a second thought assured me that he had not the slightest chance **for** false dealing with me even were he so disposed, and so my suspicions were lulled.

The announcement that I was going away, not to return,

probably, for a year, and then only for a visit, was anything but pleasant to Ruth. She made no effort, however, to dissuade me from this step. Knowing my ambition, she said she was only glad that I could gratify it, and expressed the opinion that I would always be dissatisfied unless I did so. After thus speaking, she raised her eyes in sadness to mine and said:

"But how do you think I will spend all these months of your absence?"

"In thinking of me, I hope, and in writing to me," I answered, smiling.

"I trust that you would not have that my only employment," she replied; and then added, "I shall teach. I never can endure the monotony of remaining at home without something more than I now have to engross my time and attention."

"It would be well, perhaps," I said, "since you do not regard teaching as monotonous or irksome. But how would you like teaching with me when I return."

"O, I would like that immensely," she replied, animated by the thought. "Do you know I have been thinking of that? You will be Professor then. Now won't you promise me that when you have completed your studies, you will take charge of some Academy and allow me to be your assistant."

"You tempt me to consider the proposition," I said, "but what is to become of my profession?"

"Make teaching your profession," she answered. "What more noble profession do you ask? And in what profession have you greater opportunities for doing good?"

"You forget my dislike for teaching," I answered.

" But you would find that quite different from teaching a district school."

" I hope so," I said, " but we shall have quite time enough to consider this matter."

The subject was now changed. Before leaving her, I had promised to visit her more than once previous to my final departure, and the promise was faithfully **kept.**

CHAPTER XII.

I had decided to connect myself with an educational institution in Corvette, in the southern part of Vermont.

It was not a college, but a seminary liberally endowed, and the curriculum was little below that of the colleges and universities of New England. I selected this for two reasons; first, because I could attend it at a very reasonable sum per annum; second, because, being located in a quiet country village, in which I was a perfect stranger, it presented to me the opportunity of pursuing my studies with little or no distractions.

Owing to delays and labors of manifold nature it was June before I was fully prepared to depart.

According to my custom whenever visiting any place where I could conveniently perform the journey by a trip through the Lake, I left the cars at Burlington, and embarked on a steamer. Although by thus doing I increased the distance, the comfort and pleasure were greatly enhanced. I had passed through the Lake three or four times previous to this, so that all points of note were quite familiar to me, yet I never tired of looking at them, or of dwelling with deep interest on their historic associations.

It was a matter of real disappointment to me, recently, when visiting New York, that I learned that steamers no longer run as they formerly did between the northern and southern limits of this body of water—railroads having effectually supplanted them.

It is not an easy thing for one who has long associated with men, who has been in business usually performed by those of mature years, to exchange all for the labors and experience again of his boyhood. Such was the obstacle that I had to surmount in surrendering my commission as Preventive Officer. Though but twenty years of age, my business and associations had made me feel much older, and however unwise it may have been, I could but regard it as slightly humiliating to throw up my claims to experience and maturity and become once more a schoolboy.

I shall never forget how I sat nearly all day on the deck, as we sailed up the lake, thinking of my situation, and almost regretting that I had not sought some employment, however humble, that would have secured me a livelihood, instead of taking the step I had.

It seemed incurring a great risk. I had contracted a debt, and put off the day of engaging in business to an uncertain period, and many times during the day I wished I had not done it; but, then, the adage " Nothing ventured, nothing gained," coming to mind, served to dispel my despondent feelings.

The boat having reached her destination, I engaged a private conveyance to Corvette—twelve miles distant.   It was just sunset when we arrived at the summit of a hill overlooking a large valley in which was located the village of Corvette.   It lay in quiet beauty nearly two miles distant, embowered in shade trees, the land receding from it on all hands in gently rising slopes to hills whose summits were crowned with forests. A small river ran through the valley, bordered by broad, rich intervales, and its banks likewise being lined with willows and other trees, all served to make up, at this season, when nature is clad in her richest garb, a beautiful picture—the most beautiful, I believe, that I have ever beheld.

The Seminary—a four story brick building, eighty feet in length, adorned with bell tower and clock—fronted the main street; its grounds, consisting of several acres, being covered, with the exception of the flower garden, with gigantic maples.   Though simple in its style of architecture, the neatness and symmetry of this building and the beauty of its surroundings at once struck me ; and during my long stay here, my admiration for it constantly increased.   Years have elapsed, but the impression made upon me by the scene on that memorable June evening is as vivid as if made but yesterday.

I found myself, as I had anticipated, a perfect stranger here to all--students as well teachers.   The former numbered about one hundred and twenty, all of whom, with the exception of those living in the village, boarded in the Seminary, and, as I, in consequence of being from a distance, must board in the Institution, I was allotted room 57 in the third hall.

Being fatigued with my day's journey, I retired as soon as I had enrolled myself, and made all the necessary arrangements with the financial manager, and was awakened by the gong only in time to dress hurriedly, and reach the dining hall after all the other students were seated for breakfast. Visions of the scanty fare and tyrannical government described by Dickens and Charlotte Brontë, as sometimes found in English Boarding Schools, rose before me when I received nothing but corn cake that morning for breakfast; but the recollection that I was in free and democratic New England, where boys, as well as men, assert their rights, dispelled my fears, and confirmed me in the belief that the quality and quantity of our board must be all that I could desire. The bountiful supply of vegetable and animal food provided for dinner assured me that I was right in this belief, and I learned that we were confined to corn cake, solely, but once a week, for the morning meal.

The number of young ladies attending the Seminary was about equal to that of the young men, and though they occupied different parts of the same building, and were supposed to have no communication with each other except in the reception rooms, and there only by permission of the principal or preceptress, numbers found means of evading these regulations, and thus necessitated " eternal vigilance " on the part of the Faculty. The severe public reproofs and punishment, however, which usually followed the discovery of any such offences, rendered love making here an extremely hazardous business, so that none but the most incautious ever ventured upon the experiment of writing *billet doux.*

My business here being study, and my interest in the fair

sex being confined chiefly to "the girl I left behind me," I never sought the acquaintance of any of the young lady students during my stay in the seminary; and besides the simple recognition, in the halls, of those who belonged to the same classes as myself, or a little chat at the table with the lady opposite, I believe I scarcely spoke to a lady during the space of two years. I was regarded as an anomaly by the students in this particular, and while many found facilities for getting acquainted with their lady classmates, I met several in the recitation rooms week after week without ever speaking with them, or knowing aught of them save their names and places of residence. I have now in memory one of these, Miss Burdell, whom for three months I met daily in the rhetoric class, which, being quite small, consisting of not more than a dozen members, recited to the Principal in his office. She sat directly opposite me on a sofa. She was modest and diffident but strikingly intelligent, always displaying a clear and correct understanding of her lesson, and replying to questions addressed her, or expressing her opinion on subjects under discussion in a dignified manner, with voice and articulation which never failed to command the attention of the whole class. Her essays too were always an embodiment of grace and good sense, quite unlike many others to which we listened, and which were characterized by both pedantry and silliness. All that I ever knew respecting Miss Burdell was that she lived in one of the large villages of Vermont, on Lake Champlain; that she graduated from the Seminary at the close of the term when I met her, and that she intended to engage in teaching for a livelihood.

The term closed, and Miss Burdell left us. Standing a

little away, I saw her step on the train, and a moment afterwards she was fast receding from the friends and acquaintances she had formed in her *Alma Mater*. Her seat in class was vacant, and I wondered at the loneliness which I, a stranger to her, experienced at the absence of her familiar face. But it was only **the first** of similar sad experiences for me while I was in Corvette. There were young men there from nearly every State in the Union. We met daily for three, six or nine months, perhaps a year or more; and occasionally an attachment would spring up between one and myself. We walked and chatted together, told each other our former experiences and many of our future plans, and lived as if we were to know each other and meet often through all our future years. It is wonderful **to** contemplate the amount of hope that the young possess. I believe that I had not then a doubt that I should realize the fruition of all my plans, and spend many happy days in coming time in the society of those whom I regarded as friends; friends whose homes were far off in the sunny south, away in the cities of the west, and on the Atlantic coast; but school terms expire, and so did those of which I write. Often I accompanied schoolmates to the depot, the bell rung, we grasped hands, and a wave of a handkerchief from the window, or the lifting of a hat on the platform, was the last token of regard, save, perhaps, a letter or two, that I ever received from those who had been the partners of my labors, disappointments and joys in student life. Many of these have since taken passage **on a** swifter train to another world—some on the battle field, others in the presence of friends and in the seclusion of home; but of all those that I then knew, I have since met but few.

Sad memories cluster around those partings, but the lesson which they teach is replete with admonitions more solemn and enduring than those that come from the human tongue.

I was glad to find that I was not the oldest of the male students. There were several there about my age, and a half dozen or more who were my seniors by three, four, and even six years. I have intimated that friendship existed between many of them and myself, but while this is true, I was on terms of familiar intimacy with but one— Gordon McKenzie, a young Scotchman who had been there a year previous to my arrival, and who remained a year after my departure, or until he received such a degree as was conferred by the Institution.

I was first attracted to him by his politeness and engaging manners, and as my acquaintance with him further increased, a certain congeniality of taste, and plans nearly similar with regard to the future, cemented a bond of friendship between us that has never been sundered. An adventure or two in which we were participants no doubt served to make this bond stronger, and they are still subjects to which we are pleased often to revert. He was poor but still popular with the students notwithstanding an impetuosity of temper which led him to act hastily, and which even made most of them fear to offend him ; but as he was very conscientious and frank, and reasonable withal, his indignation was seldom displayed unless his cause was one of justice. In stature he was almost Liliputian, weighing at the age of twenty-one less than a hundred pounds, but his activity, combined with his strength, developed by early exercise and by continual practice in the gymnasium, rendered him the most formidable wrestler among the students. If not the greatest in intellect, he certainly had the most talent in some directions, and while his prose essays generally commanded a tribute of praise from the professors, his poems, when recited in public with his usual grace and dignity, never failed to call forth rapturous applause. Naturally satirical, he, sometimes, gratified his personal piques in poetic satire, and no one who had **ever** witnessed this exhibition of **his** powers cared to incur his displeasure. This propensity, on one occasion, nearly cost him his place in the Seminary. **A** teacher of the classics who was **for a** time connected with the school having rendered himself odious to McKenzie, or Mack, as he was always called, delivered a lecture before the students on the classics.

The opportunity for showing his dislike of the Professor seemed to Mack too good to be lost, and the following week, at the time of the usual Rhetorical Exercises, by managing to deceive the Principal with regard to the character of his declamation, he delivered a poem on the classics—a most laughable and cutting satire on the lecture. **It was** an act of imprudence, however, on Mack's part that could be settled only by an humble apology, but this he **could** afford in view of the *éclat* his poem **had** won him with **the** students.

My friend's history was romantic. He was the son of a physician, and was born in Ayrshire, Scotland. He had a sister younger than himself, who died when he was eleven years of age, and the year following his father died. Contrary to his wishes, and in the face of his earnest entreaties and expostulations, his mother some months subsequently married a man whom he heartily disliked, and thinking that **he had** no longer any home in which he could hope for

enjoyment, he ran away, like many other boys, went on
board a merchantman, and for four years sailed on the broad
highway of nations, visiting renowned cities and countries
of almost every clime. The vessel to which he belonged
was finally wrecked off the coast of Chili, and he was taken
from the wreck with a few others by a Spanish merchantman, and conveyed to Santiago. Here he fell in with an
American sea captain, who kindly brought him to New
York, and having become tired of the sea, and being anxious
to live in the United States, of which he had heard and read
much, he determined to seek his fortune in this western
world.

The realities, however, were a sad contrast to the anticipations indulged by a boy of his romantic fancy. After
knocking about the city for a week he chanced to meet with
a wealthy farmer, living in Rensselaer Co., in New York,
to whom he engaged to take care of horses and do general
farm work. He found the position a trying one, both from
the tyrannical nature of his employer and the arbitrary
insolence of his son, a youth about his own age; yet he
remained here two years, when in a passion one day, to
which he was wantonly provoked, he severely beat the son,
in consequence of which he once more ran away. Respectable apparel and a hundred dollars in money, which he had
saved by his prudence, constituted his entire worldly possessions, and with this outfit he decided to attend school, and
for this purpose had sought Corvette. He was a good
scholar for his years when he left Scotland, and he had
improved every leisure moment, while on the farm, in reading and study. Possessed of a retentive memory, and a
careful habit of observing, his mind was stored with inter-

esting knowledge of the many places he had visited, and I
often felt a keen sense of my own ignorance when listening
to his accounts of the things he had seen in his extensive
travels. Reared in the birth-place of Burns, and familiar
from earliest childhood with his haunts and home, it was
natural that he should be his favorite poet, nor was I surprised to find that he could repeat, verbatim, many of the
poems written by that ill-starred genius.

At the time I first formed his acquaintance, the stock of
money which he had earned was exhausted, but having won
the favor of the **Rev. Mr.** Halleck, who taught painting in
the Seminary, that gentleman had kindly offered to defray
his expenses there until he graduated, and give him ample
time for the payment of the debt. It will be seen that he
thus held the same position, with respect to the reverend
gentleman, that I held towards Mr. Niel; but whatever had
been the motive that induced the latter to assist me, it is
certain that the former had acted from the purest benevo-
lence, and a feeling that the noble principles and genius of
the young Scotchman should be encouraged. **Mack's** gratitude to his benefactor knew no limits. No opportunity of
showing it was lost; and his only trouble seemed to be that
untoward fortune might prevent him from canceling the
debt he had thus incurred.

Mack and I had become well acquainted, and were frequently together previous to our fall vacation, but at that
time an incident occurred which made us warm friends.
Among the students were several from the Southern States,
sons of wealthy planters and merchants. Sixby, from
Raleigh, North Carolina, was one of these, but, unlike the
others, he had little of the proverbial civility and courtesy

of Southern gentlemen. He was my *bête noir.* Disliking his conceited and foppish air from the first, I had tried to avoid him, but, as we were in the same class in Latin, I sometimes found it necessary to speak to him. He seemed to have conceived the same antipathy towards me, and though, whenever we came in contact, I observed the same politeness that I did to others, he seldom failed to provoke me by his rudeness.

In less than a week from the time that I entered the Seminary, having learned that I was from Canada, he took occasion, in my hearing, to allude to the country as a land of barbarians; and at another time he astonished the company at table by requesting his neighbor to pass the butter to "that Canuck."

I tried to treat his insults with dignified contempt, yet resolved, if he persisted in this course, to call him some day to an account. I might have been more ready to do this had I not observed that he was generally rude to others, and that he was in favor with only a few who danced attendance on him, chiefly because he was extravagant in the use of his money, and rewarded their servility with private dinners, rides and frequent presents. A fellow named Hardwick, the son of a Boston lawyer, was the most faithful of his satellites, and, though not rich, he vied with him in the richness of his dress, and in the size and beauty of his gold-headed cane. It must be confessed that they made a fine appearance as they walked into church in their Sunday toggery, or patroled the streets together, but to those knowing them they were merely snobs, as rude and boisterous in speech as they were boorish in manner.

Sixby possessed a fine library, but its contents had effected little towards the cultivation of his mind. He was twenty-one, and had for a long time been preparing for college, in fact had presented himself the year previous for admission, but, in consequence of getting "plucked," had returned with the intention, if possible, of taking a degree from the Seminary.

Soon after the affront he had given me at the table, we were in class translating one of Cicero's orations against Catiline. I had just translated several lines, when Sixby, who had been inattentive, whispering nearly all the time to a classmate, exclaimed:

"Hold on! read that again! I didn't understand how you translated it."

"Which sentence?" I asked.

"All that you read," he answered in an imperative tone.

Having translated nearly thirty lines, which he might have heard had he given attention, I replied:

"I will read it if the professor wishes to hear it again."

He was the same professor that Mack had offended by his poem, and I knew that he was favorably disposed towards Sixby on account of many rides and presents that he had accepted from him; but he had not the assurance under the circumstances to ask me to translate it a second time, and so smiling, and suggesting to Sixby that he had better attend to his business, he requested me to finish reading my paragraph. Sixby, unused to having his authoritative requests refused by the students, was in a rage. His small black eyes flashed; his face glowed with anger, and there was in it an expression which said:

"I'll have revenge."

I met his gaze for a moment with an expression as deter-

M

mined as his own.   He lingered outside the door, in the hall, when the class was excused, and the moment I came out he said,

"You are accommodating, Styles.   Are the Canucks in Canada all so accommodating?"

"When they deal with nigger drivers," I answered.

I was prompted to this reply from the fact that I knew his father was a slave owner, and with a maliciousness akin to his own, I meant that the answer should be the most cutting I could give; though I was soon sorry for it, and wished that I had treated him in a more dignified and Christian-like manner.   He turned pale through anger, and I think he would have struck me, but just then the Principal came along and we all dispersed.

As I passed on, followed by two of the class who had witnessed the scene, I heard one remark to the other in an undertone,

"I guess Sixby has found somebody at last that he can't bully."

"It looks so," replied the other.

Sixby did not speak to me for several weeks after this, and I believed that he had concluded to treat me with more courtesy, until the occurrence of the incident to which I have already alluded.

During the fall vacation, which lasted a month, the teachers and professors, and many of the students, who lived at a distance, remained at the Seminary.   It was our custom to go out daily, during the bright days of October, and play ball for exercise.   It was while thus at play that I chanced to hold the bat, while Sixby was one of the parties catching. The ball had been knocked some distance away, and while he ran for it I turned to speak to Mack, who was not in the game, and had just come out. Sixby in returning happening to **spy a very** large potato, half decayed, which had been thrown from the garden **on** the playground, picked it **up**, and, when a few yards distant, threw it swiftly at me. **My** face being averted **I** did **not** observe him, and the potato struck me with full force on the cheek, nearly knocking me down, the decayed portion spattering **over** my face **and** bedaubing my clothes.

It would **be** difficult **to portray the intensity** of my anger when I realized the situation. **I had** only a glimpse of the diabolical grin on Sixby's face ere I had reached him and dashed him to the ground with a savage blow in the face. Two kicks, as savagely administered, followed quicker than thought, which made **him set** up a howl that might have **been** mistaken for the dirge of a red man. I never felt such rage, such strength before, nor have I since. I believe I could have thrashed Hercules, himself, **on the** spot. I was checked **in my work** of destruction just **at** that moment by **the sight of** Hardwick, sprawling **on the** ground behind me, and **a voice saying**:

"Mr. Styles! Mr. Styles! **this will never do!**" It was **Mr.** Hanson, the Principal, for whom I had profound respect. I was rational instantly.

"**I** beg your pardon, Mr. **Hanson,**" **I said,** "but you saw the provocation."

"I saw," he said, "but you did wrong, all of you. Fighting!" he exclaimed, in astonishment. "Gentlemen like you and Mr. McKenzie, Mr. Sixby, too, the son **of a** planter!"

Mack's blood was up.

"If he's got any more sons like him," he exclaimed "he'd better send them up here ; *we'll plant 'em ;* " and his eyes glared fiercely at poor Sixby, who had got up and was now limping off, his hand being pressed against his side. Notwithstanding my smarting and swollen cheek, and the presence of the Principal and two other professors, I could not forego a laugh at Mack's speech, and knowing Mr. Hanson's appreciation of the ludicrous, I glanced up at his face, and was sure I saw his lip quivering in ·his efforts to repress a smile.

Mack's part in the affray may be thus explained.

The moment I started for Sixby, Hardwick, with a heavy bat, rushed forward to defend him, and was about to strike me on the head with it from behind, when he was leveled by a blow from Mack, who had divined his purpose and hastened to my defence in the nick of time.

"You may go to your rooms now, young men," said the Principal sternly. I will attend to this affair this afternoon."

I instantly obeyed him, and so did Mack and Hardwick —Sixby having already gone. I was not at all alarmed about discipline, remembering that it was vacation, and the Principal in consequence having no control over us. And even in case he had, I was quite sure that he would do nothing, having seen the provocation on which Sixby and Hardwick had been struck, and disliking them as I knew he did.

My ill-feeling had so far subsided that as soon as I had reached my room I burst into a hearty fit of laughter, in which I was joined by Mack who had accompanied me ; still, he was too angry to enjoy it fully.

"You can better afford to laugh than I can," said he,

"for you had two kicks at that puppy Sixby, while I only had one blow at Hardwick. Why, confound it, man, he would have broken your head with that bat if I had not been there. I've a mind to go to his room and thrash him now," and he moved towards the door as if really determined on performing the act.

"Stop, Mack," I said. "You would only disgrace yourself, and get into trouble, besides we have done enough."

Lingering a moment as if meditating, he finally replied:

"You're right, no doubt, but I won't admit that they've had enough; they'll try the thing again with you, as soon as they have an opportunity."

"No, never," I said. "That fellow, Sixby, is satisfied now. He has learned that I am not to be insulted with impunity."

I was right. Ever after he treated me with respect; indeed, his shyness of me reminded me of the dog "Trip" that I knocked on the head the day that I commenced teaching in Meadville. Hardwick was likewise similarly respectful. Nearly every student remaining at the Seminary came into my room in the course of the day to congratulate me, and condemn the insulting act of Sixby and the cowardly one of his colleague. Numbers who came back at the beginning of the next term also thanked me for the deed, thus showing the estimation in which Sixby was held.

The rumor was first afloat that I had broken two or three of his ribs, and I was on the point of going to his room to express sorrow for my violence, when I learned that, beyond a very black eye, he was not seriously injured.

CHAPTER XIII.

An account of my work in the Seminary—My friend goes to engage a
school and takes me with him—A school manager—A bargain—
My friend hires out.

Up to this time I had twice written to Niel, and he
promptly answered, asking me in his last letter if I was
not getting "short," and urging me to "draw" on him if
such was the case.

But, from my economy, I had still more than half the
sum he loaned me on deposit, and I was not obliged to ask
for more until the following April, when I obtained another
sum of two hundred dollars.

Unlike many of the students, I seldom indulged in the
luxury of a drive, consequently, my livery bill was small.
During my first vacation I made a trip to Albany, where I
remained a couple of days, but this was by far the longest
and most expensive journey that I made in the course of
two years. My time was wholly devoted to study; indeed,
I gave so little time to recreation that, at the end of six
months, I discovered, from the state of my health, that I
was studying far too much and exercising too little, and so

I shortened the time that I gave to the former to nine hours per diem and increased the time devoted to the latter by an hour.

The remaining two hours I spent either in reading, chatting or in experimenting in the laboratory. I had obtained the privilege of prosecuting these experiments from the Principal, whose good favor I was fortunate enough to enjoy. Perceiving my fondness for study, he strove in every way to aid and encourage me, giving me free access to his own private library, often assisting me in my experiments, that I might not fall a martyr to science, as he jocosely remarked, and giving me advice which has saved me from many errors of action in the years that have intervened.

From Ruth I received a letter every two weeks, and during all the time that I was absent from her I made it a rule to write her as often, always devoting a portion of a Saturday holiday to this purpose ; and each letter contained a careful account of every incident of interest to me which had occurred, and of every new aspiration that had seized me during the preceding half month. She had engaged in teaching soon after my departure, and was still thus employed.

It was during the vacation of which I have spoken, near its close, that Mack one day entered my room, quite animated with a new idea that had possessed him.

"Styles," said he, "do you think I could manage a district school?"

"I do not know why you could not," I replied; "you certainly have the requisite that is regarded the most important in a teacher in many communities."

" What is that ? " he asked.

" Ability to thrash the big boys."

" Yes," he said, with a laugh, " but do you really think I could succeed as a teacher ? "

" That depends very much on the community in which you teach, and the class of pupils that you have. Amongst intelligent people, and with obedient pupils, I have no doubt you would succeed admirably ; but, in other circumstances, I fear that your stock of patience would not suffice. Would you expect to board around ? "

He had often laughed at the account of my own experience in teaching, and my question at once amused him.

" I don't know the custom in this section," he said, " but I have no fears about the board. A sailor is not particular in regard to his diet, and as to patience, I believe I have as much of that as you have. It is something I must learn to cultivate, and perhaps teaching will afford me the best opportunity for doing it. At all events I don't think I shall kill a dog the first day. But do you think my education is sufficient ? "

" Nonsense, man ! " I said, " why you were fitted for college long ago, and with the ability to write such poetry as you do, to ask me if your education is sufficient to teach a district school is most absurd."

" Well, if you deem me competent, I think I shall try it. I do not like to be so entirely dependent on Mr. Halleck for my support. It must be inconvenient for him in his circumstances to advance me so much money, and I wish to show him that I am quite ready to help myself when I have an opportunity, I have heard to-day of a place about fifteen miles from here, where they wish to get a teacher for the winter, and I have decided to drive over there to-morrow, and would like to have you go with me."

"With the greatest pleasure," I answered. "I shall enjoy the ride, and besides I shall **be glad** to see the place **where** you are to teach; perhaps, too, **as I am** quite a Yankee, **I** may assist you in making a good bargain."

The next morning we drove away **with the** enjoyment of a cloudless sky, and cool, rich autumnal air. Our road lay for some distance through a fine farming section of country, where farmers were busy securing their late crops; and the subject of agriculture being thus suggested **to** our minds, we discussed **it** with the thoroughness and zeal of experienced plowmen. The beautiful scenery often called forth our admiration, and school-teaching also claiming no inconsiderable portion of our thoughts, we talked so incessantly **that** we were at our journey's end before aware of it.

The school-house **was** located in a rough, woody **and** thinly settled part, with a mountain at no great distance from it. Unlike the structure where I taught at Meadville, **it** wore a faded coat **of** red paint, and had an apology for a wood-shed near, but in other **respects it bore the** same untidy **and** uncared-for appearance.

Having learned **by** inquiry that the school manager lived in a house about **sixty** rods distant, back from the road, we repaired thither, **and** found him near **his** dwelling with a couple **of** large boys digging potatoes. All stopped work and stared as we approached.

"Good morning, sir," said Mack, to the father.

"Good mornin'; we're gettin' some fine weather fur pertater diggin', jest now," **he** said.

"Yes, **fine; do** your potatoes turn out well?"

"Wall, no they don't," he replied, leaning on his hoe, his countenance assuming an expression of disappointment and disgust. "No, they're little *nasty* things, and half rotten at that."

"That's too bad," said Mack, sympathetically.

"And especially since they are one of the chief dependencies of the farmer in this country," I said.

"Yes," replied the farmer, and he scowled with inexpressible disgust; "we're pretty darned hard up fur everything ter eat when we haint got plenty of pertaters. I jinerly lay in fur a good stock of 'em, for it's so fur ter the boardin' places in this deestrict, we calkerlate we have ter board the teachers more nor half the time; 'specially in the winter, if we happen ter hav a woman teacher; but I'm gwine ter try and git a man this winter, if I can, one that's able ter travel. I've got a pretty good crop of corn though, so I guess I can keep him, if necessary."

"If he's as mean as the schoolmaster we had last winter here," said one of the boys, in a husky voice, "pertaters 'll be too good for him."

"Was he rather mean?" asked Mack.

"Mean! I guess he was," replied the boy, "he used ter knock the scholars round jest as he was a mind tew; they all hated him worse 'n they would pizen."

"Darn his picter, he never laid his hands on me," said the other boy, who was older and larger than the first speaker; "ef he had, I'd showed him a thing or tew. Tom Gibson and I made up our minds ter put him out of the schoolhouse ef we see much more of his pufformances, but I guess he begun ter smell the rat, fur he carried himself pretty straight after that."

" Wall, wall," said the old man, " I guess he want a bad feller if the young ones had behaved themselves, but somehow he didn't **seem** ter have a nack of gettin their goodwill, and I s'pose they used ter make him mad."

" I presume you have teachers here, sometimes," I **said,** " that are well liked."

" O, yes," replied the man, " they're allers liked well 'nuff ef they only git the hang of the scholars, and play and 'sociate with 'em as if they didn't feel 'bove 'em.

" **It don't dew fer** a schoolmaster ter go ter puttin' on style here," said the larger boy, " ef he does we take the starch out on him pretty quick."

" Well," said Mack, " you rather frighten me from the idea of teaching in this place. My business here to-day is to see whether I can engage the school for the winter. I hear that you are in want of a teacher."

" **Gosh,**" exclaimed the farmer, " be you a school-teacher ? why I thought you chaps **was** butter-buyers. **I'm** sorry yer aint, fur I've got three tubs of as nice butter ter sell **as you can** find in this **county.** The neighbors all say that my old woman can't be beat fur butter makin'."

The boys had regarded **Mack with the greatest** curiosity since they had learned the object of his visit, and as soon as the father had concluded his remark, the younger said,

" Why, you don't look big enough to keep school."

The elder boy seeming desirous of apologizing for his former remarks, and at **the** same time to put Mack at his ease, immediately exclaimed,

" O, you needn't be scart ; the boys aint bad chaps here, and ef you git on the right side on 'em you'll git along. Ennyway I shant touch yer."

It will be lucky for you, young man, if you don't, I thought, but whatever Mack's thoughts were, he discreetly replied,

" I have no fear, sir, that you and I will have any trouble. I think I can get along with any well disposed person who will treat me with the politeness I show to him.".

" I guess you wouldn't have any trouble if you used the scholars well," said the father, "but, I swow, I'm afraid you're pretty small; the boys might think they'd dew as they're mind tew on 'count yer size."

" You cannot always judge of a man's strength and activity from his size," I said. " I happen to know that there are few men of Mr. Mackenzie's strength. At all events, there is no one in the Seminary at Corvette who will venture to wrestle with him."

" You don't say ? " exclaimed the man; " well, 'tis an old sayin' that you never kin tell how fur a toad 'll hop by his looks."

" By gosh ! I don't believe he could throw Tom Gibson," said the larger boy, " he's great on square holt."

" How much be you gwine ter ax a month ? " inquired the man.

" All that you will pay," replied Mack. " How much have you usually paid ? "

" Fifteen dollars is the most," was the answer. " Last winter we paid thirteen and a half."

"'That is too low," said Mack. " I expect eighteen, and I prefer boarding at one place."

" Wall, you couldn't dew that here. The folks wouldn't give yer five ef they thought you felt tew big ter board with 'em; and, 'sides, we allers think a teacher orter go 'round and git 'quainted with his scholars in order ter keep on the right side on 'em."

"It is not that I feel too big to board around," replied Mack, "but I wish to study, and for that reason I think it would be more pleasant to board in one place."

"P'raps 'twould," was the answer; "but 'taint no use speakin' on it here; the deestrict wouldn't stand it; and we never could pay eighteen dollars. Hev you got a certifikit?"

"No, but I will get one if I engage to teach."

"Mr. Mackenzie," I said, "is an advanced and thorough scholar. He has spent four years on the ocean, and has visited the most important countries and renowned cities on the globe. If your boys could listen to accounts of what he has seen, the knowledge that they would thus obtain would be worth to them far more than they often receive at a winter's school. If you can get Mr. Mackenzie to teach for eighteen dollars a month, you are getting him at a very low rate."

The curiosity of the trio was thoroughly aroused. They began to look at Mack with an expression of awe and astonishment. The man, after a moment's silence, exclaimed:

"Wall, I swow, I guess he is quite a chap. So you've been ter sea, hev yer?" he asked.

"Yes, sir," replied Mack. "I have been on many seas— the Mediterranean, Caribbean, Caspian, Adriatic and others."

"Did you ever see a whale?" he asked with the utmost seriousness.

"O, yes, a great many of them," was the answer.

"Wall, I spose that's quite a sight. I never see one, but I'd like tew fust rate. But say, don't you think you could keep our school for less'n eighteen dollars? that's a thun-

derin' price. I'd like ter hire yer though, fur I'd be glad myself ter hear yer tell 'bout some o' them big fish you've
seen."

" Eighteen dollars is as low as I can teach," said Mack.

The school manager meditated a moment, and then turning to his sons said,

" Wall, what d'ye say, boys, shall I hire him ? "

" Dew just as you're a mind tew," replied the elder , " I'd
kinder like ter him tell some o' them stories. "

" What dew you say, Tim ? " asked the father of the
younger boy.

" Why, I say jest as Jack says," he replied, "dew as
you're a mind tew, but I'd like darn'd well to hear 'bout
them whales."

The man hesitated, thought for a moment with downcast
eyes, then dropping his hoe, and exclaiming,

" Hold on a minute, I'll see the old woman," started on a
dog trot for the house.

Five minutes afterwards the woman, in a striped woolen
gown, with sleeves rolled up, appeared in the door, her husband standing just behind looking over her shoulder.   After
carefully adjusting her spectacles and taking a good look
towards us, she exclaimed in a tone of partial contempt.

" Pshaw, he aint bigger'n a midgit."

" Yes," replied her spouse, " but that other feller says
he's *alfired* smart."

" Wall," she answered, " I don't believe it.   Law, I could
handle him myself."

" You'd better not talk quite so loud thar," yelled the
elder boy with some show of mortified feelings.

The door now closed, and the consultation was continued

inside. We amused ourselves by talking to the boys for another ten minutes, when the man walked out, and with an air which seemed to show that he was determind to follow the latest advice, said,

"**Wall,** boys, yer marm thinks we'd better hev a school meetin' 'fore I hire, and **then thar want** be any chance fur grumblin'."

"That's **jest** what **I've been thinkin,"** said his eldest. "If yer should hire, and give such a tarnal **price,** like enuff some ov em in the deestrict would be so mad they wouldn't speak tew yer. **If yer call** a school meetin', and talk it over, why, then, **they** kin dew as they're **mind** tew 'bout payin' sich wages, and they can't blame you any way."

I here thought that I might again interpose with profit to Mack.

"You have been appointed as one of the committee with power to **engage a** teacher, have you not?" I asked.

"**Yas**; but hang it all, I don't like to go so much above our usual figger."

"I suppose if the school should prove to be a good one, the inhabitants of the district would find **no fault with the** price," I continued.

"**Wall, I** 'd'no; mebbe **they would and** mebbe they wouldn't," he answered; "but the thing ont **is, we** can't tell what the school will **be now.**"

I could but admit **that his reasoning** was good, but believing that I could persuade him to give the price demanded, I was not at all inclined to yield.

"For myself, I have no doubt," I said, "that your school will be **all** that you **could** wish. Mr. Mackenzie is not only **a** thorough scholar, but he is energetic, and has the faculty, beyond most men, of imparting the knowledge that he possesses. He can furnish you the very best of recommendations from the professors at Corvette, and it is my opinion that if you hire another only half as well qualified because you can get him two or three dollars a month less, the people of the district will feel that they have more cause for complaint than they will if you pay the price he asks."

He seemed to be undecided, but soon said,

" I don't see why it aint jest as well ter hev a school-meetin'. I kin tell em all about him, and then they kin dew as they're a mind tew 'bout hirin' him."

"That would be well enough," I replied, "if it were not for the delay. It will require two or three days to do what you propose, and then a day or two more to let Mr. Mackenzie know the result of the school meeting, and, in the meantime, he may loose the chance of getting a situation as there are but few schools remaining that are not engaged for the winter."

The man hung his head again and deliberated. He evidently felt that he was in a trying position.

At length, turning again to the elder boy, he said, in a nervous tone,

" Wall, what d'ye say, Jack ; if he'll take seventeen would yer hire him ? "

The boy hung his head and deliberated ; and then looking up with a simple half-smiling expression, exclaimed,

" Darn it all, I don't know but yer might as well."

" Wall, will yer take it ? " the man asked with an anxious countenance, addressing Mack.

It was now the latter's turn to deliberate, but only for a moment, when he answered, " I will take it."

The man seemed frightened. He spit two or three times fiercely, bit off a huge piece of tobacco, and dug a hill of potatoes before uttering a word, and then, with a half-frenzied look, ejaculated,

"Wall, I s'pose I shall hav ter dew it, seein' as how I've said so much. I b'lieve though if I'd stuck tew yer I might have got yer for fourteen or fifteen; but darn' yer picter, I want yer ter dew yer best. Give em a good school so't they cant cuss me."

"I shall do my best, sir," replied Mack, with a serious face, half regretting that he had agreed to undertake the task.

The bargain having been made the man felt it necessary to give Mack the following instructions.

"Now, sir," said he, "I want yer ter give the scholars their orders as soon as school begins ter keep way from my well this winter. The darned critters come sloppin' round it every winter, and they git it so slippery thar cant any on us git within a rod ont to draw water without choppin' half-a-day. I had a yearlin' hog that I wouldn't took eight dollars in cash for, slip inter it last winter and drown."

"Is there no well or spring belonging to the school?" asked Mack.

"No," he answered, "but thar's a brook over 'cross the road, in the paster thar; 'taint more'n a quarter of a mile off; they kin jest as well go thar arter their water."

"I'll see to that," replied Mack with a dubious look.

"And another thing," pursued the committee, "I want yer ter keep em outer my barn. The plagy boys git in thar and jump on the hay, and they've scart my sheep so I can't git within a mile on em."

N

"Yes, sir," said Mack obsequiously, "I'll see to that, too. Anything else?" he asked.

"No, I don't thing of nothin now, but I want yer ter be on hand in the mornin', and git the fires built in season."

"Certainly, sir," was the answer in the same deferential tone.

At this juncture the kitchen door opened, and the housewife, in a sharp shrill voice, called out,

"Dinner's ready, Jim."

Being very hungry, Mack and I were not slow in accepting the farmer's invitation to dine with him, and after seeing our horse cared for, we followed him to the house.

Time will not permit me to detail to the reader the conversation that occurred between the family and ourselves; it will suffice to say that we enjoyed it as we did our coarse but bountiful dinner.

As we were again seated in the carriage, and about starting off, Jack, the elder boy, as a final address to Mack, called out,

"Yer mustn't forgit 'bout them whales 'fore yer come on ter keep school."

After assuring him that he would not, Mack touched the horse lightly with the whip, and we were off at a brisk trot. Scarcely had we entered the highway when a loud "Halloo!" caused us to halt and look back.

Our friend, the school manager, was swinging his hat energetically, and the moment he saw that we observed him, he approached us on the run. As soon as within speaking distance, hat still in hand, nearly breathless, he said,

"Thar's one thing I want ter ask 'fore yer leave; have yer got any religion?"

It was a moment before Mack could control himself enough to inform him with a grave expression of countenance that he was nominally a church member, but regretted that he was not as active in the performance of Christian duties as he should be.

"Wall," said the man, "it don't make a darn's odds with me whether you be er not. I only tho't I'd ask 'cause thar's tew or three families in the deestrict that's kinder pious, and they kinder think that a feller that keeps school orter pray a little in the mornin when he commences."

"Well, as to that," replied Mack, "you may say to them that I shall at least feel it a duty to open the school with the Lord's prayer."

"Wall, I'm glad on't," he replied, "'cause it'll suit them folks fust rate, and I'll tell 'em." His curiosity being thus gratified, he put on his hat and returned.

CHAPTER XIV.

Mack regrets his bargain, but sticks to it—A letter containing an amusing account of his experience in teaching— Copies of letters he receives from his patrons—His second letter, in which he gives a little experience in " boarding around."

MACK was to begin his school on the last Monday of November, and the Saturday previous to that he bade his friends at the Seminary good-bye, and set out for the scene of his labors. Poor fellow, I pitied him, knowing as I did how much he enjoyed congenial society, and understanding better than he did the number of annoyances to which he would be subjected.

We had learned, after his engagement, that the locality in which he was to teach was generally regarded as an out-of-the-way place, inhabited chiefly by poor and uncultivated people, and that on this account the district had been nick-named by its neighbors "The Lost Nation."

Mack had once or twice expressed to me his regret at not having applied for a school earlier, when he might have secured one in a different community, but he had a great desire to learn the character and customs of different peoples, and whenever inclined to repent of his promise to teach in this particular district, he always consoled himself with the reflection that **he** would have an admirable opportunity **to** learn the characteristics of lower life in Yankeedom. **He** had often remarked that what he **saw** and heard on the day he engaged to **teach** was worth **to** him as much as his winter's wages, and he avowed his determination to keep a diary, during his stay in the district, with the view of some-time making up a quarto volume from the incidents of that winter. His enthusiasm, however, on this subject began sensibly to diminish as the time for his departure drew near, and on the day that he was to leave he would gladly have cancelled his engagement, could he honorably or consistently, with his circumstances, have done so. But he went to his work, and in two weeks after he commenced it the following letter announced to me his success.

M——, —th Dec., 1856.

My DEAR STYLES,

I still live, but whether I shall continue **to do so at the** expiration of another two weeks is **a question that** I am now prepared, seriously, to consider. **I have had** opportunity to discover the comfort and pleasure **to** be enjoyed in "boarding around," and I confess I like **it.** Doughnuts for dinner every day except two, when **their** presence was supplied with cold johnny cake, with a pig's foot for dessert. Unlike yourself, I have not yet experienced the comfort of sleeping with two boys, but have always had the company of one, and during a period of four nights, when **my** sleeping apartment was warm, bed-fellows of another **kind** made a change to a cold room exceedingly pleasant. **I find,** however, that there are several farmers in the district who live in good houses, and from the neat and respectable appearance of their children, I venture to hope that I shall have all the comforts in boarding with them that I could wish. My present number of pupils is fifty-six, and I understand that there are four or five more boys coming " as soon as their threshing is done." Should their conduct prove anything like what it is said to have been in school in former times, I imagine that the threshing will be done chiefly after they have become my pupils. On the whole, I cannot complain of the deportment of those who are already in school, having been obliged to resort to extreme measures in only one instance. You doubtless remember Tom Gibson, who is "great on square holt." Well, having become tired of his familiar remarks and the advice that he volunteered to offer about the management of classes, etc., I ventured to inform him on the fourth day that I could manage the school without his aid if he would kindly permit me, whereupon he coolly said :

" I guess you're gittin' stuck up, aint yer ? "

He was evidently astonished at the display of indignation which followed, but not much cowed, he insolently remarked :

" You're pretty small, bub, to make so much noise."

His right eye is robed in mourning now, and I think he has concluded to waive the discussion of the question as to the probability of my being " stuck up."

But, my dear fellow, I need your advice about one thing, —the multitude of text books.

I have four different kinds of arithmetics, five reading books, three geographies, and three spellers, all of the same, or nearly the same grade, and I am expected to hear the lessons in all the different sorts ; what am I to do ? It is

by far the greatest annoyance that I have; causing me, as
it does, to perform a great deal of unnecessary work, and
thus depriving me of time to make the recitations interesting and instructive to the pupils. By giving much oral
instruction and the use of the black board, I get along very
well with the arithmetic classes, but the other recitations
are not so easily managed. I appealed to the committee to
aid me in establishing a uniform series of text books, but I
might as well have expected an appropriation from New
Zealand to build a chair factory in Vermont. They had
never heard before, of too many books being an objection
to a school, and even after I had explained the case they
failed to see the difficulty, and one of them thought if I
knew much about school teaching I would have no trouble
with regard to the books. Now, as you have had a little
experience in teaching, I have no doubt that you can make
some suggestion that will be profitable to me.

Are all the district schools of this country in the same
state as mine with regard to text books?

I enclose two notes which I have received since teaching
here, which will show you at the same time the annoyances
I have to meet, and the literary status of my patrons.

Yours ever,

MACK.

The following are copies of the letters enclosed:—

Mr. Makkensy, Sir,

i wish you would let james
set on nuther seet. i doant want him ter set with the Snider

young ones. They call him names and sa his father and
mother is fools an you no that aint very plesant.

Yours effectionetly,

LYDI S——————

Mr. Makenzy my boy sez you wont hear his jografy
leson caus its a old won and their haint enny more like it
in school and tell him that ive gotter by him a nu jografy.
now i shant du it. i studded that jografy miself And i no
its good won. i haint got no muny ter fool way and ef you
want him ter hev a nuther you kan jest by it yerself er ile
take him out yer school.

i perscribe miself yours

respecfully

ERNEST ————————

The reader will understand that I sympathized with my
friend in his troubles, but I certainly felt unable to relieve
him.   Every one who has had much experience in teaching, knows the embarrassment of having a variety of text
books in one class.   This drawback to the teacher's success
was formerly very common, and though it is now seldom
seen in the more advanced and cultivated communities, it
still exists in many rural districts.

The best advice that I could give was that he should
explain to the parents the difficulty under which he labored,
and, if possible, persuade them to purchase new books, but
if they refused, to get along as best he could with those
already in use.   He certainly could not be justly blamed
if his pupils, under the circumstances, failed to make the
progress that they would had his wishes in the matter been
observed.

Reforms in school may be effected in a short time by a teacher who has had experience, and is well known in the locality where he teaches, provided he has an intelligent school board or a goodly number of intelligent patrons to sustain him; but old customs and theories can be abolished in a community like that where my friend was teaching, only by wise and persistent efforts through several terms of school.

Mack subsequently informed me that he adopted my suggestion, and succeeded in persuading two or three to purchase new books, but as others refused, he was obliged to continue his work with constant regrets that he was compelled, by their ignorance, to misemploy much of his time.

Three weeks more passed, when the post brought me the following letter:

MY DEAR STYLES,

I am becoming attached to my school. There really is some pleasure to be found in teaching, notwithstanding the many annoyances. One frequently becomes tired with the monotony of his labors, discouraged and vexed at the want of interest displayed by many of his older pupils, whose want of knowledge is really shocking, and he feels that his life is one of ceaseless drudgery; but then when he finds among his pupils those of bright minds who strive earnestly to learn, who listen with profound attention to what is said, and seem grateful for the instruction imparted to them, he is encouraged, and realizes that his mission is a noble one—that he is helping to mould the minds of those who may eventually be numbered with the wise and good. Really,

I believe that there is no other pursuit in which one can engage with such perfect assurance of leaving

" Footprints on the sands of time."

I find that my travels are of immense value to me in my present labors.

You would smile to see my large, awkward pupils listen sometimes with gaping mouths to the descriptions given them of things I have seen in foreign lands. I am glad to entertain and instruct them in this manner, but they are so curious and importunate in their questions, that I often get weary, and to relieve myself of the labor of giving them orally, the information they desire, I have loaned several of them books, and I think that, by so doing, I have awakened in them a taste for reading. I am certain that they all show me more respect than they would, did they not feel that I am possessed of knowledge much superior to their own.

Since writing you my last I have boarded at two different places, and have been entertained as pleasantly and made as comfortable as I could wish. I must not omit, however, to give you an account of a night I spent with a diminutive Englishman, who, but a few years since, resided in Canada. His name is Peacock, and, owing to his generosity, six young Peacocks, equally divided as regards sex, are members of my school. He brings his progeny in stormy weather on an ox sled, and as he is very loquacious I find it difficult at times to get rid of him in season to commence my work at the proper hour. Having heard, he said, that I was a Scotchman, and a great traveller, he felt much interest in me, and in fact claimed relationship, inasmuch as we owe allegiance to the same flag. He had

urged me frequently to visit him, and as I was pleased with
the old fellow I decided to do so.

The people **with** whom I was boarding tried to dissuade
me, assuring me that I would find neither comfort nor clean-
liness in his domicile. Curiosity, however, and a desire to
fulfil my promise led me to make the visit, and one evening last week, at the close of school, I accompanied the
young Peacocks to their home. The road branches off from
the main road, at a short distance from the schoolhouse, and
leads first across a wide rough field, and then through a belt
of woods to a small clearing near the base of the mountain.

The house, a small log one, scarcely displays its roof
above the high snow drifts which surround it, and the entrance to it on the occasion of my visit could be effected
only by a slippery path, almost perpendicular, commencing
at the summit of a drift and terminating at the threshold.

Notwithstanding a word of caution which was given me
by one of the children who followed as I mounted the drift,
I lost my footing, slid swiftly down the opposite side, burst
open the door, and brought up in a sitting posture on the
floor **of** the Englishman's kitchen. **My** début **was** first
acknowledged by **a** large yellow, half starved looking dog,
which dashed **at me** with a fierce growl and seized me, as I
was rising, by the coat tail. His short, stout mistress first
assailed him over the head with a heavy brush broom-stick,
but it was not until his master had administered several
lusty kicks that he was disposed to relinquish his hold. An
apology was first offered, then salutations were exchanged,
after which my host offered me the best chair the **house**
afforded, which was once, no doubt, well bottomed with
rough bark, but in its present state of dilapidation I was

obliged to rely on the front round for support, on which I tried to balance myself while I answered his questions and surveyed the furniture of the apartment.

It was the only room in the house, and served the triple purpose of kitchen, dining room and sleeping apartment for the whole family. There were two beds besides a huge trundle bed in it, a roughly made table, three or four old chairs, a long bench and an old stove at which the mistress was engaged in frying large slices of pork.

Their few dishes were chiefly of tin, but a blue earthen plate of antique pattern was placed on the table for my own special benefit. I had proceeded thus far in my inventory of mine host's personal property, and was changing my position in the chair to a more comfortable one, when the door again suddenly burst open and in slid a full grown pig, his bristles, from cold and hunger, standing on end

> " Like quills upon a fretful porcupine."

The only difference between piggy's entrance and my own was that he maintained a standing posture. It was an opportunity again for the faithful yellow dog to display his vigilance. The long curly tail of the pig affording the most vulnerable point of attack, to this he fastened himself, and to the music of a prolonged, terrific squeal, accompanied by surly growls, the quadrupeds commenced the circuit of the room. The broom-stick, wielded as before by the hostess, was again brought into requisition, the Englishman followed with his heavy boots, while the eldest boy, seizing the fire-shovel, formed the rear of the assailing party. Round and round the table went the animals, and round and round they were followed by the trio of excited bipeds. Blows fell in rapid succession; the Englishman shouted and kicked alternately, and the squeals became more piercing at each successive shaking piggy received at his caudal continuation by the unrelenting dog. The children, with the exception of the one engaged in the attack, sought refuge on the beds, while I, for safety, removed my chair into a corner of the room, where I was just preparing to take notes, when the elder Peacock gave a furious kick, intended for the pig, but which, unluckily, missed it, struck and overturned the table, and left the man himself, from the violence of his effort, sitting, with flushed face, on the floor. The frightened pig at this juncture dashed off at a tangent, and running beneath my chair bore it off on his back, and landed its occupant on his head near the stove. I rolled over just in time to witness the romantic exit of the animal from the door, the dog still clinging to his tail.

The excitement having thus subsided, and the Englishman, as well as myself, being once more on his feet, we were prepared to contemplate the scene. At first he expressed his indignation in sundry ejaculations, interspersed with half stifled oaths, but at length, incited perhaps by my own merriment, which I struggled in vain to conceal, he seemed to comprehend the ludicrousness of the occurrence, and burst into a hearty laugh. His wife, however, was not inclined to take a ludicrous view of it, especially since she had lost her earthen plate; and her sorrow seemed the greater since the loss involved the necessity of my eating like the rest on a tin one. But I soon put her at her ease regarding this matter, and the subject was speedily dismissed.

The supper consisted of fried pork, baked potatoes, cornbread, and milk. I confess that my appetite was not what it might have been under other circumstances, but recollecting that I had fared less sumptuously many times on shipboard, I believe that I ate a meal at which you would have been astonished had you been present.

After supper the old gentleman engaged me in conversation, which was prolonged till nearly midnight. Born in Yorkshire he still retains much of the uncouth dialect of the lower classes of that county, still his accent has been modified considerably by his long residence on this continent. Intelligent far beyond his appearance he talked fluently of his native land and of my own country, which he has visited, and he related many amusing and interesting stories.

The most trying part of my stay with him was my experience in retiring. Previous to that hour the children, with little or no appearance of modesty, had doffed their raiment in our presence and sought the spacious trundle bed before mentioned, all lying crosswise in it. Shortly after eleven, the old fellow informed me that one of the beds in the room was to be occupied by myself, and then stepping to the side of the other he proceeded to divest himself of his garments and was soon ensconced beneath its coverlets. The woman was still up enjoying a pipe before the stove ; and how to get into bed without wearing the clothes I still had on became with me a subject of serious consideration.

I might have had less hesitation about sleeping in my suit, had it not been a black one, but the project was too suggestive of work with the clothes brush the next morning to make it seem at all feasible ; especially, since I had no brush with me, and knowing that there could be none in the house. I sat long pondering the situation, when finding that it became no better, I threw off my coat and vest, jumped into **bed,** and then relieving myself, **with** some difficulty, of my nether garments, I kicked them out at the foot. This difficulty surmounted, I at **once** dropped asleep.

The whole family were up **and stirring,** in the morning ere I awoke, and then how I was to make my toilet without violating my natural **modesty,** became a more serious ques. tion than the one of the preceding evening. While thinking over the probabilities of **being** able to don a portion of my attire before rising, fortunately I saw my hostess step out of the door. It was my only chance. If you have ever had any doubts of my activity I think they would have been dispelled could you have witnessed the expedition with which I put myself into my pants on that occasion. I was horrified, however, on seizing them, to find that one of the legs was wrong side out. The misfortune caused, perhaps, a second's delay, **yet to me it seemed an** hour; but by the time the woman returned, though **not in** the condition in **which I** would prefer **to be** were I going to enter **a** gentleman's drawing-room, my **appearance for that place** might be **termed** respectable.

My first **work,** after completing my toilet, was to rid my pants of the **lint with which** they were literally covered. To do this without the aid of a brush, I went out, waded through several snow drifts, and then brushed them with my hands.

For breakfast that morning, we had baked potatoes, fried pork and "johnny cake." What was left of the latter, after being besmeared with a bad quality of butter, was thrust into a huge basket for the dinner of the children and my-self at the schoolhouse.

On my departure, the mistress of the house, evidently wishing to ascertain whether I intended to board with them for the next two or three weeks, asked me if they should look for me with the children again that evening. I had been fearing the question, and so was prepared to answer it. I said I thought not, pleading the long distance and bad road.

Her husband came to my rescue at this moment with the following admonition :

"It's nonsense, Becca, for ye to be expectin' a gentleman like Mr. Mackenzie to come such a long way to git 'commo-dations like ours when he can be made comfortable in the families of gintle folks nearer the schoolhouse. Becca and I have seen hard times, Mr. Mackenzie, but, thank God, we now have enou' to eat and drink, and I hope we shall be able to do something for our young folks to make them respectable in the world. At any rate, we shall be glad to have you come and see us now and again, for I like to talk with them that knows the old mother land."

There was something pathetic in this frank speech of the honest Englishman which touched a tender cord. His hint at the struggles he and his better half had maintained against poverty excited my sympathy, while his desire to make their "young folks" respectable in the world de-manded higher admiration than is due to the efforts of the opulent to bequeath to their offspring wealth and respecta-bility. I am conscious that there was far more sincerity in my reply—"I shall be happy to come again"—than there often is in this old stereotyped expression. At all events, whether I ever **repeat** the visit or not, I shall remember this as an amusing episode in the experience of " boarding around."

Write me soon,

Yours forever,

MACK.

CHAPTER XV.

IT was spring once more. Mack had long since closed his school, which he had taught to the great satisfaction of his patrons, and he was again at the Seminary pursuing his studies, like myself, with diligence and increased ambition.

Everything seemed to be going on smoothly, and according to the wishes of our professors, when another individual was connected with the institution; and as through him Mack and myself became the heroes of a notable incident, it is proper to introduce him to the reader. Be neither astonished nor disgusted, my aristocratic friend, when I inform you that he was neither a professor, count, or millionaire—but a colored man—a veritable darkey—a fugitive slave, who was always called Tim.

Remember that it was many years ago, long before the proclamation of the martyred President had loosed the chains of the sable bondmen in the "Sunny South," and while the

Fugitive Slave Law remained as a foul blot upon the Statute Books of the famed Republic, that this occurred.

Tim's history may be briefly recounted as follows :—He was born in North Carolina, on the plantation where he had always lived till the time of his escape. Though flogged sometimes, and otherwise ill-treated, his lot had been a pleasant one, compared with that of many of his unfortunate race ; for he had a wife and two daughters, and had never been compelled to separate from them, all being slaves of the same master. But Tim, notwithstanding his ignorance, had a proud spirit and high ambition. He had heard of a land of liberty where the poor black was allowed to possess a home ; to go and come when he liked ; to enjoy the society of his family without apprehension of being torn from it by the selfishness of cruel men, and for these blessings he earnestly longed. He sighed for them the more, from the fact that his master was growing old, and might soon die, in which case he would be left to the entire mercy of his cruel and profligate son. The master was also on the verge of bankruptcy, and should this disaster occur he foresaw that a separation of his kindred would in all probability ensue : and into whose hands they would fall, or what sufferings, besides that of parting, they might have to undergo, he knew not. He had heard of the " Underground Railroad," and of the assistance the fugitive slave often received from kind friends at the North, and believing that if he could himself escape he might, in some way eventually procure the release of his wife and children, he resolved to make the attempt. This resolution he put into execution one day when, for some trivial offence, he expected a flogging from his master's son.

It is needless to recount the long and toilsome marches which he performed on foot in the night, the hairbreadth escapes from recapture, the painful watchings, and sufferings from thirst and hunger which he endured in securing his freedom.   But at length he reached New York, and having remained concealed there a few days, he pushed northward to Albany, where he was introduced by a friend to the President of our Seminary, who chanced to be in the city on business.   The latter being in want of a servant, and thinking that it would be difficult for the pursuers of the fugitive to kidnap him at the Seminary, where the students were nearly all abolitionists, he brought Tim with him to Corvette.

Once there, he felt quite secure, and, much to his gratification, he soon became a person of no little notoriety.   Like most of his race, he was an enthusiast in religion, and though it was noticeable that he was not on all occasions strictly observant of the ninth commandment, he was, on the whole, more exemplary than many professedly Christians, who had ' had the advantage of education and cultured society.

He had often preached in the South to his colored brethren, and though he could read but very little, he was quite familiar with the Bible, especially the New Testament, and could quote scriptural expressions with a readiness that would do credit to a theological student.   His conceit was unbounded, and, not being admitted into the pulpits, he sought to enlighten the minds and soften the unregenerate hearts of the white people, who assembled in school-houses in rural districts on the Sabbath to listen to his addresses. Curiosity, and an appreciation of the ridiculous, alone impelled them to hear him, as there was often not the slightest relevancy between the subjects chosen for his discourses and the lessons drawn from them.

Owing to his conceit and credulousness, he was **very** easily imposed upon, and incidents were occurring almost daily in which he was made to minister to the fun-loving propensities of mischievous students. His highest ambition was to be regarded an orator, and an invitation, accompanied by a little flattery, never failed to call **him** up **for an** impromptu lecture on any subject his audience might suggest. Another **weakness** of his was to imitate the eccentricities of noted men. Being present on a certain occasion when I chanced **to** be speaking to some of the students respecting the peculiarities of Beecher and Spurgeon, he listened attentively, and decided, it seems, to increase **his** notoriety by adopting a method **of illustration** which he then heard described; **and the following** Sabbath **he** astonished **his** congregation by sliding **down** the old-fashioned high desk in the school-house where he was preaching: thus **imitating** the great English divine **who,** to illustrate **some point, slid** down **the** railing of his pulpit.

Naturally loquacious and lively, **he sometimes** surprised his acquaintances by fits of taciturnity lasting two or three days, during which time he **would assume a** most melancholy air, taking notice of no **one, and often** in the night startling the other servants by loud and frequent groans. As an explanation of this mysterious conduct, he informed his interlocutors that he was "pressed in spirit."

One **of** the arguments advanced by pro-slavery **men** against emancipation was that a colored man could not be treated with respect and kindness without assuming a degree of familiarity and impudence that no respectable white man could tolerate. With due respect for Tim's good qualities, I must say that my short acquaintance with him rather tended to make me a proselyte to this pro-slavery opinion. He was engaged as a general servant at the Seminary, consequently, came daily in contact with the students. The majority of them treated him kindly, though, as before stated, many of them were too much inclined to seek fun at his expense. A few, among whom were Sixby and Hardwick, regarded him with the greatest contempt, and their ungentlemanly treatment of him was only counterbalanced by the kindness shown him by a few others— Mack and myself being among the latter.

In consequence of this kindness, Tim regarded us as intimate friends, and his manifold wants and secrets were so often made known to us, that we found ourselves obliged to request him to visit our rooms only in cases of necessity. He often came to us to write letters for him, and as he was anxious to give his family a full account of all that he did and saw, it became no slight task to pen an epistle according to his dictation. I once wrote to his master for him, giving a glowing account of Tim's present happy condition, indulging in a tirade against slavery, and closing with a moral admonition to himself. Mack and I also spent considerable time in teaching him to read and write, but the most irksome of the labors he imposed upon us was reading to him the chapters from which he chose his texts for the following Sunday, the task always being greatly prolonged, until we forbade it, by his frequent interruptions to deliver a homily, which the passages he heard had suggested.

But Tim soon grew vain and arrogant. In gaining his

liberty he forgot that he owed a duty to his present employer, and the latter often said that it seemed as if Tim, in order to convince himself that he was a free man, would desert the work at which he had been placed, just at the time when his services were the most required. In his enthusiasm, he had already planned for purchasing the freedom of his wife and children, and so sure was he that this was soon to be accomplished, that he one day visited the President, and, to the amusement of the latter, demanded to know in what capacity his spouse was to be admitted into the "institootion," as he always called it. He claimed that as the wives of the other clergymen in the Seminary were permitted to board, and receive attention as ladies, his own should be accorded the same right; and unless this social status was granted her, he should be obliged to change his quarters.

About this time an incident occurred which, while it afforded no little amusement to the students, greatly increased the conceit of Tim. A clergyman of some note, but of peculiar religious tenets, had been holding a series of meetings in Corvette, and in the flush of success at making proselytes, he sent an invitation to any one of the ministers at the Seminary to hold a public discussion with him respecting the doctrine that he was promulgating. No one being inclined to accept it, I casually suggested to Tim that he should do so.

He showed no hesitation; and as he was urged by other students who earnestly desired the fun, he at once commenced preparations for the discussion. The suggestion, however, which I had thoughtlessly made, caused me more trouble than I had anticipated; for, in order to prepare himself properly for the occasion, he requested me to write down the scriptural passages that were to be used in flooring his learned opponent.

At first I declined, and tried to dissuade him from his purpose, but, at the solicitation of my fellow students, I finally assented, and so laid aside my own work for the entire day. The Professors knew the plan that had been projected, but said nothing; and I was certain that they secretly enjoyed the scheme, and wished the darkey much success in subverting what they considered heterodox opinions.

Evening came, and Tim, with a bundle of notes that looked like the manuscript of a quarto volume, repaired to the hall in which the clergyman's meetings were held.

In order to avoid the suspicion of being at all connected with the affair, I prevailed on Tim to go early, and I went sometime afterward with several other students. On entering the hall, which was well filled, to my dismay, Tim, who was sitting near the door, rose and followed.

Down one passage I went, across the hall, up another alley and sat down in a vacant seat near the platform. Tim seated himself beside me, and Mack became his nearest neighbor on the other side. I had made this long journey hoping that my colored friend would take a seat eleswhere, as I knew that he would become conspicuous through the display made with his papers, and that he might thus awaken suspicion among the clergyman's friends, many of whom were acquainted with me, that I was the instigator of the attack that he was about to make. My fears were not groundless, for he had already attracted much attention, and no sooner was he seated than he pulled forth a page of foolscap, produced a pencil, and as soon as the minister commenced his address, began to write down hieroglyphics which none but himself could decipher. The attention of the audience was equally divided between him and the minister, as it was evident what was coming. In taking notes he often appealed to me for the definition of a term which he did not understand, and thus I, unwillingly, became as prominent as himself. While thus situated, finding it almost impossible to repress my risibility, my fellow students were enjoying the scene immensely, knowing, as they did, the pains I had taken to avoid the awkward position in which Tim had placed me.

At length the sermon closed, and, according to his custom, the minister invited discussion. All eyes were turned towards Tim, and as he sprang to his feet, his huge face and rolling eyes exhibiting signs of great excitement, a suppressed titter ran through the audience.

"I wants to know," he began, "ef you sez that when the wicked dies he aint punished?"

"Certainly not!" was the emphatic reply. "'The wages of sin is death.' It is eternal punishment."

As this was the point Tim had prepared himself to prove, he was nonplussed by the minister's declaration; but as he was determined that such an opportunity for displaying his learning and eloquence should not be lost, he pulled down his waistcoat, ran his fingers through his woolly hair, glanced around the audience, ahemmed two or three times, and then with grave deliberation began again as follows:

"My very intimate frens heah on my right han' and on my lef', Mr. Styles and Mr. Mackenzie, tells me dat you don't believe dar is a literal lake of fire and brimstun where

God frows de wicked and punishes dem fur ever ; now I wants to know ef dis is so ?"

"Certainly, sir, I believe in no such punishment as that," was the reply.

"'Zactly, sah," exclaimed Tim, with a triumphant smile ; " I've brot you to de pint now, and I'm gwine to show dese poor unfortinate, ignorent peoples, heah, dat you am tryin' to mislead, dat you am a 'postor, a big humbug, an when dey comes to de day ob ressurrekshun dey'll bless de Lord dat He's raised up a culled man, and bro't him all de way from Norf Carliny, and giv' him de 'bility to save dem from de error of dar ways, and to axpose you."

As the audience was composed largely of intelligent people, and the minister himself was highly educated, Tim's estimate of their mental condition was hardly just, but many among them enjoyed the scene, and though some person cried, " Put him out," no one seemed disposed to obey the order, or even to second it.

Encouraged, Tim now stepped up on the seat and with stentorian voice commenced his harangue. He referred to his notes but twice, and then, finding that they interfered with his rapid gesticulations, and regarding his victory certain without them, he threw the bundle of papers disdainfully on the floor, and launched out into a declamatory speech of ten minutes length, which might be aptly compared to a thunder storm. Sometimes he struck upon an idea that might be termed appropriate, but taken as a whole it was about as senseless a jargon as could possibly be conceived. At length, after he had become nearly exhausted with his effort, and had quite deafened those who were sitting near him, he fastened his eyes on the minister, who had been

standing all the while with a confused look and wondering
when the storm was to subside, and dropping his voice to a
moderate **tone,** said,

"**Now,** sah, if I **be not right, I** wants you to 'splain to
dese poor bredren heah, dat you have deceibed, what our
Savyah meant by the pahable of de rich man and Lazarus."

"**My** friend," replied the clergyman, "if you will come
and see me at my rooms, I will be pleased to talk with you;
but **as it is now late, I** think we had better bring the meeting to a close."

"**Ah! ah!**" exclaimed Tim. "**You see, my** belubbed
bredren, dat he feels scared. Dat's de way de Lord delib-
bers de Flistines into de hands of Samson. He's beat, **my**
frens, and yet he don't dare to 'knowledge it. He wants
to git me 'lone, **an'**, probly, he'll give me five or ten dollars
to **hol'** my tongue, **so** he **kin go on** and deceivb **de** whole **ob**
ye; but I shant do it, my bredren. De Lord hab raised me
up to save ye, and ef you don't listen to me, dis 'postor
will take ye **to hell,** dat awful place of fiah an' brimstun,
ebbry **one** ob ye."

The minister **took no further** notice of him, **but imme-**
diately dismissed the audience with a benediction.

I was the first to leave the room, and, **as I** pushed through
the crowd, **I noticed** much laughing, and heard remarks
like the following:

"The darkey did well."

"**I was in** hopes he would go on."

But others looked displeased, and gave vent to their feelings in expressions like this:

"It was mean."

"I say that **those** fellows at the Seminary should **be**
ashamed to **get that** nigger **up here to insult Mr.** ———"

I was not anxious to listen to the various opinions entertained of the lark, and, consequently, reached my room in the shortest time possible. As for Tim, he believed that he had achieved a brilliant victory; and as no one attempted to undeceive him, he was permitted to remain in the enjoyment of his happy assurance. The students never forgot the incident, and as long as Mack and I remained at the Seminary we were frequently greeted with the quotation—

"My very intimate frens, Mr. Styles and Mr. Mackenzie."

In less than a month from the occurrence of the above incident, Tim had good reason to regard us as friends; and, had it not been for our friendship, his future lot would, in all probability, have been the saddest he had ever experienced.

I have already stated that one object of his friends in removing him to the Seminary was to lessen the chances of his being kidnapped. Although the Fugitive Slave Law was in force at the time, such was the odium against it at the North, and such was the sympathy felt for the poor slave who had escaped, that the slaveholder cared not to incur the hatred of the New Englanders, and meet the storm of indignation they were sure to raise should he come openly before the courts and ask the restitution of his property; hence, he preferred, with a semblance of justice, to have the arrest made as secretly as possible, and then hurried the prisoner back to bondage ere his friends had missed him. It was, virtually, kidnapping; yet it was attempted in more than one instance with success. Fears were entertained for a while that Tim might thus be taken back to his former master, but as time wore on, both he and his friends became less wary, and, indeed, I think he had dismissed the thought of any attempt being made to recapture him.

One evening in midsummer, during the twilight, Mack **and I** had strolled away on a road leading southward, and had sat down near a bridge which crossed the stream nearly a mile from the Seminary. Farther on was a rocky slope, and this was covered with a belt of woods through which the road passed. While sitting here, chatting together, a covered carriage, drawn by two horses, rolled rapidly down from the village and passed us. There was nothing unusual in the occurrence, and doubtless it would **soon** have been forgotten, had not subsequent events rendered it an incident of no little importance. Twenty minutes, perhaps, after the carriage had passed, the voice of some one beyond the woods, singing an old familiar hymn, was borne to our ears by the still evening air. We listened a moment, and then Mack said,

" It is Tim, coming **from** his prayer meeting."

There was a schoolhouse about two miles beyond us, at which a weekly prayer meeting was held, and of this, Tim had charge, usually delivering a short sermon to those who were in attendance. As stated by Mack, **Tim** was returning from this meeting, and was giving utterance to his happy feelings in **one** of his **favorite** spiritual **songs.** On he came, the words becoming more and more distinct **as** sent forth by his powerful vocal organs, when, suddenly, the singing ceased, **and,** for a moment, **a** dead silence ensued. It was only for a moment; for, scarcely had the last note of his singing died away, ere the air was rent with startling cries.

"Help! help! murder!" were the words that thrilled us like an electric shock, **and** brought us simultaneously to **our** feet.

"They are taking Tim," exclaimed Mack, in startling tones. "Come on, Styles!" and away he dashed with the speed of a race horse towards the woods.

I required no second invitation. From my earliest recollection I had regarded slavery with the greatest abhorrence. Ere I was twelve years old, I had read many anti-slavery works, and my indignation had been aroused to the highest pitch by the numberless instances recounted therein of the cruelties exercised by the slave-holders against their human chattels.   I remember distinctly that even in my childish years, when my blood had been heated by these accounts, I permitted my imagination to portray the marvelous deeds that I would perform in the interests of the Southern bondmen when I had arrived at the age of manhood. It was then with me an impression, almost amounting to conviction, that I would travel through the South at some future time, become acquainted with slavery in all its aspects, display my sympathy for the slave by deeds of philanthropy and individual valor, and eventually subvert the institution by inciting the slaves to an insurrection. Such was the scheme that I confidentially disclosed to an unambitious and unromantic boy, two or three years my senior, but his practical turn of mind induced him to damp my ardor by the following exclamation :

"You'd do great things, you dunce ! Why, the slaveholders would shoot you 'fore you'd been there a week."

It might have been this damping of my enthusiasm, coupled with the barriers interposed by Providence, that prevented my meeting ere this the tragic fate of John Brown.   But my boyish plans with regard to slavery were never forgotten, and when that ill-starred hero suffered on the gallows for the too great sympathy and love that he had manifested for his fellow-man, I bemoaned my lowly lot that I could do nothing to avert his end. It seemed to me, as it will always seem, that he was deserted by his Northern friends in the hour of peril, in extremest need. One united effort on the part of the anti-slavery men might, no doubt, have procured his ransom, if they had not the force to wrest him from the toils of Southern hate. Unwise as he doubtless was in the means that he devised to accomplish his ends, he nevertheless deserves the respect and sympathy of good men ; and the future historian who does justice to his memory will place his name beside those who have died martyrs to a noble cause.

I have indulged in this digression, kind reader, to show wi'h what feelings I responded to my noble friend's request —" Come on ; " to show the deep sympathy for our wronged and imperiled colored friend that incited me—us, I should say, for I know that Mack's feelings were similar to my own—to violate the laws of the country in which we were then sojourners. Already I fancied that I could hear the cruel lash and the deep groan of the recaptured fugitive, suffering again in the land of bondage for the love of liberty which had led him to escape. I could see his wife and daughters torn from his embrace and borne away to distant States—not only to increase the wealth of brutal masters, but to punish the husband and father for the courage and wisdom that he had dared to show. I could hear and see all this, and the blood was boiling in my veins, and my fists were clenched with desperate resolve, as with swift winged feet I followed my friend.

I was not more than six paces behind him when he

reached the spot where the struggle was going on. In the twilight, rendered more dim by the presence of the woods, we descried the carriage that had passed us, and a man was standing by the horses holding them by the bits. A few steps aside, two men, one at his head and another at his feet, were dragging our friend along, despite his frantic efforts to resist them. They had already gagged, handcuffed and fettered him, and would soon have him in the carriage.

The man who was holding the horses, seeing us, gave the alarm in time for his companions to prepare for our attack. They had dropped their burden and faced us, just as Mack directed a blow at one which felled him to the ground. Bang! went the barrel of a revolver at the instant Mack came down with both feet into the stomach of his fallen foe.

They had the advantage of us in being well armed, as neither of us had any weapon whatever. I am confident that, in our terrible excitement, we never considered the chances of getting shot; our only thought being that Tim must never go back to slavery.

When the revolver was fired I recollect thinking that it must be our aim to come into close quarters with our antagonists, which would prevent their using their weapons, and making our chances as good as their own. With this intention then, I rushed on and grappled the other man a second after he had discharged his second barrel at Mack. He was much larger and more powerful than myself, and though I strained every muscle he threw his arms around me, lifted me up, and then, throwing me to the ground, fell heavily on me. My spirits ebbed when I discovered his superior strength, but to prevent his using his revolver again I hugged him to me with a grip more terrible than that received by Sinbad from the old man of the sea. Scarcely were we down when a blow on the head caused him to relax his hold of me, and unloosing my own grasp he rolled over insensible on the ground,

"Are you hurt?" asked Mack, as I sprang to my feet.

"No, are you?"

"Not a bit. But you search this fellow's pockets for the key to Tim's fetters while I search the other. Quick! for they'll be all right again in a minute, yet, we have the advantage of them now, for I have both revolvers; but we don't want to be recognized, as this may be a serious job for us."

This affray might have turned out differently with us had the man who had charge of the horses been able or inclined to come to the assistance of his companions. But, at the report of the revolver, the horses had taken fright and dragged him along with them until he was at least ten rods from us, before he succeeded in checking them. I have little doubt that he was glad of this excuse for not taking part in the fight; for as he was, probably, some man connected with a livery stable, who had been engaged to bring the other two to this place, he could care but little how the affair terminated, and, of course, would gladly seize on any pretext for keeping aloof from danger.

Fortunately, in one of the pockets of my disabled foe I found the key which released Tim from his shackles; and no sooner was this done, than springing to his feet he darted off for the Seminary as if a pack of blood-hounds was at his heels; Mack and I following at a more moderate pace.

At first I was astonished to find that Mack had received

P

no injury from the shots that were fired, for it seemed impossible that one man could fire at another, not more than six or eight feet distant, without hitting him, but on our return, I received a satisfactory explanation.

"He never aimed at me," said Mack, "for I heard both bullets whistle by me. You may be sure they dared not shoot us. If we ever learn the particulars of this matter, depend upon it we shall find that these fellows live in the North; and they had undertaken to return Tim to his master for the reward he offered. They wished to accomplish this as quietly as possible, to save themselves from the contempt and disgrace which they knew would follow the discovery of their conduct, and they would not be very likely to shoot us when they knew that, in all probability, they would be lynched for it within twenty-four hours."

His reasoning seemed very plausible, and as we never learned anything more respecting the matter, it was doubtless quite correct. When the kidnappers returned to consciousness they certainly must have felt themselves *hors de combat*, for besides the injuries they had received from Mack, they were without revolvers, as we had taken them with us. I presented mine to Tim, and he afterwards carried it for his defence; Mack kept his as a memento of the service he had rendered the anti-slavery cause.

Tim was so frightened and bewildered that, on reaching the Seminary, he went straight to his room without speaking to any one, but after recovering somewhat, he went to the President, in his office, and reported that he had been set on by several slave-holders with blood-hounds, knocked down, gagged and nearly killed—that somebody—students he thought—had interceded for him, and had been shot—

and that in the melee he had managed to knock down two or three and escape.

Jack Fallstaff never gave a more glowing account of his valor than did Tim of his on this occasion; but, poor fellow, I do not believe he intentionally exaggerated; he evidently knew but little of what had occurred. Subsequent examination showed that he had received a severe blow on the head, and it might have been owing to this, as well as his fright, that his memory failed him. He had just finished his narration to the President, and the latter was in a state of excited bewilderment, when Mack and I entered and stripped the embellishments from his tragic story. The President was profuse in his thanks to us, but at the same time he suggested, as a word of caution, that we had better remain incognito in the matter, as it might prove serious business for us, were it shown that we had resisted and beaten officers of justice in the execution of a duty for which they had been duly authorized. We thought so ourselves at first, but not learning that we had inflicted any serious bodily injury on any one, and believing that the men whom we had resisted were at best but kidnappers, we took no pains to conceal the part we had taken in the affair, especially after it had been published by Tim.

We felt less hesitation about it, too, knowing, as we did, that public sentiment in the North would exonerate us from all blame.

After hearing our story, the President sent two of his servants to the scene of the fight, to ascertain the nature of the injuries which the men had received, as well as to get such other information as the servants might be able to obtain from them or from their coachman. They were too late, however, for the carriage was rapidly disappearing in the distance when they arrived.

It was evident that Tim's enemies had been in communication with some one in Corvette who had laid the plan for his capture, and suspicion at once rested on Sixby. The suspicion was rendered doubly strong by the kindness which, from that time forward, this young gentleman always displayed towards Tim, and from the joy he pretended to feel at his lucky escape; but whether he was or was not really guilty of this villainous act no one of Tim's friends ever knew.

The affair soon ceased to be talked about, but Tim never felt quite so sure that he was in a land of liberty as he did before the occurrence. He attended the prayer meeting, as usual, but never went alone, nor did he trust himself away from the Seminary alone or unarmed.

In the early part of the ensuing autumn, Tim's employer having little for him to do, and finding a good position for him as servant with a friend in Ohio, he gave him due notice of his intention to send him to that State. Tim received the tidings with sorrowful feelings, but he soon became reconciled to the proposed change, and made ready for his departure. Some one of the students suggested to him that he should lecture to us before leaving, and as he readily assented, a stand was erected in the park from which he was to speak. The students, to flatter him and send him on his journey with gladness, all assembled to hear him, and one of the young gentlemen came forward to introduce him; but when he wished to announce the subject of the lecture, it was found that the lecturer had not yet decided on one. Tim gave as a reason for his delay that he presumed the audience would prefer selecting a subject, and he then expressed a wish that some one would do so. One of the boys, noted for his waggish propensities, stepped forward, **hat** in hand, and gravely suggested—

"The Cedars of Lebanon."

The lecturer smiled, bowed and declared himself profoundly grateful for **a** subject so **near** his heart; and then, stepping back a little, **and assuming a** grave expression of countenance, he opened his discourse. **For** nearly half an hour he stormed, frothed, stamped and gesticulated, **only** taking **breath** when he was interrupted by rounds of applause. His peroration was, perhaps, hardly what might have been expected, as it consisted of a recapitulation of the happy times he had seen in the "Institootion," and in portraying how the "Cedars of Lebanon" must have suffered for the want of a just description had not his intimate friends, Mr. Styles and Mr. Mackenzie, gallantly rescued him from slavery, and thus preserved him to do justice **to** those "magnificent and bootiful trees." All declared themselves delighted with the lecture, and after a collection had been taken up, he was escorted to the depot with fife and drum. Here he made a short farewell address, shook hands with all the students, stepped on the train and was borne away, doubtless the happiest man in all New England.

CHAPTER XVI.

IT was near vacation once more, and I began to contemplate
a visit to my home. I had been absent nearly eighteen
months, without having seen any of my Canadian friends.
It was a long time, and I wished to see them; the frequent
kind letters that I received from all hardly equalling the
pleasure I could experience by one hour in their society.
I had about decided to go home, when the President, who
had quite an amount of work to do in the way of writing,
such as copying, posting books, making out bills of account,
&c., offered me fair wages to engage to him through vacation. It was unwise in me to accept the offer, for I needed
rest from mental labor, and recreation; but the thought of
my financial affairs, and the assurance that I would even be
obliged to call on Mr. Niel for money to pay my travelling
expenses in case I should visit Canada, caused me to engage
in the work, and, consequently, to postpone my visit.
Notions of prudence and economy often lead us to do that

which it would be far better for us not to do, and thus it proved with me. Had the time I took to earn a small sum been given to active out-door exercise, the benefit resulting to me, eventually, would have been vastly greater; for during this period I grew nervous and debilitated, so that when the winter term commenced I was in poor condition for study. I did study, nevertheless, and though about this time I caught a severe cold, which left me with a cough from which it was long before I recovered, I kept my position in all my classes, receiving as high marks as I had at any time since I became a student.

The announcement that I was not to go home was received by Ruth with feelings of disappointment bordering on vexation. For a long time she had fancied that my attachment to my new home and friends was growing stronger and stronger, and, consequently, that the tie which bound me to the home and friends of my youth was becoming weaker, and she regarded my decision to spend my vacation in Corvette with no little sorrow and displeasure.

"But little more than a hundred miles away," she wrote me, "and the idea that you cannot find time in the period of a year and a half to come home **seems to** me almost absurd. It is to me evidence of what I feared when you left us—that you have allowed your ambition and friends in Corvette to weaken your attachment for the objects which you claimed to hold dear in your earlier years; and I can foresee that if you go to college, as you now say you hope to do, you will forget Canada with all its once pleasant associations."

As I read and re-read this letter, as I always did her letters, I weighed the charges she preferred against me, and

I could not conscientiously deny that they were in a measure correct.

That I should forget her, though, even were I to go to college or be separated from her a lifetime, I could not for a moment believe. I had become deeply interested in my studies, and was contented and happy while pursuing them, and my desire to go on and complete a college course had become sufficiently strong to induce me to postpone the day of marriage, and settling down to business; yet all my ambitious projects were associated, as in former times, with her, and I felt that every success I gained in life was another step taken towards making her happiness more complete. A young man of more practical turn and less pride than myself would doubtless talk much more with a young lady to whom he is engaged about his pecuniary circumstances than I did, but so reticent had I been on this point that she knew nothing whatever of the way in which I was meeting my expenses at Corvette, and consequently nothing of the self-denial I was practising in remaining there instead of going home. In my next letter, however, I informed her of the way in which I was engaged, and hinted at the necessity of economy in order to carry out my plans, and she thus not only became satisfied, but regretted sincerely that she had attributed my long absence to a disinclination to visit her.

"You will pardon me, I trust, for my unkind accusations," she next wrote me, "and especially when I tell you that you have always appeared to me to have so little regard for money, that I have really believed you never could have known the want of it as most poor mortals do. Not because I thought you were unwise and extravagant in the use **of** it, but because you have never spoken of **it, as** others do, as being at all necessary to the consummation **of** your plans; and so I naturally received the impression that you never regarded it of any consequence. Do not laugh at me, but often when you have told me what schemes you proposed to accomplish, though conscious that they could be effected only through the agency of wealth, I have never doubted your ability to do all, believing that the means would be provided in some way, either **in** the mysterious manner in which the widows cruse **was** replenished, or else through some magician's aid. But when you spoke of economy, in your last letter, and of money in a way which showed that you sometimes feel the need of it, I was pleased, for it made you seem more like a real tangible being, with wants like myself and others. I feel less awe of you now than I once did."

Dear, frank, noble-hearted girl, I thought as I read this letter; how unlike many of her sex who have arrived at a marriageable age. So far from regretting my want of wealth, and discarding my attentions on account of it, she seemed pleased that my circumstances were humble, not dissimilar to her own. I believe that she had never thought of the comforts and advantages found in a home of affluence, compared with one in which life is sustained by a constant struggle against the grim, unpitying monster—want.

My correspondence with Mr. Niel still continued, and a few weeks after the commencement of our winter term, at my request, he sent me a draft for another hundred dollars.

It was given apparently with as much cheerfulness and pleasure as he had loaned me the first, and the closing words of his last letter were a request, as usual, to ask aid of him whenever I felt inclined, and that I would deprive myself of no comfort or pleasure that I desired, so long as he could supply me the means requisite for the enjoyment.

The winter was a long one, and unusually severe, so that I was outside of the Seminary much less than I would gladly have been, and less than my health required. My cough grew worse, and becoming weaker gradually, much to my regret, I had to limit myself to five hours' study per day.

Towards spring, as I became pale and emaciated, my friends declared that I had the consumption, and advised me to leave the Seminary at once and return to the farm; but as I had never been at all alarmed respecting my health, I laughed at their anxiety, and assured them that I would be all right when the warm weather of spring came. The approach of that season showed that I was partly correct in my conclusions, for ·I recuperated rapidly under the influence of the balmy air and the active exercise I took; but my cough never fully left me, and as the warm weather of summer came on it increased, and I relapsed into my former debilitated condition. The last term of our school closed in the middle of July, and as many besides myself, who had long been students in the Seminary, were then to leave it to return no more, it was an occasion of unusual sadness. Partings of school friends are always sorrowful, partly because they occur at an age when the affections are keen, and partly because the result is seldom considered and prepared for as by persons of maturer years. My own sorrow was greatly enhanced, no doubt, by ill-health, for, notwithstanding the hopeful frame of mind which I had hitherto enjoyed, despondent feelings had recently taken possession of me, and I suffered from continual forebodings of misfortune.

It had been my desire to get thoroughly fitted for the Sophomore class of some New England college before returning home. Before the term closed, I was gratified to receive the assurance from our Principal that I **had** accomplished this object, and I now intended to engage **in** teaching or some other business for a year, and then **carry out** my plan with regard **to the college course ; but I had a sad** premonition **that** this would never be.

Several of the students who lived along the shores of the lake had arranged to take the night boat going north, and I joined the company. I spent the greater part of the day on which we left with Mack, and though there were many heart-aches and much hand shaking during the last hour of my stay, the parting that I had with him when the coach arrived which was to take us to the point whence the boat started was the saddest of all.

As we climed the hill from whose summit I first beheld the village and Seminary more than two years **before,** I looked back and saw them, just as I did then, clothed in the mellow light of the setting sun, and my heart sank at the thought that it was beyond doubt the last view of them I should ever enjoy.

Grief and anxious thoughts that night deprived me of sleep, and though I tried to enjoy myself with my fellow students, I succeeded but poorly ; every attempt at a smile, laugh or joke being too obviously mechanical to conceal the condition of my heart.

From time to time the boat landed, one or more of my companions bade the rest of us farewell, and so they went **until I was alone.**

CHAPTER XVII.

TWENTY-FOUR hours after leaving Corvette I got out of the stage, and, giving the driver orders to leave my baggage at a certain house further on, I set out for a walk of two miles across lots and through a piece of woods to my home. My object in so doing was, first, because the stage route did not lay by our house; second, because I was tired of riding; and third, because it was a path I had travelled hundreds of times before, and I wished to see the old familiar objects, hoping that they would revive the happy feelings that I enjoyed in my boyish days. I was not mistaken. The streamlet, now diminished to its smallest size by the dry season, still gurgled along its pebbly bottom through the forest as of old; the same gigantic elm spread its branches across it, and further on, half uprooted, the leafless, dry old hemlock was still leaning over the path, while the thrush yet warbled his familiar song. Emerging from the woods, and passing on through a meadow, I reached a corn-field, and beyond this ran the road, a few rods in front of the house. Prince, the house dog, descried me just as I entered the cornfield, and down he came with his loud **bow-wow** to show his indignation at the presumption of the stranger in thus trespassing upon private grounds. He was greatly attached to me before I went away, being then only a year old, and **I had** often **wondered** whether he would recognize **me on** my return. **I was not** long in doubt, for when about two rods distant **he stopped,** looked at me earnestly, and then, giving a sharp **bark of** delight, bounded forward and, having reached me, leaped up to lick my face. For five minutes there was neither cessation nor moderation of his expressions of joy, and the destruction of several corn hills attested the gladness of our reunion.

The recollection of my troubles had forsaken me, and not until reminded of them by my mother did I remember that **I was** not so well and happy as at the time of my depar-ture.

Prince had announced my arrival, so **that my parents** were awaiting me in the front door, and **ere** I reached it my mother met me. I could not repress a tear, especially when I discovered **her** sorrow at seeing my pale face, emaciated form, and hearing my hollow voice.

"Why, what is the matter, Frank?" she exclaimed, in tones of alarm.

"O, nothing," I replied. "I am not well just now, but I shall soon be all right again."

My father was not less pleased to see me than she, **but** like all men he had a different way of showing it. **His** anxiety, too, for my health was plainly discernible, and notwithstanding my efforts to convince them that I was not seriously ill, and that my bad appearance was owing to confinement and hard work, he was incredulous, and maintained that **there should** be something done for my cough.

I **had** not been at home a day ere **my** mother had com**menced** preparing her excellent cough and tonic syrup for me, and I confess that its use, together with my systematic course of bathing and exercise, **made a** marked improvement in my health in the course of a month. I was overwhelmed with sympathy and attention. Every old man, and woman in the vicinity, all of whom entertained the most kindly feelings towards me, had some expression of sympathy to offer, some new remedy to suggest. It was the general opinion, however, that I could never recover. **Many shook their** heads dubiously when any one ventured to assert **that I** was getting well, and now and then an aged person proclaimed that my sickness **had** all come from my devotion to " them tarnal books."

Better a thousand **times, they claimed, not to know** quite so much, and be well, than to drag out a miserable life with a great amount of "book larnin," and I was frequently alluded to as another example of a promising young man sacrificed in the morning of life on the altar of foolish **ambition.**

The Saturday following my arrival in Foreston, pursuant **to the** notice which I had given her in **my** last letter, I went **to see** Ruth. She was at the front gate awaiting me, when I arrived.

As I approached a smile lighted up her face, but it quickly passed away, and was succeeded by a deep flush and look of fear, as her eye rested on my thin, care-worn face. Ere salutations had been fully exchanged she stepped back, and regarding me with a sad and wondering expression exclaimed,

" What is the matter with you ? "

Smiling, I made the same reply that I did to the similar question of my mother.

" But your voice ! " she then said, in tremulous tones.

" Yes, I **know it is very** weak," I replied, " but it is owing to my debilitated condition. When I get stronger, it will return to its former tone. I have been at home but three days, and I begin to improve already."

" Are you sure ? " she asked, in **a tone of** eagerness.

" Yes, quite sure," I replied with a smile, yet it was not a smile springing from the fountain of a happy and contented heart, for I was not quite certain that it was a permanent improvement.

" O, I hope so," she replied, taking my hand in both her **own** and looking **up at** my face, her eyes suffused with tears.

There was something so pathetic in her tone and manner that, in my present state of weakness, I was almost incapable of restraining my emotions; but fearing that I should betray unmanly weakness, I nerved myself, laughed at her fears, and then went with her **into the house.**

" Lie down on the **sofa,**" she **said,** as **we** entered the parlor. " You must be very tired with such a long walk."

Being nearly exhausted from fatigue, I was glad to accept the invitation. I had walked the whole distance from home for the reason that our horses were engaged— it being the busy season of haying—but more especially for the reason that I had many times before taken the same walk, and I was not willing to acknowledge, even to myself, that I was not as strong as ever. I had resolved, too, that I would take as much exercise of this kind as possible, in the hope of being benefited thereby, and I thought that this journey might be of advantage to me. I had greatly over-estimated my strength, however, and it was many days before I fairly recovered from the effects of the over-exertion.

"I forgot to tell you," she said, as she drew an arm-chair up near the sofa and sat down "that your friend, Mr. Niel, is here. I think he is now out in the field with uncle."

"Mr. Niel here!" I exclaimed with surprise. "I shall be very glad——" I checked myself, for I knew that I was about to utter an untruth.

I could not say that I would be glad to see him then, even though I might have been on another occasion and under different circumstances.

I intended to visit him, but not until I had so far recovered my health that my hope and ambition were fully restored and my appearance would not alarm him. I believed that he was my friend, yet I owed him, and I could not persuade myself that, seeing me as I then was, he would not naturally conclude, as others did, that I could not recover, and in that case his seven hundred dollars were gone. I know not how it is with others, but as for myself I always have an unpleasant sensation, in the presence of a man I owe, especially the man of whom I have had to borrow money. It is a sensation at once humiliating and goading.

The feeling of course is confined to the man in humble circumstances, one whose ability to pay depends wholly, or almost wholly, upon these things—honor, health, and success in business.

I know of nothing more harassing to a proud spirited, sensitive man in the above circumstances than debt.   In the presence of his creditor, although the day of payment may still be distant, he labors under a consciousness of inferiority. **He is** sure that he **is** looked upon as **one** wanting in calculation and economy ; in short, as one devoid **of** good judgment ; otherwise he would have no necessity for borrowing **or** hiring **money.**   There **is a** feeling, **too,** even **in** health, that his chances of life, his honor and success in his undertakings are all subjects of daily consideration **with** the creditor, and are things uppermost in his mind when he meets him : and he thus lives in constant bondage to a watchful, heartless tyrant—debt.

Had I been in more prosperous circumstances, I certainly would have experienced something of the feelings I have described on meeting Mr. Niel, but at the present time, notwithstanding his repeated assurances of friendship, notwithstanding the fact that he **had** urged me to take the **money,** my feelings were unpleasant, painful **almost** beyond endurance.   I have said that **I** checked myself when **about** saying that I would be glad to see him.   **I did so,** and substituted for it the following expression :

" I would much rather have seen him at some other time."

" I am very sorry that he is here," said Ruth, almost pettishly.   " I trust that you will not feel yourself obliged to divide your time between him and myself *to-day,* although he is your friend.   You know I shall insist on monopolizing your attention on this occasion," she con-

tinued, laughing; "besides, I think you need rest.   I am
afraid that I shall make you talk too much."

"O, do not fear that," I replied; "you cannot frighten
me into the feeling that I am an invalid if you try."

"But you are, Frank, however much you may scout the
idea," she said, soberly.   "Why did you not write me that
you were so ill?"

"Because I did not believe that I was very much out of
health, nor do I yet believe that I shall not be well in a
few weeks."

"Well, I do not wish to discourage you, but you certainly look bad, and your voice indicates great weakness.   You'll be so careful, will you not?" she asked,
looking at me with the most anxious expression on her
face.

"Yes,—for your sake," I smilingly replied.

"Not only for my sake, but for your own sake, and for
the sake of all your friends.   But wouldn't you like to go
to sleep, while I go to the kitchen and assist my aunt about
dinner?" she asked.

"I would, thank you, but it seems a strange thing to do
when I have not seen you for so long a time, and have
walked so far this morning to visit you.   I thought as I
was coming that I would not have half the time during
this visit to say what I wished to say to you, even if I
talked all the while; but I am very tired, and perhaps
when I awake I can talk enough faster to make up the
time I lose while asleep."

"Well," she replied, "I only hope you will get well
rested," and then, closing the door, she left me alone.

My thoughts instantly reverted to Mr. Niel.   I was

vexed that he should be there that day; indeed, I felt that it was intrusive, for I wished to see no one but Ruth. I must confess that I exercised but little reason, for he knew not that he would meet me there, and even if he did, what right had I to be displeased? He was an old friend of the family, and had a right to visit them whenever he saw fit, and besides, he might have come on business. I am conscious now that something of my former jealousy of him must have **been** roused within me, and that I could not shake off the impression that **he** came to see Ruth. I fell asleep, however, but still he was in my mind. I dreamed that he came into the parlor, stood before the sofa, and with a triumphant, demoniacal expression on his face thus addressed me:

"So you are sick, young man, ha, ha, ha! Well, I'm glad of it. You are going to **die!** You think that you will get well, but you never, NEVER can;" and he pointed his finger at me, as he slowly pronounced the last sentence, giving to me the impression by his solemn demeanor that **he** was uttering **a** prophecy, **the** fulfillment of which had been decreed by the Invisible, Immortal. He then paused, and looked long and steadily at me, his countenance indicating an intensity of pity and contempt. Again he broke forth in derisive laughter, after which he said, as if in reply to an allusion I had made to my indebtedness to him:

"Yes, it is true you do owe me **a large** sum—a very large sum for a sick, incapable youth like yourself to pay; but what care I for that? You are going to die; the spell that you've thrown around her by your romantic, sentimental nonsense will then be broken; she will return to her reason, and seeing her true interest will marry me." He here gave a chuckle which showed the extent to which he enjoyed his anticipated triumph. Placing his hands behind him, he now began to stride up and down the parlor, with an insulting air of superiority. Finally, he stopped before me once more, and spoke again as follows:

"No, young man, if you owed me seven thousand instead of seven hundred dollars, I would have you die; yes, DIE!" he repeated, with emphasis, his small eyes flashing with fiendish, malignant hate.

"You are a Shylock!" I shouted, no longer able to control myself. "If the sum which I owe you was ducats instead of dollars, your words, like your manner and principles, would show that you are almost a perfect reproduction of that relentless, develish Jew! You are unfit to live!" and I strove to rise and rush at him, but I could not move.

Divining my object, he retreated towards the door, and opening it, backed slowly out, repeating as he did so, with the same malicious smile, his former exasperating, terrifying prophecy—

"You'll die, young man! yes, DIE!" and then quietly closing the door, left me once more alone.

I remember nothing of intervening acts, but the scene was changed. I stood at a little distance from a neat, white country church, before which were assembled quite a number of people, arrayed in their Sunday suits, apparently, with the intention of attending the services which had not yet commenced. The slow, solemn, mournful sounds of the church-bell assured me that it was tolling, and that the persons before the church had come to pay their last respects to a departed soul. Looking away in the distance, on a road running at right angles to the one on which the church was situated, I saw a hearse approaching, followed by a long procession of teams, and this, in turn, by people on foot. As I stood there, wondering who the deceased **could** be, a waggon with two men in it, strangers to me, passed, and having gone a little further, halted near a farmer sitting on the roadside near the church. The men seemed to know him, and after saluting him, one asked:

" Whose funeral is this, Mr. Saxe ? "

" **It is** Frank Styles'."

The shock thus given me broke the chain that bound me to the land of dreams, and I awoke.

Ruth was standing before me. Smiling, she said :

" I have this instant come here, and was deliberating whether I had better awaken you or let you sleep and have you dine with me bye **and bye.** Will you go out now ? " she asked.

" Yes, I will go now," I replied; " I have no desire **ever** to go to sleep again if I have to witness such horrid scenes as I have witnessed since I have been sleeping here."

" What did you dream ? " she inquired.

" I prefer not to tell you now," I said, as I accompanied her to the dining room.

The family and Mr. Niel were all there, and they greeted me with **all** the kindness I could possibly wish. Once more I had to go through the ordeal of talking about my ill health, and accepting proffered sympathy. I was beginning to get nervous and sensitive respecting this subject. My dream might have had something to do with it, but I sincerely wished that no one would mention it in future ; I had become tired of speaking of it.

Mr. Niel seemed to be in his usually friendly mood. He expressed a great deal of sympathy for me, and inquired particularly as to the nature of my illness and the length of time my cough had troubled me. Was it from a fear that I might not get well, and that he would lose the sum he had loaned me? or was it from a fear that I might get well, and that he would thereby sustain a greater loss?—that he was so particular in catechising me? These were questions that disturbed me during the whole time that I was in his presence that day.

The question respecting his fear that I would get well certainly must have been suggested by my dream, for it had never occurred to me before; and even then, I felt ashamed and guilty of meanness in harboring such a thought; but in vain I tried to banish it; in vain I tried to feel that the interest he showed in me was the natural result of his friendship, of which I had abundant proof; my horrid dream, in which he had appeared as a demon rather than as a man, still haunted me. My latest suspicion of him, too, was heightened by discovering what I believed was a gleam of satisfaction in his eye, when Mrs. Edgarton, in reply to something I said, remarked,

"I do not know, Mr. Styles, but I fear that your cough is far more serious than you imagine. You know that consumption is a very subtle and deceptive disease."

One thing pleased me. I observed Ruth closely, and never discovered the slightest indication that she gave Mr. Niel any encouragement to pay her more than passing attention. On the other hand, she rather avoided entering into conversation with him, always answering his questions in monosyllables. I even began to fear that she was rather wanting in that respect which was due him, unless she had reasons that I knew not of for wishing to keep him at a distance.

Not long after dinner she went into the parlor, and taking advantage of a pause in the conversation I soon followed her. When I sat down beside her on the sofa I said,

"I have learned from Mr. Niel's letters that he has seen you sometimes during my absence; but has he been here often?"

I noticed a slight change in the expression of her face, and detected, I thought, something of displeasure in her tones as she answered,

"Yes, quite often; I believe he has never been absent longer than six weeks at any one time."

"And does he come to see you, or your uncle?" I asked, with an air quite too serious to lead her to suppose that I was indifferent as to the nature of her answer.

"My uncle, I suppose," she replied, with a laugh which indicated that she was not quite in earnest, and then after a moment's thoughtfulness she said, "I do not like that man."

"I am very sorry," I replied; "Mr. Niel has been kind to me, and I am under great, very great obligation to him."

"How so?" she asked, with an expression of much curiosity on her face.

"Well, since it is right that you should know all about my circumstances," I replied, "I will tell you."

I then related to her in detail the way in which he at first induced me to become indebted to him, and all the subsequent transactions by which I had become his debtor to the amount of seven hundred dollars. I was puzzled as

I proceeded with my story to perceive that she changed color, and as I completed it, that her eyes beamed from excited emotions, and she seemed strangely sad. I asked for no explanation, however, presuming that she sympathized with me in my present anxiety with regard to the matter, and that it seemed quite improbable to her that I could pay so large a sum. That I was wrong, however, in my last impression was evident by the following remark :

"I see no reason why you should feel despondent respecting your circumstances if you are well, but I do wish that it was some other person to whom you are indebted than Mr. Niel."

"Will you not give me your reason for this wish?" I asked.

"I would much rather not," she answered, "for I may be greatly mistaken in my estimate of him, and, for the world, I would say nothing to awaken a prejudice in you against him after he has shown you so much kindness. His motive may have been the purest one, and until you have positive proof that it was not, he is entitled to your friendship and respect; but, for the present, I think you had better dismiss this subject entirely from your mind. When you get well, it will give you no trouble whatever, and from what you say, I infer that Mr. Niel expected to give you a long time for payment, at least all that you require. Let us talk of this no more, but tell me all about your school and the friends you have formed during your long absence. Surely you have not told me in your letters all that you have to say of them."

"No, I think not," I replied; and as the subject was one

of which I was glad to speak, I was soon so fully engaged with it that I forgot my troubles.

After we had thus talked for an hour, Ruth asked:

"But why did you decide to go **to** college? If I remember rightly, when you went away, you only thought of spending a couple of years in study, and then taking a profession."

"Yes, that is true; but my thirst for knowledge increased when I began to study, and I saw what **fields of** learning were still left for me to explore, and it seemed **to me** that the advantage **I** might gain **by so** doing would richly repay **me for** the expense and labor it would incur. Besides, **so** many of my friends and classmates have gone to college, that it is hard for me to think of being left in the background."

"Yes," she said, with an air of sad thoughtfulness, **" I can** understand your feelings and appreciate your ambition; but it seems a long time to have you absent—three years! think of it, and you will not enter for a year, which will make four."

"I know," I replied, "that it seems **a very long** period to look forward to, but it will soon glide away, and you may be assured that I will not stay away from home again so long as I have this time; I shall return at least twice every year."

"O, that will be pleasant," she said; "but have you really decided to go?"

"I had made that decision before leaving Corvette," I replied, "but fears of my health make me less determined about it now than I then was. It requires a good constitution to do all that I intended, for in order to pay a part of

The Frontier Schoolmaster.

my expenses, it would be necessary that I should teach, or
engage in some other business a portion of the year. You
know many students do this, and keep up with their classes
during the time they are thus absent, but none but the
strong can endure such extra exertion."

"Well, then, when there are such obstacles in the way
of your gratifying your ambition, why not change your
plans and do what you proposed before you went away?
Have you forgotten that you said you would consider my
proposition to engage in teaching and allow me to be your
assistant?"

"No, I have not forgotten it," I replied; "on the contrary I have thought much about it, and that is just what
I design should I take a college course. Much as I dislike
the vocation of teaching, I think the pleasure of having you
for an assistant would be a sufficient inducement for me to
follow it. As I hardly consider myself educated now,
should I go no further with my studies, I think I should
take the time required in college to fit myself for some profession."

"Well," she said, "I do not wish to influence you to do
anything of which you will repent, but with your present
education, and ability to impart knowledge, I think many
communities would be glad to obtain your services as
teacher, now, at a good salary."

"Possibly," I said; "but then in every community there
are those who always measure a man's ability by the diploma
that he carries; and, consequently, a man who has none is
at once set down as an ignoramus. A teacher, above all
others, is estimated by this unreliable criterion, and so with
my present acquirements, I should feel a continual sense of

humiliation were I to take charge of a high school or an academy, and I would teach no other.

"You forget," she said, "that many of those who are the most successful and popular teachers are men who have never received a collegiate course, but have risen to their present position, like those in other business, by industry, and by showing their fitness for the pursuit which they are following. And on the other hand, those who have diplomas from college often make signal failures in attempting to teach."

"Well," I replied, "**I know** not what I shall do as yet. My first work will be to try to recover my health; if I succeed there will be sufficient time for deciding as to business."

"Do not speak, Frank, as if there were any doubt about your recovery. I know that these things rest with the Lord, but I am sure He will spare you, and give you much work to do yet in the world."

"Are you quite sure of that?" I asked, almost feeling that she was endowed with prophetic vision.

"Yes, quite sure," she replied.

"I know you say this to encourage me, Ruth, and I confess that I do receive encouragement from it; but as it is now getting late I must return home."

"You certainly will not think of walking home," she said.

"No, I cannot," I replied, "although I had no doubt that I should do so when I left home this morning. I shall ask Mr. Niel to take me, and remain with me over Sunday."

We now repaired to the sitting room where we found him *tête-à-tête* with Miss Edgarton, Ruth's maiden aunt.

It was unnecessary to ask him to grant me the favor that I desired, for he kindly placed himself and carriage at my disposal as soon as I had mentioned the thought of returning home. When I invited him to remain over night and spend the Sabbath with me, although he assented at once, I noticed a slight suffusion of the face, as if it were not the most agreeable thing for him to do. He gave no further evidence of disappointment, however, and during our ride he was as pleasant and affable as I had ever seen him.

He talked encouragingly to me of my prospects, said he had no doubt that I would soon be in good health, and even tried to persuade me to enter college that year, offering me money to defray my expenses.

Surely, man never gave stronger evidence of friendship for another than did he for me. But the seeds of distrust and suspicion had been received into my mind. I thought that Ruth, with her far-sightedness and good sense, would never have expressed a dislike for him, had she not had some good reason for so doing; and then, too, I could not shake off the impression my dream had made on my mind, reason and argue to myself as I would. I tried to remember and feel that it was only a dream, and the most natural one that could have engaged my mind, when I had fallen asleep thinking of my sickness, Mr. Niel and the large debt I owed him; still he was ever before me, just as he appeared uttering the words: "If you owed me seven thousand instead of seven hundred dollars, I would have you die; yes, DIE!" Even his present offer of money I regarded as evidence of duplicity, for it seemed highly improbable that he could urge me to go to college in a few weeks, and confine myself to study, unless it was from a hope that I would not get well. But then, the remark of Ruth, "His motive may have been the purest one, and until you have positive proof that it was not, he is entitled to your friendship and respect," came to my mind, and made me resolve that I would strive never to think of him other than a as a friend, until he had fully shown himself unworthy of the name.

I would not, however, for a moment think of accepting further aid from him at present. Had I been well, I would have refused it, for it seemed folly for me to plunge myself more deeply in debt, without making an effort to pay a portion of my expenses by my own industry. I argued that if my health would not permit me to do something by which I could raise money, I certainly could not study; hence, my plans must be frustrated.

Mr. Niel and I attended divine service on the Sabbath at Foreston, and he remained with me until the afternoon of Monday, parting with me, as usual, with the warmest expressions of friendship, and promising to visit me again at no distant day.

CHAPTER XVIII.

I SHALL give my next year's history briefly. It was the saddest of my life. The fall and winter succeeding my return from Corvette had come and gone, and my health was no better. For some weeks it had improved, but, with characteristic impatience, I grew uneasy, chafed at the confinement, and resolved that I would redouble my exercise in order to hasten recovery. I engaged in most severe manual labor, and persevered in it in the foolish belief that I could become strong and hardy; in short, not only acquire my former health, but build up a constitution that would enable me to endure hard mental labor.

In former years, having always gained strength rapidly on returning home from school and engaging in farm labor, I believed that I might again effect the same result in like manner, never reflecting in my inexperience on the difference in my physical condition. Reading of the wonderful development of strength and muscle in Windship and others by gymnastics, I, too, was to become like them, and with this object in view I constructed a gymnasium, and without any experienced counsellor to direct me, began a course of exercise which was enough to destroy the constitution of the most robust, and the recollection of which now appalls me. My cough grew better, and finally ceased, but, in my blind determination to recover, I **had** so overstepped the bounds of prudence that I had contracted other diseases, and suffered greatly from nervous debility.

During all these months I had fretted and bemoaned **my** circumstances, and avoided society until I had become a misanthrope. I had visited Ruth from time to time, but even when in her society, I was so sad, so prone to talk of myself and my misfortunes, that I have since often wondered that she did not dismiss me with disgust. Not she. Never was there a more striking example of womanly constancy and devotion. Her cheerfulness and meekness were a tacit rebuke to me, complaining as I always was at the decrees of Fate. Convinced, almost beyond a doubt, that I never could enjoy good health, even in a comparative degree, and, consequently, never realize the fruition of my hopes, I offered to release her from her engagement to me, but the offer was magnanimously rejected. Such proof of her affection for me, while it increased my love and admiration for her, embittered the thought that I could never do for her what my youthful fancy had pictured, and, perhaps, never marry her.

In my despondency, I found no pleasure in writing to the friends that I had formed in Corvette; indeed, the act was always fraught with so many unpleasant feelings, that I could never write a cheerful letter, and so, one by one, my correspondents were dropped until I had none. I wrote to Mack three times and received two letters in return, but my last one he never answered, and as he left Corvette in the following July, I knew not where to address him.

The first note of $200 which I gave to Mr. Niel came due in the spring, and as I had no way of meeting it, my troubles were not a little increased. He had visited me once since the time I have mentioned above, and knew well the anxiety that I felt regarding my inability to pay him, and he strove to relieve me of it as usual by assuring me that he was in no haste, and reminding me of the expressions he had used at the time I hired it.

I saw nothing of him again for a long time. I learned that he visited the Edgartons once in the spring, and then his visits to them suddenly ceased, the reason for which was concealed from me several months.

In early summer, at a time when I was bereft of hope my health, unaccountably to me, began to improve. It might have been from the rest that I was taking, for I had been obliged to desist from labor, and in my despair I even neglected to take much exercise. My recovery, however, was so rapid that I could not reasonably ascribe it all to rest. It seemed then, and still seems, that nothing but the direct interposition of Providence in my behalf could have effected so surprising a change in such a short time. I felt that He had afflicted me, thwarted my plans, for a wise and good purpose. I was self-willed, headstrong, and far too forgetful of the source whence my blessings came, and now that I had been taught my weakness and utter dependence on Him, I was permitted to recover, or so far recover as to perform the work He had assigned me.

As I grew strong, by degrees I began to do a little work, but I commenced it with great caution, lest I should again over-exert myself and blast all my hopes. In a few weeks from the time that I began to grow better, I ventured to walk to Mr. Edgarton's. Ruth was both astonished and delighted to see me under such improved circumstances, and fearful that the walk would be too long for me she insisted, when I returned, on taking me nearly home with her uncle's carriage.

In August, my strength and ambition were so far restored that I began to think of seeking some employment, and with this object I wrote to the committee of a school in Bloomingdale in Vermont, some twenty miles distant from Foreston.

The school was what is known in this section as a Select School, in which the teacher was obliged to depend on the tuition of the scholars for his salary, being granted the use of the school room free of rent. Should his fall school be so managed as to meet the approval of the school committee of the locality, if he desired, he would be engaged at a stated salary to teach the more advanced pupils of the district school during the winter, a female teacher being employed for the lower grade. In the spring, by obtaining the right of occupancy, he could use the schoolroom again for a Select School. The village consisted of about fifteen hundred inhabitants, and their school had been conducted on the above plan for nearly a dozen years.

It was my desire to remain in the school during the three terms, and in applying for it I had mentioned this fact to the committee. They replied in due season, saying that my references were satisfactory, and in case I went through

R

the fall term "all right," there would be nothing in the way of my engagement for the winter.

My decision was at once made, although my nervous system was so shattered that I feared the result of the labor and confinement; but as it was the only way I saw of reducing the amount of my indebtedness to Niel, I could by no means think of declining the offer of the school. Accordingly, I replied to the letter, notifying the committee that I would commence my labor on the first Monday of September following.

A few days subsequently, I sent him for distribution fifty circulars, which read as follows:

SELECT SCHOOL.

The Fall Term of Bloomingdale Select School will commence on Monday, September, 1859.

FRANK STYLES, Principal.

TUITION:

Common English, per term of eleven weeks,	. . .	$3 00
Higher,	. . . .	3 50
Classics,	. . . .	4 00
French (extra)	. . . .	1 00

No pupils received for less than half a term, and tuition must be paid positively one half at the beginning, and the other half at the end of the term.

For further particulars apply to the Principal, or to

G. V. SMALLET, Secretary.

CHAPTER XIX.

I WENT to Bloomingdale **on the** Saturday preceding **the**
week in which my **school was to open.** It was a lively
little village, composed chiefly of wooden dwellings painted
white, containing **one** church, **four or five** stores and two
hotels.

At one of the latter **I took** up my quarters **until I** could
secure board in a private family, **knowing that my** small
salary would necessitate the strictest economy and thus
prevent my boarding at **a hotel.** After dinner I visited the
academy, a two story building situated nearly **in** the center
of the village on the main street, and but a few yards back
from it. A carpenter **and** wheelwright's shop was **the**
nearest building on the right, **while a** small dry goods store
occupied **a** place on the left—the spaces between the academy
and these two buildings being filled with piles of lumber
and dry goods boxes. The academy had once been painted
white, but it now gave little evidence **of it,** and several

broken panes of glass and its general appearance of rough
usage and want of care showed at once its character—it
was unmistakably a schoolhouse.

Climbing dilapidated steps and finding the door unlocked,
I went up a flight of stairs and entered my schoolroom. It
contained the furniture usually found in these institutions
—several rows of rough desks, a blackboard, a cracked and
rusty stove, a chair and table. It was well lighted, but two
of the windows were without curtains, and the other four
were partly shaded by pieces of dirty, torn, unbleached
muslin.

Until this moment, I had not thought of the necessity
of putting the room in readiness, not doubting that it would
be in proper condition when I arrived, but, on glancing
around and seeing the dirty state of the floor and walls, I
immediately started out in quest of some one to set things
in order. Fortunately, I found a Frenchman and his wife
who undertook the work of cleaning, and I then purchased
several yards of cloth for curtains, and engaged another
person to make and put them up.

The next person to be engaged was a glazier, and this
being done, I sought Mr. Smallet, chairman of the committee, to ascertain whether I was to bear this expense, or
whether it was to be paid by the community; also to
learn what he knew respecting the number of pupils that I
was likely to have. He was a wide-awake, good-natured,
shrewd yankee, and after greeting me cordially, and expressing many wishes for my success, answered my first
question promptly as follows :

"The cleaning of the house you will have to pay for;
the glass and setting will be at our expense, but you will

have to pay for what is broken while you teach. As **for**
the curtains, they will probably be damaged a good deal
this term, and I guess we'll divide the expense **of** those
between us."

I **was** satisfied, and then inquired **as to my** prospects for
pupils.

"O, you'll have scholars enough," **said** he; "you'll probably have to get an assistant. Quite a number outside of
the place **have** been around here inquiring **for** boarding
places, and all the village scholars are going. I'll bet you'll
have from **seventy-five to a** hundred. I'll tell **you,** Mr.
Styles, we've heard **of** you, **and we've got** an **idea** that
you're going to teach us a good school, **and** so folks are
going to send. The school last year **didn't** amount to much.
We had **a** woman teacher, and the scholars did just as **they**
pleased; and two years ago we had **a** young fellow **who**
hadn't much ambition, and the folks got rather sick of **him,**
and began **to** send their boys and girls off to school; **but**
this fall I don't know **of one in** the village that's **going
away.** You needn't **fear but** what you'll have **scholars
enough."**

Greatly encouraged **by his** remarks, **I next** inquired for
a boarding place for **myself,** when **he offered** to take me
himself at $2.**50 per** week. He had **a** pleasant house at
no great distance from the academy, **a** small family, and,
finding that he could give me a commodious neatly furnished **upper** room containing a stove, **I** accepted his offer
and at **once** had my luggage transported hither.

I attended divine service on the Sabbath in the Methodist
church, and though **I** went in the morning and afternoon,
and attended prayer meeting in the evening, the day seemed
long; **and I** felt very lonely.

On Monday, at nine o'clock, I was seated in my school-room, now rendered more respectable by the work which had been done in it recently, forgetful of all past troubles in the interest I felt in observing my pupils, and in my anxiety respecting my success in teaching.

There were now twenty-five pupils present, and before noon the number had increased to thirty-five, ranging in age from ten to twenty-two, and possessing, of course, a variety of temperaments, habits and manners. There were uncouth, mischievous boys, indigent but industrious young men, boys of indolent habits, boys of impetuous tempers, fashionable and wayward girls, amiable girls, numbers given to study, and others to folly. All as I suppose having been sent hither for the same purpose—to profit by my example, and to be led up the Hill of Learning.

After organizing my classes I found that besides the common English branches I had two classes in Algebra, one in Natural Philosophy, one in French, and another in Latin. Giving them their lessons for the succeeding day, I addressed them for sometime, dwelling on the importance of punctuality, industry and obedience, and then dismissed them for the day.

I laid down no special rules for their observance save that which required them to be present at the calling of the roll in the morning and afternoon, and another which demanded their presence always at recitation, unless excused. Other regulations were made from time to time, as the well-being of the school demanded.

In the course of a week the number of my pupils had increased to fifty, so that, in order to devote to all an appropriate share of attention, I spent seven hours daily in the schoolroom. Like all inexperienced teachers I fatigued myself by doing far more work than was necessary, often giving assistance promptly to a lazy pupil when he called for it, thus depriving others of time which was really their due, and at the same time encouraging the pupil himself in habits of indolence and dependence. A suggestion is nearly always more valuable than full explanation, for the pupil is then obliged to exercise his own reasoning faculties and cultivate the habit of self-reliance.

Another habit, also, which I indulged, gave me much useless physical exertion, and in consequence increased the exhaustion which I usually felt at nightfall. In former years I had frequently heard severe criticisms by people, of course not the most intelligent, on teachers, because they occupied chairs instead of constantly moving about during their labors in the schoolroom. They were denounced as unambitious, inactive; in short, lazy. Dreading such an imputation, and wishing to do everything included in the line of duty, I conceived it necessary to be always on the move—on the *qui vive*, I might say, like a well drilled hotel servant, to see if somebody did not want something, wish for some assistance, that I could give.

The amount of mental labor one can endure naturally decreases as the physical system becomes fatigued, yet I overlooked this important fact in pursuing the course described above. I was not only fatiguing myself unnecessarily by remaining so much on my feet, but, in rendering assistance to pupils at their seats, opportunity was often given to mischievous ones behind me to indulge in pranks that they would have found it impossible to perform had I kept my seat, and thus had the whole school before me.

It is hardly ever necessary for a teacher to turn his back to his pupils, **except**, perhaps, when he is employed at the black-board; **and** during the rest of the time he can easily keep his pupils in view, when he is in a sitting posture, and thus be enabled to preserve better order and to perform his other labors as well, and with far less fatigue. In requiring his pupils to come to him, also, instead of going to **them** when they require assistance, he diminishes their desire to come frequently, and by prohibiting them ever to **come unless it is necessary**, and then never at a moment when he is engaged with a recitation, he maintains far better discipline, increases the dignity of his position and saves himself much labor and many annoyances.

A teacher who has tact in organizing classes, and has learned how to economize time, can far more easily manage a school of sixty or seventy pupils than one of little or no experience can a school of thirty.

These are things that I knew but little about at the time of which I write, and they were learned only by experience, the knowledge of them being gradually unfolded as I found myself obliged to husband my strength, economize time, and secure more perfect discipline. Many times since those days have teachers excited my sympathy, as I have seen them with dejected, care-worn looks responding to the calls of pupils from every quarter of their schoolrooms, and increasing their labors two-fold from want of proper discipline and organization of classes.

Things went on quite smoothly, but not to my entire satisfaction, for two or three weeks. There were many instances of tardiness and a far greater number of absences than were compatible with the interests of the school. Two or three boys and the same number of girls living in the village, and about an equal number from a distance, were invariably late, often absent from their classes, and, by their general bad deportment and lack of interest in their studies, exerted a baneful influence on the other pupils, and subjected me to much trouble.

I had spoken publicly **of these** derelictions of duty, mildly at first, and then more sharply, alluding to the delinquents in terms of sarcasm which affected all, and even wrought a reform in one or two; but the others soon forgot it and went **on as** before. I next **had** private conferences with them, and this seemed to have **a** salutary effect; but the reforms thus effected were **not** permanent, and it was evident that more stringent measures must be tried.

One of the most provoking of these pupils was a girl of about sixteen named **Mattie** Whittimore. She was **the** eldest daughter **of a** thrifty merchant in the place, and being good-looking, and quite a successful performer on the piano, she had been indulged and flattered until she despised parental authority as she always **had that of** her teachers. Indeed, **I imagined from what I heard and saw of** her, that she had been permitted by her teachers, from fear of offending her or her parents, to do whatever she pleased. She was always neatly attired, possessed faultless white hands, bedecked with rings which she was fond of displaying, and her only object in life seemed to be to try to captivate by her charming face and bewitching manners.

She, like all others of her class, had several satellites among the poorer girls of her acquaintance and admirers among the young snobs of the village. Though a poor scholar she never seemed ashamed of her ignorance, or dis-

played any ambition to become wiser; often sitting with a
dreamy listlesss air, casting occasional smiles across the
schoolroom at some love-sick youth, or, what was more
usual, spending an hour in close conversation with Lizzie
Stearns, her confidential friend, who occupied the seat with
her.   The latter was the daughter of an industrious mechanic
in the village, and she was more amiable and a much better
scholar than her friend, but Miss Whittimore had so ingratiated herself with her, and attained such an ascendancy
over her, that I verily believe she would have consented to
martyrdom, had she been told by Miss Whittimore to do so.

Mattie was always late, late in the morning, late in the
afternoon, late at her classes, and frequently absent from
them.   I entreated, exhorted, and expostulated to no purpose; she either laughed, gave some flimsy excuse, or
assumed an air of independence, often of indignation, that
I should presume to call her to an account.   One thing was
certain, she must either be made to comply with the rules,
or else I could not with any consistency or justice require
the other pupils to do so, in which case my authority was
destroyed.

One day, when hearing my class in Natural Philosophy,
Mattie, who always persisted in studying the higher branches,
although very ignorant of the common ones, annoyed me
greatly by her inattention and continual whispering to those
near her.   Desiring strict attention during recitation, and
an entire avoidance of whispering, I had positively forbidden
any communication between the pupils while in class.

For some little time I pretended not to notice her, but
this only encouraged her to more open boldness in her
transgression of the rule.   At length, exasperated beyond

forbearance, when she had spoken in a loud whisper to the
girl on her right, and at the same time indulged in one of
her characteristic giggles, I stopped abruptly in the course
of some explanation I was giving, looked gravely at her
and exclaimed,

"I beg your pardon, Miss Whittimore."

Astonished, she looked at me for a moment with a bewildered expression of countenance, and then glanced inquiringly at the faces of the other members of the class, as
if to learn the cause of this strange procedure; but they,
too, were surprised, and regarded me with awe and silence.
Finding that my eyes were still intently fixed on her, as if
awaiting a reply, she blushed deeply and confusedly asked,

"What did you say?"

"I beg your pardon," I replied; "you spoke to me, I
believe."

At first she seemed more bewildered than ever, but then,
as my object in thus addressing her broke upon her mind,
her face became scarlet from mortified pride and anger.
She replied in a haughty, emphatic tone,

"*No, I didn't* speak to you."

"Ah, indeed! I beg your pardon," I said, with an air of
great politeness; "but you were speaking, were you not?"

"*Yes, I was,*" she answered, in a defiant and provokingly
insolent tone.

"Yes, I thought so," I replied; "and since you were
not speaking to me, I beg your pardon for interrupting
you. A young lady of your refinement and pretensions
surely would not be rude enough to transgress our rules
by whispering in class, unless it were from a good motive.
No doubt you were giving Miss Stearns some important

information, which I omitted in the explanation I had just given. As you are so familiar with natural philosophy that you have no need of paying attention during recitation, to-morrow, if you have no objection, I will take a seat in class, while you give us a short discourse on the principles of statics and dynamics."

As she was conscious that she had not answered a single question of her philosophy lesson that day, and also that this was a pretty fair sample of her lessons during the term thus far, she had too much sense not to perceive the sarcasm and irony embodied in my remarks. The older pupils by this time were smiling perceptibly, and many of them, with whom she was not a favorite, heartily enjoyed her confusion. After the above address to her, I proceeded with the lesson, observing her actions without her being aware of it.

For a few moments she sat silently regarding me with an air of ineffable scorn; and then she indulged in a derisive smile, and after that, catching the eye of Miss Stearns, she fell into a fit of nervous giggling, which was followed by two or three whispers to her nearest classmates. I paid no attention to her until she leaned forward to speak to one more distant, when I said,

"You are excused from class, Miss Whittimore; you will please take your seat."

She instantly obeyed, pressing her handkerchief to her mouth, as she did so, to repress the laughter with which she seemed convulsed. I knew that it was either an hysterical laugh, caused by her intense confusion and anger, or an effort to show her utter disregard and contempt for myself. When seated, after resting her head for a short time on the desk before her, continually laughing, she looked up and began to edify the pupils by sundry grimaces at myself, when she fancied that I was not observing her; now and then throwing a kiss towards me. Becoming tired of this, she once more began to whisper to different pupils, sometimes across two or more desks. One of her friends being at too great a distance to be communicated with in this manner, she obviated the difficulty by writing on a slate, and then handing it to a young girl to be passed along. In this, too, she was treating me with disrespect, as I had strictly forbidden this method of communication, having observed that the pupils were strongly addicted to it.

"Mary, you will please bring that slate to me," I said, as I saw her take it from Miss Whittimore.

As she was about to obey, the latter sprang, snatched it from her, and then quickly erased the writing on it; the sneer on her face at the same time changing to an expression of shame and alarm.

"Miss Whittimore," I said, "your conduct is such that it would not for a moment be tolerated in a well-conducted school, and I have endured it altogether too long. You will please take your books and go home. If after the expiration of a week you decide that you can observe the regulations in a manner becoming a lady, you can return."

"Thank you, Mr. Styles," she replied, with mock courtesy, "I don't think I shall return;" and she began to collect her books preparatory to her departure.

I checked the angry reply that rose to my lips and went on with my work. Profound quiet reigned in the schoolroom during the remainder of the afternoon, the pupils evidently revolving in their minds the audacity I had displayed in suspending Miss Whittimore, and wondering what would be the result.

At the tea-table that evening, Mr. Smallet, having heard in the village of the incident, alluded to it, and expressed much fear that the course I had taken would operate to my detriment, as the Whittimores would be highly indignant, and would, no doubt, prejudice others against me.

"I am very sorry to learn, Mr. Smallet," I replied, "that the citizens of your village have so little regard for the true interests of their children that they are ready to encourage them in acts of rebellion against their teacher. Such people surely can have no correct ideas of proper school management."

"Well," he said, "you know how these things are. Half the folks now days let their children do just as they please at home, and they expect teachers to do the same thing in the schoolroom, and if they don't, why thar's a row at once. There aint any reasonable person but what'll think you did just right in this affair, but, the thing of it is, thar won't many of 'em dare say so. Whittimore is a pretty popular man here, and a good many owe him, and his wife's a very smart feeling woman, one of these women that's always talking, and she'll probably be blatin round town now that the school aint good for anything. But still, you'll have some friends. There was a man talking with me about it this afternoon, and he said he was darned glad of it, but he wouldn't like to have Whittimore know that he said so, because they are good friends."

At this moment one of Mr. Smallet's children came in and presented me a letter. I broke the seal, and read as follows:

"MR. STYLES,

"SIR, — **My** daughter Mattie came home **this** afternoon and said you had expelled her. I would like you to understand **that our** teachers that we have had here before have never treated our daughter in this manner, and I think you'll find that the people, generally, here won't uphold you if you undertake to be so smart and strict.

"**We** would have sent Mattie off to a good school this fall, but Mr. Whittimore said that he presumed you **were a** poor young man, and he thought it might be an act of kindness and charity in us to send **Mattie** to school to you, and, besides, it would give your school a reputation.

"We thought, too, that perhaps you could teach **a** good school, but finding that you cannot, we shall send Mattie away where she can learn.

"Mr. Whittimore will **pay** you her tuition if you **will** call at the store to-morrow.

"**MRS. C. A.** WHITTIMORE."

If I had been disgusted with the impression Mr. **Smallet had** given me **of** public opinion in Bloomingdale respecting schools, and the rights of teachers, I certainly felt profound contempt **for it** when I **read** the unique **epistle of** this ignorant woman. I **was** astonished that an **act** of school discipline should be **so soon known and** discussed by the entire community; especially, that the punishment of insubordination in a pupil should be regarded as such an act of impropriety on the part of the teacher, that fears were entertained that it would interfere with his success,—perhaps break up his school. It was evident that they **had** not very recently, **at least,** had proper discipline in **their** school, otherwise my action in this case would not have

excited so much comment. I could easily fancy that former teachers, fearful of affronting their patrons and of losing
a portion of the miserable pittance for which they were
toiling, had permitted Miss Whittimore and kindred spirits
to indulge their caprices *ad libitum ;* and thus to de-
moralize the whole school. Perhaps they commenced their
work like myself, with high hopes and a determination to
enforce rules and maintain good discipline, but had been
compelled by public sentiment to retreat from their position,
and had dragged through the remaining months discouraged,
harassed, and longing for their engagement to expire.   It
might be thus with myself.   Why not ?   I was in delicate
health, in debt, and could less afford to lose my situation
than they could.   Would it not be more prudent for me to
pay less regard to discipline, to humor the caprices of my
pupils, flatter and pet those inclined to be indolent and
disorderly, rather than to frown at their habits and oppose
their inclinations ?   Would they not esteem me more, and
secure for me a *cosier niche* in the esteem of their
parents ?

   I pondered these questions, but my nature revolted at the
thought of becoming a sycophant and a hypocrite for the
purpose of holding my situation, and gaining the favor of
persons whose judgment was as weak as their friendship
was unstable.

   I knew that I was right ; that my position, however much
it had been degraded by unwise management, and uneducated public opinion, was a noble and responsible one, and
rather than lower it still more, and do violence to my
judgment, I would even beg for a livelihood.   With this
determination, I went to my room and wrote the following
reply to the indignant mother's epistle :

"MRS. WHITTIMORE,

MADAM,—You complain that former teachers have never treated your daughter as I have. The fact is quite evident; had they done so, she would entertain quite different ideas respecting her duty, and the rights of teachers, from what she now does, and I think her education, also, would have been greatly in excess of what it now is. As to the question of being upheld by the "people here" in my efforts to maintain order, and command the respect of my pupils, I am not disposed to consider it, being determined to do that which my conscience and judgment shall dictate, regardless of the opinions of the "people."

Your husband is quite correct in his supposition that I am "a poor young man," but if he was induced to send to my school as an act of "kindness and charity" to me, he will do me a favor by withdrawing his patronage, as I accept no pupils on such terms. I offer more than an equivalent in the instruction which I impart to my pupils for the small amount of money I receive, hence, I could, with more reason than you display, assume that I am instructing them as an act of kindness and charity to their parents.

When I decided to teach, I knew well that, in the present state of society, like all teachers, I would be obliged to rely on the fickle, undisciplined minds of youth and children for my reputation, hence, your assertion that I cannot teach a good school does not astonish me. Were it a question, however, whether I am or am not able to do so, to be decided by any tribunal, I have pupils in my school whose testimony I would prefer to have recorded—pupils advanced in their studies who have neither annoyed me by their

s

indolence, or **provoked me** to expel them by their disorderly conduct and **insolence.**

Hoping that you may find a good school elsewhere for **your** daughter, and feeling assured that, if you do, there **will be a** decided improvement in her **habits and** manners if **she** remains in it,

I remain,

Your obedient servant,

Frank Styles.

This letter **I** sent to Mrs. Whittimore as soon as it was finished.   I heard nothing more directly from her, but was informed that she assured her guests at a tea party she gave **a few days afterward,** that they had an impudent upstart for a teacher, and expressed a hope that the committee would **not be** simple enough to engage him for the winter. Mattie **was sent away to a boarding school, but** returned after an **absence of six weeks on the** plea of ill-health ; but it leaked out, subsequently, that **she had been sent home on** account of her flirtations and disinclination to study.

Her suspension **from** my school, although it gave rise **to** some disaffection outside, had **a** good effect on the pupils. **Her** intimate friends affected **displeasure, and** displayed it **as far as they** thought prudent by scornful looks and short **answers, but they were** more studious and prompt **in** the **performance of** duties.   The next day, Mrs. Stearns, the **mother of** Lizzie, called on me, asking me to see that her **daughter was** diligent in study and obedient to all rules, at **the same** time expressing **her** approval of my course with **Miss** Whittimore.   She said she felt pleased to know that Lizzie **was deprived of** her society, as her influence on her **had been anything but good;** instilling **into** her mind, as she had, the most silly notions with regard to dress, and the occupation and ambition of ladies.

I felt encouraged by her remarks and thanked her kindly, pleased to know that all the "people here" were not as devoid of good sense and reason as was Mrs. Whittimore.

It was impossible, however, to secure the prompt and steady attendance that I desired. Three, four or more pupils were either tardy **or** absent **very** frequently, and then they walked into school **with the most** independent air, depositing on my table notes like the following:

"Mr. Styles,—Please excuse —— **for being** tardy (or absent) yesterday."

Including those which asked me to excuse pupils from recitations or from rhetorical exercises, at the end of the term I had received seventy-five notes, and probably seventy of these represented so many acts of foolish parental indulgence, being written simply because the children had requested **it,** without a thought that by thus shielding them from discipline they were encouraging them in **habits** of negligence, idleness and deception, besides **allowing them** to miss many important lessons. This pernicious custom of parents, I have found in greater or less degree in every school that I have ever taught; **and so** far from being abandoned it still is practiced to a great extent in all schools; becoming more common, in proportion as **the** youthful generation receives indulgences that were unknown in former decades. Mistaken parent, you little know to how many weeks or months of time all these absences amount during the period that your son or daughter is **at** school. You little know what disappointment and trouble your indulgence to your child may cause the teacher who has charge of his mental training. Often when a boy is behind his class, and is only brought up with it by the earnest efforts and extra labor of the teacher, he is permitted to remain at home on the most flimsy pretext, one, two or more days; or perhaps go on a visit to an uncle for a week. When he returns he is again behind his class; knowing nothing of the principles which his class-mates have gone over during his absence, he can go on with them only by giving much more than his usual time to study—a thing few boys are inclined to do—and by the teacher's devoting extra time to his assistance. In case the teacher is unable to do this, the boy must enter the next lower class, if there is one, or else strive to grasp the lessons with which his class is now engaged. In the latter event, his interest is sure to fail; he becomes discouraged, learns little or nothing, and is a continual hindrance to his class-mates.

It was my misfortune to have two boys of this description in my school at Bloomingdale. One was the son of a conceited, dissipated lawyer, the other that of a carriage maker; and they were aged respectively twelve and thirteen. Both were wild, headstrong boys, notorious for their pranks, and for often being truants from school. The fathers had spoken to me in the beginning of the term about their boys, affirming that they were "a little mischievous," and saying, as the parents of such children frequently do, that their former teachers were incompetent, feeling no interest in their work, consequently, their boys had learned nothing, or as they expressed it nothing except *deviltry.* It was with many misgivings that I took them in charge, but as I could not well do otherwise, I attempted the arduous task. They were great chums, always together outside of school, and in school insisted on occupying the same seat together. In scholar-ship, they were about equal—poor readers, ridiculously bad spellers, knowing but little of geography and arithmetic, and every page of their writing-books—to use a borrowed simile—"looking as if they had spilled all their ink on them, and then wiped it up with a curry comb."

My junior class in arithmetic I found, on examination, was tolerably well prepared to commence at fractions with the exception of these two boys, and so, for their accommo-dation, I had the class begin at compound numbers. They promised me faithfully that they would be prompt in at-tendance, studious, and would make every effort to keep up with the class. The promise was kept by frequent admoni-tions from myself for about a week, when, to my regret, one day, both of them were absent.

Fearful of punishment, they lingered all the following morning outside the academy, discussing the propriety of coming in, until near the time for their recitation in arith-metic, when **they** entered, of course, unprepared to recite. They knew that the **other boys had informed me of** their whereabouts the **day** previous, **so it** would **be useless to** trump up any excuse for their **absence. I did** nothing ex-cept to reprimand them severely for their conduct, pointing out to them the wickedness of breaking their promise to me, and then I made them study diligently through the rest of the day, and at night, remained with them an hour, or until dark, in order to make them familiar with the lessons they had missed.

Two days after this, on account of their excessive whis-pering, I gave them separate seats. This was in the morning. At noon, as I entered my boarding house, I **noticed** the carriage-maker's boy coming from the academy with several books under his arm. On returning after dinner I was informed that he had left the school because I would not allow him to sit with Johnny. The lawyer's boy was also absent that afternoon, but returned the next morning, sulky and not disposed to study. As an excuse for his absence, he had brought me a note from his mother, saying that he had had a bad headache, but on learning that towards night of the preceding day he had gone two miles with two or three other boys to rob a widow's orchard, I concluded that his illness was not of a dangerous nature. Towards noon, I received the following note:

"MR. STYLES,

"Sammy brought his books home yesterday, and said he would not go to school any more because you will not let him sit with Johnny Sargent. He and Johnny are great friends, and I hope you will let them sit together. He says he will not whisper again. Will you please try him?

MRS. MORSE."

I tossed the letter from me in disgust, determined that I would not try them. It seemed useless to undertake to do anything with boys who could take their books home without permission, and coolly tell their parents that they were not going to school any more unless — in short, they could do just what they pleased.

And then, to have the parents humor these freaks! ask the teacher to do likewise! I felt that it was unpardonable ignorance and impudence; but unless I granted the request I would surely give offence, and be pronounced like my predecessors, "incompetent," and said to have no interest in my school.

The latter thought induced me, after my first ebullition of anger had passed **away,** to decide that I would give the **boys** another trial, although feeling assured that it would soon result in another separation. Accordingly, that evening I sent word **to Mrs. Morse that** her request was granted, and that **Sammy** might return. He did so, and, as I had anticipated, I had to spend much time with them **in** school, besides **an hour at** night again **on** two successive days, to bring them **up with** their classes.

Scarcely had I accomplished this, when Johnny informed me one night that his mother was going **on** a week's visit to her sister, who lived in a distant town, and that he was going with her. **I** was dismayed, foreseeing, as **I** did, the ground he would lose, and the amount of work and annoyance that would fall to me in consequence. I determined to thwart the plan, if possible, and for this purpose I at once called on his mother, showing her the result of taking her boy from school for so long a time, and entreating **her to let him** remain at home. In vain: Johnny **had not seen his aunt** and cousins for a long **time,** he had **anticipated** the visit, had been promised that he might go, and go **he** must. I left in disgust, but the most provoking part of the affair was yet to come. On the Monday that they were to start on the visit, **to** my extreme vexation Sammy Morse was again absent. At night, I called on his parents, and learned from Mrs. Morse that Sammy found it so lonesome **at** school without Johnny, that he had "teased" to stay **at** home till he came back, and she had acceded to his request.

Mr. Morse was present, and I pointed out to them unhesitatingly, yet respectfully, the mistake I thought they were making by such acts of over-indulgence. The father was a stout, good-natured man, drawling in speech, and cared much more about a bargain by which he could pocket fifty dollars than he did the education of his son.

He replied to my remarks as follows:

"I think it would be well enough to keep Sammy at school, but I always let mother dew just as she's a mind tew with the children; I never interfere."

Mother said,

"I'd like to have Sammy go to school, but he hates to go when Johnny aint there, and I think a boy never learns much unless he feels an interest in his school and likes to attend it. But I'm sorry that he gives you so much work outside of school hours."

"Yes," said the father, "but hang it all, the schoolmaster gits paid for it. If I could make money as easy as he can I'd never do another stroke of work."

I made but little reply, but, as I was about leaving, I said:

"I have taken great pains to instruct your boy, and if I could only keep him in school I think you would see much advancement in his studies by the end of the term; but I shall not hold myself responsible for his lack of improvement, unless he is regular in his attendance."

"Of course not," replied Mrs. Morse, "but I guess Sammy will study hard and catch up with his class, when he goes back. Wont you, Sammy, my dear?" she asked, addressing her boy, who sat before the door of the sitting-room, on the floor of the kitchen, mending his cross-gun.

"Guess so," he answered, as if only half conscious of

what his mother had said, and then thrusting his hands into his pockets for something he didn't find, he exclaimed,

"Say, ma, where's my big jack-knife I let you take t'other day?"

I made no further effort to induce them to send the boy to school, but departed, considering whether I could afford to devote an hour a day extra during the **rest** of the term to these boys; for it was evident that, when they returned, they would be so far behind their classes they would learn nothing unless I did so. I knew from what I had observed, that I had nothing to expect, in way of gratitude, from the parents for the pains I might take with them; indeed, they seemed utterly unconscious of the fact that I would be doing more than I was bound to do, should I **spend** with them three hours a day outside my customary hours for labor. I would gladly have paid twice the amount of their tuition could I have rid myself of them by sending them to some other school, but as that was impossible I must make a grace of necessity and do the best I **could.**

Ten school days had expired before they returned. During their absence, a young man had joined **the school,** and as he was much more advanced in Latin than any other one of my pupils, I was obliged to give him a separate recitation; thus confining myself to the school-room from half-past eight in the morning till five in the afternoon, allowing myself the customary hour for dinner. What should I do with these two boys? I thought of declining to receive them, but that would not do, it would offend the parents, and probably this, **with** the Whittimores' antipathy to me, would be sufficient to prevent my teaching there in **the** winter. I arranged to hear the young man's recitation at my room in the evening, and gave the two petted truants half an hour at the close of my school each day for their arithmetic lesson, allowing them to recite their other lessons with the classes. A short respite of three days from trouble on their account was granted me, when once more they relapsed into their former habits of whispering and playing, and once more I separated them. At noon I pretended to busy myself in the school-room for a few minutes, but did so for the purpose of watching them. Both collected their books and with them started, at what they regarded an opportune moment, to leave; but I had observed their movements, and when they had reached the stairs, I called them back, and enquired why they were taking their books home.

Johnny Sargent boldly informed me that unless they could sit together they should not come to school.

I commanded them to replace the books on their desks immediately, and not to remove them again on pain of severe punishment. They looked sulky, and neither of them moved to obey the order. Johnny made sundry motions with his head indicative of his displeasure, at the same time remarking something in an under tone.

"What do you say, sir?" I sternly demanded.

"I say," he replied, with an insolent air, "that I *shan't* come to school if I can't sit with Sammy."

"I say jest so 'bout Johnny," heroically spoke up his ally.

"Boys," I said with increased sternness, "are you going to put those books back?"

"I don't see what's the use of puttin' 'em back, if we aint comin' to school any more," argued the undaunted Johnny.

Forbearance had ceased to be a virtue. I took his books, laid them on a desk, and then, seizing him by the collar, walked him hurriedly to my table. I regretted that I had no whip or implement for punishment except a ruler, as this—unless it is used with great caution—may sometimes inflict more serious injury than was intended. I made him hold out his right hand and struck it once, twice. He danced and roared vociferously, though the blows were not severe, and as the ruler was descending a third time he quickly placed his left hand over the other and received the blow on the back of it. By this act, the corner of the ruler happened to hit his hand, breaking the skin slightly, and a little blood oozed from the wound. It being my intention to punish him only sufficiently to command obedience, I now said,

" Will you put those books on your desk, sir ? "

" Yes, sir, I will! I will! Oh, you've broke my hand! you've broke my hand! Oh, dear! Oh, dear! booh, oo! booh, oo ! "

" Stop your noise, sir ! " I said, as soon as I could make myself heard ; several of the pupils who were standing a little distance away, and had witnessed the scene, having broke into a hearty laugh at the ado he made about so slight a punishment.

He now stumbled along, his eyes covered with one arm, picked up his books, took them to his seat, and then went home. His companion had slipped off with his books, un-observed, at the time I was leading Johnny to the table, and was now safe at home.

I expected to hear from their outraged parents, but whatever storm might result from my action, I sincerely hoped that I had got rid of their promising sons.

I had scarcely resumed my labors in the afternoon, ere I was called to the door to meet Mrs. Sargent, elegantly attired, but pale and trembling from anger.

"I have come to see you," she commenced, "about Johnny. I think it was a shame for you to whip such a little fellow so awfully for a trifling offence."

"Indeed, Mrs. Sargent," I coolly replied, "I think his offence was not a trifling one, and his punishment was very slight."

"Why, Mr. Styles, you know better than that. The poor little fellow's hands were both as red as fire inside. Mr. Sargent and I both thought they would blister ; and then there is such a fearful wound on the back of one of them. Why, you must have struck him awful blows."

"I certainly hope his hands will not blister, Mrs. Sargent," I said, assuming an air of penitence for my rashness. "Do both of them really look very bad inside ? "

"Bad ! I think they do ; I wish you could see them once. I bathed them both in camphor for a long time."

"You astonish me, Mrs. Sargent ; I cannot see how his right hand should be so bad ; I only gave that one three blows."

"Well," she exclaimed, beginning to cool down a little, as my penitence and alarm grew more apparent, "I don't think that looks quite so bad as his left hand does ; I presume that has blistered by this time, if the camphor has not prevented it ; besides, that is the one that has the gash on the back of it."

"And you think there is a possibility that his right hand may not blister ? " I asked, with feigned anxiety.

"Yes, I don't think that will blister; of course it

wouldn't be so likely to as the other, as you only struck him three times on that."

I had preserved my gravity as long as I could, and I now burst into a **hearty laugh. The** poor woman was dumb with amazement at my impudence and heartlessness.

" I beg your pardon, madam," I said, " but I trust you will feel less alarm about **Johnny's left** hand when **I tell** you that, with the exception of **the blow which bruised the** back of **it** slightly, I never struck it at all."

Her anger was at once greatly intensified **by this last re-** mark, and, with **eyes almost** emitting fire, glancing at me, she said:

" I hope **you do** not say that for truth, Mr. Styles; **you** struck him on both hands, because Johnny said you did."

"**I** cannot help what your boy says, Mrs. Sargent," I re- plied, my own anger beginning to kindle; " I never struck him except as I have told you, and if you will walk **in,** several of the pupils here **will vouch for the truth of** my statement."

There are few things for which **a spirited woman will not sooner forgive you than she will for leading** her into a position **where she unwittingly** makes **a fool of herself.** This now was **precisely** the ground **of Mrs. Sargent's** anger towards me. **When,** instead **of feeling** contrition for what I had done to **her** boy, **as** she supposed I did, she discovered that I had induced her **to** commit an egregious blunder, and then laughed at her for it, the expression of mortification and anger on her countenance was beyond description. **In** a voice tremulous **with** rage, **she** quickly replied:

" Well, one thing **is evident** to me, Mr. Styles, you are **no** gentleman. I have never known Johnny to utter a falsehood, and I do not believe he has in this instance. Why, Mr. Sargent said, when he saw Johnny's hands, that he would have you arrested. He has always claimed that we never can have a good school here till the people are liberal enough to hire a teacher who has been through college, and he said so to-day, when Johnny came home and told us what you had done."

The latter part of this speech was delivered as she started down the stairs. I deigned no reply but returned to my duties, feeling, alike, amused at her simple ideas, and indignant at her insulting remarks. The assertion that her son was not untruthful, though very like that of all doting parents, was most absurd. I had caught him in at least twenty falsehoods during my short acquaintance with him, and his habit in this respect was so well known that when he did speak the truth it was commonly regarded as a mistake. But it was not the first time that fond mothers have felt aggrieved because teachers have distrusted the word of their darling boys. Only a short time since a lady-teacher showed me the following letter, which she had received from the mother of one of her pupils :

" Miss—— ——

Freddie says you did not like to believe that I told him he might get excused from school yesterday, and wanted he should bring a note from me the next time he wished to be excused. Now, you are the first teacher that ever doubted my boy's word, and I hope that in future, when he wants to go, you will let him. I have not brought my boy up to lie."

Fond, confiding mother. Her maternal affection was certainly worthy of admiration, but, unfortunately for the reputation of her shrewdness and judgment, her boy was said, throughout the neighborhood where he lived, to be in an abnormal condition when he was not engaged in the fabrication of some mischievous and improbable story.

Mrs. Morse **being a** great **admirer of Mrs.** Sargent, and never acting contrary to her opinion, **I** had no doubt that she would sympathize warmly **with her in** her present affliction, besides being angry at the discourtesy **I** had shown her own boy. It certainly was not pleasant **to** know that **I** had seriously offended three of the most influential ladies in the place within six weeks from **the time** I had commenced teaching, **and of course had** incurred, **to a** greater or less extent, the displeasure **of** their husbands; but as I had done it unintentionally, **in the** conscientious discharge of duty, **I was** free from self-reproach. It was the lot of all teachers; and so long **as I** followed the vocation **of** teaching, unpleasant things of this sort must be looked for.

Johnny and Sammy came to school no more during **the** term. The trouble I had with **them, like** the suspension of Miss Whittimore, was freely discussed **by the** citizens, the greater part **of** them secretly, **if not openly,** endorsing my action, and expressing **the hope that I would hold** out as I had begun, and show the disorderly boys that **I was** not to be "run over." The mark on Johnny's hand was examined by different ones, until he had been so ridiculed for the "fuss" made about such a small scratch that **he** declined to show it. **The** story **of his** mother's mistake had been repeated by Smallet, **to** whom **I** related it, and was soon over the entire village, causing **many** remarks and much sport. Women who disliked Mrs. Sargent's airs and assumptions of social superiority told the **story** with much gusto, and, as usual with such matters, in a very short time it became ridiculously embellished.   As her boy was frequently taunted with it by the other boys, she, no doubt, often heard it, and her antipathy towards me naturally became stronger.

A few days after the incident, Mrs. Sargent gave a party to several of the ladies, and Mrs. Whittimore and Mrs. Morse being present, the conversation naturally turned on their school, and this presently led to a discussion of the qualities and history of my unfortunate self.   The discussion was carried on chiefly by the trio named above, though one or two of their friends, unable to forego the pleasure of participating in scandal, gave additional interest to it by relating what "they say."

One averred that I had never attended anything but a district school, consequently, was unfit to teach.

"Yes, and I dare say," said another, "that it was a district school, too, in some little French village in Canada."

"I think he is a conceited, impudent fellow," said Mrs. Sargent.   "Don't you think so, Mrs. Morse ?"

"Yes, I do," replied that lady ; "he was over to our house one night, awhile ago, and he talked to Mr. Morse and I about Sammy just as if we didn't know anything ; he seemed real mad because we wouldn't send him to school every day."

"Now, I'd like to know," said Mrs. Whittimore, with an air of great solemnity, "if any of you ever heard of his running away from any place ?"

All answered in the negative, and looked at their interlocutor with impatient curiosity.

"Well, I don't know," she said, with an air showing anxiety to avoid exaggeration and error ; "but I was in the

store the other day and heard Mr. Whittimore and a couple
of men talking about some young man's running away from
some place for stealing a watch, and I thought, from something else that was said, that it was our school-master; but
perhaps it wasn't. I meant to have asked Mr. Whittimore
about it afterward, but I forgot it."

"I never heard of that," said Mrs. Sargent, "but I
shouldn't wonder at all if it was him. They say that he
run away from Meadville, where he was teaching, two or
three years ago, because he was going to be turned out of
school for some scrape he got into." •

"Yes, I heard about that," said another woman, "and do
any of you know what kind of a scrape it was?"

"Well," said a woman who hitherto had been an atten-
tive listener, "you know the Joneses down by our house
are related to the Crosses up in Meadville, and Malinda
Jones told my daughter, Susan, that Styles courted Jerusha
Cross and wanted to marry her, and Mrs. Cross forbid his
coming to her house; and then he tried to elope with her,
but she wasn't of age, and Mrs. Cross was going to have
him arrested, and he run away."

"O, that's it, eh?" said Mrs. Sargent. "Why, I heard
that it was for whipping a boy most to death in school."

"Perhaps," said Mrs. Morse, "it was for both things. I
know he's got an awful temper, and he'd just as soon kill
a boy as not if he got mad."

"O, how is Johnny, now, Mrs. Sargent?" asked a lady
to whom the question had been suggested by the allusion
to whipping. "I heard that the school-master gave him a
dreadful whipping."

T

"Well, his hands are not quite so bad as they were," replied that affectionate lady, "but I don't believe he'll ever get over the fright that man gave him. The poor little fellow groans and starts in his sleep. I don't believe but what Styles struck him on the head, and the poor child was so scared he never remembered it."

"Yes, and perhaps he stunned him so that he couldn't remember it," suggested the sympathizing Mrs. Morse.

"Were there not several pupils present who saw the punishment?" asked another of the party who seemed disposed to say something in my defence, inasmuch as my traducers were now talking in the most unreasonable and preposterous strain.

"Yes," replied Mrs. Morse; "but what if there was other scholars there? likely, Styles could git them to say most anything for him; and then I know that more than half the scholars in this school have always been so jealous of Johnny Sargent on account of his father's wealth and position here, that they've really abused the little fellow. Sammy has often told me this, and he said the other day that he presumed most of the scholars would be glad Johnny got whipped, jest because they were jealous of him."

I shall not attempt to detail to the reader the entire conversation of these women, by which they attempted to prove to their companions, and to the satisfaction of each other, that I possessed all the characteristics of a boor, knave and tyrant; that I was not a scholar, wholly unfit to teach, and that it would be an outrage on the community should I be engaged to teach for the winter. Having advanced to this point in their conclusions, an appeal was made to Mrs. Smallett, my boarding mistress, by **Mrs.** Whittimore, in this wise :

"Now, don't **you** think, Mrs. Smallett, that we ought to have another teacher after this term ceases ?"

"For one reason, **I** think it would be advisable," replied that lady, **who had listened silently, yet indignantly,** to all the malicious remarks that **had been made concerning me.**

"And what **is** that ?" asked Mrs. Whittimore, **her com-** panions, **all attention,** awaiting **the response.**

"So that people **may have a** fresh subject **to talk about,"** was the unkind reply.

Mrs. Whittimore blushed **and seemed** displeased, but Mrs. Sargent came to the rescue.

"Of course you couldn't **get Mrs.** Smallett to say any- thing against Styles ; she is getting two dollars and a half a week for his board. **If** Smallett don't look out, I wouldn't be **at** all surprised **if we had an** elopement here **before spring."**

Mrs. Smallett was **not easily put down,** and without no- ticing this **low** insinuation, she **said :**

"I do really think it would **be cruel to keep one** teacher in our school more than **six** months, **for in that** time his appearance, dress, habits and pedigree become stale as sub- jects for gossip, and the poor creatures **who** have become worn out with discussing them require a change. Ever since I have lived **in** Bloomingdale, every teacher has been subjected to severe criticisms by somebody."

The espousal **of my cause** by **Mrs.** Smallett, aided as she **was by** another lady, detracted somewhat from **the pleasure** of the entertainment, and when the party broke up the guests were not all on the best of terms. Whether the rebukes that my friends gave the others resulted in any good to me or my successor, I know not, but they certainly inspired me with gratitude, and with the belief that all women are not lovers of scandal and gossip.

CHAPTER XX.

AMONG other trials that I had in striving to stimulate my pupils to industry, and to elevate the character of the school, was that of inducing them to remain in their rooms during the evening and devote the time to study.

It seemed to be a thing unheard of before by them, and was regarded, especially by the boys, as a wanton aggression on their time and freedom of habits. Several of the older ones, who always improved every spare moment in studying, were pleased with the requirement, and were never seen in the street after the hour designated for the commencement of their labors. These, of course, were the ones whose lessons were always understood and recited to my satisfaction; the others who objected to confinement and study, except in the school-room, seldom or never knowing their lessons. To add to the trouble I experienced from this cause, evening parties and apple cuts became quite fashionable, which were prolonged often till a late hour at night, sometimes even till nearly day-break. The effect on the school was most disastrous. The pupils not only spent the evenings, which they should have devoted to study, in this unprofitable way, but they came into school the next morning worn out with their dissipation, unfit for study, and often fell asleep in the school-room. I tried in vain to effect a reform. I exhorted, scolded, and even threatened expulsion, to no purpose. It was almost like interfering with the long established religious rite of some heathen nation. They had always been accustomed to these enjoyments; they saw no harm in them, and their parents, instead of opposing, rather encouraged them; and under such circumstances my pupils were neither to be persuaded or coerced into abandoning them.

It is needless to say that I was severely tried, disappointed. I had evidently indulged in too high hopes of my success as a teacher. The school that I was to build up in Bloomingdale had been an ideal one. I had sought to introduce discipline to which my pupils were unused, and which my patrons neither appreciated nor took any pains to support. I had not reflected that the people required to be educated on this point as well as their children, and that this could be effected only by a work of time. I laid my grievance before Mr. Smallett, as a school manager, and his advice was of service to me, though it did not help me to carry out my designs. He said that the parents themselves were mostly uneducated, and had always indulged in those practices which I condemned in the children, consequently they looked upon this quite differently from one who had been trained according to a higher standard. Their ideas of school discipline were vague, or based upon what they had seen in their younger **days**; so different, in fact, from mine, **that** if **I** sought to enforce rules which **I** regarded as necessary in the management of the school, **I** would be looked upon as unwise and tyrannical.

He would advise me under the circumstances to do all that I could by moral suasion to induce the pupils to study during the evening, and to refrain from giving or attending parties, but not **to** resort to coercive measures.

Unpleasant **as it was to** adopt this advice, **I** did it, giving up at once the hope **of seeing** my pupils, or the majority of them, at least, making rapid progress in their studies, and of building up a school which would command the respect and patronage of the intelligent citizens of all that section.

To my chagrin, I also was obliged to abandon another scheme which I regarded as essential to the proper training of my pupils, **and which** I had already taken no **little** pains to carry out. **This was to make rhetorical and liter-**ary exercises a prominent **feature in** my school. Not **so** prominent that I could be accused, justly, **of giving** them attention to the neglect of other **things,** but **I** desire to accord to them that importance that they deserve in any school in which speaking and writing are supposed **to be** taught. I was well aware that in some schools undue attention was given to this department of instruction, as it is in far too many schools at the present time. **If** the teacher has no school board to superintend **his** labors, no programme **of** exercises he is bound to follow, **he** is at liberty to **turn the** attention of his pupils into such **a** channel as may best suit **his** tastes or convenience; hence, **we** find here and there a teacher of most superficial attainments arousing a thirst in his pupils for an education wholly ornamental in its character. Aware of the fact that parents are generally pleased to have their children appear before the public at an early age, exhibitions become the order of the school. Cæsar and Sallust are at once supplanted by charades. The eliminating of unknown quantities and the unraveling of the Bi-nomial Theorem are laid aside for the fashion and pleasure of executing tableaux. The conjugating of verbs and the memorizing of capitals readily give place to the easier and more attractive study of comedies and tragedies, and thus, term after term of valuable time is expended, until, too late, the parent finds his son or daughter deficient in that substantial knowledge requisite in fighting the battle of life.

It is not to be supposed that I question the utility of blending something of the ornamental with the practical in our public schools; I only decry that excess of the former into which some teachers are inclined to run.

I found that in my school at Bloomingdale, while many of the older boys and girls were ready at analyzing and parsing, they knew but little about applying the principles of grammar in composition. So little had they been drilled in the art of committing their thoughts to paper, that it seemed an impossible task for them to do it, and nearly every essay that I obtained was crude in style and replete with grammatical errors. As in all the schools that I ever taught, my pupils there continually beset me to excuse them from writing, saying that it was impossible for them to do it—the very reason, of course, why they should not be excused and should be made to attempt it.

The same reluctance was manifested with regard to declaiming. All averred that they could not do it—they were frightened, they couldn't learn *pieces*, they saw no benefit in it, and, consequently, really thought I should excuse them. These were objections that I had expected from the pupils, therefore, they did not surprise me; but when many of the parents brought forward the same objections, and opposed my wishes in the matter, I was not only surprised but disheartened. I argued and labored to convince them of the utility of the work, but in vain. I tried to show them that knowledge without the ability of imparting it was useless; that nothing betokened higher culture or more thorough scholarship than the power of expressing one's ideas clearly, definitely and gracefully; and that this power could be obtained by youth, under careful training, more easily than if neglected till after years. Numbers who were willing to admit that writing compositions might be well enough if a scholar had time and inclination to attend to it, could not see the benefit of committing the speeches and writings of others to memory and reciting them in public, especially when they experienced great embarrassment.

I represented to them that three great benefits resulted to the scholar who engaged in this exercise :

First, he was storing his mind with the thoughts of the wise ; second, he was enlarging his vocabulary and acquiring a more easy and graceful way of expressing his ideas ; and, lastly, he was constantly overcoming that embarrassment which made it so irksome to him to declaim, and which, if it was not overcome, would always prevent his giving utterance to his ideas in public.

The truth of what I said was seen and acknowledged by a few of my patrons, but the majority of them, if they saw it, felt too little interest to co-operate with me in making it an imperative rule, that the whole school should attend to these exercises.

Finding that I was inflexible in my purpose of not excusing them, the pupils appealed to the parents, and with few exceptions found little difficulty in persuading them to intercede in their behalf. Thus the intercession was made chiefly from inability on the part of the parents to say—no.

Wearied with their children's importunities, they became accessory to acts which not only proved detrimental to my own interests, but doubly so to the interests of the children themselves. Three or four notes were brought me in which the reasons were given for not wishing their boys and girls to participate in these exercises, and the reasons thus given were these—they could afford to send them to school but a few terms, at most; consequently, they wished them to devote their attention to subjects which would be of more benefit to them. The greater number of notes, however, simply asked me to excuse the pupils, without giving a reason therefor. At first I declined to grant these requests, but after talking with my patrons, as above related, and finding that their children still had more influence with them, in regard to this matter, than I had, I thought it advisable not to make speaking and writing a compulsory part of the curriculum.

Before arriving at this conclusion several of the pupils had absented themselves twice from school on the afternoons devoted to these exercises, and two girls had left the school altogether, informing their indulgent parents that they would attend no school where they were obliged to write and read essays. I could afford to lose no more pupils, and so to avoid further vexation and trouble I reluctantly gave up my rhetorical exercises. As I have already intimated, a few of my patrons desired their continuance, but knowing that it could only be done in the face of difficulties, they concluded, like myself, that it would be better to abandon them altogether.

Here then, as in the case of the evening parties, I was constrained, by the control which children in the place exercised over their parents, to back down from a position which I was positive was right.

It was not the last time that I have had to submit to such humiliation and injustice, nor am I the only teacher who can complain of similar usage.

Among other reasons which the citizens of Bloomingdale gave for asking me to excuse their children from this important and interesting part of school work, one good lady urged the following—she feared that the act of reciting pieces, or reading essays in public, would have a tendency to destroy the natural modesty of her daughters, replacing their shyness and timidity with unfeminine fearlessness and boldness in society. Although I failed to see that self-possession, ability to read or recite a piece with ease and dignity before an audience, was synonymous with boldness and immodesty, I did not argue the point with her. Having had no experience in rearing and training daughters, I yielded without protest to her superior age and judgment, and politely granted her request.

More than two-thirds of my term had now expired. It will be remembered that my circulars announced that

tuition must be paid at the middle of the term.   As a reminder of this important fact, a little before the expiration
of the half term, I gave to each pupil a bill of his tuition,
and then in school expressed a hope that there would be no
delay about the settlement.   But only three of my patrons
responded promptly to the call.   Four more paid within
the next three weeks, and the remainder of the amount,
notwithstanding the fact that I had spoken two or three
times in school about delinquent patrons, remained unpaid.

During the ninth week I was spoken to by several
different parties, who at this late hour discovered that they
were unable to pay money, and insisted on my taking
either the products of the farm or the shop.

In three instances, where I knew that families were very
poor—the heads of two of them being widows—I presented no bills whatever, esteeming it a pleasure to aid
their children in acquiring an education, and from three
more families I received nothing because the fathers were
too dishonest to pay.

In collecting my dues, as Messrs. Whittimore, Morse and
Sargent had not paid, I called at their respective places
of business, and, strange to say, they paid me without
demurring or offering any abuse beyond saying that the
school had amounted to nothing to them, and that it was
equivalent to making me a present of the money.   At the
office of Sargent I met one of my patrons in the person of
a rough old farmer who was known throughout that section
as Uncle Jack Jones.   He lived about a mile from the
village, and was reputed the richest man in town, yet he
was always bemoaning his poverty, and, judging from his
appearance, one might easily have mistaken him for a beg-

gar. Uncle Jack was very pugnacious, hated taxes, grew furious over public improvements, and though he sent to school and attended church like a great many others, he had a decided antipathy to school-teachers and ministers, regarding them as the drones of society whom industrious men were obliged to support.

At the time I saw him at Sargent's office, he was in trouble with his neighbor, Parkins, who he said was trying to cheat him out of a dollar and a half, which he owed him as damage done to his horse-rake, and which sum he avowed he would have if it cost him a hundred dollars. He had come to Sargent for advice, and as soon as that dignitary was at liberty he heard Uncle Jack's brief story, and then gave the required advice—the time required for the latter occupying not more than five minutes.

"Well, what's your bill?" gruffly demanded Uncle Jack, after the lawyer was done.

"Two dollars," laconically answered Sargent.

Without a word of remonstrance Uncle Jack handed out the sum, and then Sargent gave it to me, being the amount I had decided to take for his boy's tuition, for the seven weeks he attended school. I accepted it gratefully, and took my leave.

The following morning I chanced to meet four or five of my patrons at the post office, and Uncle Jack was among the number. Seeing one of the men paying me tuition, the thought of his own indebtedness was naturally suggested, and he gruffly addressed me thus:

"Well, say, schoolmaster, I s'pose I'm owin' yer something. How much is it for that girl of mine? I'd 'no whether she's larnt anything or not."

"Your bill is three dollars and a half, Mr. Jones," I said.

"Three dollars and a half!" he exclaimed in astonishment. Why I thought 'twas only two dollars for the common branches. I don't s'pose she studies anything more, does she?"

"Yes, she studies algebra and natural philosophy; the common branches are three dollars."

"Is that what you've charged all ov 'em that's sent to school?"

"Yes, sir," I replied.

He hung his head a few moments in silence, the very picture of disappointment and disgust, and then looking up, exclaimed:

"Algebra and nat'ral philosophy! What the devil is she studyin' them things for? I didn't know nothin' 'bout her studyin' 'em. What good be they goin' to dew her?"

"I suppose, Mr. Jones, you might ask the same question with regard to any branch a scholar pursues at school. What good does education do any of us?"

He seemed staggered by the question, and for a moment did not answer, querying, I presumed, in his own mind whether education was really of any benefit to us. At last, having apparently settled the thing to his own satisfaction, he said:

"Wall, I s'pose readin', writin' and 'rithmetic are well enough, but I don't want my girl to fool away any more time with them things you mentioned. You don't mean ter say that I've got ter pay you three dollars and a half though, dew yer?"

"Yes, sir," I replied.

"Wall, I s'pose if you say so I shall have ter dew it, but

I didn't think you'd come in here and try ter git rich out on us in **one** term ; p'raps you'll want ter teach here again sometime."

"Very likely," I answered, "and I hope you will **be glad to** have **me.**"

"Not if you're goin' ter rob us in **this way.** Three dollars and **a** half! Why, it's perfectly ridiculous. You'll take less than **that.**"

The bystanders were observing the colloquy **with** much interest, and, though all too proud to make the same display about so small a sum, I had no doubt that two of them, at least, were in sympathy with him ; the others, including the postmaster, were intelligent gentlemanly men, who were secretly enjoying the old fellow's trouble.

"No, Mr. Jones, I could not take less than that, and I am surprised that a man of your wealth and intelligence should consider *that* too large an amount to charge for teaching a pupil nearly three months. Come now, **own up** that you were merely joking when you claimed that **the** tuition is too high."

"Of course it's too high," he said, beginning to display more evidence of indignation. "At the rate **you** charge, you'll make **two or three** hundred dollars this **term ;** won't yer ? "

"No, not half of it," I said, "but suppose I did, would you consider that a high salary ? "

"High salary ! " he exclaimed in disgust. "When I was a young man like you, I was glad ter git ten dollars a month, and I had ter **work all** day chopping tew ter git it."

"Did it cost you **as** much **to** learn to chop as it **has me to** prepare for **teaching ?**"

This was a new thought to Uncle Jack. He ahemed, hesitated, and finally said,

"No, I don't know as it cost me so much, but if it had, I don't think I should have wanted to git it all back in three months."

"You are willing to admit, I presume, that teachers are as worthy of salaries as other professional men are, and work quite as hard to earn them?"

"Yes, I don't know but I be," he answered.

"Well now, Mr. Jones, if you have no objection, I will tell these gentlemen around us a short story."

"I don't know as I've any objections," he growled rather than spoke.

I then went on to relate an incident in which an able farmer had called on a lawyer to receive advice by which he could obtain one dollar and a half from a neighbor. "The advice," I said, "was given in five minutes; the lawyer charged two dollars, and the farmer paid him without even objecting to the fee. The next day the farmer met the teacher of his school, held a long parley with him, and almost refused to pay him three dollars and a half—the amount of the teacher's tuition for instructing his daughter for a period of eleven weeks.

"Don't you think, gentlemen," I asked, "that the farmer was rather unreasonable in his treatment of the teacher, in view of what he so cheerfully paid the lawyer?"

"Of course we do," answered one of the men, and all looked at Jones and smiled, as if conscious that he was the farmer in question.

"It is perhaps needless to tell you, gentlemen," I said, "that the farmer was Mr. Jones."

"Come, Uncle Jack," said the postmaster, laughing, "you'd better pay your tuition. Mr. Styles has got you in a tight place."

"Wall," said Uncle Jack, "I expect to pay it if he's mean enough to take it. You all know that we expect to be gouged by lawyers when we have anything to dew with 'em, and I think it's gittin' to be jest as bad with school-teachers."

The old fellow did not seem anxious to quibble more with regard to my bill, and pulling out his pocket-book and counting out the money, reluctantly handed it to me. As he did so, he cast a wistful, lingering glance at the bank notes as if it was the last time he should ever see them, and then his face assumed an expression of unutterable disgust, indicative of self-reproach that so large a sum could be extorted from him for such a useless purpose. He maintained a profound and respectful silence while he remained, listening to the remarks of the others as they discussed the subject of teaching. I said nothing myself, but, like him, respectfully listened. There was not a teacher in the number, yet they all assumed an extensive knowledge of the business, and though they expressed many erroneous ideas, they were, in my opinion, correct on one point—all agreeing that it is "one of the hardest ways" in which an individual ever sought a livelihood.

CHAPTER XXI.

It was next to the last week of my term. I was sitting alone
in my room, despondent, as I had been for some time
from overwork and the harassing anxiety that I felt
respecting my school together with the prospect before me,
when a boy entered with my mail. Glancing at the
addresses, I saw that one was from Ruth and another
from Niel. I was surprised at receiving the latter as he
had not corresponded with me since I came to Bloomingdale.

I wrote him a short time before I left home, informing
him of my intention to teach, and expressing a hope that I
might be able, at the end of the term, to pay a part of the
note which was now due, but I had heard nothing from him
since. In my present state of despondency I was prepared
to imagine some unpleasant intelligence, and dreading its
effect upon me, I held the letter in my hand some minutes

before breaking the seal; still my curiosity was so great that I could not refrain from opening it before I did the others. The contents were as follows:

"CARROLLTON, October 30th, 1859.

"FRIEND STYLES,—I am sorry to inform you that I need the full amount of that note and the interest on it, immediately. I did hope that I might give you more time, but losses in business make it impossible for me to wait. As you are **now** at work, it will probably give you no trouble to raise the money. Hoping to hear from you in a few **days**,

"I remain,

"Yours truly,

"NIEL."

Having read it, I sank into a chair, feeling in my weakness like an infant, unable either to plan or execute. Had I been well and strong, with a fair prospect of business, I have no doubt that I would have felt differently; the amount of the debt would have seemed smaller, and my ability to earn something much greater; but in my present circumstances, I could see nothing but sickness, poverty and disgrace. I felt, too, that my confidence had again been abused. This man who had advised, urged, and almost forced me to take the money, who had laughed at my fears when I spoke of the possibility of ill health's preventing my paying him, and had even assured me that **in** that case the loss would be of no consequence to him; this man who had always written me letters replete with expressions of friendship, now at a time when he knew it would be most embarrassing to me, had written me a short note, devoid of all his former assurances of fraternal feeling, and demanded the immediate payment of money. What did it mean? Had he really

met with losses which made it necessary that he should call
on me in this manner? It might be, but if so what was the
necessity of the altered tone? His former letters without
exception had all commenced "My dear Styles," but this
one was simply "Friend Styles;" and then again he had
said nothing of my former letter, nor had he enquired after
my health or my success in teaching, things he would
have been sure to do in former times. There was some
mystery about it which I could not understand.

I have informed the reader that he had not visited the
Edgartons during the summer, and I learned from Ruth
that she had not seen him since I began to teach. I could
but think that his great change towards me must in some
way be associated with the cessation of his visits to them,
and I believed that things had occurred which Ruth, for
some reason, had concealed from me.

If so, she would not refuse to tell me if I was anxious
to know, and I determined to learn what I could the next
time we should meet. But whatever might have occurred,
I was still owing him; he had requested payment, and I
was bound by all the laws of courtesy and honor to use
every possible effort to cancel the debt.

After sitting a while, thinking over the matter as described above, I opened and read Ruth's letter. It was like
all her letters—dignified yet affectionate—full of sympathy
and encouraging expressions. I had seen her but once since
I came to Bloomingdale, which was at the middle of the
term, the only time I had been home; but a letter from
her came regularly every fortnight, and did much to revive
my drooping spirits, and rouse me to greater determination
"to do or die." To my surprise, she informed me in her

present letter that Niel had lately visited them and remained all night. I then saw that his letter to me must have been written very soon after the visit she had mentioned, and the conviction was deepened that his visits were connected in some way with his manner recently towards myself.

Finding myself now in a better state, mentally, than I was when I read Niel's letter, I began to consider my chances for raising the means to pay the note which he held. I should have said notes, for one of two hundred dollars which I had given him would be due in a few months. The first one, with the interest which had been accumulating more than three years and a half, now amounted to about $250 ; the second one, with the interest up to the time when the note was due was $236. Now, that he had asked me for the first amount, I had no doubt that he would demand the second as soon as it was due, unless, perchance, I paid it before—a thing that I saw no possibility of my doing.

To pay this amount, which I then regarded as enormous, I had nothing only the small sum which would be left me from my school, and as a portion of this must be used in supplying my empty wardrobe, I could do nothing more than pay the interest on the first note. I had no disposition to ask aid of my friends in this matter, for I saw no reason why, if I was unable to pay, they should lose instead of Niel, who had prevailed on me to hire the money, and who was more able than any of the others to sustain the loss. My father was the one to whom I would naturally have looked for pecuniary assistance, but, as he had been making some unprofitable investments in the way of improvements on his farm, he was himself in debt, and only managed with difficulty to make both ends meet. Such being the case, I could not for a moment think of soliciting his assistance. My decision was made, and, accordingly, I drew up to my table and wrote the following letter :

MY DEAR MR. NIEL,—Your letter, asking for the payment of my first note of $200, is received. I regret, exceedingly, that fortune has not so changed with me during the last few months that I can astonish you by making payment according to your demand ; but it has not, hence, I shall do just what you expect, and say that I cannot pay it at present. I will pay you the interest on that note in a few days, and the principal in installments as I am able to earn the money. You have always expressed yourself as satisfied with this mode of discharging my indebtedness to you, and even when I was sick you urged me to become your debtor for a larger sum, offering the same chance again for paying you.

To tell the truth, Mr. Niel, your manner towards me for some time has surprised me. I wrote you two months ago, and you have not even acknowledged the receipt of my letter, and when I compare your last with the friendly ones you wrote me while I was in Corvette, I can but think that for some reason I do not hold the place in your estimation that I once did. Trusting, if such is the case, that you will no longer withold from me the cause,

I remain, as ever,

Your friend and servant,

FRANK STYLES.

Taking this letter to the post office, I returned, and to drive away thoughts of my embarrassments spent the evening in the sitting-room of Mr. Smallett, enjoying a sociable and pleasant chat with himself and family.

The next **day** I set to work, earnestly, to close an **engagement** with **the** school committee **for** the winter. I had applied, as **the** reader knows, for the winter school at the time I engaged **to teach in the fall, but** whether I was to have it or not depended upon two things : first, as to whether the committee, or the citizens, I might **say**, were pleased with my present school, and, second, the price **I set** on my labors. The question of my teaching in the **winter had been** pretty freely discussed in the village, and I found that there were advocates for it and others against it. There were five more candidates for the situation, and **as** they all had their friends, who were urging their respective claims, **it was** uncertain who would get it. All of them offered to teach for a smaller **salary** than I **did, but** as it was conceded by the citizens, whether with reason **or** not I never knew, that I was the best qualified of the candidates, the higher price I demanded seemed to **surprise no one.** Another thing **in** my favor was the fact **that I** was now in the school, and by their custom I was **entitled to the** preference, other **things** being equal.

An attempt on **the part of a teacher to** re-engage for another season to his employers is generally a sure means **of** learning the position that he occupies in the estimation **of** all the different members of the community. It calls forth all his friends and foes. He is astonished to find that individuals whom he has seldom met, and of whom he knows comparatively nothing, are the best pleased of his patrons, and are now among his staunchest supporters; while, on the other hand, those whom he regarded as friends are working *sub rosa* to prevent his re-engagement. He learns that men and women who have met him with smiles, invited him to tea, and in various ways led him to believe that they esteem him not less as a teacher than as a man, have held private interviews with the committee, and given it as their opinion that he should not be hired. Clara and Sophia, or Wellington, don't like the teacher, he is so particular, so strict, that they can't get along with him ; and, in deference to their wishes, the parents advise a change of instructors. They would not have it mentioned "for the world;" no, it would be unpleasant to have any one discover that they are at all hypocritical in character, nor would it do to acknowledge that they are so weak and unreasonable as to oppose the interests of a person simply to gratify the caprice of their inexperienced and wayward children; so they enjoin great secrecy on the committee, which injunction they observe until they find it necessary for their own interest to lift the curtain and reveal the power by which they are, to a greater or less extent, controlled. A person who has taught for many years, and not learned much of the foibles, the weakness, the deception of mankind, is but a poor observer ; he lacks one of the essentials of a success- ful instructor—the ability to read and understand human nature at a time when it is the most susceptible to good or evil impressions. It is this power which enables him to discern the characteristics and bent of his pupils, and thus to encourage their virtues, repress their vices, and find the most direct path to their confidence and affection.

The school committee of Bloomingdale consisted of three, Smallett, Barnes, and Gregory. Barnes was under the com- plete control of Whittimore, and so opposed to me ; Gregory was a friend of lawyer Sargent, yet he sent two children to school, claimed to be pleased with their progress, and was always friendly and courteous to myself.

For a little time after Sargent's boy had left school, Smallett feared that through that trouble Gregory might be influenced in favor of some other teacher, but Sargent was one of those men who are easily excited, who say a great many foolish things in the heat of passion, and then subside into a state of passive quietness, indifferent to everything except their daily routine of business. By the time the term had closed he had so far forgotten his boy's punishment that he informed Gregory that he cared not who was engaged to teach, adding, in his characteristic way, that it was not likely they would hire any one who was fit to manage a school, and thus Gregory was left to act just as he pleased.

Mrs. Sargent, however, was not so forgetful or forgiving. She had lost no opportunity of making disparaging remarks **of** myself, and when she learned that her husband had not used his influence **to** defeat me, she was equally indignant with him, assuring her friends that she had always labored to instill some public spirit and energy into her husband, but in vain.

Morse was too much engrossed with his business to feel any great interest in the engagement of a teacher, and was therefore merely a passive objector to my wishes, leaving, like Sargent, all the talking to be done by his wife.

I learned these facts from Smallett, from whom, also, I understood that the number of those who actively opposed me was small; being confined to two besides those I have mentioned. The rest of the patrons were willing to concede

that I had taught a good school, though some of them who
had friends or relatives among the other candidates for the
winter school objected to me on the ground of salary.
Barnes, who was unwilling to have it said that he was
wholly influenced by Whittimore, also kept harping on my
"outrageous price." The other two committee did not venture to hire me until they had canvassed the entire community, and learned the opinion of every man, woman, and
child in it; and then I was engaged only by falling from
fifty to forty dollars a month, exclusive of board.

The item of board was particularly mentioned from the
fact that, previous to my coming there, teachers during the
winter and summer terms, when they were hired by the
district, had always "boarded around," unless, as in some
instances, they preferred to pay for the luxury of boarding
at one place from their own pockets. It was no small
evidence, therefore, of my influence, to be able to get the
committee to allow me ten dollars a month extra for my
board, and it was done with much trepidation under the
solemn protest of Barnes.

So, finally, after all this delay and trouble, all this canvassing, in which I had been discussed in the store, shop, bar-
room and private dwelling, by old men and women, young
men and maidens, small boys and girls, I was hired;
engaged to teach again in a community where, from a conscientious desire to do my duty, I had gained the ill-will
of several children and their parents, and where, now, many
more were displeased with me because of the high salary
that I was receiving. Yes, I was hired for thirty dollars a
month and my board to spend one-fourth of a year in an
uncomfortable, untidy old building, with three scores of

boys and girls of diverse habits and manners, with the chance of again making enemies if I always acted according to the dictates of conscience. Surely the prospect was not a cheering one, but circumstances compelled me to **view** it with the best possible grace.

Amidst all my discouragements, and the unpleasant feelings I experienced from having unjustly, as I thought, received the enmity of so many of my patrons, one thing afforded me great consolation, I had secured the confidence, esteem and friendship of a large majority of my pupils, all, I might say, who had shown any disposition to learn.

With the exception of four or five, none of my pupils had made the progress that I hoped they would in the beginning of the school, or as much as they might, had they made a proper use of their opportunities—evening parties, as I have shown, and other things, having taken their attention from their studies. This want of progress, however, I must reasonably expect in a school where the pupils were generally under so little restraint at home—coming to school or staying away as they pleased—and where about the only incentive to industry was what I was able to give in the way of advice and kindly admonitions. **It** is found in every school where little or no moral support is accorded the teacher, by school boards or patrons, and it always will be. But yet my pupils had learned, accomplished much more, in fact, than one knowing the exact state of the school would imagine; and, on the last day of the term, the many marks of friendship that were shown me testified that my labors had not been unappreciated. Had I not been going to remain as a teacher, I felt conscious then that the parting with my pupils would have been a sad one.

As it was, some of the older ones who were intending to teach bid me adieu with an appearance of regret, and with kind remarks that called forth the warmest emotions of my heart.   Two young ladies and a young man of this class came to me at the close of school that day, and expressed themselves in such terms of respect and gratitude towards me that I was surprised—never before having known that I held so high a place in their esteem.

Miss Rowell, one of the young ladies, about twenty years of age, who had taught district school three or four seasons, a good scholar and very intelligent, said, as they were conversing with me:

" One thing, Mr. Styles, should certainly comfort you; you have the enmity of no one of your pupils who likes to study.   I have observed that all those who show any disposition to learn are greatly attached to you."

"That certainly is comforting, Miss Rowell," I said, "if it is true."

" I know it is true," said the young man; "and I think all the scholars feel that your anxiety to have them learn is much greater than theirs is to learn."

There was much comfort in this assurance.   If they, indeed, feel this, as he says, I thought I certainly must have their respect, and if their parents could but know it, feel it, they, too, would respect me and honor my intentions ; but, not one of them ever having visited my school, they knew nothing of it, save what they had gathered from the pupils, being ignorant of all the persuasions I had used to induce them to study, and the many methods I had devised to simplify, explain and render attractive the studies they were pursuing.

After Miss Rowell and her two companions had bid me good-bye, two younger girls from a neighboring town, who were not intending to return in the winter, came to say good-bye, and, with many tears, thanked me for my kindness, and expressed a determination to return **to** my school again in the spring should I teach in Bloomingdale. Several of the smaller pupils living in the village, some **of** whom I had often reproved and occasionally punished for their mischievousness, also expressed, in their juvenile way, gratification that I was again to be their teacher.

"I'm glad you're going to teach this winter, Mr. Styles."

"I'm going to try and learn something this winter, Mr. Styles."

"You'll **see, Mr.** Styles, if I'm not awful good next term," were addresses that greeted me many times ere I had left the schoolroom, and assured me that my pupils were not indifferent to the place they held in my esteem.

My heart glowed with gratitude for these testimonials of regard, assuring me, as they did, that my labors had **not** been wholly in vain.

It was the greatest reward that I received, being, in my estimation, of much greater value than the money paid me, however much I needed the latter.

On closing, I found that my net profits amounted to just $87, more than half of which I immediately forwarded to Niel in payment of interest.

CHAPTER XXII.

My vacation—I ask to have my curiosity gratified, and discover a
  sheep in wolf's clothing—A noble friend—My disgust with mankind—A surprise, in the shape of a valuable present—My winter
  school.

HAVING a vacation of one week allowed me, I spent this
time at home, making two visits to Ruth in that interval.

Pursuant to the intention which I have already announced to the reader, the first time I saw her, I sought
the reason of Mr. Niel's absenting himself for so long a
time from her uncle's, and after considerable evasion on her
part, I learned the following facts.

During all the time that I was absent at Corvette, Niel
had frequently visited Mr. Edgarton on the pretence of
doing business with him, and by making many trades, such
as buying or selling horses, cattle and sheep, or introducing
some new farming implement, he had even made this pretence a specious one. Having managed to make all
these trades profitable to Mr. Edgarton, he had thus obtained
his confidence, and by making him a present occasionally
he had also acquired his friendship, and, consequently,
never failed to receive a warm and urgent invitation to

repeat his visit at an early day. While thus ingratiating himself with Mr. Edgarton, he had every opportunity of speaking of myself, and, with a great display of candor and disinterestedness, had represented that he regarded me with feelings of friendship, but had little hopes of my future success on account of my visionary propensities and want of stability. Frank and honest himself, **Mr.** Edgarton suspected nothing of duplicity and dishonesty in others, and though he had always liked me, he became impressed, through the influence of Niel, with the idea that it **would** not be for the best interests of his niece to marry me. He was very fond of her, always had her welfare in view, and reposed much confidence in her judgment, yet fear that in this case she might be sacrificing judgment to affection, he could not forbear talking with her sometimes, and, without alluding directly to myself, counseled her against a false estimate of character and ability in selecting a partner for life. With the design too, no doubt, of influencing her in favor of Niel, he often spoke in eulogistic terms of that gentleman, **and** dwelt particularly on his wealth and his pleasant home, which, connected with his amiability of nature, would make him a desirable partner for any woman.

Ruth listened to all this with respectful silence. As long as no more strenuous efforts were put forth to induce her to encourage the attentions of Niel, and as long as her opinion of him was not directly asked, she felt herself bound in no wise either to show him disrespect, or declare to any one what she thought of him. But believing, as she did, that he was secretly undermining her uncle's confidence in me, while at the same time he was affecting to be my warmest friend, she could not but inwardly despise him, and only

awaited some denouement from him, some act by which his
suspected treachery would become palpable, to let both
himself and her uncle know her true feelings.   Though this
act was long in coming, it came at last.

In the spring following my return from Corvette, while
I was yet ill, with little prospect of improvement, Niel
decided, it would seem, to have a definite settlement of his
prospects with her, and for this purpose employed Mr.
Edgarton to broach, cautiously, to her the question of wed-
ding him.   Previous to this he informed him that I had
hired a large sum of him for the purpose of prosecuting my
studies, and that as I was in no position to repay him, he
expected to lose it.   He assured him that it would be the
most egregious folly for his niece to wed me, for even should
I recover, it would be impossible for me to support her,
harassed as I would be, constantly, by debt.   In thus disclosing my financial condition to Mr. Edgarton, he very
cautiously avoided saying that it was through his advice
and solicitation that I was his debtor, leaving him to infer
that I had asked his assistance, and that he had granted it
solely on the ground of confidence and friendship.   As
there was a semblance of reason in what he said about my
not being able to support Ruth, Mr. Edgarton was justly
alarmed, and no doubt resolved on pressing the suit of
Niel with earnestness and persistency.   If such was his
resolution, however, he failed to adhere to it after his
first attempt to convert Ruth to his opinion.   She had
known Niel's object from the beginning of his intimacy
with me, reading him with all the accuracy of woman's
instinct and perception.   She had long before discovered a
selfishness and want of principle in him, which assured her

that he had sought my friendship and confidence, and finally made himself my creditor, for the purpose of accomplishing my disgrace and ruin. It was her superior knowledge of the man that caused her to express a regret when I first informed her how largely I was indebted to him, yet foreseeing that no good would result from giving me her impressions of him, she had wisely refrained from so doing.

Now, however, when her uncle related to her what Niel had said of me, she had positive proof of his perfidy; he had done just what she had anticipated, and she gave full vent to her indignation and contempt for the man. Roused to a pitch of anger which she had never before displayed, she forbade her uncle ever to insult her by mentioning the name of Niel to her again, on pain of her leaving his house for ever; and she then proceeded to give him a detailed account of all the trouble Niel had taken to gain my friendship, all the persuasions he had employed to bring me into his debt. She also described to him the anxiety I felt when I first returned from Corvette respecting my indebtedness; and expressed the belief that it was owing, in a great measure, to this anxiety, still, that my health did not improve.

Mr. Edgarton had not imagined that she knew aught of my obligations to Niel, and on finding that I had told her all, and the circumstances connected with it, his confidence in me was in a measure increased, while that in Niel was correspondingly diminished. But he had too great respect and friendship for him to believe him as bad as Ruth had represented, and in relating to him the result of his interview with her, it is quite probable that he gave him only a faint picture of the scorn with which she had treated his

v

proposal. Be this as it may, however, he seemed to have concluded that any further efforts to win her affections were useless, hence, his visits to Maple Highland ceased.

"Why did you not tell me of this treachery of Niel last spring?" I asked of Ruth, when she had related to me the facts recorded above.

"Simply because I thought it would do you more harm than good," she answered. "I knew that in your bad state of health it would be likely to produce no good effect, and so I concluded that it would be wiser to let you know nothing about it."

"And so," I said, "you permitted me to remain in ignorance of his true character, thus giving him a chance to deceive me again if he thought proper?"

"I had no fear," she answered, "that he would venture to meet you again, as he would, doubtless, think I had informed you of what he had done."

"But why did he come here again, recently?" I asked.

"I don't know," she answered; "I think uncle did not let him know the extent of my displeasure, and, possibly, he thought that, by returning in the garb of friendship, he might still be regarded as a friend of the family. I do not think he will come again," she added, "for, as uncle had concluded, from his long absence, that it was through no friendship for himself that he had formerly visited us, he received him rather coolly, as did my aunts."

"And you, of course, received him with every demonstration of joy," I said, laughing.

"I did not speak to him," she replied, with flashing eyes. "He dined with the family, but I was not at the table."

"I see now," I said, "that he went away in a state of

disgust, and immediately wrote me, asking payment of that note. And you believed all the time, Ruth," I continued, "that he **was** no friend of mine, and was merely plotting to carry out his own selfish ends ?"

"I did," she replied, "and I was alarmed when you told me how much obligation you were under to him, for I felt assured that he would in some **way use his** advantage to your harm."

I felt deeply chagrined, as she said **this, at my** want of penetration, on account of which I had twice permitted myself to be duped, just as she had imagined **and** to herself had prophesied. That **she, a** young lady **of** modest and retiring manners, living almost the life of a recluse, should know and understand men better than myself, who claimed to know much of human nature and business, was anything but flattering to my self-esteem. I almost regarded her as a superior being, endowed with more than human vision. And then she **had** acted with **so** much discretion, in **not** revealing the affair to me, realizing that it could only have the effect **of** increasing the worry and regret that **I already** experienced at not being **able** to release myself from obligation to the villain **who had so deceived me.** That he was a villain, I now had every evidence. **Besides** the baseness of disclosing a private business transaction with me, in **a** place where he believed it would have the effect of injuring my prospects, **he had** proposed to marry her to whom he knew I had long been engaged. Yes, it was now apparent that he had **wormed** himself into my confidence for **the** purpose of learning **the exact** relations that Ruth and I sustained to **each** other, and then believing that he could only **win** her by getting me **out of** the way, or by lessening her confidence in me, he had bent all his energies to the accomplishment of this object.

I believed it to be quite probable that at first he fancied if he could separate us for some time our attachment for each other might become weaker, and that during this interval if he met Ruth quite often she might conceive a fancy for himself. Her dignity and true womanly principle, however, had prevented him from making any open advances to her during my absence, and on my return in such bad health, he had no doubt hoped that I would not recover, therefore, had concluded to await the progress of events. What but a desire to get rid of me could have induced him to urge me, invalid as I was from over work, to enter college at once, and again apply myself to study? What could he have hoped, except that I would either destroy my constitution wholly, or that in case of recovery my ambition and continued absence from her would cause me to forget Ruth?

Failing in this attempt, he had waited in suspense until, thinking that my prospects of marrying were as deplorable as they could well be, he thought that by making my financial embarrassment known to Ruth and her friends, and then offering her a home, with all the comforts and luxuries which wealth could provide, he would succeed in his designs. Unfortunate man! He had found a woman whose constancy was not affected by time, whose affections were not to be purchased by gold.

His plans which he had laid with such cunning, and the maturing of which he had watched so long and patiently, had failed.

His interest in me was destroyed, and his only object

now was to get the money with which he had entrusted me. He was to me no longer the man I had regarded him, generous hearted, public spirited, an appreciator of education and laudable, youthful ambition, but a sordid, selfish, heartless knave, as unworthy the affections of a good woman as he was the confidence and respect of an honest man.

I returned home from that visit to Ruth with an indefinable contempt for mankind. Had it not been for the noble redeeming qualities I found in her, I think I would have embraced the whole human race in one general malediction. I had lost all confidence in everybody, everything but herself. I believed that there was no such thing as friendship, and I almost determined that, besides her, I would never regard any person as a friend.

Towards the last of the week, calling at the post office in Arklow, for the purpose of getting my mail and having a chat with my old friend Doctor Sutherland, I was surprised at finding there a registered letter for myself. On opening it my astonishment for a moment was indescribable when I saw the number and value of the bank notes it contained— three hundred dollars, enclosed in a sheet of paper, on which were written in a strange hand the words, " From a friend." There was no signature or other mark on the sheet by which I could tell from what friendly hand it had come. I looked at the post-mark and found that it was mailed in Foreston.

My bewilderment lasted but a few minutes. There was only one friend in the wide world who would have conferred such a favor on me, and knowing that that friend had received about six hundred dollars in the settlement of the paternal estate, and had likewise saved about half t' at sum in teaching, she was in a position to bestow this boon, if so disposed.   But the reader will naturally enquire why she had taken this method of presenting it.   Simply from a consciousness that I would not accept it if I knew the donor. She feared that she would wound my feelings and incur my displeasure by offering it to me, either as a gift or a loan, yet knowing what a great pleasure it would be to me to pay the amount to Niel, she had determined to place it in my hands in such a way that I would not be certain whence it came.

She was mistaken, however, for so sure was I that no other person than herself had sent it, that I determined to return it to her without even taking the trouble to enquire at the Foreston post office what person had mailed the letter.

I was glad that the Doctor had been engaged at his desk when I opened it, otherwise he might have noticed my surprise.   As it was he only knew that I had received the amount, and until I informed him to the contrary, long afterward, when he had nearly forgotten the incident, he supposed that it was a sum I had hired of a friend.

That evening I sat down and wrote the following letter, in which I enclosed the full amount I had received :

MY DEAR RUTH,

I appreciate your noble generosity, and the delicacy with which you have shown it.   It is only another testimony of your devotion to me, and the self-denying spirit you possess ; but you will pardon me if I decline to use the sum you have with such modesty placed in my hands.   Were I positively certain that circumstances would enable me to return it with interest at no distant day, I doubt that I would accept it; but as I have no such assurance, I cannot for a moment think of making use of it. No, Ruth: if loss is to be sustained, it must be by the man through whose advice I am where I am.

Faithfully yours,

FRANK.

The next day, looking up all the letters I had received from Niel at different times, I took them, with the one above, to Ruth. My object in taking Niel's letters was to give her an opportunity to read them to her uncle, thus proving to him that it was owing wholly to Niel's own desire that I had become indebted to him. I gave them to her as soon as I arrived, but the one addressed to herself, containing the money, I said nothing about; giving it to her only at the moment I bade her adieu.

My reticence concerning the present I had received, afforded me no little secret amusement, for she had no doubt anticipated a disclosure of the affair from me, and consequently some pleasure herself in witnessing my mystified condition and listening to my remarks. When, however, I made no allusion to it, and spoke of my relations to Niel in my usual manner, she evidently was puzzled, and began to doubt that I had received the money. To remove this doubt, after I had been with her some time, she casually, and with an air of indifference, asked me if I had visited Dr. Sutherland during my vacation. On informing her, without mentioning the letter, that I had spent an hour with him on the preceding day, a shade passed over her face. She evidently began to fear that I had not received it. Whatever might have occurred to prevent this, any inquiry from her at the post office respecting it would, doubtless, make the whole transaction public, in which case it would be most embarrassing to both of us. She felt that she had done a foolish thing, for which there seemed to be no help. Divining her thoughts, I began to relent that I had not before disclosed my knowledge of the matter, and was inclined to do so now, but knowing that this would cause her much embarrassment, I determined to carry out my plan. I cut short my visit for the sole purpose of relieving her of her unpleasant feelings; and, after promising to write her on the following Saturday, and bidding her an affectionate adieu, with a smile, I slipped the letter into her hand. A crimson flush which I observed on her face, as I went out of the door, showed me that she had divined the contents, and to prevent any impression on her part that I was offended, I gave a hearty laugh, as I once more said "Good-bye."

The following Monday I was to begin my winter term at Bloomingdale, and to avoid the loneliness of spending a day there before commencing my labors, I remained at home on the Sabbath, rising in time the next morning to reach Bloomingdale before nine o'clock. I ran into the post office on my way to the academy, and received a receipt from Niel for the money I had sent him, but there was no letter—not even a word acknowledging the receipt of my letters.

At the academy, everything was hurly-burly. Nearly one hundred and thirty boys and girls were there, filling both rooms, and making a most hideous noise from running, jumping, loud talking, and scrambling for their favorite seats.

A young girl, scarcely eighteen, had been engaged to

teach the junior pupils. This was her first school, and she had been hired for the two substantial reasons that she was a niece of Barnes, one of the committee, and had offered to teach this motley throng of eighty youngsters for a dollar and fifty cents a week and board around.

I threw open the **door** of her room **as I** entered the porch, both to ascertain **the cause of the** tumult and to quiet it, not imagining that the **teacher was** present. To my surprise, a pale, weakly looking girl stood on the platform at **the** farther end of the room crying. Going forward and addressing her, I found, as I had supposed, **that she** was Miss Barnes—the teacher, in despair, and weeping at the prospect before her. **No** wonder! she had entered the room where there was **a** countless number of urchins screaming, knocking off hats, turning summersaults and performing sundry other actions known only to uncouth children, and had timidly and modestly asked a few near her, if they were not afraid they would not get hurt **by** playing so roughly. One of them shouted, "No;" and to prove his fearlessness of such **a result of** his actions, immediately upset the table upon which three or four of his companions had climbed.

They became quiet **as** I entered, **and I heard** various whispers, while in the room, like the following:

"That's the high schoolmaster." "That's that cross Styles: he'll lick us like the —— if he gits mad."

I made a few encouraging remarks to Miss Barnes, ordered the pupils to take their seats, and after exhorting them to be good children and **obey** the teacher, I went upstairs, forgetting my own inglorious prospect in my sympathy for her.

The appearance of my room, when I entered, was hardly more satisfactory than the lower one. There were about sixty pupils in it—a large number of them strangers to me —boys and girls who never attended school except in the winter, and many of them as uncouth in manner as they were in expression. There was about the same wild confusion in the room as in that I had just left, but the din immediately subsided when they saw me, and quite a number of my former pupils came forward and expressed pleasure at my return.

If my school in the fall had been a trying one, this was doubly so. It seemed to be well understood by the pupils that this was a district school, my authority in it being less absolute than it was in the other, and they felt that their rights were assailed whenever they saw a disposition on my part to render it anything different from the winter school to which they had been accustomed. This might be briefly described as a place which they had been accustomed to visit at leisure, a sort of entertainment specially provided for them during the winter months, into which they strolled at any convenient hour, beheld, with listless, dreamy attention, one or more scenes in the play, and then went out to while away the remaining time in sauntering about the streets or gossiping in some place of favorite public resort.

Any attempt to make the school different from this was an innovation at which they were disposed to rebel, and as their parents and guardians felt less interest now than they did in the fall, simply because it affected their pockets less, it required far more tact, watchfulness and persuasion on my part to induce them to discharge their duties with any degree of dignity and industry.

Scarcely a week had passed when as I was about to step into a store, one evening, I heard loud and angry voices inside, as if some one was engaged in violent altercation, and presently there was the sound of a scuffle which was succeeded by a heavy fall. Opening the door I was both amused and alarmed at the spectacle.

Near the stove in the centre of the room was Uncle Jack Jones lying on his back, both hands clutching the hair of Smallett, who was on him, ordering him in husky, smothered tones to "let go;" punching him, at the same time, in the face, chest, stomach, or wherever most convenient, with his fist, as a persuasive to obey this mandate. Two men stood at a little distance from them viewing the scene with grave countenances and intense interest, while the merchant behind the counter was convulsed with laughter, regarding it as a good farce. Soon after I became a spectator of the scene a heavy blow in the eye of Uncle Jack produced the desired effect, he concluded to "let go," and Smallett having got off him, he instantly bounded to his feet, and glancing wildly around the room, his eye fell on me. The sight seemed to stir up his anger afresh, and augment his pugnacious desires. Dashing up to me with clinched fist he astonished me with the following salutation:

" And so, you've come, you Canuck! Why don't yer go back to Canady and stay there? Nobody wants yer here! You're a great man; so stuck up that you can't board with the people in the deestrict, and so we have ter work and drudge to git money for yer to pay to that fool thar (pointing to Smallett) fur yer board."

At first I really believed the man was insane, and stepped back in no little fear for my personal safety; but when he spoke of the subject of board, I began to understand the cause of his wrath, and was disposed, like the storekeeper, to laugh.

The latter now interfered in my behalf, and by talking quietly to the old fellow, and ridiculing his absurd actions, he soon got him so pacified that he began to evince signs of shame, and in a few minutes he left the store. The other two men I have mentioned had already gone ; and from Smallett and the merchant I now learned the cause of the fight.

It seems Smallett had dropped into the store just as Uncle Jack and the other two men were discussing the action of the school-committee in hiring me, and permitting me to board at one place, at their expense. All of them were agreed in the matter that it was a most unjust thing to do, though one of the number affirmed that, individually, he cared but little about it. The other, however, felt sorely aggrieved, while Uncle Jack was not to be reconciled, declaring that there had not been another such flagrant cause of rebellion since the imposition of the Stamp Act and Tea Tax. He averred that if there were a few more spirits like himself in the "deestrict," they would "pitch" me out of the academy, hang the school committee in effigy and compel them to resign their office, or otherwise leave the community.

Unless there was some such action on the part of the intelligent and respectable citizens, this high-handed robbery would continue until their farms, stock and everything else were sold at the auction-block, and themselves obliged to spend their last days in the poor house. He went on in this strain to Smallett for some time, when, being provoked beyond forbearance by his badgering replies, he expressed his determination to "put some sense into him," and his success in the effort has been described. His black eye and bruised face did not prevent his coming to the village, as usual, to relate his grievances; on the other hand, he seemed to regard himself a martyr to a noble cause, and he proudly exhibited these marks to his friends, as proofs of the heroism with which he had defended their rights.

If the reader has ever taught school he will understand with what emotions I learned that there was such a strong current of feeling in the district against my teaching. I assume that he will understand it, for he has experienced the same emotions, though perhaps in a less degree. He has witnessed the same objection—high salary—on the part of many in every community with which he is acquainted, and though perhaps it may not have resulted in a fight, as in this instance, it has displayed itself in various ways—resulting in estrangements, back-biting, feuds and even neighborhood quarrels. Yes, every community has its Uncle Jack, with those who either openly or secretly uphold and encourage him.

From the moment I learned the cause of this quarrel, I knew that in all probability, through the influence of Uncle Jack and his colleagues, one-fourth of the citizens of the village were my enemies, and that instead of giving me their support they would contribute, in no small degree, to make my school unsuccessful—a failure. I seldom met a person in Bloomingdale after that, who looked sour and seemed distant and cold in manner, without thinking that I was the cause of it; having been instrumental in wresting from him the dollars for which he had toiled, and which were so much needed for worthier purposes. Nor were these

thoughts all the **result of my** sensitiveness and fancy.
Having bought a coat, one evening, in a store, where three
or four men were lounging, I learned that, as soon as I had
left, one man remarked that he wished himself "smart"
enough to fool the district out of forty dollars a month, he
would wear good clothes.   Another one averred that as far
as real hardship and wear on the constitution were concerned
he performed more labor in a day than I did in a week,
and yet he was receiving less than half the salary that I did.
And so remarks went round, each one giving utterance to
some feeling of displeasure, that they had not hired a
"cheaper teacher."

But, notwithstanding these unpleasant things, I remained
and went through the school, how, I scarcely know.   That
any of the pupils should have advanced in their studies,
was a surprise to me, when I reflected how little of punctuality there was, and how many things were constantly
drawing off their attention from their books; but yet, the
majority of them had learned something—a trifle compared
with what they should have learned in the same time.

During the third week of my term, a singing school was
opened in the village by Professor ——. He was an experienced and able teacher, and, of course, all the young
people of Bloomingdale must go.   Nearly every one of my
pupils joined his class, and, to my disgust, they were to
meet him twice a week, every Tuesday and Friday afternoon at two o'clock.   None of the parents objected to this
hour on account of its interference with my school. A few
of the pupils who felt a little interest in their studies asked
the Professor if he could not meet them in the evening,
but no, he had other classes elsewhere to meet, and so he

walked in without meeting a word of expostulation. Knowing nothing of the arrangements that had been made, I was taken by surprise when the pupils came up *en masse* **at** two o'clock to get excused, and I promptly refused them ; but, on receiving the positive assurance that they had parental permission to go, and the promise that they would, individually, bring me a written notice of **that** fact the next day, I allowed them to go.   The notes were brought according to agreement, and for the next six weeks a perfect stampede of pupils occurred at the academy every **Tuesday** and Friday afternoon.   Three or four usually remained, **but as** these were my oldest pupils, who were from **a** distance, and they had only one recitation after that hour, after reciting that, they returned to their rooms, giving me an opportunity to return to mine, or remain and muse in solitude as I preferred.   **Of** course, I chose to do the former, but I had enjoyed this short respite from my labors only twice, when, as I had supposed, there was a loud complaint that **I** was neglecting my business.   **Barnes,** who lived a little distance from the village, and had not been seized with the fever for singing, or heard to what an extent **it** was raging, came to Smallett one day, saying that he **had been** informed two or three times, recently, that I **was** not in school more than half the time, leaving it for the purpose **of** attending singing school, and sending my pupils home **a** whole day twice or three times a week.   Having had his erroneous ideas corrected, he asked if it was not true that I left the school-room on those days, when I had few or no scholars, before four o'clock.   Being answered in the affirmative, he gave it as his opinion that I should remain there, as the patrons, seeing me outside, or knowing that I **was in my** room, would naturally think that I had no interest in the school, and, consequently, fear that their children were learning nothing. Others also inquired of Smallett how it was that I was out of the school-room so much, and, on being enlightened with regard to the matter, instead of expressing surprise or regret that the citizens should permit a singing school to take precedence of the other, they always evinced deep regret that I should have such an "easy time" of it when the district was paying me such "high wages."

Scarcely was the singing school in operation, ere a dancing school was opened, which occupied two evenings in the week, and as the remaining evenings were usually taken up with parties, it would have been folly to expect anything in the way of study from my pupils outside of the six hours they were in the schoolroom.

During all the time that I had taught here, the only two individuals who had visited the school were the minister of the village and the school superintendent. The former had been in three or four times, and spent perhaps a couple of hours at each visit. Though he sent no children to school, he knew more about it than any other person in the village, and his words of kindness and sympathy gave me much comfort and encouragement. I was greatly indebted to him for the good opinion many of the citizens entertained of me as a teacher, for although they had too little interest to come in and ascertain for themselves the way in which I was discharging my duties, they were intelligent enough to rely on the judgment of one who was educated and had been a teacher himself. In my experience in teaching, I have always found myself sustained by the clergymen of the localities where I have labored; partly, I suppose, from the fact that there was a degree of similarity in our respective vocations, and partly because often exposed to unjust criticisms, and generally receiving only a small salary, they know how to extend the hand of sympathy to those in like circumstances. I look back over the years that I have taught, and recall the names and faces of those who have given me their support in those times of trouble which come upon all teachers, and I find none more dear and familiar than the minister of the Gospel. None so ready to examine my work, to strive to awaken an interest in the school among patrons, or to frown at every appearance of parsimony and injustice.

The superintendent visited the school twice—once in the fall and then again in the winter, spending but one hour each time. He declared himself highly pleased, paid me many compliments—a duty which superintendents seldom forget towards teachers; and carried forth a good report of the school to the village. It no doubt did me some good, inasmuch as his report was regarded by many as a careful, correct estimate of the character of the school; but to me it seemed a farce. What can he learn, I thought, in one hour, of my method of instruction and discipline, or of the general habits and progress of my pupils?

But when I compared my lot with that of the young lady teacher in the same building, I felt that I had little cause for complaint. Not a week passed during the whole term that she was not visited by some father or mother, and called to account and abused for some injustice done to their offspring. Freddie or Katie had been punished too severely; the older pupils had misused them; their books

W

had been torn, or they had been the victims of some other misfortune, for which the teacher was wholly to blame, and for which also she must receive discourteous and heartless treatment. Often, when leaving my school at night, I found her standing in her door, meekly receiving these un-just reproofs, so intimidated by the coarse manner and angry tones of the offended ones, that she was unable to offer a word in her defence. She generally retired alone to her school-room after these unkind reprimands, and spent an hour or more in weeping and bemoaning her unpleasant lot.

I could but feel much sympathy for her, and was not backward in expressing my indignation at the treatment she received. Not one in ten of the complaints that were made against her was supported by reason or justice. Among such a number of pupils, it would be surprising if simple accidents did not sometimes occur, whatever care or vigilance the teacher might exercise, and to hold her respon-sible for them was an act of cruel injustice. It was no different, however, from the treatment which, many times since that, I have seen accorded teachers, sometimes with the same, and at others, with different results, according to the nerve and temperament of the teacher. I now speak more particularly of female teachers, as they, on account of their meekness and timidity, are more frequently sub-jected to these abusive attacks than males. While one, as if forewarned of what she is to expect in teaching, receives these complaints and reproofs as a matter of course, with but little disturbance of her equanimity, another is quite differently affected, not understanding that, in assuming charge of a school, she is to be scolded and abused by every

one of her patrons who may feel inclined to give vent to
his ill-humor.

In a territory supporting ten district schools, I have
known two teachers to be almost incapacitated for their
duties from these **unjust** complaints and censures, and yet,
from education and refinement, **they** were the best qualified **of** all the number for the labors in which they were
engaged. Sensitiveness, **and** a regard for the opinions of
others, are traits not to be ignored in securing a teacher, as
their natural tendency is to make one watchful, lest, by
omitting some **duty,** dissatisfaction should arise, and careful in deportment, lest offence, unwittingly, should be given.
Yet, owing to the thoughtlessness and ignorance of patrons,
these very traits are often made subversive of the true
interests of their school, causing the teacher many hours of
disquietude, making her dislike her vocation, and thus un-
fitting her for the proper discharge of her duties.

Miss Barnes was a representative **of this class of female**
teachers; though I must admit **that she showed much less**
tact in governing than the majority of them **do,** but as no
one ever came to encourage, only to accuse her of favoritism,
indifference to her work, **or** of severity **on the one** hand and
leniency on the other, no wonder that she was discouraged.

Many of her pupils **were** large and as old as herself; boys
and girls of poor people who had been to school but little,
or else those of French nationality, who were learning the
rudiments of English. Johnny Sargent and Sammy Morse
attended her school for a short time, or until some offence
which they committed made them fearful of punishment,
when they left, and spent the remainder of the term **in the**
street; Mrs. Sargent still persisting that Johnny would

never learn anything till they hired a graduate of Dartmouth to teach in the village, and **Mrs.** Morse entertaining the same opinion with regard to **Sammy.**

I have shown that the singing school afforded me a short rest twice a week.

Providentially for Miss **Barnes** the stove pipes in her room gave her a longer rest, if not quite so frequent. With a view to economy, old worn out stove pipes were stretched the whole length and nearly across one end of the room, and these were supported by scanty bits of wire. **Nearly every week, as** might be supposed, **the stove pipes** indulged in a general tumble, **filling the room** with smoke, **soot and** ashes. **The** event was always hailed as a jubilee by the pupils, for **they never had** less than a half-holiday on these occasions. Of course some member of the committee was sent for, **and the pipes were replaced,** usually, with the additional expense of a yard of wire, and sometimes by a new joint. **On the first** and second instance of the pipe's falling, little was said; but finally people began to grumble, blaming the committee somewhat for not making **their** stove pipe structure more firm, but generally throwing **the blame wholly on** the teacher. **In most** instances the disaster **occurred** either in the morning before school commenced, **or at noon,** and it was soon said that if the pupils were instructed by the teacher neither to jump nor run in the schoolroom, **nothing** of the kind would **happen,** hence, some meanly **insinuated that she** secretly **encouraged** these rude sports for the sake of a holiday, or at **least** did not prevent them. To prevent rough sports entirely in the schoolroom during his absence, is a thing almost **im**possible for a strict and experienced male teacher to do, and to expect this young lady, with her unruly boys, to do it, was a thing most absurd. It never occurred to any one that it was a duty incumbent on the patrons to help her to preserve order, or to put the stove pipes up so securely that they would not tumble down on the slightest jar; no, that would cheat the people of the pleasure of fault finding, **as well as** interfere with their notions of economy. The pipes had been down **seven** times, when, strange **to** say, the committee were advised by **several** of the citizens to purchase and put up new ones, and stranger still, they did it. **Hitherto they** had refrained from **so** doing, **on** the plea that they **were** to build a new academy in a year or two, and they feared that **an** investment in new pipes now would be deemed useless **and** extravagant by the district; but, after losing five days of school, and causing an endless amount of profanity and abuse of the teacher, they were suddenly seized with the thought that the pipe would not be sufficiently damaged to prevent its use in the new building.

"Stove pipe holiday" had become a favorite **expression** with the boys of the village, and the frequency and zest **with** which they screamed **it** on the **street, I have no** doubt, annoyed the committee, and nerved them **finally to** heroic action. The reminder of **duty** neglected **was too** frequent; "it was becoming monotonous."

The trouble experienced by the teacher in that district from the falling of the stove-pipe was only one of many similar instances that I have witnessed.

I shall weary the reader with no longer account of my trials at Bloomingdale. It is sufficient to say that I finished my winter term and taught also in the spring. **No event** of importance to me occurred during the winter save one.

On account of his insolence and disorderly habits, I felt obliged to expel a large, rustic youth of eighteen, which act secured me the enmity of his relatives, from his grandfather down to his baby sister.

At the annual school meeting, which was held in March, the citizens who sympathized with Uncle Jack in his crusade against expensive schools, and those who had been bored with his complaints, united to make him chairman of the new committee which they elected. A part of those who voted for him affirmed that they did so, both from a curiosity to see what he would do, and to put an end to his "eternal grumbling;" and so, on this broad and liberal platform, Uncle Jack was elected to preside over the educational interests of Bloomingdale. Barnes and a man of kindred nature were his colleagues.

I learned that the next winter they engaged a girl for two dollars a week to teach the higher department of the school, with the specific understanding that she was to "board around," and hire a boy to build her fires; and, for the lower department, they engaged a girl for one dollar and twenty-five cents a week, with the same stipulations that are given above. Barnes was in favor of again hiring his niece, provided she would teach for twenty-five cents a week less than she received in the preceding winter, but the other two objected, on the ground that she had made so little effort to keep the stove pipes from tumbling down, thus securing to herself several holidays.

In the spring I was obliged again to depend on tuition as remuneration for my labors. The school was small, but pleasant. I made rules as stringent as I thought I could with propriety enforce, and to my gratification they were very generally observed. It had become pretty well understood by this time that I strove to maintain discipline, and the cases of punishment and expulsion which had occurred showed, too, that I was not afraid to resort to such measures as I deemed necessary for the accomplishment of my wishes, so that those who sent to school, sent with the full understanding that their children must obey.

Mrs. Whittimore became so far reconciled that she even decided to send Mattie. I presume she would have sent her away again, had not the unhappy result of placing her in a distant boarding school, in the previous autumn, led her to the conclusion that she had better in future keep her under her own eye. Mattie's humiliation, in that school and in my own, had produced a good effect on her. She was far more humble, more respectful, more studious, and in fact gave considerable evidence of becoming a woman of stability and good sense. She was not altogether punctual in her attendance, but so much more so than when she was last my pupil, that I was disposed to be as lenient as possible.

Johnny Sargent was sent away to his aunt's to attend school, but his chum, Sammy Morse, attended mine. He often ran away, but his mother, fearful of the result, always brought him back, apologized and assured me that she had punished him for the offence. As she showed such a strong desire to have him observe the rules and learn, I got along with him as well as I could, although quite conscious that he was learning very little.

My school, this term, brought me as net profit just $40, the full amount of which I was obliged to use for other purposes, so that nothing remained for my creditor. About this time, I received a little more than half the amount of my winter's wages, but the remainder was not paid till September. From the entire sum I was able to transmit to Niel $70.

I believe I never enjoyed a release from school more than I did that which left me free at Bloomingdale.

I had now completed my first year of teaching High School. I had learned that it was not what, in former years, I had anticipated—a lucrative, pleasant occupation, commanding a good salary and the respect of all my patrons. I remembered how, in former times, I had imagined myself enjoying the luxury of a suite of rooms, laying aside my gown and slippers in the morning, walking to the academy, issuing orders to the janitor, and then, after devotion, stepping into the lecture room, and, with retort and crucible, unfolding the mysteries of science to a large and intelligent class of young ladies and gentlemen.

But, alas, as in most cases, the reality had been a sad contrast to the anticipation. I had learned that the high school of the country was scarcely an improvement on the district school—the teacher in the one being subjected to all the vexations and hardships that he was in the other. True, my situation at Bloomingdale was, in some respects, more pleasant than it was in Meadville, yet, in other respects, it had been more trying; and when I reflected upon all the labor I had performed, all the annoyances and humiliation I had suffered for a little more than $200, exclusive of board, I could but feel that I had sought a livelihood through the most rugged and thorny path by which it could be reached.

CHAPTER XXIII.

IN the fall, after leaving Bloomingdale, hoping to secure a
better position as teacher in another place in Vermont, I
delayed a little too long, and the school was given to another,
so that I was left with out any employment, save that of
assisting my father about his farm work.

Early in October Niel visited me, and to my surprise was
in a state of partial intoxication.

I had never known him to be in this condition before,
nor had I ever heard that he was intemperate in his habits,
so that I could easily divine that he had sought to drown
his shame on this occasion of meeting me by potations to
which he had never been accustom d. I treated him with
respect, yet not with cordiality. No allusion was made by
either of us to the events which caused the estrangement.
He said that he had come to exchange my old notes for new
ones, in which the rate of interest was to be twelve per

cent. instead of six, which I had before paid him. He claimed that this was the rate which he received on all the mortgages and notes which he held against other parties, and presumed that I would have no objection to paying the same, inasmuch as he would doubtless be obliged to wait some time longer for the principal. My first impulse was to command him to leave the house, especially as I doubted that he received twelve per cent. from others, and felt that he was only demanding it in this case to oppress me and thus satiate his thirst for revenge; but then, I knew that he would immediately sue me, and make more cost in the end, so I concluded to humor his caprice, and yield to his demand. I also had a great dread of being sued, regarding it as a disgrace. Up to the present time I have escaped this annoyance, though more than once, to satisfy rapacious creditors, I have paid interest which old Shylock, himself, would have blushed at accepting. Then, too, I thought that by yielding to this proposal I might effect a compromise with him and get an extension of time, and I quietly suggested that in case I gave him twelve per cent. he should permit me to put the whole amount into one note, payable in three years from that day. Whether he was too drunk to realize that this would be a great favor to me, or whether he feared to provoke me to a rehearsal of his villany, I know not; but he made no objection to the suggestion, and I gladly gave him the new one and received my old notes.

During the few months that I was at home, I was far from being happy, fretting because I was in no better position, and continually forming plans, and then dismissing them. Hearing of the high salaries that were paid teachers in the west, I was strongly inclined to try my luck there, but numerous things opposed themselves to this movement. I had never so far recovered my health, that I felt able to endure much hardship; indeed, it was with fear that I might not be able to complete it that I commenced every term of my school at Bloomingdale.

I was obliged to take great care of myself, being very systematic and regular in my hygienic habits, and avoiding an excess of mental labor, otherwise, I would, in all probability, have been compelled to desist from teaching. This was the chief thing that prevented me from seeking employment so far from home, among strangers. And then the uncertainty of finding a position at once, indeed, the improbability of finding one until after I had been there some time and formed acquaintances, made the prospect of going, especially in my penniless condition, anything but pleasant. Added to these, the objection of my friends to such a step, and the fact that a large number of teachers from the east were already there looking for situations, made it appear wiser and more profitable to remain in my own section. I have many times since, however, regretted that I did not go, and had I known that I would follow the vocation as many years as I since have, I think no trifling thing would have prevented me. I now regard it as one of the great mistakes of my life.

My brother-in-law, in Mayfair, once more advised me to study law, and I was so far induced to heed his advice that I took up Blackstone and became familiar with its contents. But, though I liked the study of law, I had formed a dislike to the practice from what I had seen and learned of it in various ways. Owing to this, my knowledge of law terminated with my knowledge of Blackstone.

It was another of my too common mistakes, in consequence of which I have had many regrets.

As winter approached, a neighbor who was committee of the school in my own district, where, as the reader doubtless remembers, I had formerly taught, asked me on what terms I would again take the school for four months.

Knowing their inability to pay much, I replied,

"Twenty-five dollars without board."

Having ascertained that I was in earnest he at once accepted the offer, saying, as he did so, that he had no idea that I would take the school at any price, since—as he expressed it—I had been through *college.*

I boarded at home again, and went through my school as before, though, from my superior knowledge of science, I was better able now to give my pupils short lectures which interested them greatly, and I had the satisfaction of knowing that, though I was receiving low wages, I was accomplishing good.

During the winter I usually spent my evenings in reading when I was not too fatigued, and as I read many books on agriculture, and every week devoured the contents of the "Country Gentleman" and "Moore's Rural New Yorker," I became possessed with a strong desire once more to engage in farming.

This desire was not a little increased by the gradual decline of my health from confinement in the school-room. Then, too, I was daily meeting strong, robust young farmers, my school-mates in former years, and their lively spirits and general happy appearance convinced me that they had been wiser than myself in being contented with their lot and following the occupation of their fathers—clinging to the farm. They seemed in almost every way better off than myself, being healthy, free from debt, and above all contented and happy. I was much better educated than they, but as an offset to this advantage my constitution was shattered, I was badly in debt, discontented and unhappy. **If by** any means I could acquire the health that they enjoyed, and free myself from debt, it seemed **to me** that my temporal happiness would **be** complete.

My education would heighten this enjoyment, **not** only making my leisure hours more pleasant, but affording me subjects for contemplation during my labors, and also, if rightly employed in this occupation, it would contribute much towards my pecuniary profits. Yes, I would be **a** farmer, and with my usual enthusiam, when about putting into execution a new plan, I began to revel in the anticipation of my future lot, and was vexed that I had not long before given myself to this vocation in preference **to any** other.

Ruth was now in New Hampshire. Early in the winter, having been offered **a good** situation as teacher **in that state,** through the influence of **a** friend, she **accepted it,** and had now been gone some months. **I missed her society** greatly, but desiring to be unselfish with **regard to the** matter of her leaving, I contented myself **once more** with her letters. Being, as I have already shown, much more pratical than I was, **I** knew that **she would** regard my determination to be a farmer with much pleasure, hence, it was pleasant, for me to inform her of my decision.

Having spent so much **of my life** on the farm, **I** was familiar with all the different kinds of labor connected with **it,** and, **of** course, felt myself quite equal **to** the management of it, including the stock and all the necessary expenditures.

I had not yet learned that knowing how to do farm labor and knowing how to manage a farm are quite distinct things, and require talents of different order. A carpenter may execute his work neatly, he may hang a door, put on a casing or cornice with taste and accuracy, yet, if required to plan a house, he might show himself a wretched architect ; and so a man may plow, sow grain, mow and pitch hay, or take care of stock properly, yet, if required to fence, improve and fertilize a farm, keep no more than the proper amount of stock, hire help, and do all this without overstepping his income, he may prove that he is wholly unqualified for the work. It was my unhappy privilege to exemplify the truth of this statement in the summer of which I write. I had a small sum of money at the close of my winter school, and, had I possessed more wisdom and prudence, I would have applied it at once on the large note that I had recently given, but, with the conviction that I could so invest it that in a year or two it would double in amount, I laid it out in improvements which, for the first year, paid but a small percentage on the sum invested.

Full control of the farm had been given me, so I went on buying phosphates, draining, drawing muck and soiling, with the expectation of receiving enormous crops of grain and numberless tubs of butter. But everything turned out differently from what I had expected, and, as fall approached, instead of having two or three hundred dollars left, as the result of my agricultural speculation, I had barely enough to pay the help I had hired. The only benefit that

I had derived from **my** summer's work was a decided improvement **in** health.

Disgusted with farming, I began to look about again for more lucrative employment, but, **as in former times so now, the only thing that** I could **find to do was school teaching, and to this, once more, disappointed and sad, I devoted myself.**

CHAPTER XXIV.

A leap over three years—A history of their events—My marriage—
Our baby—We lose our all by fire—My experience as book agent.

KIND reader, since last we met my circumstances have
greatly changed. I am three years older, a married man,
and the father of a bright blue eyed, flaxen haired girl—
six months old, named Dora. Her advent forms an important epoch in my history—a new phase in my emotions
and ambition. I had never been fond of children, not like
many people disliking them, but never regarding them with
anything beyond passing notice.

It might not perhaps be saying too much to aver that I
disliked very young children—babies; nothing making me
feel more awkward than to have a mother present her tiny
infant for my admiration. I could see nothing to admire. I
could not compare it with other babies to its own advantage,
for all looked alike, and having been reared alone, without the
companionship of younger brothers and sisters, I knew
nothing of the dialect in which babies should be addressed,
consequently I could only look simple, smile, ask its name,

how old it was, and whether it had teeth. This much done I usually diverted the attention of the mother to some subject, leaving her with the impression, no doubt, that I was a boor, and baby with the thought that I was very unsocial. Like most other men, however, when the baby had grown larger, had become three, four or five years old, my interest in it was stronger, especially if it had been well trained, and displayed evidence of brightness. But even then I never enjoyed more than a moment's attention to it, never entering into its sports with the zest that I had seen other young men display.

It was some time before I could assume the situation of paternity with the ease and pleasurable emotions that my companion wished me to exhibit.

My disinclination, however, to caress her soon wore off, and I began to watch her developments, and fondle her with the highest degree of paternal affection.

At her present age, young as she was, her image had become so engraven on my heart, she was so blended with my every thought of home, that future separation from her I felt would be worse than death to me.

It seemed to me that a home without children must be cheerless, comfortless—that a man who had never experienced the emotions, the cares, the responsibility of fatherhood was a creature but half developed—a being with the better portion of his nature yet dormant.

But I must not leave the reader to infer that everything had gone well with me since I had abandoned the occupation of farming.

For a year after that event I had taught in a neighboring

x

township of Canada, from the result of which I had paid the interest due Niel and forty dollars of the principal.

Returning home once more in a debilitated condition, and finding my father in poor health, I was again inclined to try my luck at farming. I believed that my former mistakes in this business would serve to make me more cautious, and I had little doubt that, if I economized and made no improvements except as means and opportunity presented, farming could be made to pay. My father being anxious to relieve himself of the care of the farm, I was induced to accept it.

My first act, after making this decision, was to get married. It was not quite pleasant to contemplate the difference in my situation now and what I had formerly resolved it should be when I led Ruth to the altar, but I was not the first who had been obliged to exchange a castle for a cottage in his transition from the ideal to the real.

My wife then asserted, and she still persists in asserting, that the only reason for my getting married was that I had nothing else to do, that I had tried everything else with the design of securing either honor or happiness and failed, hence, in disappointment and despair, I got married. That my life had been calculated to confirm her in this suspicion, I cannot deny, but the reader will understand by this time that my marriage was effected, finally, from the firm conviction, on my part, that it could never occur under happier auspices, and with the reflection that conjugal life might, perhaps, be as pleasant in humble circumstances as in the higher walks of life.

Ruth, as I have shown, had some means of her own.

The accumulation of interest on this, and what she had saved by teaching had left her, at the time of our marriage, in possession of a thousand dollars. The farm of which I was the proprietor, with stock, etc., was worth twice that sum, so that in reality we seemed to be prepared to enjoy the comforts if not the luxuries of life. As I now had, something myself, although obliged from this to provide for the support of my parents, I felt less delicacy in accepting her offers of assistance than I formerly did, and I had so far descended to the realities of life that I was ready to talk with her about the practical subject of our support.

It was decided that I should sell off part of the stock, all that could be possibly spared from the farm, for the purpose of paying a portion of the sum I was owing Niel. That Ruth's possessions should be used in enlarging the house—to make it convenient for two families, and in furnishing it, and that we should endeavor to save enough from the farm from year to year to extinguish my debt. Having mutually agreed to this arrangement we married; but before any part of the above plan had been put into execution a sudden disaster frustrated the whole scheme, and left us in an unpleasant condition.

One night, late in October, during a strong gale from the west, I was suddenly awakened by Ruth, with the startling intelligence that the house was on fire. Partially dressing myself, I flew down stairs, awakened my parents, and then rushed out with the hope that I might succeed in extinguishing the fire which had caught in the roof of the kitchen from a defective chimney. But the hope was futile. Already a large part of the roof was ablaze, and the burning shingles were flying directly on the roof of the barn, which was but a few rods distant, and this too was on fire. My first work, therefore, must be to save the cattle and horses, which were confined in it. By the time I had unloosed and driven them from the stable, all the buildings—houses barn and shed—were in flames. Our nearest neighbor was a quarter of a mile distant. I had aroused him by my shouts when I first left the house, but ere he came it was too late to render much assistance.

Besides the animals, I succeeded in saving the harness and waggons. The other members of the family had saved the clothes and bedding; except this, everything else was gone—hay, grain, farming utensils, furniture and books. I had a small library which I had collected at different times at an expense of about $400, and this was to me the sorest loss of all.

Homeless now, we spent the rest of the night with our neighbor. In the morning, when I went with Ruth to view the site of our dwelling, now a smouldering heap of ashes, I think I was the saddest, the most discouraged that I had ever been in my life. Fire insurance companies were not as numerous in those days as they now are, nor had people generally been aroused to the importance of having their property protected by them, consequently, our buildings were not insured.

Ruth saw my disheartened condition, and, concealing her own feelings, she assumed a cheerfulness and a quiet resignation to our loss that surprised me.

She adjured me not too look so sad and hopeless, saying that much worse things might have happened, and that as long as we still had each other, and my health was far better than it had been, I had no reason to despair. There was truth and wisdom in her remarks, and, inspired by her example, I rallied from despondency, and, before night, had done much in the way of disposing of the stock for which we now had no hay, and towards preparing for building.

Her money was now all that we had to rely on, and with this and the aid that was given me by kind neighbors and friends I succeeded in rearing very good buildings, though obliged to get along without the comfort of many of those things which accumulate in households in the course of years, yet so gradually that the occupants are hardly conscious that they have been obtained by a considerable outlay of money.

Contrary to my intentions, before this misfortune I taught the district school which I have before mentioned, boarding at home. Unpleasant as this work was, I was again placed in circumstances where I felt obliged to do anything by which I could honestly earn a dollar; my bad luck having blasted almost all hope of releasing myself from the clutches of Niel. I had got along comfortably up to the time I have mentioned, when our child was six months old, but the low price of farm produce that summer had prevented my paying the help we had to employ, and meeting other expenses, without contracting debts which I saw no way of canceling, except by devoting myself, for awhile, to some business disconnected with the farm. What should it be ? I was neither a professional man nor an artizan. I could neither preach, practice in the courts, treat the sick, build a house, work in a cabinet shop, or on the shoemaker's bench. I wished that I might hire out to work on a farm, cut cordwood, draw wood and bark to market, or something of that sort, but my strength was not sufficient. I could think of

nothing except teaching, but that I would not try until
positively assured I could do nothing else.

While trying to settle on some business, I picked up a
newspaper, and my eye fell on the following advertisements :

$100 *a month !* Business easy, requiring a capital of only $5.   Last
year four of our agents cleared $1500 each.
            Address,   Z. Tomkins & Co.,
                                            H———, N. H.

WANTED

Agents in every town in the United States.   No risk.   Profits immense !
            Address,   Fogg & Smith,
                                            F———, Conn.

AGENTS WANTED

To sell Livingstone's Explorations in Africa.   25,000 copies sold
last month !
                    Ferguson & Follett, Publishers,
                                            New York.

Without saying anything to Ruth, I addressed letters to
all these firms, not doubting that I would have employment
that would bring me $60 or $70 a month net profit.   Determined not to be disappointed, I placed my income at this
low figure, so that in the event of my making what other
agents had made my pleasure would be the greater.

In due time the answers came.   I was with Ruth alone
in the sitting-room in the evening when the letters were
handed me by a neighbor. I first opened the letter of Tom-
kins & Co.

It informed me that for $5 they would send me a recipe
for making a " very durable and beautiful jet black ink." I
could get the ingredients at any drug store, enough for $2

to make a quantity of ink that I could retail for $25. Everybody would buy **it.** It was so cheap that very few families would take less than a gallon, lawyers and men who had much **writing** to do often taking ten or twelve gallons. It also **gave** me the pleasant assurance that after I had obtained the recipe, if I had **not the $2** with which to purchase material, I could buy a smaller quantity, even ten cents being sufficient to start with. The ink manufactured from the ingredients **that** I could obtain **with** this small sum I could sell **to** my "nearest neighbors," **and** thus secure means to extend my trade. There was much more information given **in the** circular which I did not take the trouble to read. My hopes **of** employment began to flag. I next opened the letter of Fogg & Smith, and, **to my** inexpressible disgust, the **first sentence** that met my eye read as follows:

ONE BARREL OF EXCELLENT SOFT SOAP **FOR** FIVE CENTS.

This was enough. Thrusting these letters savagely **into** my coat-pocket, I tore open the envelope of the **last** letter. I could not be disappointed in this, as **I knew** the kind of work **in** which Messrs. Ferguson and **Follett** wished me to engage.

I regarded their **offer as** quite liberal, inasmuch as they promised **to supply me** with any number of copies of a book for **$1** each which I could retail for $2. **They** averred that one of their agents often sold ten copies in a day, and scarcely one of them had ever sold less than three. This was encouraging, and I determined to try it.

It is said that pride and poverty often go hand in hand, and I think that **at that** time I must have been a living illustration of the truth of this saying. That I should have considered it at all humiliating to be the vender of an interesting and instructive book, I can only account for on the ground that, as a rule, book agents are generally regarded as persons of little ability and very "hard up."

Taking a book agency seems to be the *dernier resort* of every body. It is the business to which all flee when they have shown themselves to be incompetent to do any other, hence, the expressions "he is nothing but a book agent," or "he is only fit to act as book agent." The fact that well educated and highly respectable people sometimes for various reasons act as book agents, does not seem to wipe out the stigma that rests upon the profession. They are not regarded as a dangerous class of individuals, but so many ill-bred characters have engaged in the business of book selling, and pressed their solicitations so much beyond all courtesy and decency; that the whole class has come to be regarded as a nuisance destitute alike of money and good breeding.

This opinion of book agents was not as prevalent in those days as it now is, yet it was generally entertained in the cities and in the most populous and wealthy districts of the country. It was the knowledge of this fact that made me decide that I would do nothing at this business except in some section where I was an entire stranger.

After reading these three letters I rose, went to the kitchen, and threw the two that displeased me into the stove. Ruth had observed the expression of disgust on my face and was naturally curious to know the contents of the letters, and when I paid no attention to her request to see them, she followed me and snatched them from the stove. She read them with much merriment and many jokes at my expense, and long afterward she never heard me express a desire to exchange my employment for some other without suggesting the manufacture of soap.

As she had learned thus much, I felt constrained to inform her of my intention with regard to the book agency. She said with a smile,

"If I believed that you would stick to it I would object to your taking a book agency, on account of your being absent from home so much, but I have no **fear** on that ground."

"Why?" I asked. "Don't you think I will succeed?"

"No," she replied. "I don't wish to discourage you, but if you will allow me to be your oracle in this case, I prophesy that you will give up the business within one week, and you will not make **a** dollar."

"Well, we shall see," I said, having a little too **much** confidence in her judgment not to feel somewhat discouraged by her prophecy.

A week after these letters were received, I was about forty miles from home, in one of the flourishing villages of Northern **Vermont, to test my** success in getting subscribers for "Livingstone's Explorations in Southern Africa."

I had arrived by stage late **the** previous evening, stayed at the principal hotel **over** night, and after breakfast the next morning sallied out to commence my labors. I shall not recount in detail that day's adventures; the rebuffs, excuses and indifference that I received, nor describe all the queer characters that I met. **At** night I had three **sub**scribers; one **of** whom I was informed always subscribed for every thing, and **paid** for nothing. I was told that I would do better outside of the village, among the farmers; and so the next day I acted on this advice.

The first house I stopped at was a fine large brick residence with commodious outbuildings, and everything around betokening such a degree of taste and wealth, that I had no doubt the proprietor would subscribe at once. He was sitting in his shirt sleeves, on his verandah, when I accosted him; a man past middle age, and looking as if he might be possessed of considerable intelligence. He took the book without making any remarks, or asking me to be seated; sent his little daughter into the house after his "specs," and then commenced reading. While he read I talked to the child. Fifteen, twenty, thirty minutes passed away and he had not raised his eyes, or spoken a word. At last I said:

"You find that a very interesting book, do you not, sir?"

"Yes, pretty fair," he drawled out as he turned another leaf and went on reading as before.

I amused myself with the child about ten minutes longer when I ventured to remark,

"I suppose I can take your name as a subscriber for the work."

So absorbed was he that he made no reply this time. I pulled out my watch and tried to show him that I was anxious to go on, but he seemed to be perfectly unconscious that I was present. Had it not been for his stoic countenance and something in his speech and manner which warded off any such suspicion, I might have thought he was indulging a freak of humor by tantalizing me, but I could only attribute his actions to meanness and stupidity, and my anger began slowly to rise. After waiting ten minutes more, I walked up to him, presented my subscription list and said,

"Will you have the kindness to put your name on this?"

Without deigning a look at it or raising his eyes from the book he replied,

"I'd 'no, its pretty hard times."

"Things about here don't look as if times are hard with you," I said.

No reply, but he kept on reading. Determined that he should continue this no longer I said,

"My dear sir, you are so int rested in this book you surely will not refuse to subscribe for it. I am in some haste to go on, and if you will put your name on this list you will greatly oblige me."

"I never subscribe for books or for anything else," he replied.

"Never?" I asked.

"No, never; I always pay down for everything I buy. When you come round with the books like enuff I'll take one."

"But I shall have none to sell, as I sell only by subscription."

"Well, then, I shan't get one," he replied, "You can't git me to subscribe for one anyway."

"Why didn't you tell me this at first," I asked, "instead of keeping me here an hour for you to read?"

"O you never can expect to sell goods unless you show 'em," he retorted with an indignant look; and this was all the satisfaction I received.

At the next house a woman came to the door, and before I had time to speak she asked in a sharp voice which reminded me of the yelp of a cur,

"Be you gittin' subscribers for books?"

"Yes, for one book," I replied, considerably abashed.

"Well, we don't want none," she yelped, and then, slamming the door in my face, retreated through the hall.

Book selling was losing its charms for me. It now ranked with school teaching as an employment in my estimation.

Proceeding to the next house, I found the proprietor, a coarse, blunt, but not an ill-natured fellow, hitching his horse to a buggy in the shed. Disclosing my business to him, he was silent for a short time, and then, in a drawling voice, exclaimed:

"Wall, I don't know, I never thought 'twas a very good plan to encourage these loafers that go round the country tryin' ter git their livin' without work. Of course, I don't mean you; you may be all right enuff, but half these fellers that go round sellin books aint any better than hoss thieves. Aint you able ter work?"

I was dumbfounded. For a moment I made no reply, but at length I stammered out—

"If I were not, I think I would not be in this business; I never did any harder work."

"Why? Don't they scribe pretty freely?" he asked.

"Not very," I replied.

"Wall, I don't know," he said, after meditating awhile; "ef I thought 'twas any charity to you I might subscribe. Haint you got no recommends or nothin' 'bout yer?"

"I did not suppose a person required any recommendation for himself in order to sell a good book," I replied.

" Wall, p'raps he don't," was the reply, " but I never subscribe for a book except ter help the feller that's sellin' it."

"That may be a very good motive," I said, " but I prefer
that you subscribe for this book on account of its value."

"Wall, let's go in," he said, after hitching his horse,
" and see what my wife says ; " and he led the **way** into the
kitchen.

"Sarah," he said to the woman who seemed to be getting
dinner, " here's a book agent. I don't know nothin' about
the book, but he don't look like a very rugged chap, and I
thought p'raps 'twould kinder be an act of charity to subscribe. What do ye say ? "

" Why," she exclaimed, " if you think its goin' ter dew
him any good, subscribe."

" Wall, I guess I will," he replied.

He then added his name to my short list of subscribers
for **a** book, **the** title **of** which I doubt if he ever knew.
Thanking him, I went in pursuit of another patron. It was
some distance to the next dwelling, and as I walked rapidly
along, anxious to get over as much territory as possible, I
passed a man **and two boys near the road** reaping wheat.
As I neared them, one of the boys espying me watched me
for a moment and then addressed his companion, who by
this time had also desisted from labor, **to look at** me, as
follows :

" I'll bet that feller's one o these—what d'ye call 'em ? "

" Book agents," suggested the man.

" Yes, that's it, book agents," said the boy. " Wonder ef
he'll sell any ter Barber's folks."

The other boy now spoke in low tones, but as **I was in**
close proximity to them I distinctly heard the remark.

" I tell yer, Jack, that aint a book agent ; he steps too spry.   Half on 'em don't move as though they had life enough to breathe without help."

" If they wer'nt lazy, they never'd try to git a livin' in that way," said the old man.

I was now too distant to hear the final verdict of the party with regard to myself and my vocation, nor was I anxious to hear more, having already become convinced that I had embarked in a business which caused everybody to regard me either as a pauper, or as one too indolent to work.

Turning in at the next house, which I presumed was Barber's, I timidly raised the old heavy iron knocker, and gave three faint raps.   A short, black-eyed and very consequential man of fifty answered the summons.   He did not ask me to come in, and as I was hesitating, fearful of making my business known, he gruffly said :

" Do you want to see me, sir ? "

" Are you the proprietor of this house ? " I asked.

" Yes," was the immediate response ; " but if you are a book agent there will be no need of your stopping ; I shant subscribe."

" Good morning, sir," I said, turning on my heel to depart.

" Good morning," he replied, and the door instantly banged behind me.

No doubt, many in my place would have meekly solicited a hearing, and in the end, perhaps, would have succeeded in securing a subscriber ; but, if persistency like that were essential to make a successful book agent, I evidently had mistaken my calling.

Had it not been for the humiliation of returning home so soon, I would at once have retraced my steps to the village, preparatory to the journey; but fear of ridicule made me decide on a few more efforts.

It was now near noon, and I began to feel considerable desire for dinner, **and,** as there was no hotel in the vicinity, I visited the next house, more with a wish to appease my appetite than to obtain a subscriber.

All the dwellings I **had** before visited indicated the possession of wealth **by the** proprietors; but this was a small, unpainted house, yet everything about it displayed neatness and taste in the occupants, and I had decided, in my own mind, that here I would get a subscriber and a good dinner. A young girl came to the **door,** and **my** first request was that she would ask the mistress if I could obtain anything to eat there. She stepped into an adjoining apartment, and I heard her make known my request to some one, evidently **a** woman.

"He's got a book, hasn't he?" inquired the person, **and** I concluded that **I had been observed from a** window **as I** was approaching. Being answered in **the** affirmative, **she** said,

"Well, if **we give** him his dinner, he **will make us** subscribe, so you can tell him we have **nothing ready for** dinner, and that he had **better go to the next** house; **and to** the next house I went before the girl returned with the message, resolved that **my** career as book agent **was** closed. The house **was a** few rods back from the road, **and,** as I turned in, I concealed my book under the **fence** by the gate, but I had been **seen** by **a** precocious urchin who was playing with his little **wagon before the door.** As I approached him, he looked at **me** with impertinent curiosity, **and** asked:

"Be you a book agent?"

"No!" I growled, feeling inclined to thrash him for indulging the thought, and then I inquired if his folks were at home.

"Yes," he answered, "and you can go in if you aint a book agent. Ma don't like them fellows, and I thought you was one 'cause I see you have a book or somethin' when you was comin' in the road."

To cut my story short, I obtained a good dinner for which they refused pay, and then I walked back to the village, and the next day I returned home, having spent four days and eight dollars in getting four subscribers. No one but my own family knew what I had been about, so that I escaped ridicule from every one save Ruth.

CHAPTER **XXV**.

IT was now toward **the last of August, and I immedi-**
ately secured **the** privilege **of** teaching **a select school in**
the town of Shirley **in Vermont, where I had been a stu-**
dent several years **before.**

As Ruth's knowledge of French was superior to my own,
and she, also, was skilled in **drawing and** painting, it was
decided that she should **teach these** in the school, and, **if**
necessary, assist me by teaching a class **or** two in some
of the other branches ; the **baby to be left** in the care
of a nurse at our boarding place. Pursuant to this arrangement, we opened our school, **and the** number **of** pupils
which came in was sufficient **to** inspire us with the hope
that we should have a prosperous **term.**

Y

A sharp letter from Niel just before we left home demanding payment of the note had strengthened our determination to practice the closest economy.

In consequence of the fire, I had been unable to pay him anything except two years' interest, since the new note was given.   After the loss thus sustained, I sold all the animals except one cow and horse, as I had neither hay nor grain wherewith to keep them.

In the spring I bought stock again on credit, and had not been able to pay for it and carry on the farm without, as I have shown, contracting other debts. It was now my decision to save what I could from my labor and in the spring to sell off everything, stock and whatever else would sell, and cancel my note to Niel with the proceeds ; trusting that in some way I might be able to support the family until I had raised more stock.

The great civil war was now raging in the United States, and everybody on the continent was looking on with intense interest, and anticipating the issue with varied degrees of anxiety.

As that was the land of my birth, and I had spent much of my life and received my education there, it was natural that I should watch the struggle with no ordinary interest, and receive tidings of every battle with excited emotions.

My sympathies were wholly and strongly with the Federal cause, and had my health permitted, I doubt not that I would have enlisted at the very first call for volunteers after the attack on Sumpter.   I often spoke of my desire to enter the army, but my friends, especially my mother and Ruth, opposed the step with all the force of admonition and persuasion.

I once mentioned my desire to a recruiting officer, but as he immediately informed me that he felt assured from my appearance that I would **not be** accepted by the examining physician, I did nothing further at that time towards becoming a soldier.

This was just previous to **my** marriage, but after I became stronger, and **had assumed a more** healthy appearance, my former thoughts of enlisting occasionally returned.

We had **been** teaching at Shirley a **week, when** I received a letter from Niel, in which he threatened to expose me to the law unless my note was paid within ten **days.** I had replied to his last **letter,** and told him in full my intentions, which I have **stated above,** and, **as he** could not possibly be pressed for money, **I** knew that he had not yet lost his desire to embarrass me. I confess that I was greatly worried by the letter, and knew not what to do. I had thought of the matter much through **the** following **day, and** in the evening was talking with Ruth **respecting it, and** trying to devise some method **of** complying **with his demand,** when our boarding mistress entered and informed me that a gentleman was awaiting me below. I **went down, and found** sitting in **the parlor a well-dressed man, who** informed me that he was a **recruiting** officer.

" Have you any idea of enlisting, **Mr. Styles ?** " he asked, after we had conversed for a moment.

" I have had some idea of it," I replied, " but I was once told by a recruiting officer that I would not be accepted **on** account of ill-health."

" Do you not think **you** would **be** able to endure the work of a soldier?" **he** again asked. " If you can, I am permitted to offer you good inducements for enlisting."

" What are your inducements ? " I inquired.

" Our Government pays a certain amount, to this the State adds considerable more, and the town to which belong, in Chittenden County, has very generously offered to pay $200 more to any one who will enroll himself as a citizen of that town, so that in case you are disposed to that, I will pay you $800.

" That certainly is a liberal offer," I replied, "and a great inducement to one in my circumstances to enlist, but I would not like to have any one imagine that I go as a mercenary soldier. Did I not feel a very strong desire for the success of the North, the money alone would be but a slight temptation to me."

" We need men of this sort, Mr. Styles. One man who fights from feelings of patriotism is worth ten mercenary soldiers ; and a man who is not rich cannot afford to refuse the bounty that is offered, as his family, or those relying on him for support, may very much need it during his absence."

" I think your reasoning is quite correct," I replied, " and I will consider your offer."

" And when can I know your decision ? "

" To-morrow morning, at eight o'clock."

Satisfied with this, I went up to our room, having decided before reaching it that I would enlist, provided I could be accepted. As I went in and sat down, Ruth, observing that I was laboring under excited emotions, asked if I had heard anything further from Niel. I said—

" No, and after a few days Niel will give me no more trouble, as I shall pay him."

"How?" she asked, with an expression of anxious curiosity on her face.

"I am going to enlist," I replied.

"Enlist!" she exclaimed, in a tone which showed her alarm at the thought.

"Yes, Ruth, I mean what I say; I know of no other way of obtaining the money for Niel, and besides, it will afford me great pleasure to do something in the cause of right and justice."

She had dropped the sewing at which she was engaged, and was now sitting unemployed—the picture of despair. At length she said:

"This is not your country, and it would be wicked for you to enter the army and fight, yes, to kill men for the sake of money."

"Come, Ruth, let us talk reasonably about this matter. This is my native country; and you know that, had my health permitted, I would have entered the army at a time when I could hope but little in the way of pecuniary reward, so I am free from the imputation of fighting merely from mercenary motives. At the present time, however, I see no way of extricating myself from the toils of Niel, only by accepting the offer that has been made me, and I confess that the money is a great inducement to me."

"Well, what will you do with your school? It would not be honorable to abandon it now after you have commenced."

"As for that," I replied, "the citizens of this country are never displeased with a person who leaves his business to enter the army; on the other hand, they rather applaud the act; and you know there is a young man in this village who came very near getting the school instead of myself, and he will take it off my hands now, if I wish."

"Well," she said, after another pause, "if you are determined to go, I suppose you will, but what will become of me and our Dora in the meantime? Can you leave that baby, Frank?" As she asked the last question, she stepped to the side of her crib where she was sleeping, and slightly removing a blanket exposed her rosy, innocent face to view.

The thought was too harrowing. I was vexed that she should thus try to make my leave so painful when she must know I thought that there was no alternative but to go. I did not for the moment consider that it had not yet so struck her, and that it was by thus appealing to my affections she sought to keep me with her. I made no reply, and a moment afterward she came up to me, and placing her hand on my shoulder said in the most pathetic tones,

"You will not go, will you, Frank?"

"What about Niel?" I asked.

At the name she started suddenly, and with a look of anger which I had never before seen her display she exclaimed :

"Oh that wicked wretch! I do not believe the Lord will suffer him to drive you into the army to be killed. If there is a place of endless torment, man surely never deserved it more richly than he."

"He has a right to his own," I said; "he should not be cursed for wanting his pay."

"I am astonished, Frank, that you should say a word in palliation of the actions of that wretch. His pay?" she repeated in a tone of scorn and contempt; "he cares nothing at all for the money. If he had it, he would either keep it in his house, or else put it out for half the interest you are paying him. And then to demand it of you just when you are beginning to recover from your misfortunes and are struggling to earn it for him! He should lose it all!" she exclaimed, being wrought up by the contemplation of his heartlessness to such a pitch of indignation that she **seemed** for the moment to have lost **her** conscientious regard for strict integrity in business transactions.

" That might be only justice to him," I said, " but you know that if I live he will never lose a cent through me,"

" I know that," she replied, " and **O, I** wonder if he never feels how much superior you are to him in honesty, as well as in everything else that pertains to manhood ; but I am sure, that if you were to see and talk with him, **he** would give you time to pay without compelling you to enter the army. Do you not think so ? "

" I do not know, but I certainly shall never **ask a favor** at his hands."

Our conversation continued long ; I might say, through the entire night, for neither of us slept, and scarcely an interval of half an hour elapsed **when** we were not thus engaged.

As soon as people were astir in the morning, I called on the different members of the school committee, to inform them of my intentions. Though they had little to do with my present school, I thought I might regard their opinion in the matter as an expression of my patrons' feelings ; and as they affirmed that they would be satisfied in case I obtained another teacher to fill my place, I immediately sought and found a successor. My resignation, however, was contingent on the circumstance of my being accepted as one physically qualified for military service, and in order to have this problem settled it was necessary to visit the town of Burlington, in Vermont. After seeing the young man who was to succeed me in school, I called at the hotel to give my final answer to the recruiting officer, and to effect a complete understanding with him in regard to the terms of my enlistment.

While waiting in the office for him to come in I chanced to glance at the names entered the previous day on the register, and was astonished to find the name of Niel, my creditor. The name below it was written in the same hand, which I recognised as his own. On enquiring of the clerk, I learned that the other name was that of the recruiting officer, and that he and Niel came together, and remained over night, but the latter had not yet left his room.

Up to that moment I had not known from what source the officer obtained his information that I wished to enlist, but it was now plainly evident. As everybody in the section where I lived knew my sentiments with regard to the rebellion, also my inclination to enlist, Niel must have been cognizant of them, and no doubt he had laid the plan for securing my enlistment. It would serve his purpose in two ways. First, he would get his money, and, second, he would have the gratification of knowing that it would give great trouble to both my wife and myself, causing, as it would, our separation for a long time, if not for ever.

He had, no doubt, written his last letter with the intention of compelling me to enlist, should the opportunity to do so present itself, and then he had taken care that the opportunity should be presented ere the first effect of his letter on my mind had time to wear off.

The discovery of the part he had thus played, in getting me to enlist, made not the slightest difference in my opinion of him, for I already despised him as thoroughly as man could despise another. I did not see him, while at the hotel ; whether because he knew that I was there and wished to avoid me, or whether something else detained him in his room, I know not. When the recruiting officer came in I asked if Niel was the **man** who informed him that I wished to enlist, and being answered in the affirmative, I knew, of course, that my suspicions of Niel's motives in so doing were correct.

From a desire to pay Niel before leaving, I insisted on having the $800 paid me as soon as my examination was made, and I had been accepted.

The day following, **I** went to obtain the note w'ich had so long haunted me, causing many days of anxiety and sorrow, producing many a sleepless night, and now contributing much towards taking me from my family **to** encounter the hardships and dangers **of** military life.

Strange power to be embodied in a bit of paper I thought, as I took it and placed it carefully in my pocket-book. I felt that I was now in possession of some vast treasure. I had not experienced such pleasurable emotions for years. It was a release from bondage ; and I doubt if **ever a** fugitive slave breathed **freer** than I did, **or** was happier on reaching a land of freedom than I was, **when** I returned home with that note in my possession.

Niel, I was informed **by** his servant, was not at home, but, in anticipation of my coming, he had left the note with him, authorizing him **to give it to** me whenever I was ready **to pay** it.

Ruth now returned to Foreston, and after spending a few days in arranging my business for a long absence, I started for my regiment. As the recollection of it is now painful to me, I shall not give a detailed account of all that transpired in my family during the preparations for my departure.

Many families along the frontier of Canada, as well as thousands in the United States, have experienced the same thing—the entire household enshrouded in gloom—sleepless nights, tears, prayers, and the sad, almost agonizing, final separation.

On the day I departed, Ruth began to display quiet resignation, and even cheerfulness; yet I knew that it was only assumed for my good, and that behind all this was—" grief that passeth show."

In trying to rouse her from her sad and gloomy state, a day or two previous, I cheerfully said:

"You do not very aptly imitate the heroism of Spartan women, Ruth."

"That is true," she said; "but I might feel differently had I been born in the States and spent my life there ; yet, I believe that then, unlike Spartan wives, my motto would be—" My husband first, and country afterwards."

CHAPTER XXVI.

I join my regiment—I meet two of my former pupils—My homesickness—Our winter quarters near Brandy Station— A betrayal and the punishment of the betrayer—A fight—I hear of my old colored friend, Tim, and am pleased to do him a favor once more.

AT Burlington, I met about a dozen volunteers who had recently enlisted, and we **all** were sent on immediately to Washington. A day or two subsequently, in company with many other new recruits, and convalescents who had left the hospitals, we were dispatched **to the army of the Poto**mac to fill up the ranks of those regiments which had been decimated by battles and disease.

The Vermont regiment which I joined belonged to a brigade encamped but a short distance south-west of Culpepper, in Virginia.

It was now early in October, and as the men were under the impression that they were to remain in this position for some time, they were sparing no pains to make themselves as comfortable as possible. Vacant houses, which were known to belong to rebels, as well as barns and other outbuildings, were demolished, and either converted into small cabins for the comfort of the soldiers or else into fuel. I was not backward in appropriating whatever I could that I conceived to be necessary for my comfort, and my experience at manual labor gave me the advantage over many of the regiment who knew but little about work.

There were members of every trade and profession in the regiment—lawyers, doctors, clergymen, teachers, farmers, merchants and mechanics; men of every degree of intelligence—from the poor young man who had barely learned to read and write, to the clever gentleman who had graduated with collegiate honors. A common cause, however, and common danger levelled all distinctions of rank among the soldiers. The country was at stake, the lives of all there were imperilled to preserve it, and the feeling of patriotism by which they were animated united all by a tie too strong to be severed or weakened by the conventionalities of society.

I was surprised soon after my arrival to be addressed by two soldiers who affirmed that they had been my pupils in Meadville, nearly ten years before. After a little time I recognised them as Tom O'Callaghan and William Sargent, both of whom had been actors in the scene in which Tom's father had shown me how they flog pupils in Ireland. Both were intelligent young men, nearly as old as myself, but Sargent was the only one married. They recollected the incident of the flogging distinctly, and we all laughed heartily over it. Tom had made a good use of his time since I knew him, so that, as unpromising as he then appeared, he was now something of a scholar, and was of sober and industrious habits. He retained considerable of the Irish accent, and having inherited no small amount of Irish wit and exuberant spirits, he was always a welcome companion when immediate danger or thoughts of home tended to make his comrades despondent.

I was very glad to meet these old acquaintances, even though I had not known them for years, for the sad and lonely feelings which possessed me during the first few days of my residence with the army made even the sight of a face that I had ever seen before a source of great pleasure.

I was not alone in my despondency; nor did I want for sympathy, for there was more than one in our regiment whose heart constantly yearned for home and the friends he had left behind.

A few evenings after my arrival, as several of us were sitting around a camp fire, Tom O'Callaghan, observing my disconsolate frame of mind, exclaimed,

"O don't be looking so sad about home and the Missus, Mr. Styles; in less than a month ye'll forgit all about it and be dead in love with one of the beautiful daughters of Dixie, that we so often see in this section."

Tom's design was evidently to arouse me into **a more** happy frame of mind by this address, and though it created a slight laugh among those present, and changed the current of my thoughts for a moment, it did **not** suffice to remove the burden of sorrow which had settled down upon my heart.

Nearly the whole night I rolled from side to side, disturbed by frightful dreams, and by deep bitter regrets that I had ever enlisted. I know not what I might have **been** tempted to do had there not been behind all these sad feelings, this anguish at separation from my family, a sort of feeling, a premonition, as it were, that God would preserve my life and give me other work to do in the future.

In the morning we received orders to march, and though I knew not but that it might be to certain danger, I hailed the order with delight. The work of marching would at least afford a momentary relief to my feelings; it was a respite from utter wretchedness and home-sickness.

It turned out that the movement we made was a retreat of the whole army. Simultaneously with this, Lee, the rebel general, changed his position, and soon there was a race between the two armies for a commanding position at Centreville; but fortunately we reached it first. Two or three days were consumed in effecting this march, and as we were sometimes attacked by detachments of the enemy, every hour was attended with more or less excitement. By the time we had reached the position desired, my homesickness had considerably decreased, and I was rapidly becoming reconciled to the life of a soldier. It was during this march that I had my first experience of having hostile bullets fly around me, and of sending the same missiles at my fellow men in return, but I witnessed only a little of the horrors of war compared with what I afterwards saw.

Early in December the army went into winter quarters between the Rappahannock and Rapidan in the vicinity of Brandy Station, and we remained there until March. The way in which we spent this winter may be learned from the following extract from the history of a Vermont regiment.

"The occupation of the men during these winter months were various—*they were Yankee.* Their quarters were all comfortably arranged; some of them were ingeniously fitted up and fancifully adorned.

Harper's and Leslie's Illustrated Weeklies furnished

many a soldier's hut with tasty decorations, after he had profitably read them. The battle cuts, views of camps and landscapes, were often carefully preserved and pinned or pasted to their cabin walls; added to them were the brilliant pictures and daubs of novel covers, and all these often interspersed with their own rude pencilings. Some of their tents were turned into cobbler's shops and tailoring establishments, where the occupant, with true Yankee enterprise, would repair the clothes and shoes of his neighbors; some of them, besides all the other purposes they served, were converted into jeweller's shops, **and watches were** actually well cleaned and repaired in the camp.

All kinds of craftsmen were found among the volunteers of our army, and details were easily made for the telegraph office, the forges, and all the workshops of the Quartermaster-General."

About six weeks after we had been encamped here, five of our regiment, after chatting awhile together one morning, agreed to take a tramp. Lieut. Stanley, a gentleman who had been a teacher and editor of a country newspaper for some years, Smith his friend, Sargent and O'Callaghan, **whom** I have mentioned, and myself, composed the party.

As the rebel army was encamped in sight, and parties of rebel soldiers were daily strolling away from camp and coming into proximity with our own, we knew that it was necessary to exercise much caution lest we should find ourselves exposed to their bullets, or perchance be taken prisoners. We were all well armed with muskets and revolvers, still we had no intention of wantonly exposing ourselves to danger, hence, we decided not to wander far from camp, which decision was strictly in accordance with **orders.**

There were many houses scattered over the country in the vicinity of our camp, some of which belonged to men loyal to the Federal cause, and others to men whose principles were not so well known, though it was pretty generally believed that they secretly desired the triumph of the Southern arms. The habitations of those men who had openly espoused the Confederate cause were quickly evacuated on the approach of our army, and their personal property left behind was as quickly ap ro riated to our use, the dwellings, as I have already shown, being demolished.

We had to walk some distance from our own cabins before we reached the outskirt of the camp, and passing two or three houses, we pushed on to a fine, large residence, standing on a hill about two miles distant.

A part of our company hesitated about going so far away, but Smith urged us to proceed, saying he had been informed that the house was owned by a staunch Union man, and that in case we were to visit him he would doubtless entertain us with a good dinner. This was a temptation, as we were all pretty well cloyed with the fare that we had had constantly for a long time, and so after a little discussion we yielded to Smith's solicitation and went on. I had some misgivings, so had Stanley and Sargent, but O'Callaghan and Smith laughed at our fears, and assured us that they should go on and enjoy a good dinner, but we might return to camp if we liked.

Nothing occurred during the walk to excite our fears, and we soon reached the old mansion, on the front gallery of which sat the proprietor in an arm-chair, smoking. He was just past the middle age, with a haughty carriage and a keen, restless black eye, which, from the moment **its** glance met my own, I felt assured portended evil to us.

Lieut. Stanley, addressing him, was received rather coolly at first, but in a few minutes the old fellow's manner changed and **he** seemed quite **sociable.** I had noticed the name R. A. Kershaw on the door-plate, and immediately remembered the surname as that of an old aristocratic family of Virginia, of whom I heard two officers of **our** regiment speaking a few days before.

" Are you out foraging ?" he asked of Stanley, whom he recognised as the only officer in the party.

" Not exactly foraging," replied Stanley, " but becoming tired of the monotony of our camp life, **we** concluded to take a stroll this pleasant day."

" Well," said Kershaw, " if you would like to rest awhile here, sit down, and I'll have some refreshment prepared for you before you go."

There were a few **chairs and a** settee on the verandah, and on receiving this invitation we all seated ourselves.

" Do you or any of your party smoke ?" **he** next asked.

Sargent and myself were the only ones in **the party** who did not smoke, and learning this fact, he went **into the** house and soon returned, followed by a colored servant, who carried a box of choice Havanas. After Kershaw was again seated, and our friends were engaged in smoking, the conversation was opened and carried on **with** considerable animation between Kershaw and Stanley, for nearly an hour. The beauty of the situation of his residence commanded much admiration from all of us, and then he gave us quite a detailed account of the doings of his ancestors, as well as himself, since this part of Virignia had been their home.

z

It was noticeable, however, that he never alluded to his political views, and as he never once spoke of the rebellion, or the causes which had led to it, it was obvious that he was a rebel at heart, even though he attempted to display friendship for us.

At length a female servant came and informed him that the refreshment he had ordered for us was ready.

"Well, show them into the dining hall," said Kershaw to her. "You will excuse me, Lieutenant," he said, addressing Stanley, "for not dining with you, for I took a very late breakfast, and as I feel somewhat indisposed to-day, I have no inclination to eat at this hour."

Stanley excused him, and then began to offer some apology for our intrusion, but he was quickly interrupted by Kershaw, who bade him not to mention intrusion, trouble, or anything of the kind, and added with a smile :

"It is only a pleasure to show hospitality to the defenders of our country."

"I thought you were a Union man," replied Stanley, "although I had no means of knowing."

Kershaw colored deeply, and after a little hesitation, stammered out, as if reluctant to do so, the following reply,

"O yes, I believe in sustaining the Union at all hazards."

He then rose from his seat and walked off to the further end of the verandah, while our party followed the servant to the dining hall. The table was supplied with everything that we could desire. Beside a bountiful supply of meats of various kinds, and all the substantial kinds of food, there was champagne and a variety of wines. The champagne and wines were not touched, as we gladly accepted tea and coffee instead. The peculiar manner of our host had not been unobserved by any of us, and most of us felt a sense of uneasiness, a desire to get back to our camp as soon as possible.

While we were engaged with dinner, another servant, a fine looking colored girl, not over twenty-two, entered the dining hall, and passing by us to the further end of the apartment, she took some article from a stand and then immediately returned. As she passed behind and near me, she quickly but cautiously dropped a note before me. Taking it up and unfolding it I read as follows:

"DEAR FRIENDS,—*For heaven's sake do not betray me.* Master Kershaw is a rank rebel, and officers of the rebel army often visit him. I think he expects some of them here this afternoon or evening. Soon after you came, he sent Jake, one of his colored servants, away on horseback, towards the rebel camp.

"Look out for yourselves.

"YOUR FRIEND."

There was no name appended to the note, but I felt that it was written by an honest and sincere friend, and that, consequently, the warning given us was not to be despised. I threw the note across the table to Stanley, and after he had read it he in turn gave it to Smith, who was sitting on his right. He then, with an expression of countenance which indicated some degree of uneasiness, looked at me and said,

"What do you think of that, Styles?"

"I think," I replied, "that we had better start for our camp as soon as possible."

Smith having now read the note and heard my reply exclaimed,

"O pshaw! I don't believe that there is anything to be feared. This servant like all darkies wants to get up a sensation." He then took up the note and read it aloud, after which he said

"Don't be scared, boys; let's finish our dinner. Tom, please give me a bit more of that bacon, it is very nice."

It was perhaps his coolness and fearlessness of danger which made the rest of us reluctant to leave the table, hence, we remained and fully satiated our appetites, although it was evident from the countenances of all except Smith that they were ill at ease. Having finished my dinner, before the others had risen from the table, I stepped to a window in rear of the apartment and looked out.

Judge my astonishment then, kind reader, when I saw, not more than a hundred yard yards distant, ten or twelve rebel horsemen approaching the house under cover of the barns and outbuildings; and just behind them rode a colored man, who no doubt was the servant that Kershaw had despatched to betray us. As he had not been gone very long it was evident he had met them. There was no time to be lost.

I immediately said in a low tone:

"Quiet boys! we are betrayed; the rebels are upon us."

Instantly every one of them was at the window and took in the extent of our danger.

"We must either escape or die fighting," said our Lieutenant. "Which shall we do, Styles?" he asked of me in startling tones.

"They outnumber us," I replied, "and have horses too. Let us escape if we can, but let no one of us be taken alive."

As I said this, I glanced at the faces of my companions, and the low but determined " No ! no !" which broke from their lips, showed plainly that my opinion was the opinion of all.

Our guns were all standing in the hall, and in another moment we had taken them and were quickly passing out of the front door. No one was in sight ; but, ere we were across the lawn, the girl who had kindly given us the warning called us, and then ran towards us with outstretched hands.

" Oh, for heaven's sake, take me with you," she entreated ; " they will kill me for telling you, if I remain."

Although our flight would, no doubt, be greatly retarded by granting her request, not one of us for a moment thought of refusing her, and as she came up, Stanley took her by one arm and Sargent by the other and hurried her away with us at the greatest possible speed. We had gone perhaps two hundred yards when we heard a loud cry and the discharge of a gun, and at the same instant a bullet whistled over our heads. Tom O'Callaghan **stopped, and,** instinctively, the rest of us halted to see if there **was any-**thing the matter. **As** Tom brought his gun to his shoulder and fired, we were not long in suspense **as to** the object o f his stopping. Standing on the veranda with a carbine in his hand, which he had just fired at us, was Kershaw. Coming around towards the front of the house, on the gallop, was the party of rebels who had descried us, and they now gave a lusty shout and came **dashing** on, thinking no doubt that they had an easy prey. Tom, with his usual accurate aim, had made sure of his mark—Kershaw threw up his arms and fell backward. We gave Tom a cheer, and as we turned **to** run again, he exclaimed :

" I meant the old traitor should be punished for his treachery if I hadn't forgot how to shoot."

He had no more than uttered these words than several bullets whistled above us. As we were so much below them we had little fear that their shots would hit us, but they were rapidly nearing, and should they be permitted to come up with us, all hope of escape was at an end. This fact was obvious to Stanley, and he at once said :

" Lie down, boys, and shoot them before they can reach us! Quick, fall flat on your faces and fire."

Instantly the order was obeyed, and as they were now on their horses, and afforded good targets, we felt that the advantage was on our side. At our first fire two men and one horse fell to the ground. As there was a slight depression of the grou nd where we were lying, we must have been almost concealed from our foes. They halted and fired, but this time their shots not only flew high above us but considerably to one side. Seeing our advantage of them, they dismounted and tried to conceal themselves behind their horses. As they were in the act of doing this we gave them another volley, and another horse with his rider went down. The fact that we had them at our mercy, and could shoot them all and escape unharmed ourselves, seemed now to dawn upon them. Mounting their horses again they galloped rapidly back, taking their killed and wounded with them. We gave them a parting volley as they retired, but without effect. Our whole party might have escaped without a scratch, but Smith, who had led us into the difficulty, with his usual foolhardiness rose, and swinging his hat gave a loud cheer to the retreating rebels. He was the only one exposed to view, and seeing him, one of our foes, evidently a sharp-shooter, turned in his saddle and fired. The ball struck Smith's thigh, but it was only a bad flesh wound which bled profusely.

As soon as the rebels had left us, we took our wounded companion and hastened towards the camp. We had gone less than a mile when we met about twenty of our men who had been out foraging, and having heard the firing, had come on to ascertain its cause. Having told them our story, it was suggested that four of the party should take Smith back to camp, and the remainder return to Kershaw's, both to destroy his buildings and, if possible, capture the rebels who had pursued us. Accordingly, Sargent remained with those who took Smith to camp, and Tom and myself, with seventeen more, all under command of Lieut. Stanley, returned to take summary vengeance for our wrongs.

As we passed the spot where we shot the rebels and their horses, we found one poor animal attempting to get up. He was severely wounded, and, in compassion to him, one of the men sent a bullet through his head. The rebels, evidently, had anticipated a return of our soldiers, and had not remained long at Kershaw's. As we reached the house, we saw them more than a mile distant, hastening to their camp.

A pool of blood on the floor, where Kershaw stood when Tom shot at him, showed the accuracy of the aim. Two servants who were in the house informed us that "Massa" was "drefully wounded," and would, no doubt, die; but that he had asked the rebels to carry him to their camp, where he could be treated by a surgeon and escape the wrath of the Union soldiers.

I had forgotten to say that Julia, the girl who went with us, had insisted on returning to the house, now that she was so well protected, in order to obtain her clothes and other possessions which remained there. After ransacking the house, and giving to her and the other servants whatever they wished, we went out and harnessed the horses to a cart and express wagon, which we loaded with provisions and other valuables for the camp, drove off three cows and a yoke of oxen which we found on the premises, and then, having fired all the buildings, departed.

The female servants informed us that Jake had gone with his master to the Rebel camp, but they accompanied us to our own camp and were placed in charge of the wives of several of our officers who were there on a visit to their husbands. As we were returning from Kershaw's to our camp the first time with the colored girl, I learned that her name was Julia Larkin. She also informed us that her father had escaped from slavery some years before, and now that she was free she hoped to see him. Being too much engaged with the exciting incidents of the day to give particular heed to what she said at the time, I dismissed it from my thoughts. Several times, however, during the afternoon I thought of the name Larkin, and fancied that it sounded familiar, yet I found it impossible to tell when or where I had heard it. Early in the evening, in thinking of the name once more, Tim Larkin, our colored friend at Corvette, came to my mind.

Here, then, the mystery was solved ; the name which had so puzzled me belonged to the fugitive slave whom Mack and myself had rescued from his kidnappers. Julia had informed me that her father had escaped from slavery.

Was it possible that she was Tim's daughter? It might be, and I decided to see her again. An hour later I sought and found her, and to my surprise and pleasure learned that she was the daughter of the identical Tim whom I have introduced to the reader. In less than two years after her father escaped, their master failed, and, in consequence, she, her sister and mother were separated, being purchased by different slave holders. She was purchased by Kershaw, with whom she had now lived some time. Though she had no particular reason to complain of ill treatment at his hands, she had never liked him, and was only too glad of an opportunity to escape. His wife, who had recently died, had been very kind to her, and through her influence she had been taught to read and write. She informed me that her father was a soldier in one of the colored regiments of the Union army, and it was now her intention to find him. She had heard from him occasionally, but had never seen him since the day he escaped. Her mother was still in North Carolina, and her sister was in Virginia, about fifty miles distant, but she had seen neither of them since the day they were sold. She knew not how the rebellion might have affected them, but she had no doubt that they were still living with their former masters. She was quite intelligent, and after learning that I had written two or three of the letters which they received from her father soon after his escape, and that I had also assisted in rescuing him from the toils of slavery after he had once obtained his freedom, she manifested great gratitude, and asked that I would assist her in finding her father. I related her history and that of her parents, so far as I knew it, to the wife of the officer with whom she was then remaining, and an interest in her being thus awakened, it was decided that the lady would take her to Washington, in which place the whereabouts of her father could easily be ascertained.

I returned to my quarters after this interview, meditating on the strange mutation of affairs which had again given me information respecting the almost forgotten fugitive slave, Tim, and given me also another opportunity of showing him a kindness. It was a pleasant, happy reflection, too, that, through the dispensations of an Omnipotent Judge, Tim's hopes of again living with his family would be realized. Yes, the poor fellow would now no longer be obliged to watch and skulk among his fellow men to preserve his own liberty, and to pray and plan for means by which he could secure that of his wife and children. God had relieved him of this burden, and not only to him and his, but to millions of his race, had he proclaimed the joyful tidings of *Freedom.*

CHAPTER XXVII.

As it is not in my province to give a history of the **American** Rebellion, I shall not detail to the reader the various changes that were made in our Army Corps and Divisions, nor the marches, counter-marches and manœuvring which preceded the battle of the Wilderness. Up to this time I had never been directly under fire of the enemy, nor had I witnessed the excitement and ghastliness of the battle field.

During the several days fight which here occurred, although our division was kept in reserve we were exposed much of the time to the shells of the enemy, and several of our regiment passed **to**

" The bourne whence no traveller returns."

The battle of Spottsylvania soon followed, and here probably occurred one of the most desperate fights of the whole war. It might perhaps, above all others, be regarded the battle in which the respective combatants strove to the utmost for the supremacy. It was here that in assaulting a rebel earthwork my old pupil, Tom O'Callaghan, was killed. Poor fellow, ever since I entered the army he had been a friend. The position of teacher, which I formerly occupied towards him, seemed never to have been forgotten; he always treated me with kindness, and never addressed me in any but terms of the greatest respct.

During the battle of Spottsylvania we received an order to capture a rebel earthwork from which sharp-shooters had harassed us and picked off many of our men.

There was no hesitation, we felt as keenly as our officers the necessity of doing the work, and although many of our brave fellows fell in crossing the space that intervened between us and the breastwork, we never hesitated but rushed on, and were soon in a hand to hand fight with our foes in their entrenchment. Tom O'Callaghan and myself mounted the parapet together, and just as we were in the act of leaping down on the other side, a tall rebel, not ten feet distant, shot Tom through the chest. I shall never forget the look which the poor fellow gave me as he fell and rolled over on his back. It seemed to say,

" Styles, do you see this ? Will you avenge me ? "

He lived long enough to know my answer. His slayer, who was just in the act of aiming his revolver at me, the next instant fell forward, and their life blood oozed out and mingled in the same pool. I would have spoken to Tom, but there was no time. I pressed his hand and was hurrying away when a rebel rushed upon me with fixed bayonet, and would no doubt have driven it through my body, had not one of our men, at that instant, shot him through the head.

It was a fearful fight, but quickly over. I recoil from portraying in detail the bloody scene. In less than three minutes after we had reached the breastwork, the rebels, although they had fought with desperation, turned and fled. Giving a loud hurrah, we followed them until we came in range of one of their batteries, when we turned back. I immediately sought **my** friend Tom amongst the dead and dying with which the ground was covered, **and** found him just in time to see his spirit take its flight.

Sargent, like myself, had gone through the fight unharmed, and seeing him a little distance **off**, I ran and informed him of our friend's fate.

We went back to his lifeless **form,** where Sargent gave himself up to the emotions of grief which filled his breast. They had been neighbors from boyhood, had enlisted at the same time, and during the time I had been in the army, they had always manifested a strong feeling of friendship for each other. It was no wonder then that he felt Tom's death keenly ; and **I could fully** appreciate his feelings too, when, after looking on the form of his companion for a moment, and then on that of the one who had shot him, **he** placed his hands over his **face, and exclaimed,** in anguish of spirit :

"Oh, this dreadful, horrid war !"

It was, indeed, dreadful, and as I looked around upon the ghastly slain, and thought **of** the households and friends that would mourn their loss, the solemn truth, embodied in the lines,

> " Man's inhumanity to man
> Makes countless thousands mourn,"

was impressed upon me with a force a thousandfold more potent than I had ever felt it before.

Tom O'Callaghan was unmarried ; his mother was dead ; his father was still the same dissipated man that he was in Tom's boyhood, hence, he probably would feel his loss but little. He had two or three children besides Tom, but, as they had long been separated, seeking a livelihood in places far apart, they had but little love for each other, and, consequently, Sargent was doubtless the deepest mourner in the world, save one for poor Tom. Like myself, Sargent had a wife and child, and, as we walked away, he said :

" It is well that Tom was neither a husband nor father. It would be hard for our families, Mr. Styles, to learn that we had met his fate;" and the tears started afresh as he thought of the grief such tidings would carry to his fireside.

The subject was too harrowing for me to speak of, and I made no reply. This was the second day of the fight, and as we had as yet gained no decided advantage, there was still hot and bloody work to be done. It seemed impossible that we could escape death exposed another day as we had been on that, and it was more than probable that the sad scene Sargent had been contemplating would soon occur.

I say that such an event seemed more than probable, yet, the inner feeling of security from death on the battle field, which I have already mentioned, buoyed me up, and nerved me for my work. I wondered whether all our soldiers enjoyed the same feeling, yet I feared to ask any lest I might find that they did, and, consequently, my reliance on the premonition would be destroyed.

The enjoyment of this assurance I thought might be a blessing vouchsafed the soldier to sustain him in his work. But through all my stay with the army, I dreaded death far less on my own account than I did for the little group in Foreston that was praying without ceasing for my preservation and return.

Fighting continued for many successive days, and numerous square miles were made gory with the blood of the best men in the contending armies. Not privates alone but officers of all ranks, those who had won laurels on other battle fields, largely swelled the lists of the killed.

Some days after moving from Spottsylvania Court House, and before crossing the North Anna, we received our mail from the North. It was a joyful event, as we had received none before for nearly three weeks.

It was a sad sight to see the scores of letters addressed to poor fellows who since we received our last mail had gone to their final resting place ; letters written by those who far away were praying for the preservation of fathers, husbands, brothers and sons, and anticipating years of comfort and pleasure in their society after their return. Sargent was standing by me when the name of Thomas O'Callaghan was called. He took the letter, and with tearful eye, glancing at the superscription, said,

" It is from ———, the girl whom Tom intended to marry when he went home. I shall write to her to-morrow and return her picture, which I found in his pocket before he was buried."

I received a long letter from Ruth, in which was the following paragraph, which displays the wonderful power of our magnetic union :

" I fear, my dear husband, that you are either ill, or that serious danger or difficulties of some kind affect you. During the last few days an indefinable feeling of uneasiness with regard to you has possessed me. Did I not enjoy that feeling which you say you enjoy, that God will answer our prayers and permit you to return, it seems to me that I must become insane. I still adhere to my resolution of not reading the war news in the papers; I never could endure it."

The date of this letter showed that the last few days which she mentioned referred to those in which our last battle occurred. I wrote to her that day, giving a full account of the fight, but never intimating that we were anticipating an immediate renewal of the scenes in another place.

At the battle of Cold Harbor, which next followed, Sargent's left arm was taken off by the bursting of a shell, in consequence of which he was sent to hospital, and after nearly recovering he was discharged. Though maimed for life, a pension which he afterward received served with his other sources of revenue to make his family comfortable.

Early in July, the division to which I belonged was ordered to Harper's Ferry, to contest the advance of the Rebel General Early into Maryland. Nothing save the close of the war and a discharge from the army could have given us greater pleasure. Owing to the long campaigns and constant fighting, the soldiers of our Corps were nearly exhausted, and a respite, however brief, was regarded a godsend by us all. For two months, twenty-four hours had not elapsed that we were not within gun shot of the enemy, and not an hour that we had not been obliged to listen either to the roar of musketry or of cannon.

As for myself, I wondered at my powers of endurance. In a few days after the above order was given the battle of Monocacy was fought. Although in this engagement two men were shot down by my side, a musket ball was sent through my coat and another through my hat, I escaped unharmed. **I began to imagine that** I possessed a charmed life.

During the first days **of** August, the campaign of the Shenandoah Valley was inaugurated. On the tenth of that month our forces, thirty thousand **strong, marched** into Charlestown, the place made famous by **the trial and** execution of John Brown, to whose memory I have paid tribute in a preceding chapter.

As the incident had rendered the place one of deep interest to me, I marched through the streets with something of the same feeling I fancy that the Moslem approaches the shrine of Mecca. As if in retributive justice for this foul deed, the marks of decay and desolation were everywhere visible in the town.

I almost fancied that **I** could hear **the voice** of a prophet proclaiming woe and desolation to it, not unlike **that** which was pronounced against Babylon. **The** whole army seemed possessed with the same feelings, and **thousands** of voices broke forth singing, "John Brown's body lies mouldering in the ground," and several bands played the **air to** which these words were set.

It was my good fortune to have the honor of participating in all the succeeding important battles of the Shenandoah Valley, Winchester, Fisher's Hill and Cedar Creek. **In** December, we returned to Washington, and soon after our division moved to Hatcher's Run as a supporting column

to those who had gone to destroy the Weldon Railroad,
which was being used by the enemy.   During this expedition, while we were standing several hours in line of battle,
in mud and water six inches deep, I caught a severe cold
which proved of serious consequence to me, and prevented
my performing further service during the war.   Neglecting
this cold too long, I was soon obliged to go into hospital at
Washington, where congestion of the lungs, fever and utter
physical prostration compelled me to remain during the
entire winter.   It was a great blessing and pleasure to me
to have Ruth come and spend a month nursing me during
the time that I was the most prostrated.   She was desirous,
as well as myself, that I should return home after I had
become sufficiently convalescent ; but my physician forbade
it, declaring that the cold, changeable climate of Canada
would be more than my constitution could stand until I
had become much stronger.   He advised that I should
remain here until the warm weather of spring had set in ;
and having much confidence in his judgment I reluctantly
accepted the advice.

   It was about the middle of March, after I had become
sufficiently strong to ride out occasionally with a friend
residing in the city, who had been in the army but discharged on account of ill health, that I was greatly surprised by falling in with an old acquaintance who has
already figured in these pages.

   A few miles out from Washington, and on a spot where
numberless regiments had encamped preparatory to being
sent on their campaigns, stands, or did stand, a building
which at that time was used as a factory for utilizing the
carcasses of animals which had died or been killed in that

section. Horns and hoofs were here made into glue ; the hair was preserved for various purposes while the carcasses themselves were manufactured into soap. An unwholesome stench pervaded the place, so that none with delicate nerves or fastidious tastes would be likely to visit it except with an eye to business. While riding near this factory one fine morning with my friend, we chanced to meet a portly looking gentleman with heavy side whiskers walking leisurely with a hickory. His face was very red, betokening indulgence to considerable extent, while his habiliments were exceedingly seedy.

He was a man something over fifty, and bore all appearance of one who had seen better days, but, either from dissipation or untoward fortune, was now in reduced circumstances. As we neared him, and he raised his eyes, I was startled ; his countenance seemed wonderfully familiar, and yet I could not tell when or where I had seen him. As he passed us I turned round to get another look. Could it be possible? Was it Baxter, the former representative of McClintock County, who had treated me so ignominiously in Montreal, some years before? He certainly very closely resembled that worthy, and I determined to learn his name. Two boys were coming in the road about ten rods distant. On meeting them I said :

"Can one of you young gentlemen tell us who that man is whom we just passed ? "

"Yes, sir," said one of them promptly, "that is Mr. Baxter, what's a boss in the soap factory over thar."

The idea was too ridiculous, and I burst into a hearty laugh. The boy's face reddened, and he evidently thought I was making fun of him.

"Don't be offended, my boy," I said, giving him a small coin, "I wish to ask you a few questions. Do you know where Mr. Baxter came from?"

"I aint sure," he responded, "but I believe he came from Vermont."

"No, Jack," interposed the other boy, "he come from Canady. Father works in the factory, and he said so."

"How long has he been here?"

"'Bout two years, I guess."

"And where does he live?"

"Up thar, in that house he's jest gwine into."

I looked back, and saw him entering an unpainted, unpretentious looking house, a few steps back from the road.

Having driven on a little further, in which time I gave my friend a brief account of my acquaintance with Baxter, we returned; and such was my curiosity to learn how it was that he appeared in that place, and in circumstances so different from those in which I had known him, I determined to ascertain from himself.

Halting at the house and alighting, I knocked, with the intention of asking for a glass of water, when Baxter himself came to the door.

"How do you do, Mr. Baxter?" I said.

He stiffly acknowledged my salutation, and after looking at me sternly and enquiringly for a moment, asked if I would walk in. As I stepped inside, I said:

"You do not recognize me, I perceive."

He replied:

"Your countenance seems familiar, but I certainly cannot say where I have met you."

"My name is Styles," I said, "and I went with you

once on an electioneering trip from Dr. Sutherland's to Hilton, when you were canvassing the County of McClintock."

Had an angel appeared to him that instant, I do not think he could have been more surprised.

At first his countenance flushed; he looked bewildered, stammered out something, and then seizing me by the hand, shook it until I thought my arm would have to be amputated.

"Who have you here," he exclaimed, looking out towards the carriage.

"A friend," I replied.

"Well, ask him in, **ask him in, by all** means; you are going to dine with me to-day."

I invited my friend in and introduced him, but declined remaining more than a few moments.

Baxter showed us into the parlor, which was provided with a faded and nearly worn-out carpet, the scanty furniture corresponding well **with it in** respect to its dilapidated appearance. A care-worn woman, who, in her younger days, might have been handsome, and **whom he** introduced to us as his wife, left the **room as we entered. As we** seated ourselves, Baxter said:

"How is it, Mr. Styles, that you chance to be down here? I am astonished to **see** you here."

"Your astonishment cannot **exceed mine,**" I said, "at seeing you here;" and I then related briefly to him how it happened that I was a soldier. "Well, now," he said, "let's have a little wine, and I will then gratify your curiosity." Saying this, he went out and in a moment **returned** with a bottle and glasses. We each took a glass of **port** with him when **he** commenced **as follows:**

" I suppose you saw a paragraph in the Montreal papers two or three years ago, about a little difficulty I had there."

I had seen nothing of the kind, yet not wishing to say so, lest it might prevent our hearing the truth of the matter, I remained silent a moment, trying to devise some ingenious answer without telling a falsehood ; when interpreting my silence as an answer in the affirmative, he continued :

" Well, they tried pretty hard to make forgery of it, but of course that was all nonsense. I knew I could easily defeat them, but as business was very dull in the city, and I did not care to remain, especially since some of my old friends had deserted me, I concluded to try my fortune elsewhere, and so I drifted down this way."

" And are you practicing law ? " I asked, as if ignorant of his present occupation.

" O no," he replied, " I am an overseer in a manufactory. I wished to have something for my boys to do, and as this seemed to be a good opening I secured it."

I did not ask what sort of a manufactory it was, nor did I ask him further with regard to his trouble in Montreal. By his own admission he was fearful of being convicted of forgery, hence, had run away. Until that moment I knew not that he had any children, and touched with pity I forgave him his rascality towards me, and cordially hoped that he might do well. After a moment's silence he said :

" You knew my political principles in Canada, and of course are quite aware that they would not be tolerated here. I refer to my sympathy for the South at the commencement of the Rebellion, and as an old friend you will say nothing that will be injurious to me in this section," and as he uttered this he cast a searching look towards both my friend and myself. Previous to that, I had known nothing of his sympathies with the South. I only remembered that his loyalty to "the old flag" on one occasion had caused him to refuse to assist me, because I was born in the States. I felt that he had need of sympathy, however, and I promised him the favor of both my silence and that of my friend.

After a few more remarks with him we bade him farewell with a promise to call again, if possible, at no distant day, and then drove off. I did not see him again. In a few days I received my discharge, and bidding farewell to the scenes of war, I made my way to Canada.

CHAPTER XXVIII.

Farming again—sad affliction.

I WAS now at home again, happy in the presence of my family, and hoping that during our earthly pilgrimage untoward fortune might never again call me from them. There was such happiness in contemplating a quiet, peaceful life in this secluded spot—the life of a farmer, so pleasant and healthful, and wonderfully in contrast to that which I had led for so long a time. Yet I could foresee that even this must have its discomforts. Hardship and exposure had shown their effect on my physical system, and it was obvious to me that I was poorly prepared to confine myself to severe labor. Though the vocation of agriculture may be all that I have said, pleasant and healthful, it requires bodily vigor and unintermitting industry in the person who follows it to make it remunerative. A man whose income is derived wholly from a small farm can ill afford to hire labor, and especially if he has a family; his own hands must do the plowing, planting, sowing and reaping; in short everything, if he would thrive. This was the difficulty under which I labored, the unyielding obstacle which had prevented me from accumulating means. The money I received on entering the army had gone to pay debts; that which was paid me afterward from time to time had been used to employ help, so that now I was without the funds necessary to carry on the farm, and was unable to do it myself.

I had a piece **of** woodland which I determined to clear and bring into pasture and tillage land, and thus be enabled to increase the quantity of my stock. Soon after returning I engaged wood choppers for the purpose; hoping to realize enough from the wood, timber, lumber and first year's crop to more than pay for the expense of clearing.

It was another instance of miscalculation; one of the unhappy consequences of possessing idealty in a too large degree. The expense was much greater than I had calculated, and the proceeds resulting from the sales I had hoped to make were much smaller; hence, I was again considerably in debt. I found that my investments, though valuable, would make returns only in the lapse of time.

There is scarcely any business into which a man **without** experience may enter with less surety of success than he can farming. And yet **the managing of it** seems so easy, so simple, that many **a novice with a** good capital has rushed into it, following his theoretical notions until he has either found himself in bankruptcy, or with his means invested in improvements which will only bring back the money in installments, in the course of a generation of time.

This disastrous experience in farming occupied my attention for a year after my return from the war, but scarcely had I entered upon it ere I was doomed to affliction such I had never before experienced.

Dora, like the only child of all parents, was the idol of the household. She had heard me spoken of so much during my absence, and Ruth had so often talked to her respecting me, that, I have no doubt, I was as much associated with her thoughts as I would have been had I always been present with her. It had been one of her favorite amusements during the time I was away to pick up scraps of paper and read imaginary letters from her "papa" to the family. Their contents, of course, were suggested by such points in the real letters as her childish memory retained, and were usually an account of marches, defeats and victories, in which the names of places and commanders were grotesquely commingled and confounded; the whole closing by affectionate allusions to the different members of the family.

So constantly had her thoughts been directed to me, that when I returned, though a little shy at first, she soon expressed as much delight as the others. From the day that I came home, until sickness prevented, she was always with me in my rambles, and, sitting on my knee, beguiled many an hour of despondency with her childish prattle.

But it was not always to be thus; her society, so dear to us, was vouchsafed only for a short time. Even before I entered the army, the wonderful development of mental power which she exhibited awakened my fears that she would die at an early age. As accounts of her precocious actions and words were written me from time to time by Ruth, I felt more certain that my fears were not groundless, and even suggested to her mother that we should regard her as a treasure we were not long to keep. Though delicate in health, she had never been sick, and, after my return, when I saw her in gleeful mood running about the yard, her flaxen ringlets dancing in the breeze, I saw no reason why she might not live to cheer us in our declining years.

While she was playful like most children, there was something **more grave and** thoughtful in her face—an expression of sadness—which we often observed with pain.

Not long after my return, **she began to** decline, and, her sickness developing into brain disease, she died in **three weeks** from the time **of** her confinement to the **house.**

It was the saddest blow I ever felt. Comrades had **fallen** at my side on the field of battle; I had seen the lamp of life go out **in** the dwelling and in the hospital—all, scenes that touched my heart, and led me to thoughts of the unknown future ; but this affliction alone stirred the foundations of my heart. Before, everything that had seemed so light, so bright and cheerful, was now enshrouded in midnight gloom.

An anxious, yearning desire seized **me to know** more **of** the home to which she was going. **My heart** longed **for** constant, familiar intercourse with **those into whose presence** she had been translated. **Where is she now?** Shall we ever see her again? **were questions continually** suggesting themselves to **our minds,** and inciting **us** to search the Scripture, the only source whence the answer could be obtained. Life with me was changed. Death seemed disarmed of its terrors. A cemetery which before had appeared so dreadful, was transformed into **a** place of beauty—the only spot on earth **where the** weary could find rest.

We placed her down beside the river bank o'ershadowed with willows, in the quiet grave-yard of Arklow, and thither for four or five successive summers, it was often a pleasure for me to retire. They were the happiest days of my life. I wonder that time and the scenes through which I have passed should in any degree have stifled the emotions that I then enjoyed. But, alas, such is the frailty, the change-ableness of the human heart.

After this blow, for a long time I had but little interest in secular affairs. I wished to retire from the world with all its cares and hardships, and live the life of a recluse; but a sense of a duty—a consciousness that the temptations of the world are not to be avoided, but to be met and overcome, led me to devote myself as usual to my labors, however distasteful to me they were.

My land clearing went on as I had purposed, and after its unprofitable termination I felt constrained to engage in some other business. Teaching, of course, was the only thing that I could do, the only occupation for which I had fitted myself.

CHAPTER XXIX.

My early preparation for teaching—The little it availed me—Individuals who think themselves qualified to teach—School buildings—Salaries of teachers.

KIND reader, since the occurrence of the events recorded in the foregoing chapters, many years have passed away, and ten of them have been devoted to teaching. I have followed it in different places along the Frontier, both in Canada and the neighboring Republic, sometimes in the little rural hamlet of five hundred inhabitants, and then again in the more flourishing and aristocratic village of three or four thousand. This long devotion to the business has afforded me many and varied experiences; some of satisfaction and pleasure, contentment with my lot; others of disquietude and disgust, arising from the occurrence of incidents similar to those which annoyed me at Bloomingdale.

In saying, as I have above, that I had fitted myself for teaching, I do not mean that I had merely attended school, and passed over certain branches which all do who acquire either an academic or a collegiate education, but I had studied with the special aim of making myself useful to others; striving to become so familiar with the branches that I would be likely to teach, that I could explain them to the pleasure and profit of my pupils. A person may think himself well acquainted with a study which he has pursued while at school, yet when he becomes a teacher, questions with regard to it are continually arising, which require thought and investigation on his part, ere he is able to answer them.

A knowledge of this fact in the beginning of my experience as a teacher, gave me a desire to understand thoroughly whatever subject I took up, and I dwelt especially on those points which were to me at all difficult or obscure. While at Corvette, under the impression that I might devote much time to teaching, I closely pursued this course, and afterwards, whenever in charge of a school, I made it a point to spend more or less time in reviewing the subjects of the next day's lessons; unless they happened to be something with which I felt myself perfectly familiar. I have always to a greater or less extent followed this course, believing that very few are competent to appear before a class and explain in an interesting manner a subject to which their attention may not have been called for months or years.

Then, also, I had not been an idle observer of the different methods of governing a school and of imparting instruction. I had made the most of every opportunity presented of learning the modes of different teachers, and never let an article in a book or paper respecting these things pass by unobserved; and whenever I found anything that was an improvement on my own ideas regarding these matters I unhesitatingly adopted them.

It is not pleasant, however, now to realize that these

efforts to prepare myself for my vocation have availed but little towards securing me situations. Such is the lack of intelligence on this subject that very few, comparatively, regard previous experience or preparation as a matter of importance in the selection of a teacher. Everybody is supposed to be capable of teaching. So prevalent is this idea that the experienced teacher, the one who has spent his nights at the lamp and his days in the schoolroom for years, in the acquirement of thorough knowledge of his profession, often finds himself successfully opposed when applying for a situation, by one who has never taught, and knows nothing whatever of the business.

Says Dr. M. H. Buckham, President of the University of Vermont, "The one thing which the largest number of those who have a little education think they can do is to teach. Let business get a little dull, and immediately there is a large accession of applicants for opportunities to teach from almost all the other employments. Clerks, book-agents, patent medicine venders, lightning-rod-peddlers, insurance agents, all appear to think that, when all other employments fail, there **are always two things that remain**—one is to teach, the other **to turn tramp.**"

While public opinion tolerates ideas like **this** with regard to the vocation of teaching, what inducement has the young man to enter it with a view of making it a life-long profession? What hope has he of securing a reputation or moderate competence for his declining years if he finds himself liable to be supplanted by the one who makes teaching only a stepping stone to something higher?

We hear loud complaints against our public schools. A hue and cry is raised against "defective education." The press teems with suggestions and moral advice to teachers; books on the art of teaching are distributed through the country, and in Canada it is obligatory on all candidates for diplomas for teaching to understand them.

Teachers themselves assemble to consider and discuss methods of governing and instructing. All this is well. Whatever tends to educate the teacher and fit him more perfectly for the duties of his profession is to be commended and encouraged. But how much has this effected towards elevating the standard of our schools?

What has it accomplished towards awakening public interest in them, sufficient to make their mission grandly successful? Very little indeed. It is like an effort to produce growth, symmetry, and beauty by pruning the branches of a tree which is rotten at the core. A sea captain may be all that the duties which he has to perform may demand, experienced, brave, energetic; but give to him an unwieldy, leaky, dangerous vessel, half manned with ignorant, inefficient seamen, and he will have accomplished no small achievement if he takes it without accident over dangerous waters in tempestuous weather to a distant port. And yet it is not more unreasonable to expect him to do this than it is to expect a teacher, in the present state of public opinion with regard to school management, to conduct a school according to the wishes of his patrons and the best interests of his pupils. The work is almost an impossible one. Until public opinion is thoroughly, radically changed with regard to the school question; in short, until society is revolutionized, we cannot look for an entire subversion of the evils which now so successfully operate to the detriment of our schools. With the hope that it may contribute in some little degree to the assistance of those who are striving manfully for the improvement of our educational system, I propose to point out some of the most flagrant of these evils. And as they have been learned and felt during a long experience in teaching, I trust that they will not be regarded as the visions of fancy.

Among the first, I would call attention to the demoralizing effects upon the youthful mind, produced by the ill-constructed, homely, untidy edifices throughout the land, to which children and youth are obliged to spend the years that are devoted to their education. A school is supposed to be the place where cultivation of good manners, as well as the culture of the mind, is effected.

In the present state of things, the former of these desirable objects, unfortunately, is seldom attained. And why? **Is** it the fault of the teacher that a boy soon becomes rough, and even boorish in his manners? Has the plain, untidy building, in which he spends several hours a day, nothing to do with it? Everybody is conscious of the surprising change produced in the manners of **one** who has retired from a **palatial residence and** refined society, and spent months or **years in** the cot and haunts of **the backwoodsman. Will** any one deny that similar results may follow in the case of **a** boy who spends no small portion of his **life** in a place destitute of all the neatness, beauty, adornments, comforts and luxuries of his home? As a rule, every home in populous districts has some pretensions to neatness and adornment, the majority of them being rendered attractive by the expenditure of no small amount of money. Take **a** boy from one of these, and place him in a school building presenting the most striking contrast to it—a building as cheap and plain as the most niggardly economy could desire, or ingenuity devise, and what may one expect?

Will the pupil respect it? Will he not rather become lax in the exercise of that regard for neatness and proper decorum which he has observed in his mother's sitting-room or parlor? Let the thousands of individuals who have attended these institutions, and the hundreds of teachers who have had them in charge, answer. The majority of experienced teachers know how much, how very much easier it is to maintain order in a new building, sustaining some pretensions to respectability, than it is in one already defaced and falling into decay. Let us advance a step further, and contemplate the pleasant situation of the teacher in the school building which will be reared when our communities have learned that education is of more value than money, and have formed a proper conception of what a school should be. We see the pupil, at the proper moment, briskly approaching an elegant and substantial edifice through the avenue of trees which adorns the grounds, donning his slippers in the ante-room, and quietly entering the carpeted or tesselated school room, which is furnished with all the improvements of modern art, and decorated with pictures, statuary and flowers. The very surroundings have a refining effect upon his nature. Inspired with respect for them at the beginning, he feels no little anxiety and pride in preserving them in their condition of order and beauty. The ruthless vandal assaults that are now continually made by pupils upon school buildings and furniture would cease to occur, and, with their departure, much of that roughness which now annoys the teacher and pains the patron would also disappear. Such should be the school room patronized by every man who has a desire for the improvement of the manners and morals of his child. What a contrast to those we now find in all the rural districts of this northern land. It is almost impossible to conceive what sort of reasoning still induces men to erect educational structures which are but a little improvement on those attended by the first settlers of our country. Almost every other building, public or private, displays in its architecture the progress of wealth and intelligence; but the educational institution gives little evidence of general prosperity. It would almost seem as if people imagine that during the hours their children are at school they are in an abnormal condition, not requiring any of those comforts which are so necessary for their enjoyment while at home. Rarely, indeed, do we find a country school supplied with curtains, and still more rarely do we find one, or even an academy, supplied with water. In many instances, to keep out the blinding rays of the sun, the teacher resorts to newspapers, or perhaps, if possessed of sufficient courage and energy, he procures curtains of more durable fabric with money raised by subscription.

Water is obtained wherever it can be found, but very seldom near the school building. The first labor of a man, after he has erected a house, is to dig a well in proximity to it, if nature has not provided him with a spring; yet this same man will send his children for years to a school which has neither spring nor well connected with it, and where the only possible chance for them to quench their thirst is by trespassing on the property of others.

It is an indisputable fact, that this want of forethought

and care on the part of school boards and commissioners is a source of vexation and trouble to almost every country teacher. The pupils in squads from two to twenty visit the nearest spring or well, to the annoyance of the proprietor. Immediately complaint is made to the teacher, and in consequence the pupils are obliged to seek water at a more distant place, and not unfrequently complaints are again entered.

The general remedy for this excessive economy is to detail two boys, three or four times a day, to bring water from some distant place, where they are permitted to get it, thus consuming a vast amount of time, which should be devoted to other purposes.

As a fruit of this culpable neglect of duty towards schools, there is a constant warfare between the pupils and those living adjacent to the school edifice. Few are the teachers who do not receive two or more letters every term from citizens, complaining of the trespassing proclivities of their pupils. And yet one can scarcely blame the latter; the torture of thirst is not pleasant, and if they are tempted to trespasses and rudeness, surely, it cannot be claimed that the patrons are altogether blameless for the conduct.

Trivial as the matter may seem, it nevertheless is productive of much discomfort to the teacher and others, and shows a sad want of the interest requisite to render a school pleasant and prosperous. It is one of those drawbacks to comfort which may easily be avoided by a trifling outlay of time and money, and, taken in connection with other discomforts and a wretched school building, produces a demoralizing effect upon the pupil.

A few years ago it was with no small degree of pleasure that I found a well, provided with a nicely finished pump, adjacent to a public school house in one of the towns of Long Island.

It was the property of the school, and a novelty **to me** from the very fact. A small cup was attached to the pump by a chain, and I quaffed many draughts from it during my different visits to the school, more from a desire to boast of the peculiar privilege of drinking from a well belonging to a school than from actual thirst, and I could not refrain thinking, as I did so, of the hundreds of teachers and pupils in this northern country who are either obliged to endure the pangs of thirst during **the sweltering** days of summer, or solicit the boon of a drink of water of some benevolent family half a mile or more away.

Generally, in these rural districts, we find that people are not negligent or parsimonious in the erection of church edifices, nor are they reluctant to embellish them with taste‧ ful and expensive adornments.

The work is praiseworthy. We can never condemn the psirit which impels man to liberality in promoting the interests of religion, or in showing his reverence for the Almighty. But if intelligence is conducive to morality, why should there be less liberality displayed **in** the promotion of those means by which intelligence is secured?

Why should communities exert themselves to the utmost even contract large debts, to erect a costly church edifice and yet permit a squalid diminutive school building to stand by its side?

If one third of the money and labor expended on churches in nearly every one of our villages was devoted to the cause of secular education, **we** might have educational institutions of which, to say the least, we need not feel ashamed. And would morality decline, the great work of the Redeemer suffer from this division of money between schools and churches? Let the intelligent christian minister himself answer.

Another of the evils I have proposed to mention in connection with our school system, and one which has elicited much discussion, is the low salaries of teachers. There is no other class of public servants in the world that should be so carefully guarded from the effects of poverty and want as teachers.

The reason is obvious. The labor of a teacher is almost wholly mental in its character, hence, whatever tends to distract or trouble unfits him for the proper performance of this work. Cheerfulness in the schoolroom has always been regarded as a most desirable trait in a teacher, yet very few persons are so constituted that they can maintain this pleasant appearance when harassed by continual forebodings of financial embarrassments, or driven to constant calculations of how to make both ends meet. That these are the circumstances under which our teachers labor can easily be ascertained by any one who makes the effort. The fact becomes still more unpleasant and startling when we learn that in some of our communities teachers are accorded a good social position, and are expected to keep up the same outward signs of respectability, and practice the same hospitalities that those do in whose society they mingle. In many instances to do this is simply impossible, and the teachers are not few who, because of their inability to gratify their most harmless tastes for luxury, and to return the hospitalities extended to them by those in better circumstances, shun the society which they most like, and almost lead the life of a recluse. We can conceive of no more unpleasant position than that of a person whose intelligence and refinement prevent him from associating with one class around him, while he is debarred by the conventionalities of society from another; and yet such is the position of many teachers. Is there nothing wrong in this condition of things? Is there nothing wrong in the education of that community which pays for everything far more liberally than it does for the labor which trains the minds of its children and youth?

To see fine and expensive residences rising in our country villages as the result of a young lawyer's devotion, for a few years, to his business, is a thing of frequent occurrence; but where is the costly edifice that has ever been reared from the salary of a teacher?

The question recalls the incident I have related, when Uncle Jack sought the advice of a Bloomingdale lawyer, and again displays to us the difference with which a man rewards the one who has aided him in obtaining a few dollars, and the one who has spent long months and years, perhaps, in developing and training the mind of the child that is to be his prop and comfort in after years.

What shall we say of society that makes heroes of those who, with the least possible claim to noble motives, perform some great physical feat, and totally ignores those who are exhausting both physical and mental energies in the accomplishment of good—training the future legislators, statesmen and governors of our land? Within the last few years public sentiment has lifted many into notoriety simply for great feats of pedestrianism, and the same perverted taste has rewarded others with wealth and honor for rowing boats a certain distance in an unusually short space of time. Where is the school teacher that has ever won wealth or distinction for drawing out and successfully developing the latent powers of the youthful mind? Where is the community that has ever raised purses for those displaying the most tact and ability in teaching or governing a school? O tempora! O mores! Let us not regard as barbarians those who delight in bull-fights, or boast of our Christian land, as long as we enrich and crown with laurels the athlete, and starve and degrade the one to whom, in a great measure, the mental training of our children belongs.

It would be unfair, however, not to give certain members of almost every community due credit for liberality in the support of schools, and an intelligent estimate of the moral support that should be accorded the teachers; but as they are usually much in the minority with regard to numbers, their efforts are not unfrequently thwarted by those holding precisely opposite views.

The one who has ever attended many sessions of school commissioners in the Canadian Townships and Parishes will have scores of amusing anecdotes to relate respecting incidents that he has frequently witnessed. Dissatisfaction arises in a district with regard to a school, it may be from the offence which the teacher has unwittingly given to an ignorant patron, but generally from an opinion on the part of some, that the salary is too high. A reckless committee perhaps has agreed to pay to the teacher in winter $18 or $20 a month and board; and in summer as high as $2.50 or $3 a week and board. The provocation being deemed a sufficient *casus belli*, a petition for the removal of the obnoxious teacher is circulated, and at the next session of the school commissioners the petition is presented, and the matter discussed by the respective friends and **foes** of the school. The scene to an intelligent disinterested observer is provocative alike **of** laughter, pity and disgust. Words **are** bandied, old feuds brought up, characters villified, and, in fact, all the disgraceful or mean acts committed by either party or their ancestors embracing **two** or three generations are recounted in detail for the edification of the commissioners and spectators.

Happy, contented teacher! How many **and** fascinating **the** charms connected with your vocation! What lofty incentives to enter it, and how rich and satisfied the parent who has struggled to educate his children, when he **sees** them duly qualified and engaged in the profession of teaching.

The troubles that I have mentioned arising from teachers' salaries are obviously the result of ignorance; not only from inability to set a just estimate on a good school, **and** consequently on education, but from inability to discriminate between a good school and a bad one. Sad as **may seem** the fact, it is, nevertheless, true that very many of our inhabitants regard one school as good as another, hence, the teacher who is willing to engage for the lowest salary is the one sure **of** a position. People like these, by uniting their efforts with those of selfish principles, who, having no children to send to school, take no interest in it, are enabled to carry their points in nearly all our communities, completely overpowering, as **I have** before said, those of more intelligent views. In the **same lecture from** which I have already quoted, President Buckham says:

" Not the least evil of the present depression of business

is the throwing into the ranks of competitors for positions as teachers thousands who have no qualifications and no love for the work, who steal the bread from the mouths of competent teachers, and cheapen and degrade the whole process of education."

In an address delivered recently at a school opening on Staten Island the Hon. Geo. William Curtis said he did not believe that in all the 20,000 school districts in the State of New York, there was one teacher who was really fit for his position that was overpaid for the services he performed. Such are the opinions of intelligent, educated men, but from the want of a proper estimation of these opinions by the masses, teachers and education must suffer. Is there no remedy? If ignorance is a national misfortune and curse, should it not be treated like other public evils? May not legislation properly step in and stay its progress as it would the tide of intemperance or any deadly epidemic? May it not say, "Thus far thou shalt go, but no farther."

If it is right for our legislators to say what the qualifications of teachers must be, is it not also right for them to say what salaries they shall receive?

When a teacher has charge of a school, and is doing his work to the satisfaction of all his intelligent patrons, would it be unjust for our lawgivers to prevent selfishness and ignorance from dismissing that teacher from his position, and supplying it with one unqualified for the work simply because he will teach for a smaller salary?

CHAPTER XXX.

In this chapter I desire to show the baneful effects of the frequent change of teachers.

According to the present system, teachers in district schools usually remain but one term of three or four months, rarely a year. Principals of academies are engaged for a year, and in some instances remain two or three years, occasionally, but very seldom, five. If the teacher is inefficient, one year is as long as he should be retained; but if, on the other hand, he proves himself a competent, energetic, instructor, no greater injustice to him, and no greater injury to the school, can be done than to dismiss him. I would present the following reasons for this assertion:

First, a teacher, to be successful, must become intimately acquainted with the dispositions and habits of his pupils. Unless it is one of his first endeavors to do this, he is not adapted to the work of teaching, and should by no means defraud his employers by remaining in the school. But that he can do this, that he can so understand his two or three scores of pupils in the short period of a few months, that he can manage each one properly—that is, repress his vices and awaken and rouse to action the better principles of his nature—no intelligent person can believe. Moral reforms can be effected only by a work of time, and however good a disciplinarian a teacher may be, he can never bring an undisciplined, rough school into a state of respectful obedience to his authority, and give to it a spirit of industry, in the comparatively short period for which teachers are engaged. Not only does the teacher require time to learn the characteristics of his pupils, and know how to adapt himself to their various natures, but they also require time to assimilate themselves to the nature of the teacher. It often happens that at the end of three or six months, a mutual feeling of discontent and dissatisfaction, a want of respect and affection for each other, exists between a teacher and his pupils, and yet, after the lapse of an equal or longer period, they have formed a strong admiration and like for each other. The pupils have learned that instead of being unkind, and needlessly strict in his dealings with them, he really has had their welfare in view, and that, in proportion as they become docile and industrious, his sternness relaxes, and he shows himself the possessor of the warmest and most friendly emotions.

On the other hand, the teacher has discovered the latent power, the hidden springs of noble feeling possessed by those whom before he regarded as destitute of ambition and noble qualities; in short, he has discovered the mainspring in the moral mechanism of each one of them, by means of which he is controlled, and he is now guiding him with a skillful hand to a goal of usefulness and honor. The removal of **a** teacher at a time when such relations exist between himself and pupils can only result in dissatisfaction and discouragement to the former, and in positive harm to the latter. The teacher's successor must go over the same ground; he has the same things to learn, the same work to accomplish; hence, every change of this kind that is made, necessarily, retards the progress of the pupil.

. In my own experience in teaching I have found it **one** of the most unpleasant features of the business to **leave the** charge, and consequently society, of those pupils to whom **I** have become attached. **Frequently** entire classes have been together under my **charge,** term after term, and between them and myself mutual confidence, respect and friendship have sprung up.

The thought of leading them on in their studies until they had matriculated into some higher educational institution, or prepared themselves for the employments of life, was pleasant, and I always felt no little pride in fitting them for either of these events. **To be compelled then to leave** them at a time when my interest in them was strongest, and my attachment for them by no means slight, was, to say the least, unpleasant, and I always entered my next school **with** a sort of feeling that there was little encouragement for me to form the same attachment for others, as it would in all probability soon be severed in the same manner. It is thus shown that frequent changes have a tendency to weaken the interest and destroy the ambition of the teacher.

It is preposterous to suppose that he can ever feel the interest in a school when he knows that he is soon to leave it,

that he would did he feel that he was to remain in charge
of it for a long time.

In order to display the proper kind of ambition he should
feel that he is a permanent citizen of the place in which he
teaches, and is identified with all its interests. In this
case the interests of the school are his, and he works with
a zeal and earnestness which shows that he is anxious with
regard to the result. Let a man a contract for construct-
ing an edifice, and he knows that he will be held responsible
for the style and durability of his work; but engage him to
work on the same structure for a few days only, and his
interest in it, and the anxiety which he feels respecting the
character of the work when fully completed, will be far
different from what they will in the former case. So with
a teacher; engage him for a term of years, and he will at
once see that he is to be the chief instructor of the youthful part of the community in which he labors, and a desire
for his own reputation, if nothing more, will induce him
to use every means to make the instruction as thorough as
possible—something to which he can point with satisfaction
and pride. On the other hand engage him for a few months
only, or for a year, and allow him to feel that at the expiration of that time he is to be succeeded by another, and how
much less the incentive for him to work. He feels that he
is to perform but a small part of the work of educating
those of whom he is placed in charge.

Where many different teachers are employed in educating
a child, all will leave impressions upon him, but no one can
claim the honor of doing a great share of the work.

The fact is, no teacher can feel contented and at home
under the present system of engaging; he is like an itin-

erant preacher, knowing not to-day where he will be employed to-morrow.

For the reasons that are above enumerated, I believe that no community having the well-being of their school in view should ever engage an experienced teacher for a shorter period than five years. One year may be sufficiently long to engage one who has had no previous experience, but then it should be on the condition that he is to remain longer in case his first year's efforts are successful. Besides precluding the evils I have mentioned such a course would prevent from entering the ranks of teachers those who have no idea of making teaching a permanent profession, and only use it as a means of obtaining something more lucrative.

The greatest of all the evils, however, connected with our school system, the one that most degrades it, and shuts out of the profession of teaching men and women of ability, is THE LACK OF MORAL SUPPORT ACCORDED OUR TEACHERS.

The prosperity of a Government depends in a great measure upon the harmony existing between the different departments of which **it is composed. As the** faithful performance of those functions assigned them by **the** various organs of the body secures health to an individual, so does the harmonious working of the machinery **of a** Government secure happiness and confidence at home, dignity and character abroad. Not only is this true of National Governments, but it is equally true of every association of individuals, whether it has for its object moral, intellectual or physical culture, or the promotion of pecuniary interests.

Discipline in the army has ever been regarded as the passport to success on the field of battle. Weeks, months and even years are required to bring a soldier to proficiency in this respect, but this end attained, he is endowed with a quality so potent that not unfrequently in the annals of warfare we see both courage and patriotism sinking before it. Discipline in the navy is one of the broad stepping stones to honors and dominion on the sea. Discipline in the prison is regarded as one of the essential means of securing the reformation of the convict, and thus of sending him forth a wiser and better man. Discipline in orphan, inebriate and insane asylums is the basis upon which their founders build hopes of relieving unfortunates of the human race.

If ends thus grand and important are secured by means of discipline in institutions like these, may we not expect grander results from its proper use in the management of our public schools? If there are any means by which good can be accomplished in our efforts to elevate the human family, where can they be better employed than in those institutions to which thousands of boys and girls are now looking, and to which millions will look for instruction in coming years?

The majority of institutions founded for the promotion of public benefits are provided with a variety of officers, upon whose hearty and unceasing co-operation the success of the institution depends. Every banking establishment must have its president, teller and cashier. Every railroad and insurance company, every benevolent and Bible society, must have its complement of officers, every one of whom is to guard with peculiar care the interests of the establishment with which he is connected. How is it with our public school? Do we find the same watchful care over it? the same liberal expenditure of money to crown it with prosper-

ity? Far from it. As regards its management, it is an
institution prominently and proverbially unique. It is
true, it has a certain number of officers connected with it
who are supposed to have its welfare in view and to make
it the subject of their supervision, but as at present
managed these officers may be considered nominal rather
than taking an active part in its support and control. The
teacher is the only functionary of this institution upon
whom any great amount of labor or responsibility devolves.
Into the schoolroom he is ushered to officiate in every
capacity, from that of corporal to generalissimo of the army
of youth who are to look to him for instruction. Filling at once
the executive, legislative and judicial departments, in order
to secure success, he must possess versatility of talent and
the power of adapting himself to circumstances, that are
rarely found combined in one individual. But whatever
the order of his talents, however strong his determination
to discharge his duties promptly and efficiently, however
sanguine his hopes of success, he will find himself sadly
disappointed, and subjected to annoyances of which he had
little thought. Speaking both from actual experience and
observation, I believe that of all his discouragements and
troubles none is so great as that arising from the custom of
his patrons of seldom or never visiting the school-room, and
of basing their opinions of his fitness or unfitness for teaching on the judgment of their children. As things now
exist, the teacher is reduced to the unhappy necessity of
looking to the vacillating and undisciplined minds of youth
and children for his reputation. Is this fair? Is it reasonable? Is it justice? Do you, farmers, who have stock to
sell or purchase, who have important improvements to make

in the way of fencing, subsoiling **or draining,** send your children **to** superintend the work for you? Do you, merchants, send your boys or girls to distant markets to make such purchases as your business from time to time requires? **Do you,** mechanics, **accept the** suggestions of your children with regard to **your work,** or allow them to make **the** slightest alteration in the plans you have projected? O **no, say you,** they are **far** too young and inexperienced to **be** relied **on** in such matters. Yes, their judgment is too feeble to be relied on in matters where dollars and cents only are concerned; **but,** my dear friend, does it ever occur **to you** that the mind of your boy or girl is too feeble, too undeveloped, to place a proper estimate upon character? **to** judge accurately of the moral or mental worth of persons of mature years? to exercise a nice discrimination between what is right **and wrong** in the conduct of a teacher?

To form **an** accurate opinion of another, to judge correctly of character, **requires ability that** very few possess. It requires not only judgment of mature years, but the keen perception and broad reflective powers resulting from **large** experience and intimate knowledge of human nature. **Yet, in the face** of these facts, have you not sent your children **to** the public school from early childhood, and permitted their opinion to bias your judgment of the worth of the **various** teachers who have had charge of their mental training?

Were youth and children always infallible in their conclusions, **genial in** their tempers and agreeable in their habits, teachers could submit cheerfully to be arraigned before **such** a tribunal to answer for their conduct; but in the present condition of human morals, we protest earnestly, **solemnly and vehemently against it.**

It is a fact to which people seem obstinately to close their eyes, that a teacher can never instruct and interest his pupils unless he is free from all those perplexities and harassing anxieties to which, in the present state of school management, he is invariably subjected. It cannot be denied that it is owing, in a great measure, to the indifference manifested by school boards and patrons to the comfort and interests of teachers, that many able men and women now refrain from entering the profession; and that from the same cause, those who do teach fall short, very far short, of doing the good which, under other circumstances, they might accomplish.

A clergyman once said to me, "I would like to teach. It would be a a great pleasure to me to instruct boys and girls in the branches in which I feel an interest, and to watch the development of their minds. I taught two or three terms, but the disrespect which many of my large scholars showed not only for the rules, but for myself also, kept me in a continual state of care and perplexity. I had no one to support my authority, and in two or three cases where I appealed to parents, they seemed displeased, and inclined to regard me as unnecessarily strict, and so I abandoned the business, leaving it to those who are more indifferent to the pranks and insults of rebellious scholars and the fault-findings of their parents."

The experience of this clergyman, as thus related, is the experience of thousands. They would gladly teach, but the manifold annoyances connected with the business make almost any other employment preferable. It is scarcely an exaggeration to say that a majority of our country schools and academies are almost as scrupulously avoided as pesthouses. I have myself taught in a country academy five successive **years** without receiving an hour's visit from any school commissioner or patron of the school, except on days of the annual examination, and then a very few came only **at my repeated** and earnest solicitation. **Is** it any wonder that under such circumstances pupils find that they can carry forth and retail the most preposterous stories respect-**ing** the school and teacher without fear of detection ? Is it **any** wonder that we find evil-disposed persons, who may have taken a dislike to the teacher, catching up and exag-gerating these tales for the purpose of gratifying some petty resentment or malignant grudge ?

Every one **knows** with what pertinacity and zeal the **teacher of a** country school is criticised. The advent of a **new teacher into a country district** or village is an era in **the history of that community.** It is an epoch in the labor **of** biographical **research and mental** speculation. I often think that **the system of** engaging **teachers** for a term of years, as advocated by some, **is a** cruel one, when applied to country schools. It deprives **many** in every community of **the** long-cherished habit of looking up annually, or semi-annually, the pedigree of a teacher, and displaying their **knowledge** of the art of teaching by indulging in the freest **and most** absurd criticisms of his school management.

The **person** who volunteers an opinion or pronounces a **stricture on** any business or profession of which he knows nothing, practically, **is** generally regarded as a conceited **ignoramus,** but this stigma is avoided when he approaches the subject of teaching. A profession which above all others demands experience and tact in the person who follows it, **is the only one** whose votaries may be criticised by everybody with impunity. So true is this, that it has become an accepted dogma that the teacher is a scape-goat for nearly all the evils, moral or social, with which the community where he pursues his vocation happens to be afflicted. If it suffers from reckless legislation, and is overburdened with municipal, railway or other taxes, the teacher being the only vulnerable object at which grumblers may level their artillery, must suffer. His *enormous* salary is the cause of the financial embarrassment, consequently, it must be reduced.

Should he seek relief for his over-worked brain and exhausted body in those simple recreations to which others resort, he is not dignified, or his morals objectionable. If he is reserved, he lacks sociability, in short, is "stuck up." If he dresses with care, he is a fop; if he fails to do so, he is slovenly. Should he get angry, and stand up for his rights, he is too independent, and must be put down; if he fails to display considerable spirit, he lacks determination, and is unfit to govern a school. In short, a person who answers all the requirements of a country district must be an anomaly—there can be nothing like him in heaven or on earth.

Certain communities are proverbial for constant warfare against their teachers. The incidents recounted in preceding chapters of this work sufficiently corroborate this statement, also, another, viz:—that in almost every, and perhaps in every community, are parents who seem to think their children are never appreciated at school, hence, are unjustly treated by their teachers. When it happens, as it sometimes does, that three, four or more families of this description reside in the same community, woe to the one who is hired to teach their school. I now have in mind a community of this kind. For twenty years the experience of their teachers has been uniform—annoyed, harassed, slandered, and happy only when the periods of their engagements have expired. No teacher has ever remained there longer than two years, and the majority of them but one, many but six months. The most experienced teachers that have ever labored there have been the least successful, and have usually lost the reputation which they have secured in other places by years of patient toil. The school is seldom or never visited save by the school inspector, and it is a matter of common occurrence that the school committee are about quizzing and cross examining pupils for information respecting difficulties in school—difficulties that never would have arisen had these guardians of educational interests visited it at proper intervals, and given the teacher their support in his efforts to elevate it to the standard of a well conducted school. This is an isolated instance of miserable school management, but what is true of this community is equally true of numberless others.

A glance at a few more instances of the treatment which teachers often meet may not be uninteresting to the reader, and it is to be hoped that it may contribute something towards showing the necessity of a reform in our system of managing schools.

Some years since, a friend of mine took charge of a high school, in which many teachers had previously labored, but only a few of whom had met with any degree of success I knew him to be profound in scholarship, unimpeachable in his morals, painstaking in his efforts, and I verily believed him to be one of the best teachers the country afforded, but, like many another of his profession, he soon learned that he was in a position where talent would avail but little. He was one who believed that system is essential to success. He felt the imperative necessity **of** establishing a **degree** of quietude in his schoolroom, and securing prompt attendance at recitation, **in** order to awaken an interest in study. To do this, it was necessary to cross the wishes of an over-indulged and conceited daughter of the most influential member of **the** school directors. His fate was sealed. The complaint of the daughter, with exaggerated details of her wrongs, was laid **before** the weakminded parent. Encouraged and pitied, rather than reproved, her conduct assumed an insolence towards the teacher which his own ideas of justice and the dignity of his position were ill-prepared to brook.

But his authority was undermined. The spirit of rebellion having been fostered by the one whose business it was to destroy it in the bud, it gradually infused itself through the school, and, at an early day, resulted in the teacher's dismissal—sent adrift at the fancy and suggestion of an ignorant and wilful **girl of fifteen.**

A few years later, **a** young friend, **whom I** knew to be the soul of honor, and thoroughly energetic in his habits, was, at my suggestion, engaged to take charge of a school in a rural district in one of our border towns. Knowing that few teachers had been fortunate enough to go through the school with a reputation unspotted, I waited with no little interest the close of my friend's labors. Embracing the first convenient opportunity, I inquired of a prominent school committee as to the character of the school. To my surprise, he informed me that it was **the** poorest one they had had for **years.** Not willing that a young man I had recommended **should be thus** traduced, I submitted my informant to a rigid cross-examination, and succeeded in eliciting from him the following facts :

First, he knew nothing of the school save what he had gathered from his children—two or three large ungovernable girls in their teens, with a younger brother controlled by as many devils as were cast out of Mary Madelene.

Second, not an **individual living in** the district **had** visited the school during the entire winter.

Third, he could not mention a single fault in the school, and only judged it to be poor from the fact that his children did not like it, and were averse to attending it.

The matter was now plain. My experience as teacher at once led me to divine the true situation of affairs. The teacher had found the school sadly demoralized, and the scholars backward in their studies. With a natural taste for order, manly deportment and study, he sought to restrain the boisterous conduct of the rustics of whom he found himself in charge, as well as to infuse a spirit of ambition into all the members of the school ; but his efforts, so far from being appreciated, were by many regarded as wanton aggressions on their freedom of speech and manners, and a useless disturbance of the ease in which they had been accustomed to spend their time. Bred in the habit of discussing and criticizing in the family circle the words and actions of their teachers, their mistaken notions were now imparted to parents ready like thousands of others to accept their children's story of the teacher's imperfections, and to unite with them in vilifying him.

The statement is often made, and made, too, by those who

are supposed to **be** people of intelligence, that if a school is what it should be, children will always take pleasure **in** attending it. If the teacher is pleasant, happy in his illustrations and explanations and attractive in his manner, there will be no need of compulsory methods to get him to school; he will go from choice. My dear sir, or madam, is it possible that in this nineteenth century, with children of your own whose habits you have observed, you can give utterance to such expressions? As well might you argue that if a minister of the Gospel is attractive in the pulpit, if he sets forth the doctrine of faith and repentance in a clear and logical manner, every hearer, no matter how vicious or depraved in character, will at once accept the views he is promulgating, and afford a striking example of a regenerate soul.

If your ground is tenable, then, a good teacher must be able to render hard, unceasing labor more attractive to youth than all the pleasures they have ever known. **He** must be a magnet so powerful that he will draw **every boy** just at the proper hour from the skating rink, the bowling alley, the race course, the bar-room, cricket-ground, depot or whatever place of amusement he has been in the habit of frequenting, and, without any compulsory efforts, induce him to devote himself to his studies with heroic and untiring energy.

So far from accepting your theory, my friend, I shall most persistently contend that the duties of every teacher demand that daily, and almost hourly, he shall oppose the wishes and plans of at least some of his pupils; and that to contradict this statement is to assert that boys and girls are always infallible, both in judgment and conduct.

Dr. Buckham says:

" A teacher may be popular for the very things that make him a poor teacher, for being slack in his requirements, over ready with his help, profuse in his undeserved commendations. A good teacher is likely to be unpopular with a certain class at all times and with all at times."

Quite in contrast to this is the opinion of those who think a teacher to be successful must always be popular, and that unless he is so he should be immediately discharged.

To flourish, a school must be the object in which much of the hope and pride of its patrons centre. If the human mind is of any value, if it is a matter of any importance that our children should be elevated to something besides a mere animal state of existence, then certainly the public school demands our encouragement and support. Its claims upon us are of such a character that we should marshal every faculty to render its mission successful. To attain this end, I believe it one of the most necessary things to elect a board of efficient managers, whose business shall be to receive competent teachers, and, with their assistance, to frame a code of wholesome rules, and see that in the minutest details these are faithfully executed. I have endeavored to show that in many instances the usefulness of the teacher is almost, and sometimes wholly destroyed by the meddlesome interference and criticisms of those who know nothing practically of teaching; and by the system I propose this evil would be abolished. It should be incumbent upon the school board to be so frequently in the school-room as to become well acquainted with the pupils, know all the delinquencies, observe the merits or defects of the teacher's method, and relieve him **in** a measure of governing the school.

By this arrangement the teacher would be enabled to devote much more time and attention to recitations, being free in a measure from those distractions which at the present time so materially interfere with the proper performance of his duties. There should be the most perfect understanding between the school board and the teacher, so that **he** will be ever ready to consult them, assured **of** their respect for his own rights, and of their co-operation in whatever promises to promote the well-being of the school. While thus assisted and directed by the school managers, and feeling that his acts have been sanctioned by them, the teacher will naturally feel a degree of quiescence, which, as things now exist, he can never experience. No pupil could successfully misrepresent him, and if censure for anything should occur, it would be shared by the managers, whom the people have selected to do their work.

Will you who advocate the idea of sustaining a school at the least possible expense tell me that a school thus managed would not form a pleasing contrast **to** the ones we now find in our communities? Will you claim that the expense and labor of sustaining such schools are too great for the amount of good achieved, or that there is only here and there a community that can afford it?

Will you claim this, and still unblushingly assert that you can justly appreciate **a** well developed, a thoroughly disciplined intellect?

Are you as careful of the expense that is to contribute **to** your material comfort? Possibly, like many others **who** advocate the closest, nay, most niggardly economy in sustaining schools, you find means to purchase a splendid equipage, or to erect a residence, which for size and architectural beauty will surpass anything of the kind in your vicinity.   You never visit the school-room where you send your children, but from the time in which you placed your material for building in the hands of the carpenter and mason, you have not ceased to visit these individuals daily, to see if they are making a proper use of that material and performing their work according to your wishes.

Do you not know that you have given the teacher a greater work to perform; a greater responsibility to discharge ?   Do you not know that in surrendering to him the work of moulding the minds of your children you have placed in his charge material finer than ivory, more valuable than marble ?   Are you not aware that every precept and example of that teacher are of more importance to you than the clink of the trowel, and the stroke of the jack-plane, you are so narrowly watching ?   Yes, be assured that every principle implanted by the teacher in the breasts of your children is to have a mightier influence in determining the weal or woe of your declining years than Doric columns or Corinthian capitals.   Perhaps that, with all your indifference to the interests of the public school, you are an admirer of the fine arts, and generously open your purse to place your son under the ablest masters of music.   Remember that in the moral and mental mechanism of that son are keys capable of sending forth diviner music than ever swelled at the touch of Handel.   It is the privilege of that teacher whom you disregard to tune them to discordant notes that will render the possessor wretched, or draw from them a soul-inspiring melody that will cheer him in all his march from the commencement of active life up to the Throne of God.

CHAPTER XXXI.

A joyful surprise—My old friend McKenzie turns up after a separation from me of several years—A letter in which he recounts his wanderings and trials.

DURING the spring of 187-, while remaining at home giving my attention to the farm, I drove one evening to Foreston village, when the postmaster presented me the following letter which had been addressed to himself. It read as follows:

YONKERS, N.Y., 3rd May, 187-.

DEAR SIR,

Will you have the kindness to give me the address of Mr. Frank Styles, a gentleman who attended the Seminary at Corvette in Vermont during the years 1856–57.

At that time his parents resided in Foreston, Canada East. By giving me his address, or any information that will lead to the discovery of his whereabouts, you will greatly oblige,

Your obedient servant,

GORDON McKENZIE.

I was wild with delight. Here was a letter from my old friend—one whom I had thought of thousands of times and longed to see, yet I knew not where he was, and even doubted that he was still alive.

The next day's mail from Foreston conveyed to him a letter embracing four sheets of foolscap closely written. A few days subsequently I received the following reply :

YONKERS, N.Y., May, 187–.

MY DEAR STYLES,

I feel at this moment not perhaps like the Morning Star, but, as the poet says.

> " As if I had this moment caught
> Some treasure, I through life have sought."

The treasure assumes the shape of a letter, and I have but this moment finished reading it. It is yours.

To say that I am very glad indeed in having heard from you, is but a faint way of expressing my pleasure. I have had nothing to equal it since I received the first letter from the one who is now my wife—married you see.

As you insist upon my giving you a complete history of my doings since I left Corvette I will attempt it. First, however, let me refer to the circumstance of my writing your postmaster in relation to your whereabouts.

The evening I did so, I had occasion, in the work of correcting the French exercises of my pupils, to consult my French dictionary. On taking it down my eye, for the thousandth time, fell on your name. The book you see is the one you presented me in the Seminary at Corvette more than ten years ago. The decision, I will learn where Styles is, flashed upon me in a moment, and I immediately addressed your postmaster. The rest you know ; and now to my narrative.

On the morning of the 5th day of July, 185-, I left the Seminary never to return to it as a student. **In** order to replenish my scanty wardrobe and procure enough money to pay my fare to Troy, N.Y., I had sold all, or nearly all my books. Two days subsequently, having no money with which to obtain a meal or a night's lodging, I pawned my watch in Cohoes for $3.00. This sum had dwindled down to fifty cents, and I was still without employment, when I entered a public house for my dinner in a village not far from Cohoes. While there, I learned that the landlord was desirous of obtaining a bar-tender. **A** chance **for** employment, however humble or menial, in my present circumstances seemed a godsend. I had walked about and sought something to do without avail, until I was completely tired out and disheartened. I had no money to pay for my lodging that night, and the prospect of beggary was before me. You know my abhorrence of the liquor traffic; well, I hesitated, shuddered, then offered my services and was accepted. My ignorance of the business, **of** course, reduced my salary to a very small sum, but it **would preserve me** from starvation, and possibly afford me an opportunity to secure other employment.

I immediately commenced my labors, but am confident that the reluctance I felt to perform them rendered me **an** unprofitable servant. I was in a place where I was liable, constantly, to **meet** those with whom I was acquainted, especially the old students at Corvette, many of whom lived in Troy, Albany and other places adjacent. They all knew **my** standing in the Seminary, the honors with which I had graduated, and **the** strenuous efforts I

had made in behalf of temperance, hence, the dread of
having them form the impression that I had willingly
settled down to the business of tending bar was harassing,
tormenting.   Luckily, I saw but very few of them, and by
being constantly on the *qui vive* I managed to keep out of
sight, and thus escaped recognition.

I lived, or rather existed, in this way two months,
when I chanced one day to hear a gentleman inquiring of
another, if he could inform him where a school teacher
might be found to take charge of a school of which he
was a trustee.   I was not long in requesting an interview
with him, and after telling my story, and showing him my
diploma and recommendations, I was engaged.   The school
was not far distant, in Saratoga County, but as it was a
district school my salary was low, yet the prospect of
getting out of my present situation made me happy.

I remained here until the spring of '61, when, the fall
of Sumpter rousing my patriotic emotions, I resigned
my situation and went to New York city with the intention of enlisting in the Federal Army.   Alas! my *defective*
stature blasted my hopes, and I fear that the disappointment somewhat diminished my patriotism.   I was declared
two inches too short.   It was in vain that I expatiated
on my prowess, ardor and agility.   The officials were inex-
orable; a man was too insignificant to be allowed to die for
his country unless he was two inches taller than myself.
Hoping that they would deduce from it the fact that a
man's value as a warrior is not in proportion to his size, I
cited them to the story of David and Goliah, but they
seemed never to have heard of it.

I assured them that I was born in Scotland—a land of

heroes whose soldiers had won glory for their country on a thousand fields, but all to no purpose. Disappointed and disgusted I walked off, scarcely knowing with which to be the most indignant—the arbitrary laws of the American Republic, or the *lusus naturæ* which in a nation and family of giants had made me a pigmy.

I believe, however, that my wrath was poured out upon the latter. I could see no good reason why I, with as large a degree of patriotism and other kindred emotions as ever animated Wallace or Bruce, should **be** permitted **to** remain **a** dwarf, so small indeed as to be regarded insignificant by my fellows. I fear that my murmuring at that time against the decrees of Providence, my complaints respecting my diminutive size, **were** the cause of my present proportions. Within the past two or three years I have been growing; **not** tall, but latitudinally, expanding to a degree astonishing both to my friends and myself. You will scarcely recognize in me, when we meet, the Mack weighing but ninety-eight pounds whom you knew in Corvette. But pardon this digression.

I spent several days **after my** disappointment in wandering about the city looking **once** more for employment. I had **just** obtained a situation in a carpet store, and was to commence my labors there on the following Monday, when I was taken sick, and **did** not rise from my bed for three weeks. **By** the time **I** was able to go to work again, my money was nearly gone, and the situation referred to in the carpet store was filled by another. One evening, sad and disconsolate, in looking over the advertisements in a daily, my eye fell on one asking for a man to drive a bread cart **in** the city. Applicants were requested to call at No. 296

R—— street, at 9 o'clock on the following morning.   As hateful to me as was the thought of engaging in this menial occupation, I was by unavoidable circumstances again placed where I was constrained to do whatever was proffered me. I knew how to manage horses ; driving was not hard work, and, in my present enfeebled condition, it seemed altogether advisable to obtain the situation if possible.

At the appointed hour with anxious heart I was at the place designated.   It was a small confectioner's shop, attended at the time I was there by a modest pretty girl not more than sixteen, but from her intelligence and dignity appearing to be at least three years older.   She informed me that her father, who placed the advertisement in the paper, had been unexpectedly called over to Hoboken, and would not return until eleven.   Having nothing to do else-where I resolved to remain there until he returned.

It wanted a few minutes of nine when I arrived, and I had been there but a short time when another applicant, and then another came, until within an hour ten had presented themselves.   Only three of them, however, stayed to see Mr. Fisk, the advertiser ; the others with disappointed, scowling looks left in disgust on finding that he was absent, and that there were four already awaiting his return.

The other applicants were hardy looking, laboring men, and it seemed to me that their chances were far better than mine, pale, effeminate looking, and slight as I was.   I made myself as agreeable as possible to Miss Fisk, hoping and believing that she was a favorite with her father, and that her intercession with him in my favor would have its influence.   I related to her incidents in my history, roused her sympathy by telling her of my recent sickness and my necessities, and finally hinted that by appealing to him in my behalf she would confer a lasting debt of gratitude on me.

Clearly comprehending the situation, smiling she said,

"I think I can help you. Many people call papa stern, but he's not so to me. I can usually make him do what I like."

You will please understand that these remarks between us were made in an under tone, while the other three were conversing together in the farther end of the shop. Soon after this a door in the rear of the shop opened and Mr. Fisk entered. I could well understand why people called him stern, for there was a frigid air about him, an unfeeling expression of countenance which made me shrink from appealing to him in the hour of necessity. He was a tall, spare, dark-visaged man with gruff voice; and every look he gave from his small piercing black eyes made me feel that he suspected me of the triple crime of theft, murder and arson.

"Mr. McKenzie, Papa," said his daughter, as he entered the shop and looked inquiringly at me, "he has seen your advertisement, and has come to apply for the situation."

He bowed, looked searchingly at me for a moment, then at the other applicants, and was about speaking to me when his daughter laid her hand on his arm and looked towards me as if she would speak to him privately. I retired a little from their presence, when, after she had talked with him for a short time, he came forward, and, speaking in a tone not altogether unkind, asked,

"What wages do you expect?"

"Whatever you think I can earn," I replied

He asked the others, individually, the same thing, and each named the amount he expected. After asking me another question or two, to ascertain whether I knew anything about the care of horses, he turned to the others and said, " I shall engage Mr. McKenzie."

I certainly felt sorry for these poor men when I saw them going disappointed away, but not many hours, subsequently, I felt that they ought to have been congratulated for their happy escape from the lot that fell to me.

I trust you will pardon me for relating so minutely the details connected with my engagement at this time, but, as the events of that day have had much to do with subsequent events of my life, you will understand why I am thus explicit.

After the others had gone, Fisk said to me :

" I am afraid you will not like my work and the accommodations I shall be obliged to give you. You do not look as if you were able to endure much hardship."

Believing it necessary to inspire him with as much confidence in my physical ability as possible, in order to get the situation, I affected a good deal of *sang froid* with regard to the fare I received, and scouted the idea of not being as able as any man to undergo exposure and hardship. I said,

" I have been a sailor four years and a farmer two, so you see, I am not ignorant of what labor is, nor am I at all particular about my fare."

" I fear," he answered, " that you will find more fault with the arrangements for lodging than for anything else. I always require a man who drives my bread cart to take care of the horses and sleep in a room which I have had fitted up for the purpose in a loft above the stable. **My** reason for this is that before I took this precaution my stable was broken into on two occasions and my harnesses were stolen, **and** once, one of my horses was badly maimed."

I shuddered **at the thought** of sleeping in such a place, yet regarding it more discreet to treat the matter as of little consequence, I said,

" I think I can get along with the lodging."

After talking with him awhile longer I returned to my boarding place, took dinner and then removed my trunk and valise to a **boarding** house near the dwelling of Fisk. I was then sent out with the man who had previously driven the cart in order that I might learn the different routes. In the evening after our return, it being quite late, we stopped at the shop a moment when, the man who had been with me leaving us, Fisk went with me to the stable. A ferocious bull dog had a kennel in it, and after commanding him **to** be quiet, and seeing the horse cared for, Fisk mounted **a** ladder which led **to the loft,** and showed me **the** couch **I was to occupy for the night,** which consisted of **a few** blankets spread **on an** old-fashioned bedstead. **As I** followed him below **to lock the** door, **he unloosed the** dog, wished me pleasant dreams, **and** departed. I had not fully realized my situation until **I was** alone. Never did I spend such a night ; sleep never visited my eyelids, and whenever I rose and paced the floor to give relief to my feelings, the savage brute below growled and roared with the ferocity of the wild beasts in Central Park when about receiving their meals.

I cursed my folly **in** hiring **out to** endure such ignominious treatment, and resolved that this should be my last night in this place. The man who had previously driven the cart was ignorant, and his rough exterior and brutal manners were quite in keeping with these surroundings, and I was not surprised that he had had no objection to sleeping in this unwholesome place.

Fearful that I might have trouble with his dog, being a stranger, Fisk, as soon as morning broke, came to the stable. The depression of spirits which resulted from my incarceration in this place gave rise to forebodings of poverty and sickness, hence, I was not as ready to dismiss myself from a situation as I was some time previous to his arrival. I only informed him that I was apprehensive of injury to my health from sleeping there, and asked if he could not change my quarters. He replied in the negative, reminding me of my assurance to him that I was willing to accept rough, hard fare.

"I can well understand," said he, "that you are deserving of a better position than the one I have given you, but regard for the safety of my property compels me to have a man sleep where you do."

I saw the reasonableness of his statement, and as his manner towards me was kind, I formed quite a favorable impression of him, but still was determined that my stay there should be short.

I remained with him a week, but I was about as unpleasantly situated as I was while tending bar. Fearful lest I should be recognized by some old chum or acquaintance, it was to me a week of wretchedness.

At the expiration of that time, I had money enough to visit Philadelphia, which I did in hopes of finding employment. In the course of my journey I happened to meet the proprietor of the carpet store to whom I had previously engaged, and he informed me that he was again in want of a man, and would hire me if I wished to return and take the place. I promised to do so at the expiration of two days, in case I should find nothing to do in the city to which I was going. Disappointment awaiting me there, I returned, on a packet boat, and in so doing formed the acquaintance of a young man who then had charge of a school in Kingston, New Jersey. He intended to enter Rutgar's College in the fall, and he thought he could obtain for me the situation he was to leave, in case he should do so. Some weeks, subsequently, while I was in the carpet store, I received a note from him informing me that if I would come immediately to Kingston he would assist me in securing his school. I started at once, and the adventures which attended me on the trip I will recount in my next letter.

Trusting that you will write me without delay,

I remain,

Yours most sincerely,

Mack.

CHAPTER XXXII.

In compliance with Mack's request, I answered his letter without delay, and a few days subsequently an answer came, in which, after a few preliminary remarks, he resumed his story as follows :

Princeton Station was the nearest place to Kingston that I could reach by railroad, and as it was nearly dark on Saturday evening when I arrived there, and too late to transact business should I go on, I decided to remain there until Monday. Shortly after my arrival several men came in, and I learned that they were about going to a neighboring village to take part in a grand political ratification meeting which was to take place there that night. Among the number was a school trustee of an adjoining district whose name was Fletcher. The landlord, knowing the object of my contemplated visit to Kingston, informed Fletcher that one of his guests was a young gentleman in pursuit of a school, whereupon Fletcher immediately solicited an interview with me.

He said their school was then vacant, and that he was making efforts to secure the services of a teacher; and then desired to know if I was at liberty to engage to him.

I replied that I would accept the situation in case they would pay as much as they would at Kingston, and without hesitation he assured me that they would do so. I was highly elated, of course, with the prospect.

Fletcher insisted on my going with them to the meeting that evening, saying that he would introduce me to his associate trustee, and added that I would be pleased with the speeches, as several distinguished men were to be present. I consented, but as I was in ignorance as to the "stripe" of my new friend's politics, I thought it best to be reticent with regard to the character of my own.

I was not left long in the dark, however, for on our way over, one of our party in the coach said,

"I'll bet the Black Republicans will get the drubbing to-night they deserve, for Charlie Ferguson is to speak."

This remark at once called forth several others, from which I learned the not very **pleasant fact** that I was in a nest of rabbid Democrats.

To add to my discomfort, Fletcher uttered a most disparaging remark about the Republican party, and then made an appeal to me to corroborate it. Having already considered the awkwardness of my situation, being a Republican, and decided that under the circumstances it might be as well to keep them in ignorance of my views, I merely laughed, and replied that his appeal to me suggested a story. By the time the story was told the former subject was forgotten, and I had not committed myself. I confess that I felt slightly ashamed of my hypocritical conduct, but I silenced the murmurs of conscience by arguing to myself that owing to my obscurity my influence was nothing, and that whatever I said would soon be forgotten if noticed at all.

That my reasoning was fallacious in part, the sequel will show. It was soon obvious that the company regarded me as a promising, warm-hearted Democrat, and the dilemna which resulted to me that night from my hypocrisy I shall never forget.

On arriving at the place of meeting I was actually forced upon the platform with the speakers, and regularly introduced to each one of them as Mr. McKenzie, " the gentleman from New York city." " Charlie " surpassed all his previous efforts in vilifying the Republicans, and was repeatedly obliged to cease speaking until the thunderous applause had died away.

Another and then another speaker rose, each striving to outstrip the other in his denunciations of the Republican party, to all of which I was obliged mutely to listen, and I began to fear that I would either have to show my colors, or be compelled even to play the role of a political Peter.

I decided, however, if called upon to speak, to refuse, but in order to save myself the trouble I intended to make my escape from the platform while the next one was speaking. Judge my astonishment and confusion then, when the next speaker rose, made a few remarks, and then said he had been requested by the chairman to make his speech as brief as possible as the meeting was to be addressed by the Honorable Mr. McKenzie from New York city ; and at the same moment he waved his hand towards me. When the applause which greeted this announcement had died away, the chairman rose and introduced me in a fulsome speech, which was received with hearty cheers.

I never fainted in my life, but I think I came nearer to it on this occasion than I ever did before, or have since.   I was mordly certain that any attempt on my part to stand, much more to speak, would be an utter impossibility.   I therefore simply kept my seat for some seconds ; then deliberately took out my watch, opened and looked at it for several seconds more, and then, still seated, begged in view of the lateness of the hour, the fact that such able speeches had been made, that I be excused, urging, likewise, that anything I might say at that late hour must only prove " stale, flat and unprofitable."   The chairman attempted to speak, but before he could utter a sentence, from every part of the house came the cry " McKenzie ! McKenzie ! " and I saw that further delay would be dangerous to my reputation.   Brief as this interval was, it enabled me to collect my thoughts and become more composed.

I had decided to make a speech without even committing myself.   It was a dangerous thing for a young man like myself unaccustomed to public speaking to attempt, inasmuch **as** it required both coolness and tact.   It was simply an effort to speak for a certain length of time in a way that would satisfy my audience, and at the same time neither do harm to my own party nor violence to my principles.

I was sufficiently conversant with the political history of the country to expatiate successfully on the achievement of the Democratic party in decades gone by.   I advised moderation, exhorted them them to unity of action, and closed by expressing the belief that, if they were united, they would undoubtedly carry many of the States by a large majority. **Of the truth of my** last remark I had not the slightest doubt.

You will please remember that in all this time I never mentioned the Republician party, nor did I express a **hope** that the Democrats might be successful. I touched lightly on some of the prominent things in the Democratic platform, but dwelt in *generalities*.

Remembering the condition of my audience **at the** time, and judging from the applause which greeted me, **I have** every reason to believe that these generalities were regarded " glittering."

Although conscious as **I was** that the speech was one that any schoolboy should make, when at last I closed, and three cheers had been given for "the Hon. Gentleman from **New York**," I was borne **from the** platform **by** the most demonstrative of the audience—among whom was my friend Fletcher—and carried to the nearest hotel. Here they all drank my health, and, will **you** believe it ? they tried to make me swallow a glass **of vile** whiskey ? Having heard, however, of " Jersey Lightning," I was firm, and respectfully declined.

That speech decided my fortunes in New Jersey, for so well pleased were they with it that both Fletcher and his **associate** insisted that I should name the price for which I would **teach their school.** **I declined** doing this until I had seen the trustees in Kingston, whom I was about **to** visit, but they were still importunate. I asked how much **they had usually** paid, and the reply was $125 per quarter ; but they **assured** me that that would have nothing **to do** with my case. I thought of asking $250 per quarter, but feared that I would be overdoing the thing, and so refused to give them my terms before I visited Kingston.

Seeing that there was no moving me from this position, Fletcher proposed that I should remain with him until Monday, when he would carry me over to Kingston and conclude the bargain with me there, in case I did not hire out to the trustees of that place. I acceded to his proposal, and accordingly on Monday was driven to Kingston and met the trustees.

They offered me $160 per quarter, saying that that was ten dollars more than they had ever paid before. I refused the offer, when, after a brief consultation, they advanced the price to $175. My friend Fletcher slyly giving me a wink, I again declined the offer, and we were about going away, when the chairman of the board asked if I would remain for $190, provided their constituents did not object to the price. I glanced at Fletcher but his eye was averted, and I then asked if they would give me two days in which to consider the matter.

"Certainly, as long as you like," was the reply.

We then returned to Morrisville—the place where the **school was** located—and found the other two trustees awaiting us at the hotel. The one whom I had never seen before was a staunch Republican, and my two Democratic friends were very careful not to let him know the part I had taken in the meeting of Saturday evening. After a long parley they agreed to hire me for a year, at $200 per quarter, which was to be raised to $210 for the following year, in the event of my giving good satisfaction.

After the bargain was closed and I had time to reflect upon the strange combination of circumstances which had placed me in this desirable situation, I could but wonder. I must confess I felt that I had been guilty of some deceit, and had displayed a great deal of assurance in contending for the salary that they finally agreed to pay me; for, as near as I can recollect, I had decided on leaving New York to accept any price that my employers were willing to pay.

I remained in the Morrisville school three years. After I had been there about six months, one morning a young lady, with a face wonderfully familiar, entered my school as a pupil. Until I had time to speak to her and learn her name, I was sorely puzzled to know where I had met her. It was Emma Fisk, the young lady through whose influence I had obtained the situation with her father, confectioner, and proprietor of a bakery in New York. It appeared that Mr. Fisk had formerly owned a farm in New Jersey, in the place where I was teaching, but had sold out, removed to New York, and engaged in business there. Finding it less profitable than he had anticipated, he had returned to New Jersey and re-purchased his farm. His daughter soon after their arrival commenced attending my school, and did so until the intimacy which sprung up between us necessitated my removal to another place.

Discovering that she possessed much intelligence and amiability of character, I naturally took an interest in her as a pupil, and in less than a year a warm friendship existed between us.

Three months afterward I had fully effected the transition between friendship and a stronger emotion, and disclosing my feelings to her I was surprised to learn that she entertained the same with regard to myself.

About this time the removal from the place of the

man with whom I had been boarding obliged me to seek quarters elsewhere, and the house of Mr. Fisk seemed to be the only available one where I could board in the future. I, of course, gladly made the change, but in the new position the relation which I sustained towards Emma could not be concealed from her parents.

Her mother never opposed us, but the father, on the contrary, sternly forbade her to have anything to do with me except as a teacher and boarder of the family; his only objection being my want of fortune. In consequence of this objection, we were obliged to dissemble, and thus eluded all suspicion for several months. One evening, however, Mr. Fisk returning home unexpectedly, found Emma and myself alone in the parlor, and at once gave vent to his feelings in unqualified abuse of myself. He also commanded me to leave his house forever, and on the following morning I sought another place. I fortunately found one with a respectable family, though living a long distance from my school. I had cherished a hope that I might find employment where I was then teaching for a much longer period, but as Mr. Fisk was now chairman of the school board, and objected decidedly to my re-engagement, I was obliged to seek a school elsewhere, and soon found one ten miles distant, of which I was given charge.

Previous to leaving Morrisville I learned from both Emma and her mother that Mr. Fisk was anxiously endeavoring to effect a marriage between his daughter and a bachelor merchant of the village, who was reputed rich, but, owing to his crabbed nature and penuriousness, was unpopular with his fellow citizens. He frequently visited the house of Fisk while I was there, but as Emma disliked him, and only treated him with courtesy to please her father, I was not at all apprehensive that he would meet with sufficient encouragement to induce him to propose marriage. Knowing, too, Fisk's affection for his daughter, I could not believe that he would advise, much less coerce her to a union which was highly repugnant to her feelings, and which would in all probability result in years of discomfort and wretchedness to her. No sooner, however, had I left his house than he began to encourage Judd, the merchant, to make frequent visits there, in hopes, no doubt, that he might succeed in winning Emma's favor, and that she would thus forget me.

Through the favor of her mother and the kindness of a friend of mine, I was enabled to correspond with her after I left the place, and occasionally I met her at the house of my friend.

I trust you will not imagine that when I was carrying on this clandestine correspondence, and meeting her thus secretly, I had lost my former respect for frankness and open, fair dealing; for I had not, and I had many scruples and questions to settle with myself about the honor of inducing her to disobey her father's positive commands, before I could feel that I was not doing wrong. The fact, however, that her mother, who was a christian lady, respected by all who knew her, was encouraging our attachment to each other, and seemed to regard our marriage as the only means of securing the happiness of her daughter, was a sufficient guarantee to me that I was doing nothing incompatible with the principles of an honest man and a gentleman. I, therefore, resolved that our union should not be long delayed.

Shortly after I had formed this resolution, I learned that Mr. Fisk had broached the subject to his daughter of marrying Judd, and on hearing her prompt refusal he had threatened to disinherit and disown her unless she complied with his wishes. I soon obtained an interview with Mrs. Fisk, and asked if she would object to the immediate marriage of Emma to myself, provided it could be effected. She assured me that she would not, yet, with deep grief and many tears, expressed her belief that **it** could never take place with the knowledge of her husband. I next saw Emma, who, after listening to my plans, and receiving explicit reasons for my course, consented to an elopement. Accordingly, on the night of the 6th of December, 186–, collecting such articles as she required, she met me at **a** place of rendezvous, where I had a coach in readiness which conveyed us to the railroad station at Trenton. Here we arrived in time to reach the Owl Train, which took us to New York. In consequence of an accident which occurred to a freight train which had preceded us by an hour, we did **not reach the** city until five o'clock the next morning.

It will be necessary here to acquaint you **with** a few facts in regard to my past history which I came near forgetting. I knew that several of my old friends resided in the city of New York and in its immediate vicinity, at the time I found employment there. A feeling of pride kept me from acquainting my former friend, the Rev. Mr. Halleck, with my whereabouts at the time I was tending bar in Saratoga County, and during that time a change of residence on his part caused me to lose his address. After I had left that situation and engaged in teaching, my low salary prevented my discharging any part of the debt I owed him, hence I refrained from looking him up ; deferring it until my circumstances should change for the better.   While engaged in the carpet store, I one day happened to meet our old friend, Scott, and from him I learned that Mr. Halleck resided in Brooklyn.   I did not visit or see him, but, after I engaged the school in Morrisville, I sent money at stated intervals until I had paid the full amount I owed him.   I corresponded not only with him, but with Scott also, and to the latter I had confided the story of my relations to my future wife.

I had already made arrangements with him to meet us at the depot when we arrived, and when he did so, to my delight he informed me that he had arranged to take us to Mr. Halleck's, and that that gentleman had promised to unite us in the bonds of wedlock at his house.   The programme was faithfully carried out, and we then removed to our boarding house, where Scott had made all preparations for us to spend our honey moon.

A few weeks, subsequently, I went to Blackstone, Long Island, to take charge of the public school there, which Mr. Halleck had engaged for me at a salary of $1,000 per annum.   I remained there until 1868, when I resigned for the purpose of securing the principalship of the school at this place at a higher salary.

I am still here in the enjoyment of good health, receiving in addition to my salary a few hundred dollars yearly from different papers for the productions of my humble pen.   My father-in-law has so far laid aside his indignation and prejudices against me that he now sometimes visits us, and always brings a present of no small value to the young Georgie McKenzie, who now enhances the happiness of our household by his prattle.

With a most cordial wish that you will visit us with your family at no distant day,

I remain,

Yours assuredly and ever,

GORDON McKENZIE.

CHAPTER XXXIII.

Two or three letters more were interchanged between McKenzie and myself, when I visited him. The following summer he visited me in return, and thus we met each other from time to time. While on my last visit to him he received a letter from Scotland which, while it was the cause of sadness, also afforded him the cheerful prospect of relief from the arduous duties of teaching.

While he was a student in Corvette he wrote to his mother, and in due time received an answer which was replete with expressions of maternal tenderness. Thus a correspondence was opened between them which was kept up until the time of which I write. A year after he commenced his labors in Blackstone his mother visited him, and remained two or three months. Soon after her return to Scotland her husband, who the reader will remember held this relation by a second marriage, inherited quite a fortune by the death of a relative. In less than two years he died, bequeathing the greater part of his property to his wife. After sending her son Gordon several valuable presents, and vainly endeavoring to induce him to come to Scotland and reside, she decided to come to America, and spend her remaining days with him. It was while contemplating this movement, and making preparations for it, that she was seized with a dangerous illness, which in the course of a few weeks terminated her life.

The letter alluded to above announced to McKenzie the death of his mother, and the fact, also, that she had left him the sum of twelve thousand pounds sterling.

It was now Mack's summer's vacation, and the day after receiving this letter he informed me that he intended to resign his position as teacher where he then was, and remove to New York; and he wished to know if I would like to be his successor in the school.

I had previously been teaching in Warsaw in Canada. My family was still there, and I had been engaged to assume the principalship of the academy at that place another year. I replied to Mack's inquiry by saying that nothing would give me more pleasure than to succeed him in his school, and would do so on condition of my getting released from my engagement at Warsaw.

He had little difficulty in securing me his situation, and I then returned to Canada, hoping to be able to obtain my own release. I was not disappointed, and immediately set about making arrangements for my departure.

A week previous to the time when I was to leave I sat alone one evening with my family, now consisting of a wife and three children.   They were to remove to our old home at Foreston, where my aged parents still resided, and were to remain there a year; then, in the event of my re-engagement at Yonkers, they were to go with me to that place to reside.

The prospect of separation was an **unhappy one** for us all, but still it was neither new nor strange.

Owing to my inability to incur the expense and trouble of moving my family and household effects every time I was obliged to change the scene of my labors, I had lived in almost constant exile from my wife and children, seeing them only at intervals of one, two or more weeks, according to my distance from them. During the last three years, however, I had enjoyed the pleasure of their society constantly, and though, if I followed teaching, it was not likely that this pleasure would be vouchsafed me long, I had no doubt until I returned from my visit to Mack that I would be with them during the ensuing year.

The education of our children had been a subject of great interest to us, and Ruth had given much attention to it when they were in Foreston.   On the evening alluded to above, we had been impressing upon them the importance of devoting themselves to study during my absence, and our two boys, Jack and Tommy, aged respectively thirteen and nine, were now lamenting my departure, and tearfully declaring their determination to be industrious and obedient to my wishes.

Ruth sat by the table with an open book near her which

she evidently felt too sad to read, and was now seemingly trying to reconcile the dealings of Providence with her ideas of love and justice. I could easily divine her thoughts, for I had long known her inclination at times to indulge skeptical feelings. Though generally maintaining consistent Christian faith, she could not sometimes forbear in hours of trial, betraying the weakness of the doubting Apostle, and these moments were always characterized by the same sad, hopeless expressions of countenance now so plainly visible. Her path like mine had not been one of sunshine and flowers, and the slight furrows on her face, and the gray hairs that were here and there discernible, showed that time and care had affected her not less deeply than myself.

"This evening," she at length said, "brings back so vividly the thoughts and emotions I experienced the night you promised to enlist, and the evening also before you started for the army."

"I hope, my dear," I said, "that the prospect of a good situation in cultured society **does not seem fraught with** the danger to me that the life of a **soldier did.**"

"**No,**" she said, "**that is** not it, but **I** cannot bear the thought of your long absence from us **again.** I am not as strong now and as well able to bear **it** as I then was," and tears moistened her eyes as she said this. "Besides," she continued, "these children require your presence and care. It seems cruel that circumstances compel us to live in this unnatural way."

There was too much of truth in these remarks not **to** affect me. The thought of being absent from my children so long, at a time when perhaps the most comfort was to be realized with them, and at a time, too, when they most required my care and instruction, had already been sufficiently harrowing, and it was made doubly so by the consciousness that Ruth so fully realized and deplored the same thing.

"I understand the truth of what you say," I replied, "but there is no use of repining at our lot, or finding fault with the decrees of Providence. We might be in much more unpleasant circumstances than we are now in, and every cloud you know has a silver lining."

"I have often tried," she said, "to console myself with these thoughts, but when I remember how long and faithfully you have worked, and I see so many of our early friends who have displayed but little industry enjoying all the comforts and ease of wealth, it seems to me that you must have been born under an unlucky planet."

"You forget," I replied, "that wealth is secured by honest industry in only rare instances, and that those who have it often come into possession of it by a combination of circumstances over which they have had no control, and for which, consequently, they can claim no credit."

"I know that," she said, "and I used to have a sort of presentiment that some such circumstances would place you beyond the necessity of hard labor in the later years of your life, but I am now bereft of even that consolation."

At this moment a neighbor's boy entered to ask our oldest boy to accompany him, as usual, to the post-office. He did so, and no sooner had he gone than Kate, our five year old, who had become somewhat distinguished for her quaint sayings, and who evidently had some conception of the cause of the prevailing sadness, climbed on my knee and with an anxious expression of countenance said :

" Papa, will you have to teach stool in heaven ? "

" I hope not, my child," I said. " But why do you ask ? "

" 'Cause," she answered, " I heard mamma say she was 'fraid you'd always have to teach stool."

I continued to chat and play with her until Jack returned with our mail, which consisted of a letter addressed to Ruth and the evening paper. I took the latter, and busied myself with it a few moments, when, glancing towards Ruth, I was surprised to see her pale and trembling from emotion, still holding the letter in her hand.

" What is the matter ? " I said. " Please let me read it, and I held out my hand for the epistle which I had **no** doubt was the **cause** of her singular appearance.

She withheld it, and said :

" Not now; I will let you see it bye and bye," and then she took a book, commenced reading, and soon displayed her usual composure.

I returned to my paper, though still wondering what the contents of the **letter could be.** After reading a few minutes, Ruth, in much better spirits than I had recently seen her, asked :

" Don't you think you will be able **to** judge by Christmas whether they will want you to remain another year or not, so that in case they do, you can send for us ? "

" It is possible that I may," I replied.

After musing a moment she said : " What a lucky fellow Mack was, he will probably never teach again. I wish that some such good fortune might be in store for you. Would you fulfill your engagement with the school trustees at Yonkers were you now to receive a legacy from some friend?" she asked.

I might not have been at all surprised at the question had there not been something peculiar in the expression of her face, an unusually bright sparkle in her eye, and I thought I detected a strong effort to suppress a smile. But thinking that this might all arise from her contemplation of the pleasure an unexpected fortune would give us, I replied:

"Certainly I would, unless they were quite willing to release me from it."

"And what would you do after they had released you?" she asked.

"I don't know I am sure," I said; "but why do you tantalize me with this idle talk?"

"O, to see what you would say," she replied, and then continued: "You have no fears I suppose that a valuable legacy would dethrone your reason as it has others?"

"I would be most happy to risk it," I replied.

"Well, then, read that," she said, throwing me the letter she had just received.

Seizing it with trembling hand, I opened and read as follows:

"CARROLLTON, Aug. 20th, 187-.

"MRS. RUTH STYLES:

DEAR MADAM,—I have great pleasure in informing you, as the attorney of Mr. Niel, that previous to his death, which occurred on Thursday last, he left you in his will, property, consisting of bank stock, mortgages and real estate, to the amount of $21,000 (twenty-one thousand dollars). There being no claims against his estate, the property is awaiting your order.

> I am, Madam,
>> Your obedient servant,
>>> R. P. WINSLOW, Advocate.

P.S.—I enclose a letter from Mr. Niel to your husband."

I gasped, took up the letter enclosed, which read:

"MY DEAR MR. STYLES,—I address you as I was wont to do years ago; for, though I have been ashamed to see you the honesty of your principles I have never forgotten, and you are still dear to me. My physician tells me that I have but a few days to live, and with a desire that I may make reparation for the wrong I have done, I shall bequeath either you or your noble wife the principal part of my property. With the exception of what I have done to you and yours I do not know that I have ever wronged one of my fellows, hence, I trust that you will not think too harshly of me when I am gone. I have sought forgiveness at the only Fount whence it can be obtained, and have the assurance that it is granted. **Could I now** feel that you too forgive, and that the amount I leave you will in a measure repay you for all the trouble I have given, I would die happy.

> Believe me,
>> Your sincerest friend,
>>> W. N. NIEL."

This letter was in the same handwriting as the other, which made it probable that it had been written after the dictation of Niel while on his death-bed.

Poor man. Not naturally vicious or unkind, he had permitted his love passion to betray him into an act of wickedness unlike anything he had ever before committed, and for which he had no doubt suffered bitter feelings of remorse.

It was too late to assure him how fully he was forgiven; but now, for the first time, we told our children the story of the sorrow and hardships which finally resulted in a temporal blessing to us, and we teach them to respect the memory of the man who was the author of all.

The day following that on which my fortune so unexpectedly changed, I received a letter from Mack containing a draft for $1,000.

" I did not present it to you while you were here," he wrote me, " knowing that, if I succeeded in getting you to accept it at all, it would only be after a long parley into which I had no desire to enter. You are on no account to refuse it, nor even to think of such a thing. You would have done the same thing for me had our circumstances been reversed, and you can do me no greater favor than to use it without ever mentioning it hereafter.

Bring hour family with you at once, fit up a house at Yonkers, and be happy."

Although now beyond the necessity of accepting my generous friend's munificent present, I was not the less grateful to him. I immediately visited Yonkers, when I returned it, and surprised and delighted him with the story of my own strange good fortune.

I procured a substitute for myself in the school where I had agreed to teach, and then removed to Foreston, to engage in the quiet and peaceful pursuit of farming, which

I had always intended to follow should my circumstances ever permit. Since that time, however, a desire to educate our children led me to remove to New York and enter into partnership with Mack in a lucrative business in which he had embarked. In our improved condition of life we are not forgetful of the trials through which we have reached it, and of those to whom our sympathy and hospitality are extended, none receive them more cordially than the teacher who is toiling over the thorny path we both have trod.

THE END.